The Lost Ancestor
by
Nathan Dylan Goodwin

I would like to dedicate this book to Robert, Sarah and Harrison

Chapter One

Morton Farrier was impressed. He had known that, when he was given an address on the exclusive Granville Road in St Margaret at Cliffe, he would find himself envious but the house outside of which he had just parked was nothing short of stunning. It was centred among a row of disparate and elite properties, the homes and second homes of the rich and fortunate. The village, perched high on the white cliffs of Kent between Deal and Dover, overlooked the invisible marine boundary of the English Channel and the North Sea and had, since Victorian times, attracted wealth and prosperity. Whatever the occupation of the house's owner, he had to be earning a decent salary.

Morton stepped from his red and white Mini and took a good look at the house. Protected by black iron gates and a cherry-laurel hedge, the pristine white-walled and oak-window-framed property was dominated by a sumptuous three-storey panel of glass, set in a concave semi-circle.

Given the apparent luxury of the place, Morton was surprised to be able simply to pull open the gates and head up the drive unhindered by video entry systems or guard dogs. Pressing the doorbell, he waited as it chimed noisily inside. A few moments later, the blurred shadow of a figure moved towards the frosted glass. The door opened, revealing a tall, slender man with an affable, pleasant face. Wearing an expensive-looking shirt and dark trousers, the man smiled and offered his hand to Morton. His hair was stone-grey, thinned at the centre and deep lines were etched on his forehead and around the corners of his eyes; Morton guessed him to be in his mid-seventies.

'Mr Mercer?' Morton asked, shaking the proffered hand vigorously.

'Ray,' he said warmly. 'You must be Morton Farrier? You look familiar from the newspapers a few months ago. Come on in.'

'Thank you,' he answered, preferring not to discuss a previous case which had made the national headlines after it had led to the downfall of a prominent aristocratic family, the sacking of an upcoming police chief and the imprisonment of a murderer. The upshot of that high profile case was that Morton was afforded the luxury of cherry-picking from prospective genealogical assignments. The intriguing email which had arrived in his inbox three days ago from Ray Mercer had piqued his interest sufficiently to warrant a meeting.

Morton followed Ray through an opulent hallway. Fractured light filtered in through the large, floor-to-ceiling windows, illuminating the marble flooring. The vast hallway fed an open staircase and a network of oak doors, some offering Morton revealing glimpses of the luxurious rooms within. Ray pulled open one of the doors, which led into a sizeable, rectangular room with one wall being made entirely of glass, offering a breathtaking view of the English Channel.

'Wow!' Morton said, heading towards the window. 'Fantastic view.' In the hazy distance the rugged cliffs of the *Nord-Pas de Calais* rose over the Channel, busy with giant white passenger ships coming and going between Dover and Calais.

Ray, arms folded contemplatively, joined Morton and stared out to the distant sea. 'Not bad, is it? I came back here to retire a few years ago. I'll never get bored with it—always something different or new to appreciate. When I was designing the house, I spent an age fussing over artwork for the walls. Then I realised that if I just had a decent window, Mother Nature would paint me a new picture every day and there would be no need for anything else.'

'It certainly is lovely,' Morton said, taking in the whole room. The three remaining walls were lined with bookshelves. Besides that, the room was minimalistic in its furnishing: a selection of silver-framed photographs stood on a desk in the centre of the room with two leather chairs neatly placed either side of the desk. A grand piano completed the room's furniture.

Ray turned to Morton. 'You can see why they called it *Hellfire Corner* around here during the last war, with France being so close.'

'Didn't the Nazis have guns stationed in northern France which could reach here?'

'That's right. I was born in a small cottage just down the road from here in 1935. My earliest memories are of war: searchlights over the Channel, guns banging, planes dog-fighting overhead, bombs landing nearby, Jerry pilots being frogmarched by the Home Guard past our house.'

'Must have been scary for a young boy.'

'Well, it was all boys' adventure stuff at first. Then Hitler put the V1 rocket launchers just across the water and suddenly we were under the flight path of the dreaded doodlebugs. That was how my father died: a doodlebug was shot down by a well-meaning American fighter

2

plane and it detonated right next door to our house. He was killed outright.'

'How awful for you,' Morton said.

'Yes. My mother had taken me out for a walk along the beach down in St Margaret's Bay that morning. The irony was that she had guessed what the American plane was about to do and pointed it out to me so that I could watch. The image of my mother's face, as the blood drained from it and horror consumed her eyes, will stay with me forever. I knew, too, of course—I wasn't silly. She sent me off to spend a few days with my granny in Winchelsea. She was my dad's mum. Though she later had a short-lived marriage to the village doctor, he was illegitimate, hence me being a Mercer, like granny. Anyway, days turned into weeks, weeks turned into months; before I knew it I hadn't seen my mother in several years. I later learned that she was incarcerated at the East Kent County Asylum in Chartham. It was in the days when mental health was something to keep hidden, to be ashamed of, so my grandmother thought it best not to tell me what had happened to her until after her death.'

Morton watched quietly as Ray brushed his eyes with his right index finger. 'That must have been pretty tough on you,' Morton said, carefully watching the old man.

Something seemed to click in Ray, catapulting him back to reality. He shrugged slightly. 'Just one of those things, happened to lots of families out there. Still, the silver lining, for want of a better phrase, was that I became very close to my grandmother. I doted on her, and she on me.'

'And it was her twin sister who disappeared?' Morton asked. 'The person you want me to try and find for you?'

'Yes, that's right, Mary Mercer.' Turning from the window, Ray walked over to his desk, picked up a framed photograph and handed it to Morton. 'That's her on the right, with my granny, Edith.'

Morton held the cold silver frame and took in the picture. Seeing the real people behind the names and dates always brought his genealogical cases to life for him. The time-faded, sepia photo was of two girls, identical in height, around the age of fifteen. However, the similarity between the sisters ended there. Mary, dark hair parted in the centre with matching decorative bows to each side, rested her head on her sister and the pair jointly held some kind of a book. In Morton's experience, it was usually a Bible. Both girls had plain, white dresses with simple buttons running down the middle. Edith had sharp,

3

angular features and fiery eyes, giving her the look of someone with a formidable temperament. Mary, meanwhile, had a much softer, prettier face with warm eyes.

Ray shifted slightly. 'That was the last picture of the two of them together. I did a bit of digging—it was taken at Pearson's Photography Studio in Hastings in 1910. Look like chalk and cheese, don't they?'

Morton nodded. 'I wouldn't ever have guessed them to be twins.'

'Well, I've got the proof over there,' Ray said with a smile, nodding his head towards the desk. 'Come and sit down.'

The pair moved to the leather chairs. Morton opened his briefcase and took out a notepad and pen. Although he always took his laptop with him on such visits, he still preferred scribing notes the old-fashioned way then typing them up at home, fleshing out the detail with further research as he went.

'Here,' Ray said, handing Morton an A3 manila envelope.

Morton withdrew a large, carefully organised pile of papers and set them down in his lap. On the top of the pile was a General Register Office copy of Mary Mercer's birth certificate. 'Nineteenth of April, 1893, 4.16pm, Winchelsea, Sussex. Mary Kate. Girl. Daughter of Thomas Mercer and Katherine Mercer, formally Wraight. Father's occupation—waggoner. Mark of Katherine Mercer, informant.' Two pieces of information struck Morton as being of interest: first of all, that Katherine, like many countryside folk in the nineteenth-century, was illiterate and signed her name with a cross; secondly, that the precise time of birth had been noted on the certificate, which usually indicted multiple births so as to prove the order of delivery. Morton lifted the certificate and took a cursory glance at the next: Mary's twin sister, Edith Jane Mercer, born nine minutes later. The rest of the certificate was identical.

'So,' Ray said. 'There's the proof that Mary was actually born onto this planet. You'll see in that pile of documents that I found her living at home with her sisters, mum and dad in 1901, then I found her ten years later on the 1911 census, then she vanishes. Mary's whole life whittled down to three official documents.'

Morton scribbled some notes on his pad. 'No marriage or death certificates?'

Ray shook his head vehemently. 'No. I've tried every combination you can think of. I actually started searching for her years ago, back in the days when you had to go to the Family Records Centre

4

in Islington. I checked every quarter of every year—not a dicky bird. I tried emigration and passenger records but that came back with nothing either. I've tried every conceivable angle but she remains completely elusive.'

'I don't wish to be insensitive here, Ray, but have you considered the possibility that something untoward happened to her? Something which left no genealogical trace for me to follow?' Morton said, carefully choosing his words.

'Do you mean what if her death was covered up somehow? Like someone killed her? Or suicide?' Ray asked, before addressing the question. 'She was at my mother's funeral in 1962, although I didn't know it at the time.'

'What do you mean?' Morton asked, his interest piquing substantially.

'Well, I'll come to that. Let me start at the beginning, so you know everything.' Ray took in a deep breath and looked to the ceiling, as if trying to extract long-buried memories. 'I clearly remember the first time that Granny told me about her sister's disappearance. I must have been about ten years old at the time and I was rummaging through Granny's bedside drawer looking for something or other when I found a locket. The drawer was full of jewellery but something about this locket made me pick it out and look at it more closely. It was silver with a small stone set in the centre. Inside, was the photo of someone I didn't recognise. Granny came in and lost her temper with me, snatched it away and sent me to my room. I remember being jolly upset by it all—I'd never seen her so angry before. A while later she came and found me, sat on my bed and I can still see her now, tears flooding down her face as she apologised for her outburst and told me that the picture in the locket was of her sister, Mary, whom she hadn't seen for a very long time. Then she told me the same snippet that she would repeat over the course of her life until the day she died: Mary was at work as usual as a live-in, domestic servant and she left to go home for her half day's leave. The people she worked for said she did her normal day's work then left for home; but she never arrived. According to Granny, the whole village came out in force to look for her. The search began to peter out after a few days then it was stopped altogether when a letter was discovered that said she had run away. Apparently, the letter was postmarked in Scotland. The search was called off and Granny was left heartbroken. I mean, imagine your twin sister just vanishing like that. I don't think she ever believed that letter to have been genuine.'

'You mean it was forged?' Morton asked.

'No, it was definitely in her handwriting. I just don't think Granny could believe her twin would write it.'

'I don't suppose you still have the letter?'

Ray shook his head. 'No, sadly not. I don't know where it went, but Granny didn't have it.'

Morton wrote the word 'Scotland' then underlined it. 'Is there any significance in running away to Scotland? I'm thinking Gretna Green, eloping with someone?'

'Not that I was ever told, no. You'll find among that stack a newspaper report in the *Sussex Express* about the search for Mary. There's no mention of a companion. Anyway, that was the last time Mary was heard of until 1962—fifty-one years later. Granny was buried in St Thomas's Church, Winchelsea with her parents. Most of the day was a blur for me and by the end of it I was entirely drained. All the mourners had gone and I just needed to be by myself, so I returned to her grave. There I was, reading all the condolence cards attached to the flowers, when I saw a simple single white rose, around which was wound an identical silver locket to the one Granny had, only this one contained a photo of Granny.'

Morton was hurriedly writing everything down. 'Was there anything else with it, a note maybe?'

'Yes, a small card which read 'I hope you are at peace'.'

Morton nodded, not wishing to express his curiosity over the turn of phrase used. *I hope you are at peace.* It could be interpreted in several different ways.

'She came back,' Ray said quietly, before turning to his desk and pulling open a drawer. He held up two silver lockets and handed them to Morton. 'And here they are.'

Morton took the pendants from Ray. Just as he said, they were identical, made of sterling silver with a precious stone set in the centre. Morton unclasped the first and saw a tiny photograph of Ray's grandmother, Edith. Inside the other locket was a photograph which was unmistakably Mary Mercer. 'May I take a photograph of them, please?'

'By all means, go ahead.'

Morton set the lockets down side by side and took a digital photo of them.

'I had the handwriting on the card analysed and compared with what I knew was her writing in an old book of hers I found. The graphologist I employed was pretty certain it was the same person: it was Mary Mercer, alive and well in Winchelsea in 1962. His report and copies of the two pieces of handwriting are in the pile for you.'

Morton looked down at his scribbled notes. The Mercer Case just got more interesting. 'I'll find her,' Morton said, almost to himself, as he took a cursory glance through the rest of the paperwork. Ray had even included a typed list of all the negative searches he had made; he had certainly been meticulous in his research.

'Will you?' Ray said. He shook his head and exhaled. An almost imperceptible moistening of the old man's eyes told Morton that finding his great aunt had become more than a hobby to him, more than a curious incident on a family tree; it had grown into something personal. 'My dear granny meant so much to me, being more of a mother than my own in the end and the thought of how upset she would get talking about Mary will haunt me until the day she's found. I know it sounds daft, but I just want to visit Granny's grave and finally tell her what happened to her twin sister.'

'I totally understand; I'd feel the same way,' Morton told him with a reassuring smile. 'Now, all these documents are great—thank you—but what I really need from you is anything that you know about Mary which doesn't come from certificates, censuses and photos. What did your granny tell you about Mary?' Anything at all: places she visited on holiday, relatives abroad, previous absconding, boyfriends, jobs…?' Morton probed, knowing that the tiniest snippet of information could lead to a breakthrough.

Ray paused and stared out of the window. After several seconds had passed, he turned back towards Morton. 'There's really very little that I can think of. I know she worked at a large country mansion in Winchelsea as a housemaid, but that she wasn't very good at the job. Like all siblings, they fell out and made up. I don't know of any relatives abroad or other people she was close to. I doubt very much the family ever went on holiday—it just wasn't done in those days. Granny would just repeat the same stories over and over until the day she died. She felt that she'd let Mary down. Even in the delirious throes of death, she was apologising to Mary for having let her go.'

Morton looked up from his notepad, curious by Ray's turn of phrase. 'Were those her exact words?'

'Well, along those lines. Obviously I don't remember precisely.'

7

Morton nodded. 'What about Mary's belongings? Do you know what happened to them after she disappeared?'

Ray shook his head sadly. 'Sorry, I'm really not much help, am I? By the time I came along in 1935 she'd been gone for twenty-four years. Her parents were dead, so I assume everything was disposed of. I didn't find anything of Mary's other than a few books among Granny's effects after she died. Sorry.'

'It's fine. Could I see the books, please?' Morton asked.

'They're all together here—there's only four of them,' Ray said, reaching for a small stack of books in a nearby shelf. He handed them to Morton. 'You can borrow them if you like. I've read them all cover-to-cover, just in case there was any kind of a secret message or hidden note. Alas not.'

'Thank you,' Morton replied, taking a quick look at the cover of the top book, entitled *Four Sisters*. 'What about other family members? Did Mary and Edith have any other siblings?'

'There was an older sister, Caroline. She married a soldier, called William Ransom; they lived in Bristol and had one child, a daughter called Rebecca.' Ray walked sombrely back over to the window, something Morton could see he did with regularity. 'Their side of the family have never been any help, though. Granny didn't really keep in touch with them—I get the feeling there was a falling out or something a long way back. Not much hope of finding what happened to her, is there?' he muttered.

'Well, I'm willing to take the case on and give it a go,' Morton said.

Ray turned, standing in a puddle of white sunlight. He smiled. 'Don't take too long about it. Not to put too fine a point on it but I've got stage four cancer of the pancreas.'

'Oh, I'm sorry to hear that,' Morton said, realising just how much finding his lost aunt meant to Ray and how little time he had in which to find her: 'I'll do what I can for you.'

'Thank you. Is there anything else you need from me?'

'This is all a good start,' Morton said, holding up the stack of papers. 'I'll get back to you if I need anything else.' Morton reinserted the paperwork back into the manila folder, then packed away his briefcase. He stood, ventured towards the window and shook Ray's hand.

'Thank you, Morton,' Ray said quietly. 'I finally feel there's a glimmer of hope at finding her.' He briefly turned to the photograph of Mary and Edith. A snapshot of history when their family was intact.

Morton said goodbye and left the house. As he walked down the driveway towards his Mini, he began to lay the pieces of the puzzle out in his mind. Unlike the bog-standard genealogical cases that he used to undertake, whereby he would research the ancestral lines of a particular surname, this type of case intrigued and excited him. The fragmented Mercer Case jigsaw in his mind needed to be reassembled. Quickly. He didn't know much about pancreatic cancer but he did know that stage four meant that Ray probably didn't have long to live.

As Morton drove the forty-three miles back home, he began to consider his first steps in the case. The bottom line for him was that someone, somewhere had once known what had happened to Mary Mercer. His job was to find that person.

Chapter Two

Monday 2nd January 1911

Edith Mercer stared into the tiny hallway mirror, her self-directed anger increasing in earnest as she tugged her hairbrush through her thick dark hair. 'For God's sake!' she muttered, regretting cursing the moment the words had passed her lips.

'Edie!' a hollow voice berated from the living room.

Edith exhaled sharply. 'Sorry, Father. It's my hair, it's awful. And my face. They're not going to want to give me *any* job at Blackfriars House, never mind a job as third housemaid.' Edith lifted the unwieldy hair and let it fall untidily around her ears. At seventeen years of age, Edith hated her appearance; she always had. She had hoped that when the change into womanhood had arrived, just like her older sister, Caroline, had once intimated, she would somehow be transformed from the plain-looking girl she saw before her into someone much more beautiful. In fact, the change had only left her with greasy, blotchy skin and equally oily unmanageable hair. Her childish naïvety had led to dreams of metamorphosing into Ellaline Terriss, a stage star with whom Edith had become enchanted after seeing her performing in the musical comedy *The Beauty of Bath* at the Aldwych Theatre. It was Ellaline's centre-parted hair which fell into neat ringlets that Edith was attempting to replicate. She rubbed her face with a *Papier Poudre* wipe, trying to render her skin the desirable, pallid complexion of Edwardian ladies rather than the hideous dark complexion that she and her sisters had inherited from their father.

'There's nothing wrong with your appearance, Edie,' her twin sister, Mary said, emerging from their shared bedroom. 'You're fine-looking.' Mary looked over her sister's shoulder, smiling and placing a gentle hand on her shoulder.

Edith shrugged her sister's hand off. 'Fine-looking. Who wants to be *fine*-looking?' The twins were polar opposites in looks. Mary was a natural beauty with fiery red hair, stunning hazel eyes and a dark complexion; she never saw the need to constantly titivate and fiddle with her hair or try to look like the plethora of glamorous women who adorned the postcards stuck to the walls by Edith's bed.

'Are you nearly ready? It's almost nine-thirty,' Mary asked softly.

Edith sighed. 'I'll have to be. It won't do to be fine-looking *and* late for the interview: I'll never get the job.'

Mary ran her fingers through Edith's hair, gently teasing apart the lank strands. She leant in and pecked her sister on the cheek. 'Let's go.'

Edith poked her head around the living-room door. Their father, in his tatty labourer's clothes, was sitting beside the simmering open-fire, smoking a pipe and attempting to repair one of his boots. 'See you later,' Edith said.

Her father nodded without looking up and said nothing until Edith reached the front door. 'Mary, you want to try learning from your sister. About time you paid your way, you two.'

A knowing, conversant glance passed between the sisters as Edith took a deep breath and opened the door. A surge of freezing, winter air rushed at Edith's face. She pulled her coat tight and stepped onto a fresh flight of snow with Mary close by in her shadow. The tiny town was even more still and calm than usual. The swathes of white snow, which had steadily fallen for the past three days, seemed to mute every flicker of life.

The Mercers lived in a small stone cottage in Winchelsea, a town whose former glory days as the premier Cinque Port, taking pride of place on the Sussex coast, were long since over. For hundreds of years the townsfolk had quietly watched the coast recede from view, taking with it the reliance upon the sea. Gone were the mariners, seamen, rope-makers, shipbuilders, tradesmen, sailors and coastguards, replaced with labourers, farmers and domestic servants.

Mary pulled her coat tight. 'Bloody hell, that's cold,' she whispered with a giggle.

'Shh, or you'll get us both shot,' Edith said with a glance over her shoulder.

Mary pushed herself into her sister's side, as icy winds scooped great squalls of fresh snow up from the low-lying fields to the exposed streets. 'He can't hear us. What's he in such a foul mood for anyway?' Mary asked.

'The usual—this weather means no work on the farm, which means we're relying on the pittance Mum earns doing the laundry for Mrs Booth.'

The girls slowly made their way past the white weather-boarded cottages of Friar's Road, their shoes crunching the unblemished snow. The only signs of Winchelsea's having a heartbeat emanated from the

11

wispy bands of smoke rising and dancing from the chimneys of each house that they passed, lacing the air with the scent of charred wood.

'Curse this wretched wind,' Edith snapped, nudging her sister away and grasping her hair at the sides. 'I'll look like such a state when I get there.'

'Why do you care so much about your appearance? They're employing you as a housemaid, not a music hall star.'

Edith's cheeks tinged with an almost-imperceptible crimson but it was enough for her twin to identify as a flush of embarrassment. 'I just want to look my best, that's all.'

Mary stopped, mouth agape in mock astonishment. 'Edith Jane Mercer! You've got a fancy man working at Blackfriars! Is that why you want to work all the hours God sends as a housemaid?'

Edith ignored her sister and continued walking, her head turned indignantly to one side. 'I've got no such thing,' she muttered.

Mary skipped along the frozen ground until she was a step ahead of her twin. 'What's his name, then? Not Charles? You don't want to be a gardener's wife do you? Or is it Jack Maslow? He is very handsome,' Mary giggled.

'There's nobody,' Edith replied indignantly, pretending to be absorbed by the bare wintry branches of passing trees.

Mary grasped Edith's arm. 'Tell me, Edie,' she said, a subtle seriousness to her tone.

Edith stopped and stared at her sister. A pregnant pause passed. 'I think Edward has his eye on me, that's all. Nothing more. No salacious gossip. No courtship. No *fancy man.*'

Mary frowned. '*Cousin* Edward?'

'What other Edwards do you know?'

'But...' Mary began.

'But what? What will the family say? I don't care what anyone says or thinks. You're allowed to marry your cousin. They need to stop being so *Victorian*,' Edith said heatedly.

Mary mumbled something under her breath, as she was so accustomed to doing when her sister annoyed her. In past quarrels, Edith would usually have taken the bait and asked her sister to repeat what she had said. On this occasion she held her tongue.

The girls continued walking in silence, the only sound being the sporadic surge of snowy wind coursing through the trees.

'Does he feel the same?' Mary enquired softly, watching as her shoes pressed perfectly into the fresh powder.

'I don't know. Maybe. Just leave it, will you, Mary?' Edith retorted.

The twins wordlessly trudged towards the dark entrance gates of Blackfriars, an icy wind carrying with it a fresh flurry of snow, only adding to the chill steadily permeating the sisters' clothing.

Edith stopped at the open gates, took a deep, chilly breath and began to walk towards the mansion with Mary a short distance behind her.

'Do you remember when we were little girls, sitting in our bedroom pretending we were Lord and Lady Rothborne?' Mary asked with a smile, hoping to thaw the atmosphere between them.

'We were young and silly,' Edith retorted, turning her attention to the large friary, which had at last come into view. The girls had been to the property on numerous prior occasions when locals were invited by the benevolent hosts to tea dances, fêtes and charity functions in the vast acres of Blackfriars. Despite their familiarity, whenever they saw the creamy-yellow Caen-stone building they were left in awe and wonderment at what went on inside such a grand place. Their cousin, Edward, had worked at the property as a footman for a number of years and had spoken of Blackfriars as if it were some exotic creature. He had often told them of the great extravagancies which took place there. He had described the sumptuous balls and elaborate birthday parties with such detail as to fill the sisters with a deep envy.

The girls neared the grand entrance where fresh snow had begun to settle on the swept stone steps. Remembering what she had been told, Edith veered away from the front door.

'Wouldn't it be wonderful just to waltz in through the front door?' Mary said.

Edith didn't answer, making her way over to the side entrance to a plain wooden door. With a short, cursory glance at Mary, she knocked on the wrought-iron ring and waited.

A great puff of warm air, laced with a morning's baking, wafted past Edith's face as the door was pulled open. Standing in full smart uniform was Mrs Cuff, the housekeeper, with whom the twins were acquainted from the village. She was a tall lady with a friendly, hospitable face. Her dark hair was pulled neatly into a bun at the back of her head. 'Come in, girls,' she said, standing aside to allow them in.

Edith and Mary stepped into the welcome embrace of the large kitchen, bustling with domestic servants busily performing their duties. The chef, a rotund man with a strong French accent and little

13

knowledge of the English language, was barking orders at three kitchen maids who scuttled around the room like terrified mice.

An impromptu smile crept up on Edith, as for the first time in her life, she felt that she belonged: *destiny* wanted her to become a part—a small part, she knew—in the carefully orchestrated running of Blackfriars House. She had plans, definite, firm plans which would see her rise through the ranks of the household staff. If she worked diligently, which she was certainly not afraid of doing, she would be promoted to second, then first housemaid, then lady's maid and would eventually become a close confidante of Lady Rothborne. In years to come, she could be the housekeeper—the highest ranking female member of staff—and *she* would be the one to welcome new applicants to the post of third housemaid. She knew the job would be arduous with long hours and few breaks but she would be paid the handsome sum of twenty pounds per year—far and above anything she had ever earned before. Finally, she would have the independence that she craved.

'I'll take your coats, girls,' Mrs Cuff said, extending her arm expectantly. 'I'll take you to Her Ladyship momentarily.'

Handing over their cold, damp coats, the girls stood awkwardly and watched the comings and goings of the staff, who seemed entirely oblivious to the new arrivals' presence, each engrossed in executing their own duties.

Mrs Cuff disappeared with the coats, returning moments later. 'Ready, Miss Mercer?'

Edith inhaled slowly, delighting in her new title. *Miss Mercer.* All the years of slaving for her mother and quietly absorbing the mechanisms of running a household had led to this moment. *Miss Mercer, third housemaid at Blackfriars of Winchelsea, Sussex.* With a slight nod of the head, Edith moved across the kitchen. 'I've never been more ready, Mrs Cuff.'

Mary, standing unobtrusively at the edge of the room, went to wish her sister luck, but before she knew it, Edith had been enveloped into the depths of the house without so much as a glance back at her twin. A few years ago Mary might have been irritated at her sister's indifference but, for some time since, Mary was growing used to her sister's increasing aloofness and detachment. She supposed that was just what happened to twins as they grew up and wanted to assert and be known for their own personalities.

Mary looked blithely around the kitchen, wondering at the uses of the implements, pots and pans hanging from giant hooks around the room. To her, many of them looked like instruments of torture. A myriad iron pipes of varying sizes led from a giant black range, leading to goodness only knew where. A huge copper pot, larger than anything that she had ever seen before, caught her attention. She went over to it, almost mesmerised by its splendour. It was so perfectly shiny and smooth that she could see her own curious face staring back at her. As she stared at the distorted bronzed-hued reflection, Mary suddenly became aware of the stillness of the kitchen. The orders had stopped and the maids had all vanished.

A stark shadow passed behind her and she felt hot putrid breath on her neck. She turned quickly to see the chef's quizzical face glaring at her.

'*Prends ça à la bibliotèque, maintenant!*' he barked.

Mary froze, staring at his harsh features, only understanding fragments of his order. The chef thrust a steaming silver coffee pot towards her.

'*Prends!*' he repeated, his cold eyes swelling intensely. '*Tiens!*'

Did bibliotèque mean library? Mary wondered, struggling to recall her French lessons from school. The idea of even catching a glimpse of the wonderful, celebrated Blackfriars' library filled her with a joy that far outweighed the potential stupidity of her decision to reach across and tentatively take the silver coffee pot. 'Biblotèque?' she said softly.

Angry yellow teeth appeared between the chef's cracked lips. 'Oui, la bibliotèque,' he said, slowly repeating each word. Spit flew from his mouth on the final word.

Mary gave a submissive nod of her head and walked purposefully from the kitchen with the coffee pot. 'What a disgusting creature!' she mumbled to herself, entirely unsure of where she was headed exactly. Ahead of her a long, narrow corridor with plain, whitewashed walls fed several closed doors. She knew that she needed to find a staircase which led to the east wing, having once caught sight of the grand library during a summer fete. As she reached the end of the corridor, Mary shuddered from the cold, having left the reaches of the hot kitchen ranges. She found herself at a corridor which ran perpendicular to the last. Standing still, Mary closed her eyes and tried to imagine a birds' eye view of Blackfriars. If she was not mistaken, then she needed to take a left turn into the bowels of the east wing, then search for a staircase to the next floor. The library should then be somewhere close by.

As Mary began to walk along the flag-stone floor, she quickly spotted a staircase and smiled. She climbed the steps and, at the top, she pushed open a heavy-set wooden door, appearing in a grand, decadent hallway which stole her breath away. Mary's eyes flitted and danced across the huge family portraits that hung on beautifully elaborate ruby and gold wallpaper, across pieces of ornate furniture, enormous porcelain and pottery pieces, which would take up most of her tiny bedroom, and a gigantic cascading chandelier. Whilst her twin sister dreamed of *working* her life in a grand place such as this, Mary dreamed of living her life in it, *becoming* Lady Mary Rothborne and owning all of these precious things. She knew that it was an impossible fatuous dream, but it was one that had failed to release its childhood grip on her ever since she had first met Cecil Mansfield, heir to the Blackfriars estate, at a summer fête in 1902 to celebrate King Edward's coronation. Although she was just nine years old at the time, and he was thirteen years her senior, that moment cemented Mary's infatuation with him and his family. The childish games that Edie had just mocked her for, the annual family attendance at the Blackfriars fêtes, were always at Mary's initiation and insistence. Her infatuation was knocked but not diminished when Cecil became married to Philadelphia Carnarvon.

The sound of laughter jolted Mary from her musings. She cursed herself for her silly daydreams and fantasies—they were always getting her into trouble. She tucked herself against a large stone pillar and peered to the side. Two gentlemen whom she did not recognise headed across the hallway, chatting animatedly as they went. They disappeared from sight and Mary quickly moved into the east wing of the house. Once there, the library was impossible to miss and, as she reached the open doorway, she had to remind herself to move inside the room where she would be out of sight, rather than stand dumbstruck at the sheer marvel of the room.

Mary set the coffee pot down and took in the splendour of the library. An eerie grey light caused by the falling snow fell through the tall, latticed windows. Her eyes danced excitedly around the room, unable to focus on any one aspect. Thousands upon thousands of books lined floor-to-ceiling shelving, set within intricately carved walnut panels. An open fire stacked with seasoned oak pumped life and heat into the room; Mary knew that if she had been the lady of the

16

house, *this* would have been the place that she would spend her days. Mary, unlike her twin, had an insatiable appetite for books of all kinds: she read about kings and queens, nature, history, science, foreign countries and, on her father's instruction, she read the Bible. Under Mary's bed was a veritable treasure trove of fiction books—stories which she read over and over, living her life vicariously through the protagonists' exciting lives. However dreary and unpalatable her life really was, Mary always knew she had a whole different, more exciting and exotic world waiting under her bed. Standing here, in the Blackfriars grand library was better than anything that she could have produced from her imagination.

Having taken in the scale and wonder of the room, Mary moved to the nearest shelf and pored over the tomes before her. Her forefinger moved carefully over the coarse spines, tracing the gold and black lettering, absorbing unfamiliar authors and titles. To her delight, Mary's fingertip came to rest on *Four Sisters*, the most recent novel by her favourite author, Alice Ashdown. She delicately pulled the book from the shelf then turned it over in her hands.

'What are you doing?' a voice whispered at the open doorway, making Mary drop the book in fright.

'Edward! Don't creep up on me like that!' Mary said.

Edward pushed the door closed. 'Mary, I'm serious. What are you doing in here?'

'Bringing up a coffee pot. I couldn't find one of the dreadful servants, so I did it myself,' she said playfully. 'I shall be having coffee, luncheon, afternoon tea, dinner and supper in here.' Mary stooped down in an exaggerated fashion to pick up the fallen book. 'See to it that I'm not disturbed, Mister Mercer.'

Edward shook his head. 'Mary, you'll get us both in big trouble if you're found in here.'

'Please address me as *Lady Mercer*,' Mary said with her head held high, staring down her nose at her cousin, the handsome Blackfriars footman. She and Edward had both inherited their grandfather's fiery red hair, a simple familial resemblance, but which others imbued with implications about shared personality traits. It was true that, as children, Edward was one of the few people who had really understood her mischievous sense of adventure. After Edie, Edward had always been her favourite relative.

A small smile appeared on Edward's face. 'Mary, put that book back. This coffee is for Lady Rothborne, she'll be in here at any moment.'

Mary flung her red hair to one side and marched in an exaggeratedly indignant fashion to the tall windows. 'In view of the impetuous snow we're having of late, I shall enjoy my coffee on this delightful window seat. Fetch it over please, Mercer.' Mary sat bolt upright in the window *chaise longue*, the book placed in her lap, with all the posture of an eminent lady.

Edward drew closer and stood in front of her. '*Lady* Mercer,' he said exaggeratedly. 'Will you *please* get out of here!' Edward gently placed his hand on her elbow and ran his fingers up her arm and into her tousled hair.

His touch sent a wave of delight through her, a feeling that shocked and surprised her. She remembered what Edie had just told her and whipped her head to one side so that his hand fell from her. She looked at the window and watched fat chunks of snow silently colliding with the window, slowly transforming into droplets of water.

A moment's silence was interrupted by the sound of the door opening behind them, quickly followed by a mild gasp. Edward immediately side-stepped and stood up straight, knowing that he had been caught.

'What in *God's name* is happening here?' a grave, female voice bellowed across the library.

Mary looked over at the doorway and there, in an elegant coal-black dress which stretched to the floor, stood the formidable Lady Rothborne, Dowager Countess of Blackfriars. She allowed her words to linger and echo among the book-laden walls like a reverberating spell. Despite her old age, she stood with perfect posture, staring at the pair of them.

Edward stepped forward with a deferential nod of his head. 'Your Ladyship, I was just showing Miss Mercer the way out. She got lost bringing your coffee up. She was doing the chef a favour.'

Lady Rothborne strode into the room and stopped before Edward. 'Miss *Mercer*?'

'Yes, Your Ladyship—she is my cousin.'

'I can see the resemblance,' Lady Rothborne said, without so much as a glance towards Mary. 'What is your *cousin* doing assisting Monsieur Bastion? I was not aware of any new scullery maids at Blackfriars. Where is her uniform?'

Edward's eyes sank to the floor. 'She was just waiting here while her sister has an interview with Lady Rothborne, Your Ladyship. She has come for the job of third housemaid.'

Lady Rothborne raised an eyebrow, her harsh features softening momentarily. 'Has she now?' She glanced across to Mary but addressed Edward. 'That will be all, Mercer.'

Edward looked uncertainly at Mary.

'That will be all, Mercer,' Lady Rothborne reiterated in a louder, more severe tone.

'Yes, my lady,' Edward said. With a slight nod of the head, he hurried from the room, closing the door behind him.

Mary stared at Lady Rothborne, anxiously waiting for her to speak; even to look at her directly. Edie would be mortified to know that she had been caught by Lady Rothborne holding a book from the Blackfriars library. Mary lowered the copy of *Four Sisters* and slowly began to push it behind her back.

Without a flinch, Lady Rothborne turned and snapped, 'And what are you planning on doing with *that*?'

'Well, I would love to borrow it,' Mary said.

Lady Rothborne could not hide a look of puzzlement. 'You want to borrow a book from the Blackfriars library, Miss Mercer?'

'Only if you don't mind.'

Lady Rothborne raised her eyebrows. 'I'm afraid there is no precedence for handing books out willy-nilly to the public.' She paused and smiled. 'For employees, on the hand, we might make an exception. May I ask, why you did not apply for the role of third housemaid?'

Mary shrugged. 'I don't have the experience. My sister, Edie has done it for years.'

Lady Rothborne smiled. 'Nonsense. I'm sure you would pick it up in a flash. Would you like a job here?'

Mary's eyes suddenly came alive, as her imagination was reignited. Books, cousin Edward, Lord Rothborne: little consideration was required. It wasn't exactly what she had dreamed of but it was a start. A way in. 'Yes, I would like that very much.'

Chapter Three

Morton was sitting in his study, sipping a large cup of coffee and steadily sifting through the wodge of paperwork provided by his new client, Ray Mercer. Having initially buzzed through the pile of papers in order to ascertain the contents, he was now working through them systematically, creating a basic genealogical chart for the Mercer family as he went. So far, so ordinary. Nothing which would give rise to the disappearance of a seventeen year-old girl. He had so far been most intrigued by the note left on Edith's grave in 1962. *I hope you are at peace.* Morton had carefully studied the script—the writer had beautiful flowing handwriting, like nothing he had ever seen before. Using skills learnt in his degree, Morton analysed the pressure, stroke and letter size on the note then compared it to the photocopy from the book, where Mary had inscribed her name and address in the inside cover. Without doubt, they belonged to the same person. Only once he was certain of this did Morton read the graphologist's report, which drew identical conclusions. He was still perturbed by the wording of the note. *I hope you are at peace* was a mile away from *rest in peace.* Morton stared up at the wall of his study that he used when working on a case. At the very centre of the wall was the photo of Mary and Edith, with various certificates, notes and census reports Blu-Tacked around it. He stuck the two samples of handwriting onto the wall then turned back to the stack of papers given to him by Ray Mercer. At the top of the pile was a photocopy of the newspaper article featured in *The Sussex Express,* dated Saturday 22nd April 1911.

Missing Local Girl
Readers are being asked to keep a look-out for a Winchelsea girl, following her mysterious disappearance. Miss Mary Mercer, in the employ of the Mansfield family of Blackfriars, had left her duties as usual for her half day's leave on Wednesday 12th April, but failed to reach her home of 3 Friar's Cottages. Readers will be saddened to learn that, despite a thorough searching of the locality on Saturday last, Miss Mercer's whereabouts still remain unknown. Family and friends joined a fruitless search, looking far and wide for the seventeen-year-old girl. Sergeant Boxall of the Sussex County Police is leading an investigation into Miss Mercer's disappearance.

Morton looked at the dates mentioned in the article and noted down the date of Mary's disappearance. The 1911 census, taken on the 2nd April 1911, would provide Morton with a tentative snapshot of those present in Mary's life, days prior to her disappearance. Returning to the principle that *somebody* at the time must have known what had happened to her, he had drawn up three lists of people close to Mary in April 1911: friends, family and work. Morton first turned his attention to the work list. The copy taken from the 1911 census showed Mary Mercer working as a live-in housemaid at Blackfriars House in Winchelsea. Above her name were written the names of three other domestic servants, which Morton scribbled down. The rest of the household had not been given to him, being on a previous page. Morton fired up his laptop, logged onto the internet and accessed the 1911 census on the Ancestry website. Moments after typing in Mary's full name and year of birth, a scanned copy of the original census report appeared onscreen, identical to that in his hands. Morton clicked onto the page before to see the full list of occupants of Blackfriars House. Mary had been in the employ of the Mansfield family. Heading the family was Cecil Mansfield, the Earl of Rothborne and his wife, Philadelphia, to whom he had been married for six years. The couple had no children. His mother, Lady Rothborne, a widow, was listed next, followed by Frederick Mansfield, cousin to the head of the house, and a plethora of domestic staff. As Morton carefully noted down each person, his eyes landed on a familiar surname: Edward James Mercer, unmarried, twenty-one years old, footman, born in Icklesham, Sussex. *What were the chances of there being an unrelated Mercer working in the same house as Mary?* Morton wondered. Not very high, he reasoned, adding this name to the list of Mary's family members; he would need further research. Morton printed the page then saved the file. A quick correlation of census reports and birth records on the Ancestry website confirmed that Edward Mercer was Mary's first cousin. Edward now featured on both the *family* and *work* lists.

Morton sat back, took a mouthful of the warm coffee and stared at the list of names before him. His eyes rested on the family list. Mary's mum, dad and sister lived at number three, Friar's Cottages, the same place in which they had resided ten years previously. The eldest Mercer girl, Caroline, was absent from the family home in 1911. Morton typed 'Caroline Ransom' into the search box and found her, just as Ray Mercer had said, living in Bristol. She was recorded as a widow having been married for two years with no children. Having printed the page out, Morton ran a yellow highlighter over Caroline's name. If Mary was going to run away from home, then an elder sister in Bristol seemed a good potential place to which to flee.

Morton stood up and wandered over to the tiny window which gave onto the old, cobbled streets of Mermaid Street, Rye in East Sussex. He and Juliette, his long-term girlfriend, had lived here for a few months now, his previous house having been destroyed in the pursuit of a genealogical case. It was a sixteenth century house, filled with all the quirks and eccentricities of an ancient property, the first being the house name: *The House with Two Doors*. That alone had almost been enough to stop Juliette from even setting foot in the place. 'Can't we just live somewhere normal, Morton?' she had pleaded. 'Why do you feel the need to live somewhere strange? We don't *have* to live in a windmill, or a Martello tower, or a prison, or a converted Methodist chapel, we could just opt for a modern house with modern things like central heating, double-glazing and vertical walls and horizontal floors. Is that *really* too much to ask?'

'Let's just take a look,' Morton had replied, as they had approached the property.

'I don't even know which bloody door to knock on,' Juliette had mumbled.

It was a fair point, Morton had had to concede. Both looked like front doors. Both had gold knockers and handles. The right one had the extra feature of a letterbox, so he had opted for that one.

It had taken Morton his first step inside to fall in love with it; it had taken Juliette two full viewings of the house and a detailed list of the pros and cons of living there before an offer was finally made and accepted. Now, eight months later, she loved it just as much as he did.

Morton spotted a tourist pointing at his front doors. It was a daily occurrence, particularly at the height of summer, when flocks of visitors would descend on Rye to spot Mermaid Street's quirky house names. He pushed open the latticed window and breathed in air laden with the outpourings of various nearby tearooms, and re-focussed his mind back on the Mercer Case. If Mary had indeed run away to her sister's house in Bristol, there would be few records to corroborate this; the 1911 census was the most recent to be made publicly available and electoral registers did not extend to include women until 1918, and even then only if they were aged over thirty and owned property. Mary would be much more likely to appear among unofficial sources, family folklore and faded photo albums than in official records: Morton needed to find out if Caroline and William had any living descendants through their daughter, Rebecca.

Returning to his laptop, he opened up a search page on Ancestry for the birth of Rebecca Ransom with the mother's maiden name, Mercer. One result.

'December quarter of 1911. Rebecca Victoria Ransom, mother's maiden name, Mercer. District of Bristol. Volume 6a. Page 103.'

Morton smiled. His next step was to ensure that Rebecca actually made it into adulthood, although from what Ray Mercer had said about this side of the family's not being very helpful, he guessed that she had lived a full life. On previous cases, Morton's exhilaration at this same point had been dashed when he had discovered that the child had died soon after birth. He typed Rebecca's name into the 1916-2007 marriage index and found that she had married a Victor Reginald Catt in 1935. Putting her name into the death search index 1916 to 2007 gave one result.

Name: Rebecca Victoria Catt
Birth date: 1st November 1911
Date of Registration: June 1993
Age at death: 81
Registration District: Bristol
Inferred County: Gloucestershire
Register Number: 13c
District and Subdistrict: 3011I
Entry number: 124

Morton was pleased to see that Rebecca had married and lived a full life. Now he needed Rebecca to have left the standard paper trail of children and grandchildren. Switching back to the birth index, Morton found that Victor and Rebecca had produced three children together: two boys and a girl, all born in the Bristol area. To save time, Morton prioritised his searches with the two boys, Reginald and Douglas.

In the time that it took for Morton to finish the final splashes of his coffee, he had undertaken searches into the genealogical backgrounds of Reginald and Douglas Catt. He had confirmed that both men were still alive, both had their own wives and children and, using an electoral roll website, he had an address and phone number for each man. He considered cold-calling them but only liked to do this in the most urgent circumstances. Before typing out a letter to each man, he carried out a quick Google search of their names.

'Bingo,' Morton said, as he clicked his cursor onto the website of 'V. R. Catt and Sons, Ironmongers.' According to their website, Victor Reginald Catt had set up an ironmonger's store in Bristol in 1948, his two sons gradually taking over the business in the 1980s. Morton saved a black and white photograph of Victor outside his shop in 1950 and a colour image of him and his sons outside the shop celebrating their fortieth anniversary in 1988.

Navigating back to their home page, Morton clicked on the 'Contact us' tab and then set about typing a message into the contact form. *'Dear Douglas and Reginald, I hope you don't mind my emailing you out of the blue like this; I am a forensic genealogist who is researching the Mercer family tree, to which I believe you belong. In particular, I am concentrating on trying to discover what became of Mary Mercer, the sister of your grandmother, Caroline Ransom (née Mercer), who disappeared without trace in 1911. At this very early stage in my investigations, I am considering that one avenue of possibility is that Mary may have visited her sister Caroline at some point in or after 1911 and would really welcome your thoughts on this. I look forward to hearing from you. Kind regards, Morton Farrier.'*

Morton clicked the 'Submit' button and the message vanished. He now just needed to wait patiently and hope that they would respond. Morton returned to the three lists of people close to Mary in 1911. By far, the longest list was the staff of Blackfriars. *Did the household and staff accounts books still survive?* Morton wondered. A brief Google search told him that the property was in the hands of the Mansfield family, the same family as in 1911 when Mary had disappeared. He had driven past the imposing property countless times, Winchelsea being on the unavoidable route between his house in Rye and his father's in Hastings, yet, despite it having been open to the public since 1960, he had never actually set foot in it. It was high time for a visit.

Morton had trained to be a forensic genealogist in the time before family history had exploded onto the internet. He loved the immediacy and speed of such a huge plethora of records being online, but for him, the biggest enjoyment came from an immersion in history: holding ancient documents between his fingers, analysing faded photographs and uncovering lichen-covered tombstones in the search of an elusive ancestor. He needed little convincing to step out of his study for some hands-on research.

He had decided to park on Friar's Road in the summer shadows of the town church. Grabbing his bag, he stepped out into the early-afternoon sun, taking in the stillness of the small town. Winchelsea, being just three miles from his home, had always fascinated him. The casual visitor or holidaymaker often came here to see a quaint, well-preserved English village; those unguided tourists left without the knowledge that it was in fact a town, once envisaged by its founder, Edward I, as one of the leading seaports in England. Further confusion often came by the unique design of the town using a grid pattern, something which often confused visitors used to associating it with modern American cities.

Morton began to assimilate his surroundings, picturing himself here more than one hundred years ago, consciously removing all traces of modern life.

It was very easy to imagine Friar's Road in 1911; but for the addition of a scattering of cars and a couple of television aerials and satellite dishes, the village was delightfully devoid of the usual modern street furniture; it even lacked street lighting. He turned his attention to the run of attractive stone and brick cottages. Number three Friar's Cottage was the penultimate house in a run of charming rose-covered properties. Having only one small window downstairs and one upstairs, it was among the smallest houses on the street, which Morton knew meant that the girls would very likely have shared a room prior to Mary's departure for service at Blackfriars. It was little wonder then that Edith was devastated at her sister's disappearance.

Morton removed his Nikon camera from his bag and took several shots of the house, all the while hoping that the owner wouldn't spot him and burst out to ask him what he was doing. It had not yet happened in his career, but he never really had a clear answer ready as to what he would say. He always thought the truth sounded too convoluted or complicated. He tucked his camera back into his bag and strolled down the quiet road. Traffic visitors to Blackfriars were directed along the main A259 road to the front entrance, but Morton knew that just past the village primary school was an unpublicised footpath into the estate. He was sure that this was the way which Mary Mercer would have walked to and from work on her days off. It had struck Morton as curious when he had first noticed on the census that she was living at the property, despite only living metres away. It was only after he had reflected on the nature of her job as a housemaid that he understood that her duties would have required her to spend almost every waking hour in service with only half a day's leave per week.

He reached a pair of stone pillars just wide enough to accommodate a standard horse and carriage, then crossed into Blackfriars. He walked slowly down the concrete path which bisected a perfectly manicured lawn. As the path drew closer to the house, a teasing glimpse of a purple wisteria-engulfed wing appeared. He continued as the house appeared inch by inch in front of him. When the full magnificence of Blackfriars came into view, Morton stopped and stared in awe. Despite the few members of the public milling about near to the building, he was able to see the estate through the Edwardian eyes of Mary Mercer. She too must have been locked in sheer admiration the first time that she walked this path. As he neared the building, he turned back on himself and stared at the winding path that he had just taken. Somewhere on that route back to Friar's Cottage on Wednesday 12th April 1911, Mary Mercer had vanished for more than fifty years. *Where did you go?* Morton wondered, as he photographed the pathway. *And why?*

Morton slung his camera around his neck and became absorbed in a growing crowd, steadily moving towards the makeshift ticket office outside the Blackfriars front door.

Every snippet of conversation emanating from the queue to enter Blackfriars centred on the television show, *The Friary,* a popular Sunday night drama about the 'upstairs downstairs' lives of an Edwardian aristocratic family. Blackfriars was used for the external shots and some of the 'upstairs' filming. Juliette loved the programme but Morton took great offence at the historical liberties taken in the name of entertainment; it was exactly the same for Juliette and police dramas. Except now that she was training to be a fully-paid up member of the police, rather than a PCSO, she was even more sceptical and deriding.

The gap shrank between Morton and the lone ticket-seller sitting behind a wooden trestle table with an open cash-box. *Not the most sophisticated ticket office in the world,* Morton thought, but he knew that a modern day ticket office would look slightly anachronistic in an Edwardian television drama.

Finally, he reached the front of the queue and was greeted with a sharp frown from a plump lady with a ruddy complexion and white curly hair. Her name badge announced her as 'Mrs Greenwood'.

'Welcome to the Blackfriars estate,' she said in a voice which told Morton that she had said it a million times before.

'Morning.'

'Have you been here before?' she asked monotonously.

'No, first time,' Morton said.

'I expect you're a fan of the show.'

'Yeah, I guess so,' Morton said vaguely, wondering why, yet again, lying was much simpler than telling the truth.

The dreary lady informed him that his sixteen pounds entrance fee bought him a ticket which was valid for a year, and a map of the estate. He additionally purchased a five pounds guide book, which, from having a quick flick through whilst he handed over his money, appeared to blend trivia from the show with factual historical information. Morton spotted an extract which seemed to be an Edwardian estate accounts list. Underneath it was a modern photo of a smartly dressed, spectacled man in his fifties. The caption to the photo labelled him as the Blackfriars archivist, Sidney Mersham.

'Do you happen to know if Sidney Mersham is in at all today?' Morton asked, snatching the opportunity.

The lady frowned. 'I don't know,' she said, without giving the question a moment's consideration, before adding, 'I come in, hang my coat up downstairs, then I'm stuck here for the rest of the day.'

Morton smiled, hoping that it might enliven the jaded cashier. 'I'm a forensic genealogist and I'm trying to find out if any staff records exist for the Edwardian period here. Do you think there's anyone I could speak to today?'

The lady sighed. 'They're not keen on opening up their records to the public,' she warned, handing him his change.

'Any chance you could ask for me?' Morton pleaded.

She rolled back her sleeve and looked at her watch. 'I'm off on my break shortly. I'll see who's around to ask.'

'That would be great, thank you. I'll be in the main house.' Morton flashed his best smile and made his way into the grand entrance hall, joining the tail-end of a snaking queue, penned in by narrow maroon ropes, which separated the public from the ornate furnishings. Strategically placed around the room were enlarged stills taken from *The Friary*, showing the approximate location the actors had stood in a particular episode of the programme. Morton would have liked to get some photographs of the house to help him build an impression of what life was like here for Mary in 1911, but numerous large signs explicitly banned it in every language possible.

The line of babbling, excited visitors wound their way past an officious custodian, who directed them into the grand saloon. The two women directly in front of Morton stopped dead.

'Oh my golly!' one them said in a thick southern American accent. 'Did you ever seen such a thing?'

'It's like I'm in *The Friary*!' her friend replied. 'Good afternoon, Your Ladyship,' she added in her best attempt at an aristocratic British accent.

The first woman turned to Morton. 'Would you look at that? Have you ever seen anything so beautiful?'

He had, but he didn't like to put a dampener on their visit. 'No, it's amazing,' Morton said, trying to sound more excited than he felt. He had to agree, though, that the saloon *was* fairly impressive. The room was long and rectangular with a high, vaulted ceiling. Stone gothic arches gave Morton a glimpse of the stream of visitors being herded through the first floor.

The line continued to move through the wooden-panelled room with its enormous stone fireplace, where the coats of arms of five generations of Mansfields were intricately carved.

The saloon opened out onto a large hallway dominated by a sparkling chandelier and several imposing oil paintings of long-deceased members of the Mansfield family. Morton took out his guide book and took a cursory glance at the information given about some of the paintings. The vast majority had been hanging since pre-Edwardian times.

Morton continued through the hallway, past several out-of-bounds doors until he reached the extensive library. When he entered the vast room, he understood why it was described in the guide book as 'the jewel in the Blackfriars crown'. It was one of the largest private collections of books that Morton had ever seen. Visitors were funnelled through the library in a one-way system, giving little time to stop and take in the splendour of the room. He looked longingly at the dusty books, tantalisingly close, yet imprisoned by lines of wire, never to be touched or read again. It seemed a tragic waste to Morton that such an impressive collection of tomes should have been reduced to a mere back-drop for a Sunday night television drama.

From his peripheral vision, Morton was aware that he was being pointed at. He turned to see the lady from the visitors' desk smiling and directing a well-groomed man and lady towards him.

'Morning, I'm Milton Mansfield; this is my wife, Daphne,' the man said, in a perfect Etonian voice, as he shook Morton's hand. He looked to be in his late sixties, wearing an expensive-looking suit and a red bow-tie.

'Morton Farrier, pleased to meet you,' he said, a little dumbfounded that his request to speak to someone about the family archives had reached the upper echelons of the house.

Daphne Mansfield stepped forward and offered her hand. 'Lovely to meet you,' she said with a smile. She was a good twenty years Milton's junior with perfect make-up and a short blonde bob. 'You look familiar. Mr Farrier, did you say?'

'Yes, that's right. I'm a forensic genealogist...' Morton was interrupted by a raucous laugh coming from the other side of the library. He turned to see one of the Americans taking photos of the other draped over a life-size cut-out of *The Friary's* leading man.

'Excuse me a moment,' Daphne said, about to intercept a pink-lipstick kiss being planted on the cut-out.

'They love the show over there,' Milton said. 'So, how can we help you, Mr Farrier?'

'Well, I'm really after looking at any staff or household accounts and records which you might have here pertaining to the period around 1911. I'm assuming they're here as there is very little for Blackfriars at East Sussex Archives,' Morton said. To his right, he noticed that Daphne, mid-way through a polite chastising, was looking at him. She cast a doubtful smile in his direction then returned her attention to the Americans.

Milton nodded enthusiastically. 'Yes, all of our records are still kept in-house. A small fire in 1939 did some damage, but pretty well we've got a good collection down there. We've got an archivist, Sidney Mersham, who oversees it all. I don't know off-hand exactly what we've got for the period you're interested in. I'm afraid Sidney is rather busy today, the poor chap's being hounded by the writers of *The Friary*. I'm sure he wouldn't object to a quick discussion at another time.'

'That would be great,' Morton replied. He fished in his jacket pocket and handed over a business card. 'Perhaps Sidney could give me a call?'

'I'll pass it on to him right away.'

Daphne, having subdued the Americans, returned to her husband's side. 'I've realised from where I recognise you. You're the one who brought down the Windsor-Sackville family, aren't you.' Her smile had faded, leaving her disapproval etched on her face.

'That old bunch of crooks!' Milton said with an exaggerated guffaw. 'That needed doing centuries ago!'

Morton noticed Daphne firmly squeeze her husband's arm. 'May I ask what it is you're looking for at Blackfriars, Mr Farrier?' she asked.

'Not *what* I'm looking for—*whom*,' Morton said, before briefly explaining about the outline of the Mercer Case.

'I see,' Daphne said. 'And what is it that you hope to find among our records?'

'Anything which might give a clue to her daily routine here, particularly people she worked with. I'm working on the premise that somebody at the time knew what happened to her.'

'Well, we've nothing to hide, unlike the Windsor-Sackville rogues,' Milton laughed. 'Have a good rummage, you've got your work cut out trying to conduct a missing person's enquiry more than a century later.'

Morton smiled. 'I'll find her,' he said confidently. 'I look forward to hearing from Sidney in due course.'

'Yes, we'll let you get back to your tour. Enjoy,' Milton said.

Daphne nodded with a cautious smile and then threaded her arm through Milton's and led him from the room. As soon as they were out of his earshot, she turned to him and instigated what looked to Morton like a very animated conversation. He had a gut feeling that had Daphne remained in the conversation, he would not have received the invitation to meet with Sidney and possibly search among their archives; he hoped that her influence would not now jeopardise his access.

Morton took one final look around the library before continuing the tour upstairs past various bedrooms, which were all well-appointed with full Edwardian splendour and many of which he recognised from *The Friary*.

Having completed the tour of the house, Morton made his way to the tearoom, which was located in an airy, converted barn a short distance from the house. Morton ordered a large latte and took a seat at a round metallic table. He sat in a warm shard of sunlight, which cut through the glass front. But for an elderly couple queuing at the till, the tearoom was deserted. Sipping on his drink, Morton began to read the Blackfriars guidebook. He quickly learnt that the Mansfields had resided here since shortly after the Dissolution of the Monasteries, when they were gifted the property and the title Earl of Rothborne from Henry VIII. At the centre of the guidebook was a pull-out genealogical chart of the Mansfield family. The current owner and title-holder was Milton Francis Mansfield, Earl of Rothborne, who had inherited the property from his father, George Richard Mansfield. Morton studied the chart carefully: during Mary Mercer's time at Blackfriars, the property was held by Cecil and Philadelphia Mansfield. Morton flipped to the index page and searched for further references to Cecil and Lady Philadelphia; predictably, there were several, as their tenure at Blackfriars neatly coincided with the period portrayed in *The Friary*. Morton went to the first reference and found a photo of the couple alongside a similar modern image of the actors playing Lord and Lady Asquith in *The Friary*. The accompanying information wove a potted history between the Mansfields and the Asquiths, largely, it seemed to Morton, where interesting contrasts and comparisons could be drawn.

Morton tucked the guidebook away in his bag, intending to finish reading it later, and left the tearoom to get a better feel for the whole estate. He followed the gravel footpath and slowly meandered through a patchwork of tall pines, low rhododendrons and great swathes of tidy grass upon which a sprinkling of visitors were picnicking. The path turned and opened out onto a large lake in the shape of a pinched oval. It was filled with lilypads and bordered by a variety of plants, flowers and trees whose low-slung branches dangled inches from the water's surface. Morton felt compelled to take a seat on one of several benches slightly set back from the path facing the water. He sat and watched as a small flock of Canada geese pushed off from the water and elegantly flew off into the distance. Across the water stood a charming, evocative and slightly dilapidated boathouse. The gabled, wooden structure gave Morton the impression of an ancient church, swallowed up by the murky depths, leaving only the peak still visible. He guessed that the boathouse was once used by the Mansfields to access a tall cylindrical stone building situated on a small island in the centre of the lake. The building had no windows, only an arched wooden door. Curious to know more about the strange building, Morton opened his guidebook and read that the tower was a folly, serving no useful purpose. Inside, a metal staircase rose to the

31

top, giving an unobstructed view of the formal rose gardens and Koi fish pond further down the estate. It had been built in the 1850s and so was certainly here during Mary's time as a housemaid.

Morton continued his journey around the periphery of the lake, sauntering slowly and enjoying the fresh air and warmth from the hot sun. The path took him past a Victorian heather-covered ice-house and into the orchard, which contained an array of traditional English apple, pear and plum trees. Close to the path by which he had entered Blackfriars were the ruins of the oldest part of the abbey. The guidebook informed him that it was the ruins of a thirteenth century Franciscan chapel. Morton entered the ruins—just two stone walls and two arches were all that remained. With little else to see, Morton made his way back to the main path to leave. The quickest route back to the car would be the back path which he had taken to get here, but Morton decided to leave via the front entrance, just to get a different perspective on the estate.

The main road into Blackfriars was heaving with cars, coaches and pedestrians, such was the popularity of *The Friary;* Morton, the only person heading in the opposite direction, was like a determined salmon, fighting its way upstream. Finally, he reached the main road, Monk's Walk, and turned right towards the church.

Winchelsea church, dedicated to St Thomas the Martyr, had always seemed out of keeping to Morton, incongruous in the small town, as it was originally built to cathedral proportions. Only the chancel of the original church still existed, following years of ravaging raids by the French and Spanish. Like most of the town, the church sat in a neat square parcel of land. As Morton entered the churchyard, a cool breeze rose around the monstrous church buttresses. He pulled on his jumper and began to search the churchyard for the Mercer family grave.

Despite knowing the age of the graves for which he was searching, Morton still conducted a meticulous search, intending to log any instances where the Mercer name cropped up. In the event, there was only one grave with that name. After fifteen minutes of searching, he found it on the south-east side of the church. Weathered grey with spots of orange lichen, the grave was slightly tilted, but otherwise legible and in good condition.

Morton took several photographs of the grave and also jotted down the inscription. *In loving memory of Katherine Mercer, born 2nd March 1870, died 8th December 1932. A wonderful mother and wife. Also, Thomas*

Mercer, husband of the above, born 21ˢᵗ April 1870, died 1ˢᵗ November 1938. A small open book made of stone had been added to the grave and summarised the life of one of their daughters: *Edith Leyden (née Mercer) 1893-1962.*

Here they were, a small splinter of their fractured family, gone to the grave with no knowledge of Mary's whereabouts. Morton's thoughts turned to what Ray had told him about Mary returning for her sister's funeral. She had stood here, on this very spot in 1962. He wondered if that had been her first visit to Winchelsea since 1911. *What kept you away, Mary?* Morton thought to himself, wrangling with the seemingly unanswerable question. *Why did you only come back when all of your family were dead and buried?* Morton's gaze turned to the enormous church but his mind was firmly on Mary. She had disappeared without trace in 1911, never showing up again on official documents. The most obvious and likely scenario was that she had changed her name. The chances of her *legally* changing her name and leaving a paper trail were not likely but still needed investigating. Morton knew that it was perfectly legal to change your name without registering the fact, so long as it was not for illegal purposes. He knew that the records were not online or even digitised as yet; it would require a personal visit to the National Archives at Kew or the use of a paid researcher.

He took one last look at the grave, then made his way across the diagonal path in the clawed shadow of the church until he reached his car on Friar's Road. Morton opened the Mini, climbed in but did not fire it up. Instead, he sat in the peace of the town, allowing his mind to sew and weave a mental collage of the case. It had always helped Morton to visualise his cases, to bring them to life from the bare boring bones of names and dates. The tapestry in his mind contained the sepia picture of Mary and Edith as children, 3 Friar's Cottage, Blackfriars and the churchyard. The answer to the disappearance of Mary Mercer was woven somewhere into the fabric of this.

Within an hour, Morton had arrived home and sent a research request to the National Archives to search among the indexes of J18—name changes 1903-2003. He had considered visiting the archives in person but with currently only one research avenue to pursue there, the twenty pound search fee per fifteen minutes seemed a better option. He had poured himself a large glass of red wine and then set about the task of making his and Juliette's dinner. Although he had officially stopped work for the day, the case was always being worked on in the back of his mind, as new avenues and ideas were produced.

Juliette arrived home just before six o'clock. 'Wine,' she said, strolling into the kitchen and kissing Morton on the lips.

Morton pointed to the glass waiting on the worktop. 'And how was the Initial Police Learning and Development Programme today?' he teased. Juliette was in phase three of a four-phase training programme to become a police officer and, despite the odd moan and groan, she was loving it. She was born to do it. Juliette kicked off her boots and perched herself at the kitchen table.

'After having a few brilliant days of supervised patrol with the guys from Ashford, today we were back in the classroom at Maidstone. *Class-based learning*. Hence the need for wine. I just don't take it in very well coming from a textbook or the ancient ex-police wheeled in from retirement to share anecdotes. I want to be out on the streets, learning from real life.'

'It won't be long,' Morton reminded her, as he dished up their dinner and carried it over to the table.

'Thanks—looks lovely. How was your day?'

'Not bad,' Morton said, relaying the main highlights of his day. After more than two years together, Morton could now gauge the very thin line of giving just the right bullet-pointed amount of detail about his day before her eyes glazed over and he lost her. He almost crossed the line when he told her that he had hired a researcher at the National Archives to search the records of the Supreme Court of Judicature, then hastily added 'Name change records.' Ever since his last high-profile case, which involved a great deal of illegal activity on his part, she had demanded to know his every move. Now that she was training to become a police officer, she insisted that he *always* stayed on the right side of the law.

'I think we've got an episode of *The Friary* in the Sky planner to watch. Fancy it after dinner?' she asked.

Morton couldn't tell if she was joking of not. 'Only if we can follow it with an episode of *The Bill*.'

Juliette smirked. 'A film it is, then.'

'Perfect. Cheers.'

Under the focussed light from a desk lamp, a man methodically searched, read and printed every page on Morton Farrier's Forensic Genealogist website. With a thirsty concentration, he pored over the printed papers, absorbing and digesting every word. Then he ran a Google search, pulling up pictures and quotes from Morton's past cases. Opening up a new tab in his browser, he logged into a family history website and used some of Morton's own tricks to find out everything about him, including where he lived and with whom. With some difficulty, owing to two bound, broken fingers, the man scooped up all the papers and pushed them into a manila envelope. 'Morton Farrier, I'm coming for you,' he breathed.

Chapter Four

Tuesday 3rd January 1911

Mary Mercer's alarm clock sent its shrill tones into the silent room. She switched it off and sat up in bed. From the other side of their small shared bedroom, Edie emitted a protracted and irritated sigh. Mary had slept very little, the weight of her decision to steal her sister's coveted job preventing her mind from succumbing to sleep. When the two sisters had reconvened in the Blackfriars kitchen, Mary had been assured by Lady Rothborne that the housemaid's job would be hers. She had waited for Edith with her eyes fixed to the floor. Minutes took hours to pass, until she finally arrived. Seventeen years without separation had told Mary everything that she needed to know from her twin's face: Edie already knew that she had lost the job to her sister.

'Edie! Wait!' Mary had cried, as she had bolted through the kitchen door into the blustery Winchelsea snowstorm.

A hand had grabbed Mary by the wrist and prevented her from following. Mary had twisted around to see Mrs Cuff, a polite yet forceful look on her face. 'Let her go. She'll just need some time.'

Mary had given her sister time; she had walked back home so slowly that the freezing air had penetrated through her coat, deep into her very core so that her skin was pink and prickly. Silently, she had headed straight to her room, like a scolded puppy. She had lit the fire, tucked herself under layers of woollen blankets and remained there until bedtime. Such was the weight of her guilt, she could not even bring herself to read the pristine copy of *Four Sisters*, given to her by Lady Rothborne, which she had stared at on her bedside table. It was the first time in her life that Mary had really stood in defiance of Edie, having never previously had the courage. Her heart was heavy and she was filled with remorse for the way that it had happened, yet underneath it all, she stood by her decision. *Why should Edie always get everything handed to her on a plate? It was high time that she learnt to be in someone else's shadow for once.*

Her father and mother had visited Mary on separate occasions last night. Soon after she had arrived home, her father's explosive diatribe blasted the air. 'What do you think you're playing at, my girl? That job was Edie's, not yours. You was only going to keep her company. She's devastated.' Her father's canine-like face had moved closer to hers. 'What have you got to say for yourself, Mary?'

The blankets on Mary's shoulders had moved fractionally with her shrug, as she watched bubbles of angry spittle forming at the corner of her father's mouth.

'Answer me!' he had bellowed, loudly enough to wake the dead in St Thomas's churchyard.

'Lady Rothborne said I would be perfect for the job, so I took it,' Mary had said meekly.

'Perfect on what grounds?' he had seethed. 'I ask you… those stuck up idiots, they don't know nothing. A housemaid, Mary… you can't even keep your own room tidy. You can't make beds, sweep room after room and clean fire grates.'

Mary had drawn in a big lungful of air and risen from the bed, like a caged lion being taunted through the bars. She had levelled with her father. 'Those things can be taught, Father. I'll learn them in a matter of minutes. How hard can it be to put some blankets on a bed or push a broom around? Have you ever thought that maybe I got the job on my personality? That Lady Rothborne thinks of me as the right calibre for Blackfriars? Did it ever occur to you that your precious Edie might not have been right for the job?'

Her father had laughed in mock indignation then slapped Mary hard across the face, sending her tumbling backwards onto her bed. 'My goodness, girl. I don't even recognise my own daughter stood in front of me. You're deluded if you think you're one of them. *Calibre?* That a word your Lady Rothborne friend taught you, is it?'

Mary had yelped in pain and clutched at her face, determined not to cry. 'You said I needed to get a job, to pay my own way…' Mary's voice trailed off, having nothing left to add.

'Not Edith's job! That was meant for her. It's a disgraceful way to treat your sister. What's she ever done to you?' her father had seethed.

Mary could have listed a thousand times that Edie had taken precedence over her, got her own way and been treated more favourably, but she chose to say nothing.

'Disgusting behaviour,' were her father's parting words before he had slammed the door shut; the roaring fire in the grate had responded by scattering a fiery burst of orange ash into the room.

Some time later, her mother had quietly pushed open the bedroom door. 'Are you awake, Mary?' she had asked.

Mary, wide awake but with a blanket pulled over her head, couldn't tell from her mother's expressionless tone how she was going to act towards her.   In past family quarrels, her mother's default position was to sit back in quiet but steadfast support of her husband. Very rarely had she opposed him in an argument because, when it happened, the ill after-effects were felt in the Mercer household for days or even sometimes weeks on end.

'Mary,' her mother had said more loudly.

Mary pulled down the blanket and had hardened herself in readiness for another scolding. 'Come on then, get it over with.'

Her mother had perched herself down on the edge of the bed and taken Mary's left hand in hers. 'Look at me, Mary.'

It was a polite request, not an order, so Mary had looked at her mother and waited for the tirade to begin.

'No, I mean *really* look at me.   Look at my face.'   She had paused, allowing time for Mary's eyes to study the features. 'I'm forty-one, yet when I look in the mirror, an old haggard woman stares back at me.   I've done domestic work all my life.   The job of a third housemaid is jolly hard.   It's relentless.   I watched domestic service slowly kill my own mother and vowed that my three girls wouldn't be taken by it.   It's a poison, Mary.   They may seem like a lovely lot, but they're not cut from the same cloth as us.   They don't care about the likes of you.   Once you put that uniform on, you belong to them. They'll take everything from you until you've nothing left to give, then they'll send you to the Rye workhouse where you'll wait for humiliation and shame to take you to a pauper's grave, just like what happened with your gran. The same will happen to me if your father goes first.'

Mary had been staggered by her mother's beseeching outpouring.   Stories of the workhouse had always haunted and terrified her.   'If that's true, then why did you send Edie to work there?   Why's it okay for her and not me?'

Her mother's face had scrunched slightly, revealing deep-cut wrinkles and lines around her eyes.   She was right; domestic service *had* worn and jaded her.   'It's what Edie's always wanted.   Her whole life, she wanted it and I thought that if that's what she wanted, then she can jolly well be the best she can and climb up the ranks to be a housekeeper—at least they're treated and paid better.   I've prepared her for that life.'   Her mother's voice had softened.   'But you, Mary— you're better than that.   Like Caroline, you could be more than an old laundry maid like me.   You always talked of travelling and getting a decent education.   What's suddenly changed?'

'Maybe I've just grown up,' Mary had replied. Then she had considered her words against the truth of taking a job because she might one day get the chance to run away with Lord Rothborne and in the meantime she had a library full of books to keep her entertained: she was anything but grown up. She was a silly, immature *girl*. Mary had suddenly burst into tears.

'It's okay,' her mother had said, pulling Mary into a comforting embrace. 'It'll work itself out. Something else will come along for poor Edie. Maybe even another job at Blackfriars.'

Through her watery eyes, Mary had thought that she noticed a shadow move from outside her bedroom door: someone had been listening.

The fire in the tiny bedroom hearth was long since dead: all that remained of it now was a handful of unburnt wood and a pile of black and white ash. Mary pulled a blanket around her shoulders and opened the curtains. A glimmer of moonlight peered in through the window, tinting the room with fine white edges. The snow had continued to fall overnight: a new spotless carpet of powder had covered the streets. She needed to wrap up warm, even for the short journey to Blackfriars. She was told by Mrs Cuff to start promptly today at six-thirty, which meant packing a suitcase and preparing to live in. Mary caught her ghostly reflection in the window and remembered what her mother had told her about life in service and how it would take everything and leave nothing unless she worked hard and rose through the ranks of the staff. *It is time to grow up, Miss Mary Mercer. Stop those silly fantasies and dreams of grandeur. You're a servant now. Prove that you can do it.*

Mary took a deep breath of cold courage and began to get dressed. Once she had pulled on sufficient layers to stop herself from shivering, she took a battered brown suitcase out from under her bed and began to fill it. She tiptoed around the room as quickly and quietly as possible, but she knew the creaking floorboards and groaning chest of drawers must have woken Edie a long time ago. Yet Edie did not move. She kept her back to the room, with sheets and blankets held tightly up to her ears.

Her suitcase filled, Mary made her way out of the bedroom. She paused before closing the door and looked at her twin sister. *It's now or never, Mary*, she told herself. *Say something to Edie. Apologise. Make amends.* Yet no words came from either sister. Indignant, Mary pushed the door closed and crept downstairs to the front door. As she slid back the metal bolts on the front door, the sound of a chair creaking came from the lounge. Mary turned to see her mother standing in the haunting light of a muted lamp. Her eyes were swollen and red.

'Mary,' her mother said softly. She opened her arms and pulled Mary in tightly.

'Mother, I'm only going a quarter of a mile down the road! I'll be back next week.'

Her mother released her and smiled as tears streamed down her cheeks. 'Goodbye, love.'

Mary kissed her mother on the cheek. 'Bye.' She turned, tugged open the heavy-set door and stepped out into the freezing darkness.

Through the upstairs bedroom window, Edith watched her sister trudge towards Blackfriars, her wild red hair contrasting with the bright white snow. Then she was gone.

Mary arrived at the back entrance to Blackfriars, expecting to be greeted by the warm smile of Mrs Cuff. Instead, she came face to face with the ugly scowl of Monsieur Bastion. '*Quoi?*' he barked.

Sweeping back her windswept hair, Mary stepped confidently into the kitchen, pushing past the fat Frenchman. 'My name is Mary Mercer, and I am the new third housemaid at Blackfriars. Where will I find Mrs Cuff?'

Monsieur Bastion grunted an incomprehensible reply and raised his hands in disgust.

'I'll take you to her,' said a diminutive girl wearing the full black and white uniform of a domestic servant. She approached Mary and smiled. 'My name's Clara. I'm second housemaid here. Mrs Cuff said I was to show you the ropes.'

'Nice to meet you, I'm Mary Mercer.'

Clara smiled. 'Follow me and I'll take you to our bedroom.'

Mary received a reproving scowl from Monsieur Bastion as she followed Clara out of the kitchen. She led Mary along the narrow dimly-lit corridor until they reached a flight of wooden stairs.

'They go on for an eternity,' Clara said with a small giggle. 'Prepare yourself—there are ninety-six of them—I counted once.'

Each time the steps levelled out, Mary tried to get her bearings, but failed before they were off again. Finally, when the stairs terminated at a roof pitch so steep that she had to duck down to enter

40

the corridor, Mary realised that they were in the attic and had entirely bypassed the main sections of the house.

'This is where the female staff sleep,' Clara explained. 'This one's ours,' she said, pointing to the second door of eight along the corridor. Clara led them into a room which reminded Mary of her own bedroom. Two single beds, set and perfectly made, dominated the small room. Between the two beds were a pair of wooden bedside tables. A thin wardrobe next to the door completed the room. Clara must have noticed the look on Mary's face. 'It's a bit bare but it's comfortable enough.'

'It'll be fine, I'm sure,' Mary said, setting down her case. 'Which bed's mine?'

Clara pointed to the bed which Mary had hoped would not be hers; it was the furthest from the fire and underneath the window. Mary lay her suitcase on the bed and popped open the brass clasps. 'Want to help me unpack?'

Clara winced apologetically. 'No time, I'm afraid. We need to be downstairs to start work at six-thirty sharp.'

Mary nodded and reluctantly closed her case. 'Maybe this afternoon?'

'We don't finish until nine o'clock. I'll help you with it then.' Clara smiled again. 'We should probably head downstairs now.'

Mary stood aside to allow Clara past and took a quick look back at her new room. To all intents and purposes, this was her new home. Not exactly what she had dreamt of, but at least she was now living at Blackfriars—under the same roof as Cecil Mansfield, Earl of Rothborne.

'Come on, or you'll get us both into trouble with Mrs Cuff,' Clara called from the corridor.

'Coming,' Mary answered. Mary followed Clara back down the ninety-six wooden steps into the innards of the house. In her naïve stupidity, Mary had assumed that the servants had full use of the main house, that she would be using the grand central staircase to get to her bedroom, which would be on the same floor as the ladies of the house. How wrong she had been.

Clara stopped at a closed door along the corridor which led to the kitchen and softly tapped a finger on the brass plate which said 'Housekeeper.' Moments later, Mrs Cuff pulled open the door. 'Hello, Mary. Welcome to Blackfriars. Come in.'

Mary watched Clara intently, mimicking her pose by standing, hands held together behind her back, with a slight deferential bow of the head. The two girls stood silently as Mrs Cuff opened a tall mahogany cupboard and retrieved a full set of uniform, which she handed over to Mary with a smile. 'Here you go, now you're a fully paid up third housemaid!' Mrs Cuff closed the cupboard and, turning to face Clara, said, 'Take Mary to change then you need to get a move on with your duties, ladies.'

'Yes, Mrs Cuff,' Clara said, bowing her head and leading Mary back out into the corridor.

Clara moved closer to Mary and whispered. 'She's nice, just don't get on the wrong side of her.' Clara pushed open a door opposite. 'Go and change in there—it's an *inside* female toilet—bet you've never seen one of those before! I'll wait here. But be quick—we start duties in four minutes.'

Mary hurried inside and changed into her uniform. A tiny hand-mirror rested on the side of the sink. Mary held it up and was shocked to see what she looked like in uniform. Her mother's words came flooding into her mind. *Once you put that uniform on, you belong to them. They'll take everything from you until you've nothing left to give, then they'll send you to the Rye workhouse where you'll wait for humiliation and shame to take you to a pauper's grave.* Her heart began to pound in her chest as she saw her mother's and grandmother's hoary, exhausted reflections staring back at her. 'I can't do this,' Mary uttered to her reflection. 'I can't do this. I won't end my days in an unmarked pauper's grave, nobody knowing or caring about me. I won't do it.'

Mary took a deep breath, set down the hand-mirror and began to pull off her uniform. *Now I don't belong to anyone!* she thought, as the black dress tumbled to her ankles. *I belong to me and to nobody else.* She was just in the process of removing the ties from her hair when the door crept open.

'You nearly done, Miss Mercer?' Clara said playfully, before she spotted that Mary was half-naked, her uniform cast aside on the stone floor. Clara hurried inside the toilet and closed the door. 'What are you doing?'

'Going home. There's been a terrible mistake. This job was my sister, Edie's. She's spent her life training to be a housemaid. She could do it standing on her head. It's like my father said, I can't even make my own bed,' Mary said breathlessly. 'I'll run home. Edie can be here in fifteen minutes.'

'Stop!' Clara shouted, grabbing Mary by the arm. 'It's too late to change your mind: you're one of us now.' Clara's demeanour changed and Mary could see anger in her pale blue eyes. 'Get dressed now, or I'm going to get into serious trouble if I'm not sweeping the drawing room floor in two minutes' time. You're not leaving here unless you're in full uniform, ready to work.' Clara turned sharply and left the room.

Through gritted teeth and watery eyes, Mary bent down and pulled on her uniform.

Five minutes later, the girls were in the drawing room, diligently sweeping up every morsel of dust. Mary silently observed and copied Clara's actions, trying to ignore the heavy doubts that weighed on her mind about taking Edie's prized job. Once swept, Clara showed Mary how to dust furniture and ornaments and how to wash the oak panelling. When the room was complete, Mary rested her elbow on her broom and sighed. 'Can I get a quick glass of water, please?'

Clara emitted a half-mocking laugh. 'No. Now we do the same to the dining room, the front hall, followed by the sitting room, the saloon and finally the smoking room.'

'Today?'

'Today and every day. It's also the duty of the third housemaid to clean the fire grates in each of those rooms and to light and maintain a fire. I'll help you this week, but next week you're by yourself. Let's get a move on—we need to have all of that complete by half-past eight breakfast.'

Mary stared at Clara incredulously. It would take her a month of Sundays to sweep and dust all of those rooms. To have them completed by breakfast was plainly absurd.

'Come on,' Clara called. 'Put your back into it.'

When the breakfast bell finally sounded and the girls headed to the servants' hall, Mary sank back into her chair, closed her eyes and groaned. She was seated at the end of a long wooden table. Her seat at the far end, reflecting her position in the household staff, did not go unnoticed by Mary, or indeed some of the other servants seated at a higher position. At the head of the table were Mrs Cuff and Mr Risler, the butler. As she moved her eyes down the line of servants, Mary spotted her cousin, Edward, smiling in her direction. To his right, two men were staring at her and laughing. Edward elbowed his immediate neighbour and said something to them which made them pull mock-

43

dejected faces. Mary briefly returned Edward's smile, then turned to Clara, seated beside her.

'Can I get myself a drink now?' Mary asked.

Clara cast a quick uncertain look along the length of the table then shook her head. 'You have to wait to be served. Eliza, the upper housemaid, will serve us tea or coffee, while the butler, Mr Risler, carves the cold meat. Sit patiently. And don't talk so loudly; it's not the Blackfriars way.'

Mary matched the deportment and posture of the other maids, her back up straight and head held high, and waited to be served.

Once the tea, coffee and cold ham had been served to the table of almost twenty-five servants, quiet, discreet conversations occurred between seated neighbours. Mary realised that however much she might like to converse with her cousin, it would be considered entirely inappropriate. *Not the Blackfriars way,* she thought.

'Why must we speak so quietly?' Mary asked a young girl opposite her, wearing a white uniform with a mobcap on her head.

'So we don't disturb the family,' the girl said, as if she were answering the most obvious question in the world.

'What's your name?' Mary asked.

'Joan,' came the short reply.

'And what's the nature of your slavery?'

Clara and Eliza's soft conversation stopped and they looked curiously between Joan and Mary.

'What?' Joan said.

Mary fully understood the look from Clara and Eliza. *It was not the Blackfriars way to be talking in this manner.* 'What is your job here?' Mary rephrased. Clara and Eliza turned back to each other and continued talking.

'Scullery maid.' She lowered her voice so that it was barely audible to Mary. 'Lowest of the low, that's why I'm down here with you. Welcome to the bottom of the pile.'

Mary looked uncomfortably along the table at the line of domestic servants, convinced that she had made a catastrophic mistake in accepting the third housemaid's job. *If only I had just gone home this morning,* Mary thought. *If only I hadn't been so bloody stupid and gone off exploring Blackfriars while Edie had had her interview.*

Mr Risler, a lank man with black greasy hair, walked behind the line of servants opposite Mary, forking out extra pieces of ham, making polite conversation as he went. 'Some of my meat, ladies?' he asked with a smirk when he reached Mary and Joan.

Joan shook her head vehemently. 'No thank you, Mr Risler.'

Without looking up, Mary could feel the penetrating stare of the butler.

'And you, Miss?'

Mary met his eyes. 'No thank you, Mr Risler.'

Mr Risler licked his lips. 'Pity,' he said, walking behind Mary to begin the line of servants on her side of the table. 'Nice to see a new addition to the *virgins' wing*,' he muttered, barely audibly, before moving on to Clara and Eliza.

Mary shot a glance at Joan, who quickly lowered her eyes. 'What does that mean?'

'It means he's a bit of a letch and someone to keep at arm's length,' Joan mumbled.

For the duration of breakfast, Mary tried in vain to talk with anyone other than Joan, the curt and rude scullery maid opposite her. However, distinct hierarchical lines sliced the table into conversation pockets, most of which excluded Mary. She was actually relieved when breakfast was formally declared over.

'Now what?' Mary asked Clara, as they proceeded from the servants' hall in the order at which they had been seated.

'Female servants' quarters followed by the male servants' quarters.'

'What about them?'

'We make the beds, replenish the candles, dust then sweep the floors.'

Mary swallowed back her exasperation and silently followed Clara up the ninety-six stairs to the female servants' rooms. The daily harsh reality of the role of the third housemaid at Blackfriars was slowly becoming clear to her. She recalled, with sufficient embarrassment to flush her cheeks, her behaviour in the library with Edward and the informality with which she had addressed Lady Rothborne. She was *very* fortunate that Lady Rothborne had humoured her and even offered her a job.

At the top of the stairs, Clara opened the first door to reveal a small cupboard stocked with a host of cleaning items, bedding and candles. Reaching inside, she pulled out two soft-headed, hair brooms and passed one to Mary. 'It's your duty to dust and sweep and to clean and stock the fire grate. It's my job to do the bed linen and candles. You start in our room, I'll start in Eliza and Sarah's.'

Mary pushed the door shut and stared at her bed, sorely tempted to bury herself under the blankets and forget that she had ever agreed to this awful job. She wandered over to the window and looked outside, barely able to take in the brightness of the morning. It had felt like days since the sun had bothered to rise, having capitulated to the gloomy winds and heavy snow that had poured across the channel for days on end. The concrete-grey clouds had vanished, leaving a beautiful turquoise sky. Even the beading of snow which ran along the window pane was now beginning to thaw. From the corner of her eye, something moved. Mary shifted her focus and saw an elegant female form in a crimson dress walking through the rose gardens. It only took a split-second for Mary to identify her as Lady Philadelphia. From her meandering and unhurried gait, she guessed that she was taking some gentle exercise and fresh air. Mary stared at her, transfixed, feeling as incongruous as a caged animal at London Zoo. *I don't belong here*, she lamented. *At least not like this, sweeping and cleaning; I belong down there, in a beautiful silk dress, enjoying a walk in the winter sunshine.*

Behind her, the door creaked open. It was Clara. 'Are you nearly done here?'

The reality of her new life suddenly returned to Mary: she was nothing more than a housemaid. A *third* housemaid at that. *The bottom of the pile.* 'Not quite. Sorry.' Mary could tell that Clara was annoyed.

'It's okay, I'll give you a hand. I remember my first day here, I think I was next to useless,' she said with a smile. 'I'll try and be as patient as Eliza was to me. Then in two years' time, you can show the new third housemaid the ropes. Just remember how you're feeling today.'

Mary was sure that, for as long as she lived, she wouldn't forget today. The very idea of doing this job, day in, day out for another two years horrified her. *There had to be an alternative*, she thought.

Working together, it took the girls ten minutes to finish their room before moving on to the other six female bedrooms. Once completed, it was time to move onto the male servants' quarters. Mary was intrigued to learn the location of their rooms and to catch a glimpse of her cousin's bedroom. Unexpectedly, she was led back down the ninety-six steps, along the gloomy corridor to another door.

'Don't ask me how it is, but there are ninety-eight steps up to the boys' rooms,' Clara said with a little laugh. 'And I've triple-checked.'

At the top, an exhausted Mary realised that they were, in effect, on the same corridor as the female servants' quarters; the hallway having been permanently bricked up to segregate the sexes, which seemed entirely over the top. 'God, if they knocked that thing down,' Mary said, indicating the brick divide, 'we'd have less clambering up and down stairs to do.'

Clara laughed. 'We'd be horsewhipped if we were found within a mile of the boys' rooms when they're there.'

Banging her fist on the wall, Mary said, 'But we are within a mile—our room is just the other side of here! Let me guess, *it's not the Blackfriars' way?*'

'Come on, stop chatting, let's get on. It's basically the same as our rooms', dust, sweep—'

Mary interjected, 'Clean the grates, make up the fires, check the candles.'

Clara grinned. 'You've got it.'

Just as Mary was about to enter the first room, a thought entered her head. 'Which room is my cousin Edward's?'

'That one,' Clara said, pointing to the third room along the corridor. 'Usually the most untidy one.'

'Must run in the family.' Mary smiled and began to rush through the cleaning of the first bedroom so that she could move on to his. She had been taken by surprise when he had touched her in the library yesterday; a twinge of feeling had stirred inside her that she had not been aware of before. *But no! Edie was sweet on him and, for all she knew, he was sweet on her, too.*

Mary hastily threw the broom around the floor, dusted only the areas which were visible and restocked the fire without first emptying or cleaning the grate. Quietly, she pulled open the door and crept along the corridor to Edward's bedroom. From the second bedroom she could hear Clara softly singing to herself. Mary cautiously tugged open the bedroom door, as if she were unsure of what might lie behind it. However, Edward's room was nigh on identical to all the other servants' bedrooms. Angular shafts of sunlight streamed in through the small window, situated between two single beds. Mary looked at them, wondering which one belonged to him. She spotted some postcards and pictures to the sides of both beds. Carefully casting her eyes over the images, Mary soon identified which bed belonged to Edward. Dominating the pictures of various female music hall stars, was a photograph taken at Caroline's wedding of Mary, Edie and Caroline standing outside St Thomas's, shortly after the ceremony had taken place; it was one of her favourite photographs of the three of them and was widely distributed among the family after the wedding. Mary looked long and hard at the picture, tracing her finger over the sepia outline of Edie's face, wondering when her twin might forgive her. *If* she might forgive her.

Mary sighed and slowly lowered her face to the indentation in the pillow left by Edward's head. She inhaled, gradually drawing Edward's scent through her nose and into her waiting lungs. The same stirring feeling that she had felt yesterday reappeared in her stomach.

Though she knew that she shouldn't, she carefully opened his bedside table. Without disturbing the contents, she could see a stack of letters. Mary recognised the handwriting: Edie's. It appeared from the quantity of letters that she had taken quite a fancy to Edward a long time ago. *Did Edie have a similar stack from him in her bedside table?* Mary wondered. Edie had certainly been more guarded and private in recent months. *Was Edward the source of her distraction?*

The definite sound of a bedroom door closing to the adjoining room sent Mary to her feet, pulling and pushing the broom back and forth rhythmically.

Edward's door opened and Clara stood with an impressed smile on her face. 'See, you're getting the measure of it alright. Keep going. Just another three to go before lunch.'

Mary half-heartedly smiled back and returned to her haphazard sweeping.

By the time the girls had returned to their specific places at the table in the servants' hall at one o'clock, Mary was worn out. She looked at every individual seated on the opposite side to her: not one of them looked as tired out as she felt. Even trying to converse with Joan or Clara was nigh on impossible. She was struggling. Her eyes inadvertently locked onto Edward's and he smiled reassuringly, as if he could sense her dispiritedness. She wondered if she had imagined that the moment yesterday was anything more than friendliness.

Something lightly touched Mary on the shoulder and she turned to see the disdainful face of Mr Risler. 'How are you getting on, my love?' he asked, his dark brown eyes searching her face hungrily.

Mary nodded. 'Very well, thank you.'

'Good, good. You can always come to Mr Risler if ever you need any help with anything—day or night,' he said, placing a subtle emphasis and intonation on the word *night*. He gave Mary's shoulder a squeeze, probing his long bony fingers into her flesh before moving back to his chair at the head of the table.

For a good while after Mr Risler had returned to his chair, the spot of skin where he had touched on her shoulder was crawling with repugnance. Unable to look up or talk, Mary was unwilling to eat much of the chicken, carrots and potatoes in front of her and spent much of the mealtime moving them around the plate and piling them in such a fashion as to appear more had been eaten. She sipped her beer and prayed that lunch would soon come to an end. Finally, it did.

'Now what?' Mary asked Clara, as they made their way from the servants' hall.

'Now we check all the fires are burning nicely, restock or relight as required and stock up candles ready for tonight. Then, from three until five we do needlework in the servants' hall.'

Having checked that each fire was lit and restocked all the candles, Mary and Clara joined Eliza in the empty servants' hall at three o'clock sharp. On the table, Mrs Cuff had placed a mountain of linen, livery and clothing in need of repair. Mary's heart sank; she hated needlework. She was useless at it and at home, it was always Edie or their mother who attended to the household haberdashery. Edie delighted in their mother's oft-repeated tale of how she had never met a girl incapable of sewing a hem until Mary had first tried a running stitch. 'Practice makes perfect,' her mother would say, night after night, as the three of them attempted to repair torn clothing by candlelight in the lounge. In Mary's case, practice did not make perfect. Practice made Mary despise even holding a needle and thread.

'Are we supposed to get all of that done today?' Mary asked incredulously.

'As much of it as we can, yes. There'll be another stack there tomorrow—equally as large,' Eliza said, reaching for the first garment.

Mary took a white apron from the pile and, copying Eliza and Clara, ran it carefully through her fingers to identify the repair required.

'Are we not allowed to talk while we work?' Mary whispered after several minutes' silence.

Eliza shook her head. 'We might become distracted from our duties.'

49

And so Mary worked with the two girls in near-silence for two, torturous hours. To Mary, a thousand minutes might have passed in those two hours. At ten minutes to five, Mrs Cuff entered the servants' hall and began to inspect the neat pile of completed repairs whilst the girls stood, arms folded behind their backs, and watched expectantly. Only minor nods of the head gave Mary any indication of her approval or otherwise. She picked up the white apron which Mary had started with and raised an eyebrow.

'Is this your handiwork?' she asked Mary.

Mary nodded.

Mrs Cuff threw it to one side. 'Not good enough,' she said reprovingly, continuing through the stack. Every repair that Mary had undertaken ended up in its own jumbled heap. 'Well, you certainly weren't employed here for your needlework skills, were you?'

'No, Mrs Cuff,' Mary mumbled.

'This stitching is very shoddy, look,' she said, tugging at a loose thread on an overcoat. One pull and the stitching came apart. 'I can see you're going to take a lot of work, young lady. What have you got to say for yourself?'

'Sorry.'

'Eliza, Clara—you need to have these garments corrected before you finish for the day,' Mrs Cuff said.

'Yes, Mrs Cuff,' they responded in unison.

Mrs Cuff left the servants' hall carrying the approved clothing. The still maid entered and began setting the table for tea. Mary could feel Eliza and Clara's disapproval.

'What *did* they employ her for?' Eliza whispered to Clara, as she scooped up the garments in need of correction. 'Come on, we'll work through tea.'

'Let me help,' Mary begged.

'I don't think so, Mary,' Eliza said frostily.

The two gaps beside Mary at the dinner table only heightened her feelings of isolation and segregation from the rest of the staff. Nobody, not even Joan or the awful Mr Risler attempted conversation. Mary sat in cold dismal silence, eating her bread and butter and taking small sips from her cup of tea, desperately hoping that the day would just end. But it didn't end, it kept on going. Half an hour after she had sat down and the sun had given way to darkness, Mary was back up on her feet ready to return to her duties. Once all the other servants had departed the room, Mary left and was collected by Clara at the door.

'Did you manage to get them done?' Mary asked in the muted, flickering glow of the corridor lamp.

Clara nodded. 'Eliza's just taken them in to Mrs Cuff.'

At that moment, the housekeeper's door opened and Eliza stepped out. 'Back to work, girls,' she instructed haughtily. 'Let's not repeat that tomorrow.'

Clara led them back upstairs to the female servants' quarters and pushed open their bedroom door. Inside was dark and freezing: Mary shuddered.

'It does warm up,' Clara said. 'Our duties now are to turn down the beds, close the curtains and light the fires. Watch and copy.'

Mary stood back and watched as Clara carefully pulled one side of the bedding into a neat diagonal line before pulling out the creases.

'Your go,' Clara instructed, as she tugged closed the curtains.

Mary copied with her own bed.

'Perfect. I'll light the fire, then I'll show you what's next.'

Once the small splinters of kindling had ignited, Clara showed Mary where to fill the water jugs. As soon as all the rooms in the female servants' quarters were ready, they repeated the task in the male quarters.

At eight o'clock, the girls returned to the servants' hall for supper, which consisted of cold ham and hot vegetables, but Mary was too tired to eat a single thing. All she wanted was her bed, irrespective of how cold or uncomfortable it was: she just wanted to lie down and close her eyes.

'What's the matter with you?' Joan whispered.

'I'm exhausted. You've no idea how many times I've been up and down those wretched ninety-six stairs. It must be at least a hundred,' Mary said, a little too loudly.

Joan put her forefinger on her lips. 'Keep it down, or you'll get into trouble.'

Mary rolled her eyes and emitted a small sigh.

Supper in the servants' hall lasted precisely half an hour. By the end of it, Mary had gulped down three cups of tea, but not touched her food. Without uttering a word, she followed Clara for the final duties of the day into the main bedrooms of the house.

'We need to check the water jugs, the fires and take a hot can of water to each bedroom,' Clara told her, leading Mary into a large, warm bedroom. A four-poster mahogany bed with fine, delicate cotton sheets stood in the centre of the room. Beautifully decorative

51

curtains covered the tall windows which, in daylight, afforded views across the lake. A carved wooden dressing table, chest of drawers and a writing desk completed the room.

'Whose room is this?' Mary said, mentally comparing it to her own insignificant bedroom upstairs. *This* should be her bedroom. It was perfect. Mary approached the bed and stroked the soft fine linen.

'Don't touch it,' Clara warned. 'It's Lady Rothborne's bedroom.'

'And Lord Rothborne's?'

Clara shook her head. 'His bedroom is next door.'

Mary puzzled as to why they would not share a bed. *Maybe it wasn't the Blackfriars way,* she reasoned. She had once read that most of the former kings and queens of England slept separately from their spouses and thought it must be common practice among the upper classes. Mary had a sudden, intense desire to see Cecil's bedroom. 'You finish up here and I'll do the next one,' Mary said quickly, hurrying for the door. She was in the brightly lit hallway before Clara could answer.

Mary entered Lord Rothborne's bedroom, closed the door behind her and smiled. The size and layout of the room was comparable to Lady Rothborne's, yet somehow it struck her as definitely belonging to a man. The wallpaper, carpets and curtains all exuded masculinity. She approached the bed and ran a finger over the crisp, pristine pillow. Unlike Edward's inferior bed, there was no revealing indentation. Unable to help herself, Mary lowered her face down onto the pillow and closed her eyes. Over the sterile scent of fresh laundry, she could detect the faintest whiff of an expensive cologne. Never in her most fanciful childhood dreams did she imagine such intimacy with Lord Mansfield, Earl of Rothborne. *Cecil.* For just that single moment, they were together. Mary took a long, deep breath, yearning to hold the fragment of his smell inside her for as long as possible, then stood and returned to herself: Mary Mercer, third housemaid of Blackfriars. She turned down the bed, added logs to the fire, refilled a jug of water and brought in a hot can of water. She did her duty, took one last longing look into the bedroom, then moved on.

When, at last, Mary climbed the ninety-six stairs for the last time that day and fell into bed, sleep would not come. Clara had fallen asleep the moment she had crawled under the blankets, but for Mary, the emotion and difficulty of her first day plagued her. It had, without doubt, been the toughest day of her life; every muscle, every joint, every bone throbbed with pain. Her mother's words and a flashback of a visit to see her granny in the Rye workhouse filled her mind. Now she understood why Granny, spirit and body broken, was dead and buried in a pauper's grave at the age of sixty-two.

The chunks of willow in the grate had all but disappeared when sleep finally came for Mary. She had cried for what seemed to her like an eternity: she cried for the pain in her body; she cried for her granny; she cried for her sister, Edie; she cried for the life she wanted; but most of all, she cried for the life to which she had given herself over.

Chapter Five

Wednesday 18th January 1911

Mary's first half-day off had finally arrived. She was granted half a day in the previous two weeks but, under pressure from Clara and Eliza, decided to spend it on needlework practice which, as far as Mary was concerned, had made no difference at all to her inability to stitch.

It was one o'clock, just when the rest of the servants would be settling down for lunch, when Mary Mercer flung open the kitchen door and bound out into the fresh air.

'*Eh! Ferme la porte!*' Monsieur Bastion called after her.

Mary gasped at the air like a miner who had been trapped underground for weeks on end. At last, she was free, albeit for just half a day. She didn't need to be back until nine o'clock and she intended to make the most of every single second. She hoped to goodness that her letter to Edie had arrived on time, giving warning of her imminent visit. Maybe they could go for a long walk together. There might even be time to get a ride into Rye for the afternoon.

The pervading snows had now completely vanished, leaving no trace of ever having been, and today, the sun shone brightly. As Mary hurried up the back path from Blackfriars towards her home, she looked out at the beautiful sun's rays, illuminating the manicured lawns and the orchard around the ruined abbey in the distance. She was so happy to be free that she felt sure that the sun was shining just for her.

Mary ran the final few yards, wanting to spend as much of her precious time at home as possible. She quietly pushed open the front door, wanting to surprise her mother and Edie. Her father would likely be out at work but she hoped to see him at teatime. Tiptoeing silently into the passageway, Mary closed the door without a sound and peered into the lounge: empty. She crept along the short hallway to the back of the house and opened the kitchen door. To her surprise, she found her father eating lunch at the kitchen table with her mother and Edie.

'Surprise!' Mary cried, bursting into the room.

'Oh my godfathers, you scared the living daylights out of me!' her mother said with a smile. She stood and hugged Mary.

Over her mother's shoulder, Edie looked up, briefly met Mary's eyes, then flicked her gaze to meet their father's eyes: Mary was perturbed by the conspiratorial look that passed between them. Her mother, as if sensing that Mary wasn't about to receive the same welcome from Edie and her father, kept her held in a tight embrace. Letting her arms fall limply to her side, Mary let go and was waiting for either her sister or father to look back at her. Finally, her mother released her grip.

'Sit down, Mary dear, there's tea in the pot. Thomas, fetch Mary a cup,' her mother said. 'We've had some very sad news reach us.'

'What's happened?' Mary asked.

'It's Caroline's William: he's dead from consumption.'

'Oh,' was all Mary could think to say. She barely knew William but was mightily grateful that he had taken her horrible sister all the way to live in Bristol. She hoped that this didn't mean Caroline would be making a return. 'Is Caroline coming back?'

Her mother shook her head. 'I don't know—it's too soon to say,' she said, pouring Mary a cup of tea. 'I'm minded to go and stay with her a few days, but your dad's not keen on the idea.'

'Who's paying for you to get there, then?' he barked. 'Better that she comes home here if anything.'

'We'll see,' her mother said. She smiled and changed the subject. 'Will you be wanting some food? There isn't much, but you're welcome.'

Mary glanced at the bare plates on the table. Her family were existing on scraps of bread and the merest sliver of butter between them. Her father's presence at the lunch table usually meant no work, which meant no money. As hungry as she felt, she couldn't possibly take their food. 'No, no lunch for me, thank you—I've already eaten.'

Her father snorted and mumbled, 'Bet you have, some fancy three-course meal or other, I shouldn't wonder.'

Mary knew what might cheer her father. She reached into her bag and pulled out a handful of money—it was every penny she had earned so far at Blackfriars. She placed it on the table in front of him.

'It's my wages so far—' Mary began. She stopped mid-sentence when her father reached up, snatched the money from the table and pocketed it without so much as looking up.

'Thank you, Mary,' her mother mouthed softly.

Edie finished her last mouthful of bread, stood up and left the room. Mary hurried after her. 'Wait, Edie!' she called, chasing after her sister. Edie continued up the stairs and into their shared bedroom without so much as a glance back at her twin.

Edie stood defiantly at the window, her shoulders dramatically surging up and down with every angry breath. 'Just go away!' Edie cried. 'Go back to Blackfriars; I don't want you here.'

'Please talk to me, Edie,' Mary pleaded, reaching out to touch her sister's hand. 'I hate the job and I wish to goodness that I hadn't taken it from you. One of the reasons I came home today was to beg you to go back there tonight instead of me; they'd take you on in a flash. I'm terrible at being a third housemaid.'

Edith turned to face her sister, her raging eyes red and watery. Her jaw was clenched and a small purple vein throbbed at her left temple. 'Oh, it's alright for me now, is it? Have you got something much better, then? I heard you and Mum talking about how the job was alright for me but you're capable of so much more. Maybe you're not so clever, then, if you can't even be a third housemaid.'

'Please, Edie,' Mary said quietly.

'I don't want the wretched job. I don't want anything from you ever again.'

'Edie, please…'

'Just go!' Edith yelled.

The gentle groaning of the wooden floorboards in the hallway made the girls switch their attention to the door, both realising that the outcome of their argument rested with whichever parent was standing at the top of the stairs. It was their father; Mary had lost the battle and no more words were needed.

'Think it's time you went back to Blackfriars,' her father said.

Mary knew from the tone of his voice that it was not a suggestion but a command and that the slightest rebuttal on her part would result in a violent outburst. As she had done on so many prior occasions, Mary conceded defeat, pushed past her father, down the stairs and straight out the front door. She desperately wanted to hug her mother, but she knew that remaining in the house a minute longer would make her mother's life a misery for the next month.

Mary maintained her composure as she walked from the house towards the gates of Blackfriars. She was fully aware that she had the entire afternoon and most of the evening to herself, yet the gravel path to Blackfriars drew her back in. Somehow, it seemed the only logical and sensible place to go. The moment that she crossed into the estate, every angry, incredulous word that she had just suppressed, every spiteful glance between her father and sister and every angry rejection from home flowed out of her as hot tears.

Without having consciously gone there, Mary found herself sitting in the ruins of the ancient abbey. There was now little to see of the former complex, razed to the ground by the Reformation in 1558. One solitary three-arched wall and another perpendicular flint wall were all that remained, having defied history and the elements for hundreds of years. It was to here that Mary and Edith would sneak as children, providing them as it did with cover from the house, before scrumping for apples and pears in the nearby orchards. Mary sank down with her back to the wall and, knowing that she was protected from view from prying eyes from the house, allowed herself to cry and cry. Since starting work at Blackfriars, Mary had never cried as much in her entire life. Each and every night when she went to bed, the woes and anxieties from the day manifested themselves as tears. Most recently, she wept for the fanciful relationship that she now knew that she would never have with Lord Rothborne. Four days ago, her childish fantasies had been dropped like a delicate glass vase onto a marble floor, smashing into a thousand pieces. Mary had been working in Cecil's bedroom, as she had managed to do each day since starting. She had always wangled it so that it was she who prepared his room. She had diligently cleaned the fire grate and restocked it with the best seasoned wood that she could find, swept his floor and dusted his furniture before saving the best part for last: Cecil's bed. She had carefully washed her hands prior to touching the soft sheets, then pulled them back ready to be turned down. As she had done on each occasion, Mary had laid her head on his pillow, closed her eyes and imagined that he had invited her into his bed. In her mind, he was asleep next to her, tenderly breathing on the nape of her neck. Mary had then dared to pull her legs up into the bed and, even through her coarse uniform, she could feel the softness of the sheets, which Clara had told her were made from the finest Egyptian cotton. All of her childhood dreams had come rushing back into her mind, as though a dam had suddenly burst. All things for which Edie had mocked her. *Now look at me, Edith Mercer!* Mary had thought. *You're moping at home with Father and here I'm in Lord Rothborne's bed!*

With a gloating smile, Mary had opened her eyes. In the doorway stood Lord Rothborne, Mrs Cuff, Clara and Eliza. Horrified, Mary fell out of the bed onto the floor, gasping at various words to try and formulate a sentence which might justify what she had been doing.

'Out. Now,' Mrs Cuff had barked.

Mary, still unable to speak, had regained her exterior composure, while the inside of her mind raced and jerked manically, unable to hold a single thread of thought. As her heart pounded inside her chest, she had walked calmly towards the door, her eyes following the contours of a lavish Turkish rug on the floor. Despite all that had happened, a small part of her had still believed that Cecil would smile, reach out and take her in his arms, dismissing the other servants.

At the last second, Mary had thrown her head up to look him square in the face. He was stood in a core of light, as if illuminated by God Himself. She saw his beautiful boyish face and striking dark red hair up close for the first time since 1902. She had locked onto his pale blue eyes. A tiny gasp of breath had escaped when what she saw shocked her, like a knife to the heart. There was nothing there. Not even simple affection. His eyes had reflected repugnance and repulsion, as he had looked her up and down as though she were a dirty street vagrant.

Mary's eyes had fallen to the floor as she left the room in disgrace. A wave of nausea had rippled through her body, biting at her stomach as the realisation that they would never be together came crashing down upon her.

A faint shadow passed across the ground in front of Mary, jolting her back to the present. She turned and stared towards the sunlit silhouette of a male figure. Despite all that had happened, a small part of Mary wondered if, at last, Cecil had come for her. Come to make amends. Come to take her away. Come to make her his. Yet, she knew it was not true. She recognised the shadowed form.

'Mary, what's the matter? What are you doing here?' It was Edward's voice.

Mary wiped her eyes on her sleeve. 'Nothing. Resting.'

Edward stepped out of the sunlight and crouched down beside her, placing his hand on her wild red hair. 'Why didn't you go home? It's your afternoon off.'

The softness of his touch and the sentiment in his voice sent a fresh torrent of emotion flooding out. She fell, like a weak child, into his arms.

Edward carefully placed his hands under her elbows and pulled her towards him.

Mary allowed Edward's gentle hands to guide her up. As she stood, any pretences of grandeur fell away and she returned to being Mary Mercer, a bashful seventeen-year-old girl. She looked into

Edward's dark eyes and saw a fragment of what she knew he could see emanating from hers. She stood, frozen to the spot by a burgeoning feeling inside which set her heart beating faster, his eyes exerting total control over her.

Edward leant in and kissed Mary lightly on the lips. The spell was broken.

'Don't,' Mary said, taking a step backwards. 'We can't.'

Edward's brow furrowed and his grip on her arms tightened. 'What's the matter?'

Mary turned, freeing herself from his hold. 'It's Edie.'

'What about Edie?' A few seconds of silence passed between them before Edward repositioned himself in front of her. 'What about Edie?' he repeated.

Mary's eyes returned to his. 'She likes you and she thinks you like her back.'

'What? Where has that come from?'

Mary shrugged.

'Well, I don't like her like *that*,' he said. 'But you...' His voice trailed off into the quiet of the ruins, then he leant in and kissed her again.

Mary allowed his warm lips to rest on hers. Neither of them spoke. Neither of them moved.

Edward gently lay her down in the grass, his lips moving from her mouth to her neck, his hands exploring increasingly intimate areas of her body.

Mary exhaled, closed her eyes and gave herself to him, as reveries of Cecil and realities of Edward collided in her mind.

Chapter Six

It took Morton less than thirty seconds to close his front door and arrive at the *Mermaid Inn*, almost dead opposite his house. Without a shadow of a doubt, it was the shortest distance that he had ever had to travel to work on a case. In ten minutes' time he was due to meet with Douglas Catt, son of Victor Reginald, grandson of Caroline, great-nephew of the illusive Mary Mercer. Morton and Douglas had exchanged a small flurry of emails which had resulted in Douglas and his wife, Susan's impromptu visit to Rye for a short break. Morton bounced up the brick steps past a sign which announced 'The Mermaid, rebuilt 1420' and entered the Virginia-creeper-smothered building. It was another big draw for the tourists, coming as it did with the medieval exposed black beams and white wattle and daub walls, crooked floors and a plethora of ghost and smuggler stories. Inside, Morton headed to the lounge bar and took a cursory glance around. The occupants—two men, whose outfits suggested that they were builders, and a young couple with a baby—did not fit the bill for Douglas and Susan. He headed to the bar and received a welcoming smile from a petite brunette with excessive eye make-up. She looked like she should either be on stage or on the streets.

'Hi,' Morton said. 'I'm due to meet Douglas and Susan Catt; they're guests here. Is it okay if I wait for them to arrive?'

'By all means, please take a seat,' she said.

Morton thanked her, chose a seat by the window and produced his notepad and pen. While he waited, he reviewed the notes that he had made on the case so far. Starting at the beginning of the pad at his meeting with Ray Mercer and working his way forward, Morton familiarised himself with each step of the Mercer case. It was the printed equivalent of an animated flipbook: each page adding or changing the story slightly. He reached the last page with writing on it, where he had scribbled the response from the National Archives that he had received this morning, concerning a legal name-change: rather predictably, Mary Mercer had *not* legally changed her name. It still didn't rule out an unofficial name change, however. Morton had also noted the bones of a phone conversation with the Blackfriars archivist, Sidney Mersham, who had called yesterday to discuss Morton's interest. He had sounded affable enough and agreed to allow Morton access to the archives this afternoon.

Behind him, Morton heard the mutterings of a conversation between a woman and a man. He turned to see a middle-aged couple tentatively looking his way. They fitted the profile for the Catts. Morton stood. 'Hi. Douglas and Susan, by any chance?' he ventured with a polite smile.

Douglas marched over and thrust his hand into Morton's. He was of average build but with a rather large pot belly which pushed and stretched the front of his navy-blue t-shirt. His hair was dyed a peculiar shade of brown, swept dramatically over in a side-parting. He was definitely a golf-playing, football-watching man's man. 'Guilty as charged! This is my better half, Susan.'

'Pleased to meet you,' Susan said, placing her hand delicately into Morton's, as though it were made of fine porcelain. *The hands of a fine artist or a pianist,* Morton thought. She was a thin, fragile creature who looked to Morton like she needed a good meal inside her.

'Lovely to meet you,' Morton agreed.

'Right, drinks. Is it too early for a Scotch, dear?' Douglas asked with a grin, which revealed gleaming white, cosmetically enhanced, perfect teeth.

'Doug!' Susan said in a quiet voice. 'It's barely mid-morning—coffee time. Honestly. Sorry, Morton.'

Douglas pulled a mock-incredulous face at Morton, then smiled at Susan. 'Yes, dear. Whatever you say, dear. What about you, Morton?'

'Just a coffee will be fine. Latte, if they have it.'

'Right-o.'

Douglas turned to the brunette barmaid and ordered the drinks.

'Take a seat,' Morton said to Susan. 'How's the hotel?'

'Oh, it's just beautiful. Our bedroom is magnificent. Four-poster bed, beautifully carved furniture. Amazing,' Susan said. 'I suppose, since you live nearby, you've never had the need to stay?'

'No, maybe one day we'll take a holiday over here,' Morton said with a grin. 'It would certainly keep the travel costs down.'

'It really would,' Susan agreed.

Douglas arrived back at the table. 'Three lattes coming right up! Maybe if the good lady wife permits it, we can follow it with a Scotch or two later,' he said, playfully nudging his elbow at Morton.

'Bit too early for me, I'm afraid.' Morton smiled and reached down for his notepad and pen. Pleasantries over, it was time to start angling the conversation towards the Mercer Case. 'Well, I'm really

61

pleased that you were able to come down this way and meet up like this; it could help a lot with this case I'm working on.'

'No problem at all,' Douglas said. 'We don't need much of an excuse for a weekend away, do we, dear?'

'Especially not somewhere so beautiful,' Susan said meekly.

'To be honest, I'm pretty well retired now anyway.'

'Ironmongery still doing well, is it?' Morton asked, somewhat surprised to hear of a traditional shop doing so well against the big supermarkets and online retailers.

Douglas laughed. 'Oh, not that—my brother makes a couple of quid from that—I've been in stocks and shares since the early nineties.'

Susan gently tapped Douglas on the leg. 'We haven't come here to talk about that, Doug.'

'Sorry, fire away,' Douglas said, pulling a mock-reprimanded face.

Morton picked up his pen, then posed his first direct question: 'What do you know about Mary Mercer?'

Douglas drew in a long breath. 'Well, obviously I've not got a *personal* memory of her! I might look old but I'm not so ancient that I actually recall her. Everything that I know comes from family lore. I think there was some kind of a family bust-up so our side down in Bristol haven't really kept in touch with the rest of the family.'

'What were you told about what happened to Mary?' Morton probed.

'Basically, from our position outside looking in, Mary was driven away from Winchelsea. Either she got into a row at home or work, I don't know which, then decided to up sticks and leave. She went to Scotland to get some peace and never returned. Simple really.'

'And, as far as you know, she never came to visit your grandmother, Caroline, or made contact at all?'

'No,' Douglas said assuredly. 'Never. Mary was always the odd one out in the family, bit of a loner. She didn't really bond with either of her sisters. From what my mum had said to me over the years, it would have been really out of character for her to have suddenly made contact with our side again after she left.'

'That's a bit strange, wouldn't you say?' Morton said. 'To just up and leave and never return. That must have been some huge argument.'

'But it's only unusual because of the type of people we are, Morton. I mean, I know my old ball and chain is a bit of a handful at times, but I couldn't leave her,' Douglas said, smiling playfully at Susan. 'But that's because of the type of person I am. I expect you couldn't leave your girlfriend either. Mary wasn't like us, though. As I said, she was the odd one out: a loner.'

Morton smiled but wasn't convinced. Every family had its share of trials and tribulations, but, to his mind, it would take one cataclysmic event for anyone to voluntarily disappear and never make contact with *anyone* in the family ever again. 'Do you know if anyone on your side ever tried to find her?' he asked, taking a mouthful of his latte.

'I wouldn't know for certain; I would imagine so. My mum spoke of her on and off over the years but I don't think *she* was very minded to try and track her down—she'd not ever met her. I think they just respected the fact that she didn't want to be found.'

'It would be nice to know what happened to poor Mary,' Susan said quietly.

Morton looked at Douglas's ambivalent face. He clearly didn't share his wife's interest. Either Douglas was helping keep a family secret well concealed, or he actually didn't care at all about what happened to Mary Mercer. The fact that he had so willingly dropped everything to make the trip to Rye, suggested to Morton that Douglas might be more interested than he was letting on. It was a long way to come, even if you were semi-retired and in need of a short break.

Douglas sipped his drink and cast a look to Morton. 'Look, nothing personal to you, Morton but I'm not quite sure why Ray's so hell-bent on finding someone who, *whatever* the circumstances, is now dead. What does he think he'll do if you do find out what happened to her? I mean, come on, talk about overkill!'

'I think...' Morton began, searching for a diplomatic answer which didn't reveal Ray's terminal illness, 'that he feels he's getting on a bit now and just wants to know where she is. Lay flowers at her grave, that kind of closure. He was close to his grandmother, Edith, who in turn was close to her twin, Mary. I think he feels he owes it to Edith somehow.'

'But he never even knew her! That's what makes me laugh; he's acting like she was his sister.' For the first time, Douglas's face turned serious. 'I tell you what, from what Mum and Dad said, *that* side of the family know more than they're letting on. *A lot* more.'

Morton set his mug down and looked up. 'What do you mean?'

Douglas received something resembling a warning look from Susan and seemed to calm visibly. He smiled. 'I suppose I just mean that over the years for some reason, whether through their own guilt or what, they've played around with the truth of the matter. I expect you've heard this old fanciful tale that Mary came back for her twin's funeral and left a locket on her grave? It's all nonsense. Romantic poppycock to tie up the story.'

Morton was unsure of how to take the new serious tone of the conversation. Douglas, clearly nettled with red cheeks and a furrowed brow, received a reassuring look from Susan.

Susan shifted uncomfortably in her seat, then began to forage in her handbag, which Morton presumed to be her exit strategy from the sticky conversation. A slightly uncomfortable silence lingered in the air between them, which Morton was about to break when he saw Susan pull something from her handbag and hand it to Douglas. Addressing Morton with a polite smile, she said: 'She clearly didn't want to be found.'

Douglas took the small white envelope from Susan and passed it to Morton. 'Take a look at that.'

Morton turned the envelope over in his hands. It was addressed to Mr and Mrs Mercer, 3 Friar's Cottages, Winchelsea, Sussex. He recognised the writing instantly: it was a letter from Mary. The pen pressure, the size and stroke all unequivocally matched the note left on Edith's grave and the name and address inside the book. The envelope, off-white and mottled with light brown patches, had a red penny stamp in the top right corner and bore a smudged, black postmark, dated 17th April 1911. The word *Scotland* was smeared but just about legible.

Morton felt a surge of excitement fire through his veins as he carefully withdrew the letter through the neat incision made by a sharp letter opener. As he withdrew the letter under the watchful eyes of Douglas and Susan, Morton caught the signature. *Your loving daughter, Mary.* The letter existed. Morton unfolded the time-stained and creased letter, holding it so gently in his hands that he could barely feel it. He began to read. *Dear Mother and Father, It is with great sadness and shame that I write you this letter. I have behaved and acted in an unforgivable manner, which, if you were to learn of the whole matter, would bring embarrassment to the Mercer name. Please know that in taking on the role of housemaid at*

Blackfriars, I only wanted to earn your love and respect. In this, I have failed and ask that you respect my decision to leave Winchelsea. I hope to start a new life in Scotland, where I may be disconnected from the life and pains of Mary Mercer. I pray that I will one day receive your forgiveness. Your loving daughter, Mary.

Morton finished reading and looked up. The self-satisfied look on both Douglas and Susan's face told Morton that they believed they had just laid down a winning hand.

'Case closed,' Douglas said arrogantly.

It was anything but case closed, Morton thought, becoming slightly riled by the conceited couple. Morton rubbed his chin and cast his eyes over the letter again. 'How did you come by this letter?'

Douglas shrugged. 'I guess it passed to my grandmother, Caroline, when her parents died.'

'And what do you suppose Mary did that was so unforgivable?'

'Your guess is as good as mine,' Douglas said, finishing the last of his latte. 'If anyone in the family knew, they didn't pass that information on.'

'Do you mind if I take a digital photo of the letter?' Morton ventured.

'Go ahead,' Douglas said.

Morton withdrew his mobile and took a series of photographs of the envelope and the letter. He would later undertake a detailed analysis of it to make sure that it was genuine. From his initial assessment, though, it seemed real enough. As Douglas had said, it clearly read as though Mary were starting a new life and didn't want to maintain contact.

'Notice there's no contact address,' Susan said, almost inaudibly.

Morton had noticed and nodded his agreement, not wanting to give away that he still found it odd that she should remove herself from her entire family and nobody attempted to find her. 'You said that you thought the story of Mary returning to her twin's funeral wasn't true, but I've seen the locket that was found on the grave,' Morton said, carefully studying Douglas's reaction.

Douglas shot a quick uncertain glance in Susan's direction. 'Doesn't mean it was found at the grave, does it? I could hand you one of Susan's lockets and make up any kind of a tale about where I got it.'

He had a fair point, although Morton felt that Ray Mercer was speaking truthfully and from the heart. *Besides, why would he lie?* Morton asked himself.

65

Another pregnant pause lingered between the three of them.

'I said we should have had a whisky!' Douglas said, gently squeezing Susan's knee. 'Heavy going, all this! It's why my mum didn't used to speak much about old Mary: there are just some family secrets that need to remain just that; a secret.'

Morton scribbled more notes on his pad, then finished his latte. 'Is there anything else that you can think of that would help me?'

Douglas looked taken aback. 'Help you do what?'

He really did think he had laid the winning hand, Morton thought. *Case closed.* 'Help me find what happened to Mary.'

Douglas took a lengthy breath in and his cheeks flushed crimson. 'Look, I don't want to fall out over this, Mr Farrier, but I do urge you, in the strongest possible terms, to drop this ridiculous quest of yours. It's going nowhere.'

'It says so in the letter,' Susan added feebly.

Douglas leant over, reached around to his back pocket and pulled out a leather wallet. 'Here you are,' he said, pulling out a wodge of notes. He handed them to Morton. 'For your trouble. I know you've got to earn your money like anyone else.'

Morton took the money and quickly ran his thumb through the bunch of fifty pound notes. There was at least five hundred pounds in his hand. Morton placed it on the table between them. 'Thank you, but I'm being paid by my client to find out what happened to Mary, and that's what I intend to do.'

'How much is he paying you? I'll match it,' he said, turning to Susan. 'Get the chequebook, love.'

Susan began to rummage in her handbag again.

'Please, stop,' Morton said. 'I'm not interested. I'm working for my client.'

'You might regret that,' Douglas said, standing up and signalling that the meeting was over. With his left hand, Douglas scooped up the pile of cash and Morton noticed for the first time that his two fingers, index and middle, were bandaged together. Morton sat and watched as the couple hurried from the hotel out onto Mermaid Street.

Well, that went well, Morton thought. At least he had digital copies of Mary's letter to add to the growing jigsaw puzzle that surrounded Mary's life. His uneasiness about the letter was only compounded by the fact that Douglas had driven nearly two hundred miles to deliver it personally, believing it would put the nail in the

Mercer Case coffin. Morton didn't trust the letter and he certainly didn't trust Douglas Catt.

Morton finished his latte, packed up his bag and left *The Mermaid*.

A hulk of a man blocked the entrance to Blackfriars with unnecessary drama, standing with his legs apart and hand raised defiantly towards Morton's Mini. The man, wearing a thick black bomber jacket, came over to the driver's window. 'Shut,' he said eloquently.

'What is?' Morton asked, unable to resist a gentle goading.

The hulk flicked his head back towards the building. 'Getting ready for filming.'

Morton nodded politely. 'I've got an appointment to see Sidney Mersham, the archivist.'

'The what-avist?' the hulk asked with a snarl.

'Archivist,' Morton reiterated.

The hulk didn't move. Or blink. Morton had a flashback to childhood staring competitions and looked belligerently into the hulk's menacing eyes. Seconds passed. The hulk blinked, sniffed loudly then spat the contents of his nasal passages onto the shingle beside the car. Nice. Pulling a walkie-talkie from his belt, he muttered something inaudible, all the while keeping his gaze fixed firmly on Morton.

With a minute nod of his head, the hulk stood back and allowed Morton to drive towards the house. *What a lovely maître d',* Morton thought, as he parked up close to the house. He had the choice of pretty well the whole car park today; the only vehicles on site were the monstrous trucks belonging to the television company here to film *The Friary*. A handful of casually dressed people milled about carrying television-making paraphernalia to and from the house. Morton followed one lad, with jeans inexplicably suspended halfway down his legs, into the main entrance of the house.

The grand saloon appeared very differently to Morton's last visit; all of the photographs, life-size cut-outs and rope barriers had been removed and replaced by Edwardian-era furniture. Morton might have felt that he had stepped back in time but for the plethora of cables, monitors, lights and cameras directed in the general direction of the fireplace, ready for the next scene. A motley bunch of men and women all purposefully busied themselves about the set. Morton recognised the actors who played Lord and Lady Asquith; they were sitting on a *chaise longue* in full Edwardian garb, anachronistically tapping at their mobile phones.

'Can I help you?' a voice asked from beside Morton. He turned to see Mrs Greenwood, the sullen woman who had been on the entrance desk when he had last visited.

'Hello again, you probably don't remember me from my previous visit, but you kindly arranged for me to meet with the archivist.'

A flicker of recognition illuminated her eyes. 'Oh, yes.'

'I've got an appointment with him—do you know where he might be?'

Mrs Greenwood seemed slightly taken aback. 'They're letting you in, are they? Aren't you the lucky one,' she said with a smile. 'I'll take you down there—follow me.'

'Thank you,' Morton said, following her, as she dodged her way through the organised chaos of a television set.

She led him through the large hallway to a door with 'Private' written in large black letters. Beside the door was a security keypad, which Morton couldn't help but stare at as she punched in the four-digit code: 1536. *Was that a nod towards the beginning of the Dissolution of the Monasteries?* Morton wondered. *The beginning of the end for the Catholic Church's ownership of Blackfriars?*

The door led to another shorter and simpler corridor with four closed doors. Mrs Greenwood marched towards the one at the far end. 'I'd love to get a look in those archives for my own family history,' she muttered, her voice echoing around the low vaulted ceiling. 'I have managed to take a peek but not quite what I'd like,' she said, pulling open the door and beginning a short descent of a stone spiral staircase. 'They're a bit funny about people prying, even staff. Consider yourself very fortunate.'

Morton was sure that luck played no part in his admission but rather the Mansfields' knowledge of a previous case which had gained him entry. 'I can see why these parts aren't open to the public,' Morton said, almost banging his head on the ceiling.

'You get used to it.'

As they neared the bottom, Morton tried to get a representation in his head of their exact location within the depths of the house. He reckoned that they were almost in the dead centre. The protected and concealed heart of the house. Another key-padded door awaited them at the bottom. Mrs Greenwood, making no attempt to conceal the code, tapped in 1540. The end of the Dissolution of the Monasteries and the granting of Blackfriars, eighteen years later, to the Mansfield family. Genius.

As Morton suspected, the door opened into a windowless room. It was a small and simple office, just a desk, computer and a few filing cabinets. There was no way that hundreds of years of history had been stuffed into those few metal drawers. At least, he hoped not. To the right of the desk was yet another door, behind which, Morton suspected were four hundred and seventy years of Blackfriars and Mansfield archives.

'Mr Mersham,' she called out. 'Visitor for you.'

A man dressed in tweed trousers and jacket appeared at the door. Morton recognised the geeky round glasses and swept-over black hair from the picture in the Blackfriars guide. 'Sidney Mersham,' he said, offering Morton his hand.

'Morton Farrier. Thank you for seeing me.'

'You're quite welcome. Please, take a seat.'

'I hear you don't usually open up the archives to researchers?' Morton said, taking a seat on a cracked green leather chair opposite Sidney.

Sidney scrunched up his face. 'Not really. We have in the past. It's just not practical or manageable. I think on this occasion Daphne took a shine to you and your quest.'

Morton considered the brief conversation he had had with Milton and Daphne Mansfield: it was hardly worthy of his gaining unusual access to hundreds of years of personal papers.

Sidney must have sensed Morton's uncertainty. 'I think it was the nature of the case that swayed her. Essentially, it's a missing person's enquiry for a young girl. She's got daughters and I think she empathised. Most of the requests we get are from people just wanting to be nosey. Although, now a lot of the requests are from people interested in *The Friary.*'

Morton nodded and Sidney opened his hands in a gesture which said *fait accompli.*

'Let's get started, then,' Sidney said. 'You tell me what you know already and I'll tell you what we've got that might fit with what you're looking for.'

'Right—' Morton began but was interrupted by Sidney frowning and raising a finger to stop him.

Sidney's attention had turned towards the door where Mrs Greenwood was still standing, quietly absorbing the exchange between the two men. Sidney removed his glasses and stared at her. 'I'm sorry, Jenny, was there something else?'

Her cheeks flushed. She shook her head, mumbled something incoherent then scuttled from the room.

'Sorry, do carry on,' Sidney said, remounting his glasses upon his nose.

Morton felt bad for the poor woman but, when he was about to speak in her defence, decided that the end of his appointment time might be a more appropriate time to suggest that she be allowed to conduct some personal research. Morton pulled his notepad from his bag and began to recount the salient points of the Mercer case.

As he wrote, Sidney nodded, made noises of agreement and scribbled his own notes. 'A sad case for the family,' he said solemnly when Morton had finished. 'I think we should have a few bits and pieces which might show Mary's life here. I doubt very much that the answer to her disappearance lies in there, though,' he said, pointing to the room behind him. He shrugged. 'We'll see.' Sidney smiled, stood and gestured for Morton to follow.

The room in which Morton found himself was much larger and somehow more modern than he had imagined that it would be. It was at least forty feet long with no windows and no other doors. A low, whirring sound emanated from a complicated labyrinth of tubes and vents, which Morton suspected was controlling the humidity and temperature of the room. On each wall were tall metal filing cabinets.

'You look impressed,' Sidney said, pushing his glasses onto the bridge of his nose.

'Yes, I am,' Morton said. 'It must keep you busy.'

Sidney laughed. 'Very much so. I've spent the last fifteen years trying to get the archives into some kind of order and to catalogue what we have. When I started here it was in one hell of a mess. Generations' worth of paperwork. Of course, at the moment it's the writers of *The Friary* that are keeping me busy, asking questions about the ins and outs of life here in the Edwardian period. That's how I know exactly what we have here that might show your Mary.'

My Mary. Morton brought the photograph of Mary to mind. He supposed she was becoming *his* in some strange way. It always happened with an interesting assignment like the Mercer Case; after just a few hours of research, he was hooked. Juliette often said his passion for genealogy was like an addiction and she was right. Douglas Catt would have needed to offer him an awful lot more money for him to back out now. He was a forensic genealogist, employed to find Mary Mercer, and that's just what he was going to do.

'Right, most of the information on the domestic servants is in here,' Sidney said, making his way towards a filing cabinet near the back of the room. He took out a silver key from his pocket and pushed it into the lock, then tugged open both doors. Inside were neat rows of books, boxes, ledgers and papers, bundled and wrapped like any decent archive.

Sidney held the sides of his glasses and scrunched up his face as he darted his head up and down like a curious meerkat. 'Ah, here we are,' he said with a grin, as he plucked a small leather book from the shelves, followed by an A4-sized ledger. 'Let's have a look.'

Morton followed Sidney back out into the small office, where he carefully set the documents down onto the desk. Morton watched patiently, as Sidney opened up the first book. It was a light-brown, calfskin-bound book about the size of a paperback. Sidney turned past the marble-effect endpapers until he reached the first handwritten pages. Slowly, he ran his index finger down the side of the page. '1909,' he muttered, turning the page and beginning his search again. '1910.' On the next page he held his glasses and leant in to take a closer inspection. 'Here we are, wages for the year 1911.' He pushed the book over to Morton. 'See if you can't find your Mary.'

Eagerly, Morton grasped the book in both hands. He loved the feeling of touching history, making a special connection with the past, with the person who had held this very document in their hands more than a century ago. He scanned down a list of names, which seemed to be arranged haphazardly. The name *Mercer* jumped out at him. Morton moved his eyes across the line, *Mercer, Edward, Second Footman.* Mary's first cousin. There then followed a run of dated, weekly columns, showing Edward's pay of fourteen pounds. Then Morton spotted something curious. Edward Mercer's pay ceased on Friday 19th May 1911—alarmingly close to Mary's disappearance. Morton skipped forward to the remainder of the year, into 1912 and then 1913. No Edward Mercer. 'Interesting,' he said, capturing Sidney's interest. 'Her cousin, Edward worked here as a footman. He seems to have stopped work here the month after she disappeared. Could be a connection there.'

Sidney nodded emphatically, thrust his glasses back onto the bridge of his nose and leant in for a closer look. Morton took out his pencil and notepad and began to scribble down the information. Working backwards, he found that Edward's first pay at Blackfriars had been in 1908; there were no breaks in employment until he left in May 1911. Finding what happened to Edward was definitely a priority, but for now he needed to continue his search for Mary. Morton returned to 1911 and ran his finger further down the page until he found her. Her wages, twelve pounds per annum, began in January 1911 and, as Morton had expected, ended on Friday 14th April 1911. He quickly checked if her name appeared elsewhere in the book but found no further trace.

'Is it okay if I take a quick photograph?' Morton asked.

'By all means. I'll hold it open for you,' Sidney said.

Morton took a photograph of the relevant page, showing both of the Mercers' terminated employment. 'Thank you, that's very helpful.'

Sidney slid the wage book to one side then picked up the A4 brown brushed-velvet ledger. 'Now this…' he said, stroking the front of the book as if it were a pet dog, 'might well have been your saving grace. It's the Blackfriars Day Book, the butler and housekeeper's account of daily life in the house. It's of varied usefulness, recording stock levels of wines and spirits, the purchasing of fruit and vegetables, household repairs and also the comings and goings of staff.'

Morton's excitement about the promise of the Day Book was tempered by Sidney's use of the word 'might', clearly meaning that the book would, in fact, be of no use to him. Although historically interesting, the quantity of claret and champagne consumed by a wealthy Edwardian family in one week was of no use to the Mercer case. 'Go on,' Morton urged.

Sidney flicked to the back of the book. 'This one ends in January 1911.'

'And the next one?' Morton asked, already fearing the answer.

'Still in use in 1939—' Sidney began to explain.

'The fire?' Morton interjected, remembering what Milton Mansfield had told him about certain records having been destroyed.

'Exactly. A lot of the burnt records were kept and catalogued but I'm afraid nothing exists of that Day Book. Still, this one might be worth a look,' Sidney said, pushing it across the table to Morton.

Morton opened it at the first page, dated 1907 and began to assimilate the type of information on offer. As suggested by Sidney, it told of the general life at Blackfriars, signed off each week by the housekeeper, Mrs Cuff and the butler, Mr Risler. Morton turned to the back few pages where 1911 began then skimmed through it until the first mention of Mary occurred. Morton felt compelled to read aloud so that Sidney could share in his discoveries. '*Monday 2nd January 1911. Employed new housemaid, Miss Mary Mercer, little previous experience—will need a great deal of support.* Another entry for that week: *Wednesday 4th January. Miss Mercer's limited experience in any domestic area is putting a strain on the other domestic staff. Her haberdasher skills leave plenty to be desired.*'

'Oh dear,' Sidney said with a grimace. 'Doesn't sound like your Mary had a good start here.'

'Nor a good end…' Morton said solemnly. 'Is it okay to take a photo?'

'Go ahead.'

As Morton took out his mobile phone, the sound of the keypad being pressed was followed by a mechanical release and the door opening. In the doorway stood a smiling Daphne Mansfield. She was dressed impeccably in high heels, short patterned skirt, blouse and jacket. Every garment shouted its origin as Knightsbridge.

'Mr Farrier,' she greeted. 'Good to see you again.'

'Hello, Lady Rothborne. Thank you for allowing me in here. I know you must be up to your eyes with the filming.'

'Oh, no worries at all,' she said, dismissively waving her perfectly manicured fingers at him. 'Have you had any luck in your quest to find this lady of yours?'

Morton considered the question. He had certainly become more acquainted with Mary Mercer and the wages ledger had offered a new lead for her cousin, Edward. 'Yes, very profitable, thank you.'

'Smashing. So you'll have no need to break in at some ungodly hour, then to raid the archives?' she said with a wry smile.

'No, I don't think that will be necessary,' Morton said, feeling somewhat sheepish at her reference to a previous case where breaking and entering seemed to have emerged as a natural and obvious part of his research strategies. He hoped that the Mercer Case would be strictly legal, if only to make his home-life easier. Now that Juliette was training to be a police officer, there was no way she would be undertaking anything remotely illegal.

Daphne smiled. 'Sid, I'm sorry to interrupt, but the producers have just halted filming over some historical inaccuracy or other in the script. Is there a chance Mr Farrier could spare you for five minutes upstairs?'

Sidney looked uncertainly at the open archive door. 'Er, can it wait at all? Half an hour or so?'

'I think it needs sorting now, don't worry about your precious archives, Mr Farrier will watch them for you.'

Morton smiled as Sidney reluctantly followed Daphne from the room. The door closed behind them with a heavy clunk.

Morton continued to scan the ledger, disappointed that the one book he really wanted had been consumed by the 1939 fire. *What were the chances?* he thought. Then he flicked back to the start of the book. It started in 1907 and ended in 1911. Four years. Four years in one ledger. The next one apparently ran from 1911 until 1939. Morton considered that there were three options at play here: one, that record-keeping had changed between those years and little was recorded each week; two, that Sidney had made a mistake in believing the ledger destroyed or three, that he was lying. The first option seemed flimsy to Morton. The last two options meant that there was a real possibility that a Day Book commencing in January 1911 was currently sitting in the filing cabinet in the adjacent room, the door of which was open. He was fairly sure that what he was about to do could not be considered illegal since all doors were open. He recalled Juliette once enlightening him to the fact that you couldn't be prosecuted for breaking and entering if a door was already opened.

Morton couldn't waste this golden opportunity to take a look for himself. He stood, listened quietly for a moment, then darted inside the archive room. With his heart beating fast, he pulled open the cabinet doors and began to run his eyes across the archives, searching for something resembling the other Day Book. His eyes settled on a ledger of similar size and colour. Morton pulled it down and opened the first pages. *Bingo!* It began where the previous had ended. As much as he would have dearly loved to have searched every page, time was not a luxury he had, so he hurriedly flicked through until he reached the week beginning Monday 10th April 1911—the week of Mary's disappearance. Morton quickly took a digital photograph of the page.

A noise close by came from the office.

Someone was tapping at the keypad.

He heard the clunking of the heavy door opening.

Morton quickly took a photo of the week prior and following her disappearance, before hastily placing the book back where he had found it.

Time up.

'What are you doing in here?' came the sound of Sidney Mersham's agitated voice.

Morton held up the wages book. 'Just being helpful and putting this back. I didn't like to keep reading the Day Book without you there,' Morton said, amazed at his own composure.

Sidney looked doubtful. 'Right, come on, let's get this done. There can only be another few pages left. I've got work to do now upstairs. Honestly, you'd think they would have done their homework *before* filming.'

Morton heaved a sigh of relief and headed back into the small office. In doing his best to appear calm and cool, Morton failed to spot the CCTV camera just above the door, fixed on him and following his every move.

Chapter Seven

Wednesday 8th February 1911

Mary had been working at Blackfriars for more than one month. The desperate, daily ache in her muscles had gradually eased, but the ache in her heart had not; she still despised and resented every moment of her time as a third housemaid. Each day ended the same, with Mary crying herself to sleep, attempting to stifle her sobs from Clara, who was growing increasingly irritated by her emotional outpouring. After the last failed attempt, Mary had given up using her half days off to go home. Instead, she spent as much of her free time as possible with Edward.

Just like today, at precisely one o'clock, Mary would flee Blackfriars via the kitchen entrance and steal her way up the back path in the direction of her home. Part way, when a screen of firs temporarily eclipsed the house, Mary would sneak through the orchard and into the abbey ruins, where she would await him. Sometimes he came, sometimes he could not get away without being seen and they had to wait another week to be reunited.

Today, he was late and Mary was beginning to doubt that he was coming at all. She had been cowering in the wintry ruins for more than twenty minutes, sitting on a cold chunk of sandstone that looked as though it had once been a window lintel, rubbing a shard of flint back and forth, rhythmically creating a short gully. She had wrapped up as much as she could but it was not sufficient to keep out the cold; she longed for warmer days when intimacy did not mean having every part of her body frozen to the bone. Last week, she had been so deeply chilled that it had taken almost half an hour trembling in front of her bedroom fire for the painful surge of blood to return to her extremities, which had aroused Clara's suspicions. 'Have you not got fires at home?' she had asked, taking pity on Mary by donating blankets from her own bed to wrap around her shoulders. Mary had responded by saying that her father was still out of work and there the conversation had ended.

Mary recoiled with fright as someone jumped out from behind the ruins wall.

'Mary!' Edward called.

'Oh, don't do that!' Mary said, laying a hand on her chest, as if to slow down the sudden change in her heart rhythm.

76

There he was, standing in full black and white livery, as handsome as ever. He had, by far, the most pleasing appearance among the male domestic staff.

Edward grinned. 'Did you think I wasn't coming?' he asked, huddling down beside her and placing his arm over her shoulder.

'I'm just glad you made it,' she said, pushing her body into his warmth.

Edward closed his eyes and pressed his lips to hers. Mary kept her eyes open, desiring that each of her senses absorb and soak him up. Finally, she opened her mouth and allowed their shared passion to flow between them. Grappling exploring hands led, as it always did, to a fervent union.

Afterwards, Mary always regretted how quickly it was over, that no time could be allowed in a normal warm bed for the closeness to continue. Maybe in the summer months they could take themselves off to a secluded woodland where prying eyes and arctic temperatures could not reach them.

Hurriedly, the pair dressed and returned to the stone seat, where they sat like a pair of owlets huddled together for warmth. Mary picked up the piece of sharp flint and returned to scratching at the sandstone, carving the letter M.

'What are you going to write?' Edward asked. 'Mary loves Edward?'

Mary giggled and nudged him playfully.

Edward held her hand and waited for her to look up. He had a serious look on his face. 'Do you...' Edward began, his gaze falling to the floor. 'How do you feel...what do you feel towards me?' He kicked at a small pebble. 'Because... well...'

Mary laughed. 'Well what?' She knew, of course, the words which would not come. She felt it too, that unmistakable fluttering and desire deep inside her that consumed more and more of her thoughts.

Edward stood up, his back to her. He paced to the edge of the ruin and stared out. 'I...' he stammered. 'Oh, God!'

'Just say it, Edward!' Mary pleaded.

'Your sister's walking down the path!' he blurted, ducking behind the stone wall.

'What?' Mary said, jumping up and heading towards him. 'What's Edie doing here?'

'Get back!' Edward said in a hushed whisper. 'It's not Edie; it's Caroline.'

Mary, body tucked behind the wall, stuck her head out just enough to see the unmistakable black figure striding down the path towards the house. 'What's *she* doing here? She should be at home in Bristol.'

'I don't know, but we'll be rumbled if she reaches the kitchens and they find out you haven't been going home. Quick, you need to catch her up and stop her before she gets to the house.'

Mary ran her fingers through her squally hair, pecked Edward on the cheek and dashed from the ruins. Once she had reached the path and was a safe distance from Edward, she called out. 'Caroline! Caroline!'

Caroline stopped, just yards from the kitchen door and turned, placing her hands on her hips. Her husband, William had died a month ago and Caroline was still wearing full black mourning clothes. She waited until Mary was within earshot then demanded: 'Where have you been?'

Typical Caroline, thought Mary, *haven't seen her in months and she storms down here like she owns the place.* 'For a walk,' she answered. 'What does it matter to you?'

Caroline seemed to have aged terribly since Mary had last seen her. She had, in Mary's quiet opinion, had the misfortune of inheriting their father's fiery and unpredictable temperament and their mother's haggard looks. 'It matters to me because *you* haven't been home in weeks. Mother's not well.'

'What's wrong with her?' Mary asked, taking a furtive glance back at the abbey ruins. She could just make out Edward's red hair poking from behind the wall as he tried to catch their conversation.

'Tuberculosis. The doctor sent her to the sanatorium last week. She's not good, Mary,' Caroline said. 'The house is so cold it's a wonder she hasn't died already.'

Through the Victorian black veil covering her face, Mary could just see into Caroline's grey eyes; they had always seemed empty to her but now they appeared entirely devoid of life. 'Will she be okay?' Mary asked, realising then that she could have made more of an effort to make amends at home. She chided herself for her weakness. Now her mother, her only ally at home, was unwell.

Caroline snorted. 'If you really cared, you would know the answer to that.'

Mary gritted her teeth, resenting her sister's self-righteousness. 'So what do you want?'

'I *want* nothing,' she said haughtily. 'I *need* money. Money to keep the household going. With mother away and father out of work we have nothing other than your wages.'

Mary had been saving all of her wages in the hope of buying something nice for Edward's birthday. 'How much do you need?' Mary asked.

'Everything you have,' Caroline retorted. 'I don't think you realise how bad the situation is at home. I'm having to use the pittance I get for my widow's allowance to pay the rent here. If the situation continues for much longer, I'll have to let my own house in Bristol go.'

Mary nodded; she understood. If Caroline having all of her wages meant the family were able to hold onto the house and put food on the table, then that was what must happen; Edward's present would have to wait. She still had several hours of free time left—plenty of time to collect the money, spend some time at home and be back at Blackfriars by nine. 'I'll go and get it now.'

'See that you do.' Caroline sighed, turned around and marched back up the hill.

Mary walked quickly, instantly deep in thought, back to Blackfriars. She would have to explain herself to Edward later. *How had life become so desperately miserable so quickly?* she wondered. The final visit to her ailing grandmother in Rye workhouse, coupled with her mother's words about her being consumed by domestic service entered her troubled mind. 'I just want to go,' Mary recalled her grandmother pleading. 'I've done my time. I need to sleep.' Mary now realised that her grandmother saw her time as a housemaid as a prison sentence, something to be served before the welcome salvation of eternal sleep. At the time, Mary had no grasp of what the old woman was feeling, having a naïve and youthful outlook on life. But if the rest of her life had to be spent like this, Mary understood her desperation for it all to come to an end.

'*Quoi encore? Qu'est ce que tu veux maintenant? Tu t'crois à l'hôtel?*' Bastion shouted at Mary, brandishing a long silver knife in her direction. The repulsive, rude man was mid-way through beheading a pig carcass, a job he seemed to relish a little too much for Mary's liking.

Mary turned her head and strutted through the kitchen, having learned quickly to simply ignore the disgusting man. She darted up the ninety-six stairs to the female servants' quarters. As expected, she found her bedroom mercifully empty; she didn't want the hassle of explaining herself to Clara or the other servants. It was a very rare thing for a servant to return from time off a moment before absolutely necessary. Mary headed over to her bedside cabinet and pulled open the drawer. Carefully wrapped inside an old blouse, she found the Rowntrees Cocoa tin in which she had been diligently saving her wages. Tugging open the tin, Mary tipped the money onto her bed and momentarily stared at it. Reluctantly, she took out a handful of the money, leaving a few paltry coins behind—at least *something* towards a gift for Edward. Then she thought of her poor family, struggling to exist, whilst she lived rent-free with almost as much food and drink each day as she cared to consume. Taking every last coin from the bed, Mary set the tin back and was about to slide the drawer shut when she noticed her locket. It was sterling silver with a fake diamond set in the centre. Mary clasped the locket to her chest for a moment. The twins had received the lockets as a birthday present from their parents last year. Mary recalled the day fondly. She and Edie had woken early and travelled by train to Hastings to have a *carte-de-visite* taken at Pearson's Photography Studio on the West Hill. They had spent the rest of the day on the seafront, enjoying ice cream, a walk along the crowded promenade and a Punch and Judy show on the stony beach.

Mary pulled open the locket. Inside, was a tiny photograph of Edie looking unduly severe. The girls, giggling like mad things, had been chastised by George Pearson and told not to smile for the pictures. In Edie's locket was an identically stern photo of Mary. Mary closed the locket and placed it carefully back inside the drawer.

After sitting down with Caroline in the chilly kitchen and receiving a tirade of criticism, Mary had sought a moment's sanctuary in her old room. But she did not find any refuge there; a thorny discomfort bit at her stomach. The house was so terribly cold: all of the fire grates were as empty and redundant as at the height of summer. Mary looked at her room as though it belonged to a stranger and felt sure that she was warmer sitting on the piece of sandstone in the abbey ruins than in her own home. Yet that was not the cause of the unsettled feeling which was troubling her. She felt stifled. She shuddered and hurried from the room, trying to work out the cause of her malaise. On the landing, she could hear her father gently snoring in his bedroom. Caroline had given strict instructions to not disturb him. He was suffering from melancholia and hadn't left his bed in days.

'You didn't disturb him, did you?' Caroline asked Mary when she returned to the kitchen.

80

'No, I did as you asked and let him rest,' Mary said quietly. She pulled out a chair to sit down, but quickly changed her mind. The sooner that she was gone from this lifeless place the better. It pained her even to think this way, but right now she longed to be back at Blackfriars. She hurriedly poured all the money onto the table. 'That's everything.'

Caroline prodded at the heap of money with a mild sneer. 'Not much, is it? Are you sure you didn't keep anything back?'

Wild anger boiled in Mary's blood but outwardly she remained calm. She had to make allowances for her recently widowed sister's behaviour. Meeting Caroline's eyes, she spoke clearly and confidently. 'That's everything. I can assure you. I have nothing left for myself.'

Caroline seemed taken aback at her temerity. 'What do *you* need money for anyway? You have everything given to you on a silver plate. The best French chef in the parish cooks you the finest meats and vegetables, which are then served to you by another servant. You sleep in a warm bed with wood burning in the grate all night. You're not a poor widow with ailing parents and two lots of bills to pay. If only you'd *earned* such a luxurious life.'

Mary desperately wanted to argue back, to fight her corner, to tell Caroline just how bad life was at Blackfriars, but she knew that it was an argument that she could never win. Instead, she changed the subject. 'Where's Edie?'

'Out looking for work. She's gone to stay with Lucy in Eastbourne for a few days to see if there's anything there. Poor girl's been out each and every day, looking. She's even resorted to doing laundry.'

'Oh,' Mary said. Lucy was an old childhood friend with whom Edie had fallen out years ago. Things must have become desperate for Edie to seek help from her.

As she watched her elder sister placing dishes into the sink to be washed, Mary realised her uneasiness at being home: it wasn't the temperature, her mother's or Edie's absence, or her father's melancholia, it was the haunting return of Caroline. Mary could still recall, with great clarity, the day that Caroline left home to be married to William. The house immediately felt bigger and lighter for the lack of her oppression. Their father acted like he ran the Mercer household but in reality it had always been Caroline's domineering presence that dictated the mood of the house. Mary had a sudden urge to see her ailing mother. 'Can I go to the sanatorium and see her?' she asked Caroline.

'Absolutely not. She's confined to her bed and needs rest. If she pulls through, you can see her back home.'

Am I really to blame for all this? Mary asked herself. Surely she couldn't be held responsible for her mother's tuberculosis and her father's melancholia? 'I might as well leave, then,' Mary said, genuine in her words.

'Yes, you might as well,' Caroline said, keeping her back to Mary. 'Make sure you come back on your next half day's leave and bring your wages.'

Just like the previous two occasions, Mary left the Mercer household with tears rolling down her face and a horrible nauseous feeling writhing in her stomach. As she hurried down the back path to Blackfriars, the only thought which could assuage her fatigued mind was that of Edward.

Mary read the note over and over again, the wonderful, delicious words becoming engrained on her memory. *I love you, Mary Mercer! There, I said it. You're all I think about, Mary! I just want to be with you every minute of every day. Edward x.* She had found the note under her pillow when she had returned to her room. She lay on her bed, the note resting on her breasts, rising and falling with each breath. In the eerie light of a fading, solitary candle beside her bed, she wordlessly mouthed the words, *I love you, Mary Mercer,* just in case Clara was not yet asleep. Mary was in love and the best thing of all, he loved her in return. The love she felt for Edward thwarted the silly, childish feelings she had held for Cecil. She knew now, with absolute clarity, that her feelings towards him were nothing more than an immature crush. The note had dried the tears and subdued the pain caused by the afternoon at home. Thinking of Caroline made her teeth clench and a bilious feeling surge through her body. She wondered what had made Caroline into such a nasty, bitter person and was grateful for her closeness to Edie growing up. Although maybe now it seemed that bond was broken, too. The twins had never been separated for so long before and Mary hated it. She leant onto her side, pulled open her drawer and removed the silver locket. For a few moments, Mary held it above her and watched as it gently swayed from side to side. Finally, she undid the clasp and placed it around her neck. *Now you're close to me, Edie,* she thought. Edie and Edward were both resting on her heart.

Mary smiled and fell asleep without tears for the first time since she had started at Blackfriars.

Mary was elated to hear the breakfast bell sounding. Having achieved the first chores of the day, she hurried downstairs, eager to see Edward for the first time since he had left his love note to her. She had repeated it so many times that she knew it off by heart. When she thought about those few precious words, they replayed in her mind in Edward's beautiful voice.

There was an unusual bubbling of conversation filtering from the servants' hall as Mary approached. As she entered the room to take her seat, she noticed that Mrs Cuff and Mr Risler were not yet at the table. She suddenly became aware that the eyes of the other servants had fallen upon her and the level of conversation had suddenly dropped. Her cheeks flushing red, Mary sat opposite Joan, keeping her eyes firmly on the table in front of her. In time, as the noise level rose, she dared to look across to Edward. His face crimson, he tried to smile reassuringly, but something in his eyes told Mary that all was not quite right or usual.

'Ah, ain't that sweet,' Joan said, much more loudly than she had ever spoken to Mary at the dinner table.

Mary flushed again, sensing that the other servants had somehow found out about her and Edward. *Had he told them?* She looked again at Edward but his gaze was fixed firmly to the floor.

'I love you, Mary Mercer!' Joan roared, standing from the table. Mary slumped in her seat as Joan continued her dramatic performance. 'There, I said it.'

'Joan!' Eliza called. 'Stop it!'

A male servant, whose voice she did not recognise, joined the agonising display. 'You're all I think about, Mary!'

'What is the meaning of all this noise?' Mr Risler bellowed, suddenly appearing in the room with Mrs Cuff at his heel. 'Joan Leigh, sit down *at once*.'

Joan sheepishly returned to the table.

Mary glowered at Clara, her Judas Iscariot, her whole body tensed with anger and betrayal.

'I don't know what's been going on in here,' Mr Risler ranted, 'but I could hear what can only be described as an unholy cacophony coming from this room. I sincerely hope that the household were spared hearing it. This will *not* happen again. Is that clear?'

A general murmur of agreement rose from the rebuked servants.

'Before we begin breakfast,' Mr Risler bellowed, 'I have just been informed that Lord Rothborne's cousin, Frederick Mansfield, will soon be paying the family a visit.'

There was a low, almost imperceptible groan from around the table at the mention of Frederick's name. Mary looked around the room, trying to gauge the reason for the disquiet at his visit. 'We will, therefore, need to ensure that the guest rooms are all adequately prepared,' Mr Risler said, picking up a large tray of cold meats and beginning his usual route around the table.

'Sorry about *her*,' Eliza said, as she poured Mary a cup of tea. Joan scowled but remained quiet, more interested in filling her mouth with as much pork as she could cram in.

Clara turned to Mary. 'I'm sorry, too, Mary. I didn't mean for Joan to overhear. I thought I was whispering it just to Eliza.'

'I don't want to talk about it,' she said quietly. Mary was hurt by what had happened; she was not yet ready for the whole staff to know about Edward and her. For one thing, the news would now surely filter through the village and get back to Edie. For another, Edward and she would be watched with hawk-eyes to ensure that nothing untoward ever happened. It felt to Mary like a giant conspiracy that nobody wanted them to be together. She didn't care a jot about Joan, but Mary knew she would forgive Clara in time. Just not right now. On top of all that had occurred at home yesterday, Mary was in no mood for more upset.

Chapter Eight

It was a great struggle for Mary not to fall asleep. Her weary body pleaded with her to surrender to her tiredness but she fought it. Taking a fold of skin from the palm of her left hand in her right forefinger and thumb, Mary rammed her nails in as hard as she could stand. She winced and almost yelped with the pain, but it had done the trick; she was awake again and her muscles' pleas for sleep subsided. The faint clanging of the grandfather clock on the floor below told Mary that it was half past eleven. Just fifteen minutes to go and she would get up.

There was just enough of a glow from the fire and from the pale moonlight pushing its way in under the curtains for Mary to see that Clara was in a deep sleep. A gentle snore came from her throat as she took in a long inhalation. Mary smiled and considered what she was about to do. After the humiliating breakfast that morning, she had returned to her work with a sagging despondency inside her. As usual, she had engineered the duties so that it was she who cleaned Edward's bedroom. As always, she had paid scant attention to the cleaning of the room, to the fire grate nor to the bed occupied by Edward's roommate, Jack. Instead, the majority of her time was always spent on Edward's bed, allowing her senses to absorb the fragments of his presence. She would usually then make his bed, fastidiously ensuring that there was not a single ripple in the linen sheets, followed by placing a delicate kiss on his pillow. This morning, however, her routine had been disrupted at the discovery of a note under his pillow. *Meet me at the boathouse at midnight, Edward x.* Having read the note, she had quickly concealed it under her uniform.

Minutes passed where Mary's mind wandered through a future life with Edward. She saw them both standing in the summery garden of a small cottage, full of bright flowers, watching their children playing together. Happily married: that was her future. Her stomach leapt with exhilaration for what she knew what was about to happen tonight.

The clock finally struck eleven forty-five. Carefully and slowly, Mary swung her legs from the bed and placed her bare feet on the cold boards. At bedtime, she had rushed up to the room and climbed into bed, pulling the sheets and blankets tightly up to her neck so that Clara did not notice that she was fully dressed.

With the merest of movements, Mary stepped away from the bed, picked up her shoes and silently crept towards the door. Before she opened it, Mary stood still and listened. Clara's breath rose softly into the still air. Mary unlatched the door and gently pulled it open. Again, she stopped still and listened for the rhythmic sound of Clara's breathing. When she was sure that she had not disturbed her, Mary moved into the hallway and pulled the door shut. Clutching her shoes in one hand, she snuck down the ninety-six steps into the basement. The downstairs corridors were eerily quiet and almost pitch-black but for a solitary wall-mounted candle close to the kitchen door, guiding Mary in the right direction. Enough adrenalin pumped around her veins to fight off the muted feelings of fear and trepidation at being in the depths of the house in the dead of night. A sudden thought of bumping into Bastion made her shudder, a cold sensation tingling down her spine. *Who knows what a wretch like that would do to me down here, with nobody within earshot?* Mary thought. Her fear abated when she remembered that Edward was somewhere nearby, also making his descent from the upper floors. But he would not likely go out through the kitchens, but rather through the meat larder, which had an exterior door and was much closer to the male servants' staircase.

Mary was relieved to find that the kitchens were mercifully empty; the only sign of life came from the flickering flames from the open fire, creating strange, unnatural shadows from the array of pots and culinary implements suspended from the ceiling. She hurried to the door and retracted the large metal bolts which held it closed: she had made it outside. As she closed the door behind her, she gasped at the freezing February night. She thought that she had wrapped up well, but she hadn't prepared herself for this level of coldness, already seeping through her layers of clothing like an insufferable, invasive creature. *Why does my courtship with Edward always have to involve being frozen to the bone?* she wondered, as she made her way across the courtyard towards the path which ran around the outside of the lake. The moon was like a squashed orange, still days away from its full voluptuousness, yet the skies were sufficiently clear to guide Mary around the lake's periphery. On the island the great folly stood, its majestic beauty incongruent with its apparent uselessness as a building.

As Mary approached the boathouse, she slowed her pace, wishing that her eyes would adjust to the light, demanding of them more clarity from the shadows. Her steady pace came to a halt just yards from the boathouse. The door was open and she was sure that she could see someone inside. A nervous tension rose inside her as she considered that it might not have been Edward who had left her the note. *Why wasn't he turning around or speaking?* Mary took a step back, a low panic rising inside, as she tried to bring to mind the note that she had found under Edward's pillow. *Had it definitely been his handwriting?* She was sure that it had been, but the image in her mind was blurred and confused. The black form inside the boathouse shifted slightly. It was definitely a person. *Maybe he hasn't seen me,* she thought. Mary took a deep breath in and bolstered herself mentally. She would say his name once and if he didn't answer straight away, she would run. 'Edward?' she said, unable to conceal the quiver in her voice. She knew that there was no way the person in the boathouse could have heard her pathetic mumbling. 'Edward!' She spoke more clearly and more confidently.

The figure in the boathouse had heard and moved towards the door. Mary struggled to see any facial features but she thought it looked like Edward's body shape.

'You made it!' It was Edward's voice.

Mary emitted a much bigger sigh of relief than she had intended, rushing up and throwing her arms around Edward. 'Oh, thank God it's you!' In his tight embrace, Mary suddenly felt safe and warm, her silly fears instantly dissipating.

'Who did you think it was?' Edward asked. She could tell from his voice that he was smiling.

Mary shrugged. 'I just got worried, that's all. I think I got a bit scared by the darkness.'

Edward pulled her in more tightly. 'My little Mary,' he said quietly.

'You do realise we'll be given our marching orders if we are caught out here together?' Mary asked. 'Never mind that you've got the boathouse open.'

'You're worth the risk. Come on,' Edward said, taking her chilly hand and guiding her inside the boathouse.

'Where are we going?' Mary asked.

'Not far!' Edward released her hand and fumbled in his pockets. A moment later he struck a match and an amber hue lit up the small enclosure. Holding the match in one hand, he carefully stepped inside the Mansfield family rowing boat. Taking a moment to get his balance, Edward offered his hand to Mary and she climbed in.

'Where to, me lady?' Edward asked as he sat in the centre of the boat and pulled up the oars.

Mary grinned. 'I think somewhere in the Mediterranean would be rather lovely,' she said. She'd once read a book about the coastal towns and islands in that stretch of water. She had a fanciful idea of one day exploring the romantic harbours of Spain, France, Italy and Greece on one side and the exotic ports of Algeria, Morocco and Egypt on the other.

'The Mediterranean it is, then, madam.'

Mary sat back and let her mind relax. As exciting as a trip to the shores of Europe and North Africa would undoubtedly be, she actually didn't want to be anywhere other than sitting on a cold rowing boat on the Blackfriars lake with Edward. Deep down, Mary knew where they were headed and what was about to happen but she stopped herself from thinking too deeply, wanting to savour each second as it unfolded before her. She gently swayed from side to side, making the boat rock in response.

'Stop it!' Edward whispered.

'Ah, poor Edward,' Mary teased, rocking the boat even more. 'Are you getting seasick?'

'Mary! I'm serious, I can't swim!'

Mary giggled but stopped rocking. 'Peace has returned.'

Edward continued rowing the short distance.

'Here we are, Your Ladyship,' he said as they reached the wooden landing stage on the island. 'We've reached one of the Greek islands. Hope you enjoy your stay.' Edward stood, tied a loop of rope around the jetty, then stepped out. With one hand he steadied the boat, the other he offered to Mary to assist her out.

As she had expected, Edward led her through the tall dewy grass towards the old folly, his hand tightly gripping hers. She could feel the damp from the passing undergrowth rising through the hem of her dress. She could tell that he was nervous from his clammy hands and lack of conversation. She knew from his fixed expression that he was conceiving of tonight being a special, magical night that she would never forget: a night which would mark the start of their future together. They reached the oak door set at the base of the folly and Edward tugged it open.

'Madam,' he said, holding the door open.

Mary stepped into the gloom of the folly, squeezing Edward's hand for comfort. The faint glimmer of moonlight faded into black as

Edward pulled the door closed behind them. Mary shuddered and waited for her eyes to adjust.

'Don't worry, I'm here,' Edward said softly, sensing her reticence. 'This way.' He took her to the side of the room where she had just managed to glimpse the spiral staircase before the light had diminished and placed her hand on a metal rail. 'Carefully does it. You go first.'

Mary slowly climbed the staircase with Edward just behind her, their footfall on the metal steps echoing unnervingly around the cylindrical wall. Mary took the final step on the staircase and found herself in a small unfurnished room. A wicker chest stood close to the centre of the room. Opposite them was another door.

'Open it,' Edward encouraged, leading Mary across the oak floor.

Mary gently lifted the latch and pushed open the door. She inhaled sharply at the sight before her: she was standing at the edge of an exterior stone terrace giving views onto the Blackfriars estate. At the base of the stone battlements, which enclosed the terrace, were dozens of chunky candles, burning brightly into the night sky. Scattered at her feet was a dusting of white rose petals. 'Edward!' was all that she could bring herself to say.

Edward led her to the edge of the battlements and placed his arm in the small of her back as she took in the breathtaking view of the moonlit lake and rose gardens. She was overwhelmed with joy and excitement; she knew that the moment was coming. The start of their future. Her heart raced and she began to quiver.

'You're cold, Mary,' Edward exclaimed.

'No, I'm fine—honestly,' she protested, but Edward headed back through the door, returning moments later with a thick blanket, which he tucked over her shoulders.

As she had hoped that he would, Edward bent down onto one knee and took her left hand in his. In the glowing orange light from the surrounding candles, Edward's boyish face had never looked more handsome to Mary. She thought then of how stupid she had been with her immature fascination with Lord Rothborne, then instantly castigated herself for potentially spoiling this wonderful moment thinking about *him*.

'Mary Kate Mercer,' Edward said in a trembling voice. 'Will you do me the honour of becoming my wife?'

Mary smiled and tears welled in her eyes. 'I would be delighted,' she said, almost unable to vocalise her acceptance.

Edward leapt up and threw his arms around her. 'I'm so happy you said that, Mary!'

She watched as he withdrew a ring from his pocket and slid it onto her finger.

'It was our great grandmother's,' Edward said.

Mary held it close to her face. It was a solid gold band with a stone set in the centre. It was simple, but where it came from made it the most beautiful thing on earth. She loved it. 'It's beautiful, thank you.'

'I'm sure she'd be delighted to see that you got it from me. More delighted probably than the rest of our family will be about the situation.'

Our family. Her euphoria, her belief that her future had just started crumbled in the instant Edward had mentioned her family. She allowed herself to be held by him but her thoughts had returned home. Her stifling lifeless home. She could only imagine her father's reaction at the news she was to marry her cousin. *What would that do to his bout of melancholia?* Then she thought of Edie. Her twin sister who was also sweet on Edward. How would she ever find the words to tell her? Only her mother would understand and she was miles away, locked up in a sanatorium.

'What's the matter, Mary?' Edward asked, sensing her sudden detachment.

'You mentioned our family. What on earth will Caroline, Edie and Mother make of it all? I doubt they'll talk to us ever again.'

'Your mother will be absolutely fine, Edie will come round eventually and Caroline—well, who cares about *her* anyway?' Edward squeezed her hand. 'At least you won't have to worry about getting used to a new surname!'

Mary smiled and hoped that it was enough to cover the growing discomfort inside. She knew, as soon as she saw the note, what Edward was going to do tonight. Perhaps she had known sooner, when they had first made love. But now it was real and serious, they would have to tell people. Tell the other servants at Blackfriars. Tell Mrs Cuff and Mr Risler.

Edward began to kiss Mary's neck, moving his lips slowly up towards her mouth. Mary banished thoughts of the future and reciprocated his kiss. Edward gently lifted the blanket from Mary's shoulders and allowed it to fall to the petal-strewn floor before beginning to unbutton her dress.

An unfamiliar sound woke Mary. Birds singing unusually close by. She opened her eyes in horror; she was lying on the wooden floor in the upper part of the old folly. 'Edward!' she gasped, leaping up and pushing away the pile of blankets under which they had slept. She pulled open the door and peered outside. The dark, night sky was beginning to yield to daylight. The other servants were bound to be awake by now. 'Edward, get up! We need to get back to the house.'

Edward's eyes pinged open on hearing the urgency in Mary's voice. Instantly he knew what had happened. The pair quickly pulled on their clothes. Mary began to scoop up the blankets.

'Leave all that, I'll come back for it later,' Edward urged.

'What about the candles? Someone might see them.'

'It'll be okay, nobody ever comes over here.'

The pair dashed back down the spiral staircase, aware that they were running out of time. Edward rowed back to the boathouse as fast as he could, the oars chopping desperately and noisily at the water. Mary's eyes darted all around them, certain that someone would see them. *Everybody*—even the gardeners—rose early.

'Let's split up. I'll go the longer way round past the ice house and back in through the meat larder. See you at breakfast,' Edward panted, kissing Mary on the lips.

'Bye, fiancé!' Mary called after him, hurrying back towards the kitchen.

Although her son, Cecil was now the Earl of Rothborne, Lady Rothborne occasionally liked to flex and exhibit her seniority within the Mansfield family. Following the death of her husband, she insisted on having his former bedroom, located as it was in the most favourable position of all the rooms in Blackfriars. It was situated on the first floor with windows facing south over the main gardens and windows facing east over one edge of the lake. Since being widowed at the age of fifty-two, she had found the need for very little sleep; she was usually the last family member to retire for the night and the first to rise. Today, like most mornings, she enjoyed standing at the east window watching as the faintest glimmers of the morning sun began to penetrate the night sky. On warmer days, she would open the window to let in the wondrous sound of the blackbirds' dawn chorus on the early morning breeze. For Lady Rothborne, there was no time of day quite like it. Everything was still. The world was at peace and happy. She looked out of the window, absorbing the minute changes and new things that she could see, suddenly made visible by the rising sun. She spotted something moving on the path beside the lake. *A deer, perhaps?* she wondered. She squinted hard and pressed her face to the window. Two people walking. Running. They began to grow into focus.

'The footman and the third housemaid,' she said quietly. 'Very interesting.'

Lady Rothborne continued to watch until the pair had separated and disappeared inside the house using two different entrances.

A wide smile erupted on her face.

Mary pushed open the kitchen door and braced herself for a tirade in French, but Bastion was nowhere to be seen. The kitchen thankfully looked deserted. Mary closed the door and heaved a sigh of relief. She'd made it back in without being seen. Now she just needed to get back upstairs. *What was the time?*

'Nice night for it,' a booming, hollow voice said.

Mary leapt with fright and turned in the direction of the voice, which she did not recognise. An unfamiliar man was sitting at the table clutching a bottle of red wine. 'I just stepped out for…something,' Mary stammered.

'Of course you bloody didn't,' he said, slurring his words. Whoever he was, he was very drunk. 'I've been here since… God knows. Could be days. Enough time to know that you've been out all night,' he accused with a lopsided grin and pointing his finger. 'Naughty. Very naughty.'

Mary stepped closer. He was well-spoken and, despite being in a dishevelled state, was clearly not a servant or tradesman. He was handsome in a rugged, masculine way with tousled, slick, black hair and a white shirt, almost entirely unbuttoned, revealing a well-toned chest and stomach. 'Are you Lord Rothborne's cousin, Sir?' Mary ventured.

The man grinned again. 'Yup. But please don't tell me I look like that ugly little cad. I rather hoped I'd inherited Mummy's beauty.'

'I'd heard you were coming—I'm a housemaid here,' Mary said, wanting to soften him up in the hope that he wouldn't then tell anyone about her nocturnal foray, but also desperate to get back to her room.

Frederick's eyes lit up. 'A housemaid. How delectable.'

Mary shrugged, unsure of how to respond. 'It's okay.'

'What's your name?' he asked, taking a gulp of wine from the bottle.

'Miss Mercer.'

'What's your *real* name? Surely your mother didn't name you *Miss Mercer?*' he said with a laugh.

'It's Mary,' she said, a little uncomfortably.

'Mine's Frederick.' He stood and offered her his hand to shake. 'Pleased to meet you, Mary.'

Mary reluctantly shook the proffered hand out of duty to her employer and deference to his class. 'Nice to meet you. I'd better get on.' Mary began to move towards the door.

'Of course, keep the Blackfriars' wheels turning,' he muttered, taking another swig of drink. 'Before you go, could you tell me something?'

Mary stopped close to the door and faced him. 'Of course.'

'Being a housemaid, you must know a bit about the bedroom department.'

Mary's face flushed. 'Pardon?'

'I know, bloody crude of me to ask, but does my dear cousin actually bed his good lady wife? Hmm? I mean, they've been married for what six years and there are no signs of any mini Mansfields yet, are there? Most peculiar.'

'I don't think I'm in any position to talk about that,' Mary answered.

'They have separate rooms though, don't they?'

Mary nodded.

Frederick took another swig of wine. 'I only ask because I'm next in line to the Blackfriars throne you see. If Cecil doesn't produce an heir, then this—' Frederick said gesturing the wine bottle around the room—'all comes to me. Every last piece of God-awful furniture, every last servant. *You'll* be mine, Mary Mercer. How would you like that?'

Mary was desperate to leave the company of this awful drunk. *How can I get away from him? Time's running out!*

Mary's heart sank: her time had run out.

Standing at the door, mouth agape, was Mrs Cuff.

'Miss Mercer, what are you doing in here with Mr Mansfield? Where's your uniform?' Mrs Cuff stammered, quite unable to believe her eyes.

'So, sorry, Lady Housekeeper,' Frederick said, turning his attention to Mrs Cuff. 'All my fault. Miss Mercer heard a noise and came to see what the bother was. I was the bother. All my fault. Now I'm keeping her chatting. My humblest, most sincere apologies.'

Mrs Cuff glared at Mary, seeming to accept the absurd notion that Mary could possibly have heard a noise from three floors up in the attic. 'Right, well, you'd better get into your uniform and get to work.'

Mary slunk from the room.

'Cheerio, Mary,' Frederick called. 'Time I went to bed, I think.'

Mary hurried up the stairs to her bedroom, certain that she would be for it when Mrs Cuff finally caught up with her. She opened the door; Clara was just in the process of lifting her dress up over her body.

'Where have you been?' Clara asked.

'Nowhere exciting,' Mary replied. She no longer trusted that what she said to Clara wouldn't be gossiped about in the servants' hall.

'Look, I'm sorry about what happened yesterday, Mary,' Clara began. 'I didn't mean to betray your trust. Can we be friends again?'

'Just forget it. Let's get to work,' Mary said.

Chapter Nine

Morton inserted the memory card from his camera into his laptop and plugged in his iPhone. He was sitting in shorts and a t-shirt in his study, sipping at his fourth cup of coffee of the day. He drank too much of the stuff; Juliette was always telling him that he needed to cut back. She was right, of course, but it was the one thing that helped him through the eye-straining slog of staring at a computer screen for hours on end. The low bubbling of tourist chatter filtered in through the open study window, the warm day having brought the visitors to Rye by the coachload.

Morton navigated through the file directories on his computer until he found the photographs that he had taken on his camera at Blackfriars. The first picture was of the back path to the estate, with the house looming large in the distance. He lingered on the image for a few seconds, then turned to the wall of his study covered with notes, pictures and information from the Mercer Case. He looked Mary square in the eyes, almost pleading for the time-frozen image to reveal what had happened on that path that fateful day in 1911. Turning back to the laptop, he clicked onto the images taken on his phone; a dull yellow tinge on each revealed that they were taken in the dimly-lit depths of the Blackfriars archive. He knew the contents of the first page: an excerpt from the Blackfriars wages book. As he scanned down the page, he caught Edward Mercer's name again and scribbled down the date of his last wages: Friday 19th May 1911. *Where had he gone, just one month after Mary's disappearance? Sacked? A new job? Dead?* The thought then entered Morton's mind that maybe, he too had vanished without trace. The desire to know more about what happened to Edward was enough for Morton to hold off temporarily looking at the rest of the images. A change of employment would be almost impossible to ascertain; a death search would be simple. Opening up the Ancestry website, Morton ran an open-ended death search and found Edward immediately. His death was recorded in the June quarter of 1911 in the Rye registration district. He knew that the death may have had nothing to do with Mary's disappearance, but since Edward featured on both the family *and* work lists for people close to Mary around the time of her disappearance, it was certainly an intriguing lead.

Having become momentarily sidetracked, ordering a next-day priority death certificate for Edward from the General Register Office website, Morton switched his focus back to the photographs taken at Blackfriars. The second image was of the Day Book, which mentioned the disastrous start of Mary's work at Blackfriars. Morton re-read the contents of the page then held his breath as he clicked onto the next image, which he had taken covertly; he hoped that his haste to take the pictures hadn't resulted in their being out of focus or illegible. Thankfully, the image was clear. The entries for Monday 10th and Tuesday 11th were brief and routine: food supplies purchased and landscape works completed around the estate. Then he came to Wednesday—the date of Mary's disappearance.

Wednesday 12th April. Lady Philadelphia and some of the female staff returned prematurely from the hunting trip to Scotland. Lady Philadelphia suffering from morning sickness. Discovered one of the housemaids, Miss Mercer, in Lady Philadelphia's bedroom wearing her finest ball gown and some of the most precious Mansfield jewellery. Servant dismissed. Replacement currently being sought. Lady Philadelphia much improved upon return to Blackfriars. Mrs Cuff.

Morton re-read the entry several times, trying to absorb the content. He didn't know what he had been expecting to find, but something so trifling and bland left him with a sagging feeling of disappointment. Mary had been found wearing the lady of the house's clothes and jewellery and was then promptly sacked. It was understandably a dismissible offence, but why did Sidney Mersham not want him to see the entry more than one hundred years later? Morton stared at the screen. The document clearly added new information about Mary's last known hours, but its revelation to Morton would not now have damaged the Mansfield reputation: it was hardly a headline-grabbing scandal. If it hadn't been for her subsequent disappearance, it would have been almost a comical end to her employment with them. *What happened next?* he wondered. *Where did you go from there, Mary? What am I not seeing that they don't want me to see?* There was clearly something he wasn't quite getting. Morton read the entries for the rest of the week: nothing of any consequence had been noted but for the return of the rest of the household from the hunting expedition.

Saturday 15th April 1911. Household all returned from hunting trip to Scotland. Mr Risler remained in Scotland with Mr Frederick Mansfield for extended break.

Morton looked at his copy of the letter that Mary had written from Scotland. It had been postmarked Monday 17th April. There was

96

a definite overlap in time when Mary was sacked from Blackfriars and wrote the letter from Scotland whilst the family were also in that country. *Did Mary go to Scotland because the family were there? Was there someone there she ran to?*

He clicked the previewer on to the next image. It was for the Day Book commencing Monday 17th April. Only one entry stood out from mundane estate business:

Tuesday 18th April. Doctor visited and confirmed that Lady Philadelphia is expecting a child.

Morton looked at the final image taken secretly at Blackfriars. It was for the week prior to Mary's sacking, commencing Monday 3rd April 1911. He carefully read the page. Among the routines and incidental comings and goings, he noted down the entry detailing the Mansfield expedition to Scotland.

Wednesday 5th April. Lord Cecil, Lady Philadelphia and Mr Frederick Mansfield departed for Boughton House for the annual deer hunt. Accompanying staff: Mr Risler, Mrs Cuff, Jack Maslow, James Daniels, Edward Mercer, Thomas Redfern, Sarah Herriot, Clara Ellingham, Eliza Bootle, Susannah Routledge, Agnes Thompson.

Morton examined each name. *Did Mary go to Scotland to be with one of you?* he wondered as he stared at the entry. He looked curiously at the page as a whole. Something was different between the first week and the following two weeks. He clicked back and spotted it: the handwriting was different. The week's entries beginning Monday 3rd April and Monday 10th April were written by the same person and signed off with Mrs Cuff's signature. The week commencing Monday 17th April was written by a different hand and signed by Mr Risler. When he looked again at the Day Book for early January, he saw that it had also been signed off by Mrs Cuff. He could only surmise that up to the week of Mary's sacking, Mrs Cuff was solely responsible for the Day Book, the entries afterwards being completed by Mr Risler, the butler. Not that exciting, but again worth noting. Morton's rising fear that Mrs Cuff might have also died around the same time was allayed when he confirmed her continued employment as housekeeper in the wages book. *If she hadn't died or left Blackfriars, was it then a simple coincidence that she stopped being the person to sign off the Day Book after Mary vanished?* Morton thought maybe not. He scribbled the information on a Post-it note and stuck it to the wall. He clicked 'print' on all the images taken at Blackfriars, ran a yellow highlighter over the relevant parts, then Blu-Tacked them to the wall.

Morton moved to the open window and watched the plethora of summer tourists pushing their way up the cobbles of Mermaid Street. With casual glances to the growing patchwork of evidence attached to his wall, Morton allowed his mind to wander around the puzzle of the Mercer Case. The Scotland coincidence bothered him. Mary had apparently written a letter from there, severing all ties with her family in Sussex at a time when the majority of the Mansfield family and their domestic servants were on a hunting trip in the same place.

Returning to his laptop, Morton used the Scotland's People website to run meticulous searches in their archives using a variety of name combinations for Mary. Of the various Mary Mercers that showed up, each was demonstrably not the correct person. Yet she had written a letter postmarked in Scotland.

Drinking the dregs of his coffee, and vowing it to be his last cup of the day, Morton opened up the digital image of Mary's letter. In the new knowledge of Mary's dismissal, one phrase stuck out. *I have behaved and acted in an unforgivable manner, which, if you were to learn of the whole matter, would bring embarrassment to the Mercer name.* Wearing the mistress of the house's clothes and jewellery was not behaving in an unforgivable manner, even by Edwardian standards.

It didn't take a degree module in graphology to work out that Mary Mercer was the definite author of the letter, although having a degree module in graphology compelled Morton to look more closely. He zoomed in close to the letter and studied the formation of the letters carefully. As he worked, he retrieved lectures from the stored repositories of his mind, given by his esteemed lecturer, Dr Baumgartner, whom Morton greatly admired. Dr Baumgartner had taught him to study everything as if through a slow-motion macro lens: meticulously, painstakingly and intricately. It was because of those lectures that Morton spotted the anomaly. Yes, the letter was written by Mary Mercer, but there was a subtle underlying stress and tension in the way that she had formed the strokes on the page. Morton then compared her handwriting to that found on the note left at Edith's grave. That the letter revealed that she was more stressed and anxious than when she wrote the note placed on her twin's grave, spoke volumes to Morton. He considered the possibilities: that Mary really did go to Scotland to escape an embarrassing exit from Blackfriars; that she went to Scotland to go *to* someone from Blackfriars, or that somehow she was forced to write the letter. The only way that Mary could have remained in Scotland was under a pseudonym, since she failed to appear in any official records there. *Unless she used Scotland as a stepping stone to somewhere else*, Morton thought. He remembered that Ray Mercer had told him that emigration records had drawn a blank, but maybe he was searching *English* disembarkation records. Morton opened up the Outward Passenger Lists 1890-1960 on the Findmypast website, filtering the results with a departure place of Scotland. Although he was hopeful with this line of enquiry, he was unsurprised to find that there were no good matches for Mary Mercer. Spending a lot of time changing the search parameters returned the same frustrating answer: zero matches.

Morton noticed that he was slumped in his chair, having spent a ridiculous number of hours gaping at the laptop screen. He rubbed his eyes and stood from the desk. He returned to the open window and drew in a long, deep breath, holding it before slowly releasing it into the still air. The streets below were much quieter now. Morton looked at the time: 4:46. Juliette would be home any moment; it was almost time to stop searching. Almost. He decided to use what little time he had left until she arrived throwing the search wide open. He removed all the search filters and searched all outward passenger lists under the name Mercer. Eight thousand, five hundred and thirty one results. A needle in a haystack and a pointless waste of time. He removed the forename and surname and simply searched under the exact birthplace of Winchelsea. One match. Edith Leyden. Morton clicked to see the original image. The page pertained to a crossing of the *RMS Celtic II* from Liverpool bound for Canada, disembarking 18th December 1925. Morton scanned down the alphabetised list of passengers until he found her.

Name: Mrs Edith Leyden
Last address in the United Kingdom: Wisteria Cottage, Winchelsea
Port at which passenger has contracted to land: Halifax, Canada
Proposed address at destination: 4 West Street, Halifax, Canada
Profession, occupation or calling: Housewife
Age of passenger: 32
Country of last permanent residence: England

Morton printed the page then found her return voyage to England two weeks later on board the *Albania*. To some family historians, the record provided an interesting snapshot of a two-week holiday in

Canada. For Morton, it provided another potential avenue for research. He now needed to know who was residing at 4 West Street, Halifax in 1925. Morton wrote the Canadian address on a post-it note and attached it to his laptop screen. He was about to start up a new search when he heard the front door slamming shut. Morton smiled and went downstairs to meet Juliette. A sharp, wonderful smell of fresh chips wafted out from the kitchen. Morton followed the scent and found a sweaty Juliette in tracksuit bottoms, casual t-shirt and no make-up, running herself a glass of tap water.

'Hiya,' she said, pecking him on the lips. 'Good day?'

'Hi. Yeah, it was good thanks—spent most of it staring at a computer screen. How was yours?'

Juliette sighed and downed the water. 'More in the classroom—not bad though. We spent the day doing role-play. The supervisors threw various situations at us and we had to go through it as though we were on the job, deciding whether an arrestable offence had been committed, or not.'

'Fish and chips?' Morton said with a grin.

'Yeah, I was driving past the Kettle of Fish and couldn't resist.'

'Good—I'm starving.' Morton sat up to the island in the centre of the ultra-modern kitchen. It was this room which had sold the house to Juliette, which Morton found ironic since she was such a dreadful cook.

'Here you go, sir,' Juliette said, thrusting a wrapped parcel towards him.

Morton unwrapped the packet and ravenously tucked into the cod and chips. 'Delicious, thanks.'

Juliette nodded her agreement and smiled.

'This arrived today,' Morton said, pulling an envelope from its position, tucked behind a magnet on the side of the fridge.

Juliette wiped her hands on a piece of kitchen roll and opened the envelope. 'Oh, wow! They're getting married. How lovely.'

It was an invitation to his adoptive brother Jeremy's wedding. The thought of the wedding brought back a sensation of mild nausea akin to that felt prior to a job interview. It had been just a few months ago that Morton's adoptive father had finally revealed the truth about Morton's past. Believing himself to be on death's door, he had revealed that Morton's Aunty Margaret was in fact his birth mother, giving him up when he was just a few hours old. His adoptive brother, Jeremy, whom he had previously felt little connection with, was in fact his cousin. His own flesh and blood. Following his father's near-death experience, Morton had worked to restart his relationship with his adoptive brother, not easy with Jeremy being in the army and away for weeks at a time. And now here he was getting married. 'What do you get for your brother when he's marrying a man?'

Juliette smiled. 'What would you have got your brother if he was marrying a woman?'

Morton shrugged. It was a fair point.

'You're not actually bothered about it, are you?' Juliette asked with a quizzical look on her face.

'Course not,' Morton said. It was kind of the truth. He actually didn't care at all about his brother's sexuality. He was still feeling a little miffed that he was the last person in the family to actually find out. It reminded him of the feelings that he had had when he was told that he was adopted, that he was the family's extra limb, surplus to requirement. Most of all, however, he was dreading seeing his Aunty Margaret for the first time since being told that she was actually his biological mother. The thought of seeing her made his stomach lurch. *What would he say? What* could *he say? Did she even know that he knew their true relationship?*

'Good.' Juliette picked up another chip and muttered under her breath, 'At least he's getting married.'

Morton rolled his eyes and pretended not to have heard. Since very early on in their relationship, Juliette had wanted to get married. She wanted the big fairy-tale, white wedding. He, though, wanted none of it. For years, he knew the block emanated from his past, that he couldn't give his betrothed a surname which did not belong to him. But since discovering that his surname actually belonged to his mother at the time of his birth, his feelings on the matter had begun to thaw.

Juliette, not quite willing to accept Morton's silence as reluctance to speak about the subject, draped a chip over the ring finger on her left hand. 'What do you think?'

Morton took her hand and kissed the chip. 'Suits you.' Then he snatched the chip in his mouth and swallowed it. 'Fancy going for a walk after this?'

'Sure. We could walk along the river past the windmill.'

'Great.'

Chapter Ten

Morton watched Juliette leave the house. He didn't take his eyes off her as she climbed into her car and headed down the uneven cobbles before disappearing out of sight. He had asked her to text him as soon as she got to work, which had immediately aroused her suspicions. 'What's up with you?' she had asked.

'Nothing, just want to make sure you're okay,' he had replied. She had frowned incredulously at him, but let the matter rest. He hadn't told her that, when they had returned home last night from a walk along the river, a brown A4 envelope had been waiting on the doormat with his name handwritten on the front. Thankfully, Juliette had been in the toilet when he had opened the envelope or else had she seen the contents, she would have leapt back on duty and turned into police constable-in-training, Juliette Meade.

With Juliette gone for the day, Morton padded up to his study wearing his night boxer shorts and t-shirt. He picked up the envelope, which he had hidden below a stack of Mercer Case papers and withdrew the contents. On the top was a simple note which read, 'We can all dig, Morton.' Next was an incredibly neat, hand-drawn family tree for his branch of the Farrier tree. Morton's name was at the base of an inverted pyramid, which then split into two for his parents. Whoever had compiled this tree hadn't done their homework. The parents listed were his adoptive parents, *not* his biological ones. At the bottom of the stack, and most alarming of all to Morton, was a photograph of Juliette taken yesterday as she queued at the Kettle of Fish chip shop with the words, 'Juliette Meade, 1975-?' The threat was made real. Only one person had wanted him to stop researching the Mercer family enough to warrant this: Douglas Catt.

Morton dialled the *Mermaid Inn*. 'Hello, I'd like to speak to a guest of yours please, Douglas Catt,' Morton said, trying to suppress the anger in his voice.

'Okay, one second,' a polite female voice on the other said. The line went quiet and Morton was treated to a few random bars of an unidentifiable piece of music before the voice spoke again. 'Hello. I'm sorry, but Mr Catt checked out two days ago.'

'Two days? Are you sure?'

'Yes, absolutely. Sorry.'

'I don't suppose he left anything for Morton Farrier? A message of any kind?'

There was a small pause and Morton heard some computer keys being tapped. 'No, nothing. Sorry.'

'Okay, thank you for your help.' Morton hung up, reflecting on what he had just heard. Just because he had checked out, didn't actually mean that he had returned home. *He might well be staying at another hotel,* Morton thought. He remembered then that Douglas's home phone number was in an email sent to him. Bringing up his emails on his iPhone, Morton skimmed through until he reached the exchange between him and Douglas. He quickly located the correct email and then dialled Douglas's home in Bristol. The phone rang for several seconds before being picked up.

'Hello?'

Morton hung up; in hearing that single word he'd ascertained for certain that the voice on the other end had belonged to Douglas Catt. Morton was perplexed. *If Douglas hadn't sent the packet, then who did?*

He tucked the contents back into the envelope and slid it out of sight from Juliette. He wasn't sure how or even *if* to tell her about it. He didn't want to worry her unduly. *Was it reckless to* not *tell her? Especially when the threat was ostensibly aimed at her?*

Morton headed downstairs to his en suite bathroom. As he showered and the hot powerful water pelted his nape, Morton allowed his mind to wander around the Mercer Case. It was often at relaxed times like these that he had his *Eureka!* moments and an avenue of research which he had previously overlooked might jump out at him. However, no such revelatory moments happened today. He couldn't stop his mind from vaulting between seeing Aunty Margaret at Jeremy's upcoming wedding or the haunting words written below the image of Juliette in the chip shop. By even referring to a possible date of death for Juliette, the author of the package had, presumably as intended, slid a cold knife into Morton's heart. Allowing his mind to drift without direction today was not a wise idea. He switched off the shower, dried himself and pulled his towel around his midriff.

As Morton crossed the hallway, he spotted something at the foot of the stairs on the doormat. His heart began to beat faster as he padded down the stairs, fearful of the contents. As he drew closer he could see that it was a small white envelope. He bent down to pick it up and was relieved to see the familiar blue stamp of the Office of National Statistics emblazoned on the front. Panic over.

Morton tore into it and pulled out Edward Mercer's death certificate.

When and where died: 18th May 1911, Blackfriars estate, Winchelsea RD
Name and surname: Edward Mercer
Sex: Male
Age: 20 years
Occupation: Footman
Cause of death: Accidentally drowned certified by J. D. Leyden MRCS
Signature, description and residence of informant: John William Mercer, father, Old Post Office, Icklesham
When registered: 24th May 1911

Edward had drowned little over one month after Mary had vanished. Morton reasoned that his death must have compounded the loss already felt in the Mercer family by Mary's absence. He wondered if Edward had died trying to find her. Morton knew only too well how wildly unpredictable and dangerous the nearby River Rother could be. He looked back at the death certificate. It said that Edward had drowned in Winchelsea, *not* Rye. Morton considered the geology and landscape around Winchelsea; being situated on a hill, there were no large tracts of water or flowing rivers. *How did Edward accidentally drown in a town with no large areas of water?* Morton wondered. His curiosity was aroused: he needed to know more. He carried the certificate up to his study, then quickly changed into fresh clothes and prepared his laptop and a bag for a trip to The Keep—the repository for archives and records pertaining to parishes within the county of East Sussex. When he reached his bedroom he saw his phone screen light up announcing the receipt of a text message. It was from Juliette. *'Got to work, Weirdo. Do I need to text regular updates?! xx'* Morton smiled and replied, *'Glad you got there okay. No need for updates. Text when you leave! Off to The Keep. xx'*

Morton arrived at The Keep, situated just on the outskirts of Brighton, and found the car park pretty well empty. The archives had thankfully shifted from the inaccessible and unsuitable building in Lewes to a brand new, purpose built repository, opened by Her Majesty the

Queen. They had even upgraded their archive request system to a digital, computer-based one. At last. Morton parked his Mini in a quiet corner, gathered up his belongings and made his way into the light and airy building.

'Morning,' a jovial receptionist greeted from behind her semi-circular desk.

'Morning,' Morton replied, marching into the cloakroom area, placing all prohibited items into one of the large grey lockers. Carrying just his laptop, notepad, pencil and Edward's death certificate, Morton walked through the lobby area with its round wooden tables and chairs, through a glass door and into the main body of the repository. The archive was principally comprised of two main sections: the Reading Room and the Reference Room. The Reading Room, in which genealogists and members of the public could come and go freely, housed rows of large tables on which were sited digital microfilm readers and large computers giving access to various online resources. To the side of the room were rows of tall shelves containing books and photocopies of parish registers pertaining to East Sussex. The Reference Room housed several large map desks and rows of research desks, allowing work with original documents.

Morton walked into the Reading Room and took a seat in the front row at one of the digital microfilm readers. His first avenue of research would be in the local papers in the hope that Edward Mercer's death had been reported. He set down his laptop and other belongings, switched on the reader then headed to the bank of short metal filing cabinets, whose drawers were filled with mile upon mile of microfilm reels. Morton searched the drawer-edge labels and found *The Sussex Express*. Pulling open the drawer, he was greeted by the sight of dozens of yellow boxes. Having selected the box which said 'Jan-Dec 1911', Morton returned to his desk and loaded the film onto the reader. Gone were the old arm-numbing days of hand-winding a whole roll of film; the entire process could now be conducted using the large, touch-screen computer in front of him. Morton pushed the film through on fast-forward, stopping at regular intervals to check that he hadn't overshot the relevant month. After just a few short bursts, he was at the beginning of May 1911. Advancing slowly through the black and white print, he stopped at the Friday 26th May 1911 edition of *The Sussex Express*. In its original form, the paper would have been a broadsheet, jam-packed with stories, adverts and snippets of county news. Morton found the section of the newspaper he was looking for:

the part in which the smaller villages and towns of Sussex told of their parish news. As he had hoped, in this edition there was a bold heading for Winchelsea. Morton placed his fingers on the screen and splayed them apart to zoom in on the story.

Found Drowned

This was the verdict of the Coroner's jury which inquired into the circumstances of the death of Edward Mercer, a footman, 20 years of age. The deceased was a well-known inhabitant of the Icklesham parish, but having latterly worked at Blackfriars House in Winchelsea since 1908. Deceased was only missed a few hours before his body was found floating in the lake at the aforementioned property. It appeared that the deceased had been depressed lately through the continued absence of his cousin, Mary Mercer, but he had never been heard to threaten to commit suicide. Drowning (according to the police surgeon) was the cause of death.

Morton was transfixed by the short story. Edward, feeling depressed, yet not suicidal, drowned in the Blackfriars lake. *Could* he *be the person that Mary ran to in Scotland the day that she was unceremoniously sacked from Blackfriars?* Morton pulled out his phone and took a picture of the screen, recalling his visit to the still waters of the Blackfriars lake. *Was it really deep enough to kill a man?* he wondered with incredulity. He supposed that any amount of water could drown a man if he couldn't swim. To ensure that there was no further mention of Edward's drowning, Morton searched the rest of the newspaper and the adjacent weeks, but found nothing more. He rewound the film, put it back into its yellow box and returned it to the filing cabinet. Collecting his things, Morton went to the small help desk. Unfortunately for Morton, not all the outdated relics had been left at the old repository: behind the desk sat his arch enemy, Miss Deirdre Latimer. Morton had hoped that when The Keep opened, Miss Latimer would have taken the opportunity to retire. When he had eagerly arrived for his very first visit to the new building he was dismayed to see, among the huge display boards dotted around to celebrate the opening, a picture of Miss Latimer standing chatting to the Queen. The worst part for Morton was that both the Queen *and* Miss Latimer were laughing in the picture, something in her that he had never witnessed in all his time visiting the archives.

'Could I have a username and password for the computers, please?' Morton said, dispensing with any attempt at pleasantries.

Miss Latimer reciprocated their mutual dislike and didn't even bother to open her mouth. She picked up a pre-cut strip of paper and handed it to him with a surly thrust.

Morton mumbled his inaudible gratitude, then headed to a computer. He typed in the username and password, and then pulled up The Keep search page. In it, he typed *Blackfriars, Winchelsea.* Just sixteen original documents were open to the public to do with the property, owing to the large collection which remained at the house itself. Morton slowly moved the mouse down the page, reading the synopsis for each document. He passed over land tax documents, sixteenth century manorial records, aerial photographs of the abbey ruins, a collection of charcoal drawings and various land registration documents: nothing piqued his interest. On the final page, he spotted a document that made him sit up. It was for a draft contract of a seven-year lease, rent-free to Joshua David Leyden in 1911. Morton clicked the entry. *Was this the same Dr Leyden who had signed Edward Mercer's death certificate? Didn't Edith Mercer marry a man called Leyden?* It might mean nothing, but since it was the only document in the right time period, it needed checking. Morton clicked 'Order Now', grateful that the old systems for document retrieval had been left behind at the old building and a new, digital system had been created. Returning to the main screen, Morton ran a search for the parish registers of Winchelsea and Icklesham, hoping to find the location of Edward's burial. He ordered two sets of burial registers for Winchelsea January 1813—October 1934 and November 1934—July 2009. He also ordered the Icklesham burial register, December 1874—December 1975.

A few minutes later, Morton watched on-screen as the status of the documents changed from 'In transit' to 'Available'. He now needed to make his way into the Reference Room, which, much to his consternation, was now being guarded by Miss Latimer. Quiet Brian was also on duty at the desk and Morton desperately hoped that it would be him he would need to deal with.

Morton signed off the computer terminal and headed to the floor-to-ceiling glass wall which separated the Reading Room from the Reference Room. He pulled his reader's ticket from his wallet, wafted it vaguely in the general direction of a stout silver pillar which permitted entry, and a glass door glided to one side.

Morton glanced at the long wooden helpdesk to his left. Miss Latimer was nearest to him, standing in her usual stance with her arms

107

folded, scowling out at the world like a caged animal. At the far end of the desk, talking inaudibly on the phone, was Quiet Brian. Morton decided to avoid potential conflict and waltzed past Miss Latimer as if he had not seen her and waited patiently in front of Quiet Brian. As seconds of waiting turned into minutes, Morton could see in his peripheral vision Miss Latimer looking at him from the corner of her eye. Just as Morton began to feel self-conscious and silly, Quiet Brian finished his conversation and hung up. To Morton's horror, he turned and darted through the opening behind the desk and out of sight. His cheeks flushing, Morton stood in front of an empty desk, whilst Miss Latimer stood on the opposite side, running her fingers through her hair.

'This is ridiculous,' Morton muttered to himself. He moved down the desk in front of Miss Latimer, who continued the charade of having not seen him. 'I've got some documents to collect. It doesn't matter which first.' As usual, he had lost the battle with Miss Latimer.

'Reader's ticket,' she said flatly, holding open her hand. Morton handed over the ticket and watched as she scanned it, placed it down on the counter between them, then went out the back and retrieved the file and an A4 record of the document. Wordlessly, she handed him a bundle of papers contained in a blue wallet, bound with a white ribbon.

'Thank you,' he said, in spite of himself. He hated being nice to her. He headed over to a vacant table, set down his things and began to unwrap the package. Setting aside the protective blue wrapping, Morton carefully withdrew the contents. There were three original documents: all typed in black ink on thick, off-white paper. Years of diligent preservation had failed to stop a smattering of small brown marks creeping into each of the papers. At the top of each sheet was a red stamp for two shillings and sixpence.

Morton picked up the first paper and carefully read it through. It was written in a standard legal way and set out that a house in Winchelsea, called Wisteria Cottage, be given rent-free to Doctor Joshua David Leyden. At the foot of the document was the signature and address of Lord Rothborne of Blackfriars, dated December 1911.

Morton moved on to the rest of the bundle. The second document was identical to the first, but for the dates: it provided a further seven-year, rent-free extension to the lease of Wisteria Cottage to Dr Leyden. Morton set it aside, then studied the final deed. It was much shorter and provided a simple termination of the lease of

Wisteria Cottage, the property reverting back to Lord Rothborne. Morton took out his camera and took digital photographs of each of the records and briefly pondered their content. They seemed of little value to the Mercer Case, but Morton was curious to know if Dr Leyden's tenure at Wisteria Cottage coincided with his marriage to Edith Mercer. Running a marriage search online, Morton quickly confirmed that the pair had married in the June quarter of 1920, so Edith would have partially benefited from the benevolence of the Mansfield family.

Morton gently repackaged the bundle of papers into the protective blue wallet, then wrapped the white ribbon around it. He looked over to the helpdesk. The lovely Miss Latimer was the only person on duty. Great. He momentarily considered leaving the documents in front of her and silently walking out, but he still had research avenues to pursue and wasn't going to let her get in his way. Morton approached the desk and set the package down in front of Miss Latimer.

'Done?' she asked flatly.

'Yes, thank you,' Morton replied.

Miss Latimer looked down at the document, raised an eyebrow and proceeded to unravel the ribbon and re-tie it in an almost identical fashion to how Morton had bound it. Having repackaged it to her satisfaction, Miss Latimer turned and headed out behind the help desk. Morton was left wondering how their relationship had got to this point. He had known her for more than ten years now and in all that time she had never once been nice to him. To the best of his recollection, Morton couldn't recall anything specific which had founded her acrimony towards him; he had always put her virulence down to her infuriation when the head of the archives, Max Fairbrother, would bend the rules for him. He wished Max had been on duty today.

Finally, Miss Latimer returned to the desk, seemingly unaware that Morton was still standing where she had left him moments before.

'Could I have my next document, please?' Morton asked.

'Reader's ticket,' she repeated.

Morton again handed over the ticket and waited patiently for Miss Latimer to return. She handed over the burial register for Winchelsea, which Morton duly took and set about devouring. It would have been very easy for him to dive straight into 1911, but that would have gone against his training. He was a *forensic* genealogist and needed to be exacting and precise in his searches. Starting at the beginning, in January 1813, Morton studied every aspect of every page, noting down anything and everything of interest. Each time the name Mercer or Blackfriars cropped up, he wrote the information down and took a digital photograph of it. He also had open his three lists of people around Mary Mercer at the time of her disappearance and noted down the burial of some of the domestic servants. When he reached the page detailing all of the burials in 1911, Morton took extra care to ensure that nothing was missed; he even photographed the relevant pages for future reference, but there was definitely no sign of Edward Mercer. Morton continued until October 1934, then exchanged the register for the next one. In it, he found the burial notifications of several Blackfriars employees and members of the Mansfield family, which he diligently scribbled down against the list in his notepad. He found the burials of Lady Rothborne in 1928, Philadelphia Mansfield in 1953 and Cecil Mansfield in 1959. The register ended in July 2009 and Morton then switched his attention to the Icklesham burial register. Having logged the burial of several members of the Mercer family, Morton located Edward.

Date: 28th May 1911
Name: Edward Mercer
Residence: Winchelsea
Age: 20 years

As he had predicted, the register had added nothing to the Mercer Case, other than confirming Edward's date and place of burial. On past occasions, Morton had been delighted to find a descriptive vicar annotating burial registers with his own unique take on the world. He recalled finding the burial of one George Barton who was buried in 1844 in East Peckham. The vicar had added to the usual perfunctory information something along the lines of: *the last of 3 brothers all of whom were too fond of drink to live long, see 1840 and 1836.*

Morton photographed the record and continued searching in the register, noting down people of interest. All the while, Edward's death, so close to Mary's disappearance, played on his mind. *Were there really no other records that showed what had happened to him?* He allowed his mind to mull over the question, considering then dismissing possible research avenues. When he had finally ended the register in 1975, Morton returned the ledger to Miss Latimer.

110

'*Deidre*, I've got a research question that I wonder if you could help with,' Morton said, relishing the way that she winced when he addressed her by her first name.

'It's Miss Latimer, as you have been told before. What is it that you need help with now?' She didn't even try to hide her annoyance with him.

Morton glanced at his notepad. 'I'm looking for a record of an inquest that took place in Winchelsea in 1911—do you know if it still exists?'

Miss Latimer frowned. 'I doubt it,' she said. Perching a pair of glasses on the end of her nose, she turned to the computer and began tapping at the keyboard. After a while she removed her glasses, looked up at Morton and shook her head. 'Nothing at all for that period. We've got bits and pieces for the Brighton district and Lewes district, but nothing for the Rye district. Those are the only two districts for this county.'

Morton saw the tiny hint of a satisfied smile on Miss Latimer's face. She really was an obnoxious woman who should have a restraining order on being within fifty miles of the general public. 'Okay. How about police surgeon reports?'

Miss Latimer sighed, remounted her glasses and began tapping at the computer keyboard. 'Again, nothing. I assume you've tried the *Sussex Express?*'

'Yes, I have.'

'That's probably all you're going to find, then,' she said, ending their conversation by picking up a booklet and reading.

Morton returned to his desk. There was little other research he could conduct here at this point in the Mercer Case. It was time to go home and investigate other potential avenues.

Having collected all of his belongings, Morton headed out of the Reference Room. 'Could you open the door please?' Morton asked as he passed the helpdesk, avoiding an inevitable stand-off.

Without looking up, Miss Latimer pressed the release and the glass door rolled open.

'Thanks, Deidre,' Morton called, striding through the opening, through the Reading Room and back into the main lobby. He collected the remainder of his bits from his locker and left The Keep with a smug smile on his face at having had the last word with Miss Latimer.

His smile dropped when he saw his Mini. The front passenger-side tyre was flat. Brilliant. Just what he needed, to waste time changing a tyre in The Keep car park. As Morton approached the boot of the car, he noticed that the back passenger tyre was also flat. 'Damn it!' he said, circling the car and discovering that every tyre was flat, each with an inch-long incision just above the metal alloys. Morton flicked his head around the car park: he couldn't see anybody suspicious loitering in the shadows. He marched back inside the archive. 'Do you have CCTV here?' he asked the kindly receptionist.

She smiled. 'Absolutely. Why's that?'

'Excellent, I've just had all four of my car tyres slashed,' Morton said.

The lady's smile faded. 'Oh. We have CCTV *inside* The Keep, *not* outside. Sorry. Do you think it was deliberate, then?'

Morton nodded, trying to contain his consternation at the stupidity of the question. That would really have to be some bizarre pot-hole. Morton thanked her, although he wasn't sure what for and returned to his car. The image of Juliette in the fish and chip shop flashed in his mind. Instinctively, he dialled her mobile.

'Hi,' she answered. 'You were lucky to catch me—I'm just about to go back in from lunch. You okay?'

He was relieved to hear her voice. *Should I tell her about the tyres? Should I tell her about the contents of the envelope sent yesterday?* Morton knew he needed to tell her, but not now. Not on the phone.

'Hello? Are you there, Morton?'

'Sorry, yes, I'm here. Just wanted to say hi and see how you were getting on today. Not too boring is it?'

'We're doing more role-play and mock arresting. It's quite fun, really. I've been arrested for aggravated assault and possession of a Class A drug so far today. How are you getting on? Did you say you were at The Keep?'

'Yeah, it's going okay. Going to go home shortly.'

'Okay, I'd better get back in. See you tonight.'

'Try not to get arrested for anything else. Bye.'

Juliette was fine. *But what if...?* Someone out there clearly meant for him to stop working on the Mercer Case. *But why? What secrets was he threatening to resurrect in investigating Mary Mercer's disappearance?* When this had happened to Morton in the past, his tenacious personality had forced him to persist with the case, to use every research method, including illegal ones, to finish the case. *But I lost so much*, Morton reminded himself, *almost including my life*. No case, however interesting, was worth such a risk. *And yet...* Morton's obstinate nature resurfaced. It came down to a simple matter: he had promised a dying man that he would find what had happened to his aunt, Mary. And that's just what he was going to do. The fact that someone out there wanted to stop him only made him more resolved to find her.

Chapter Eleven

Wednesday 5th April 1911

After two months of Frederick Mansfield's presence at Blackfriars, Mary Mercer knew why the domestic staff had groaned when told of his impending visit. When sober, he was a delightful, intelligent man who treated the staff with respect and kindness; these moments, however, were seldom witnessed by Mary. For the most part, he was an unpredictable drunk who ate, drank and slept when his erratic mood dedicated and, at those times, he expected the domestic staff to implicitly intuit his desires and react to them accordingly. Ever since Mary's dawn encounter with him, she had feared that, when in one of his drunken stupors, he would let on about her secret, but he had said nothing. After seeing him on several occasions, both inebriated and sober, Mary decided that he was probably so intoxicated that morning that he actually didn't have any recollection of it at all. Still, she would be mightily relieved when he left for Scotland today with the rest of the family on their annual deer-hunting trip. According to the gossip among the other servants, Frederick had been told that he was to stay on with Mr Risler at Boughton House, the family's Scottish home, until he had sorted himself out. As far as Mary was concerned, getting rid of Mr Mansfield *and* Mr Risler was no bad thing. She felt mean to think it, but she hoped that it would take a long time to get him back on the straight and narrow.

Mary and Clara were preparing the female servants' bedrooms, waiting for the breakfast bell to toll. Like so many of their mealtimes during Frederick Mansfield's stay, it was already very late.

'I'm desperate for a sit-down and a drink,' Mary complained. 'I don't feel too well.'

'Well, it's all down to the whim of Mr Mansfield,' Clara retorted. There was no attempt to conceal the anger in her voice.

Mary stopped sweeping and rested her arm on the broom. 'I don't understand why Lord Rothborne puts up with it. Why would he allow his drunk cousin to just turn up here and dictate what goes on? What right does he have?'

Clara shrugged. 'Haven't the foggiest. If he were my cousin, I'd have told him to shove off a long time ago. Family or no family, this is just ridiculous. Maybe Lord Rothborne feels sorry for him. Apparently, and this is only the gospel according to dear Saint Joan, he's squandered all of his father's money on gambling and *London liaisons* with *amateurs*.'

'Well, if it came from Joan, then it *must* be true!' Mary said with a laugh.

'Exactly.'

When the breakfast bell did finally sound, the domestic staff all hurried to the servants' hall and sat down, grateful for the rest and eager to eat and drink. With everyone hushed, Mr Risler, looking flushed in the face and slightly short of breath, stood to talk.

'Uh-oh,' Joan whispered. 'This doesn't look good.'

Mr Risler took in a deep breath before beginning. 'I'm afraid that we're going to have to postpone breakfast this morning,' he began, being quickly cut off by the low murmur of discontent among the staff. 'Quiet, thank you.' He waited until he had total silence. 'His Lordship has explicitly asked that, whilst his cousin, Mr Mansfield is otherwise engaged, we take the opportunity to finalise preparations for the family to leave on the hunting trip today. He has said that you will be granted extra break time when Mr Mansfield retires to his room later.' Mr Risler turned to the male staff. 'Maslow, Daniels, Mercer, Phillips, Readfern, Wiseman—you all need to come with me so we can fetch the cases from the attic and transport them to the correct rooms. Ladies, Mrs Cuff will inform you of your duties.'

'That dreadful man!' Clara said when she and Mary were out of earshot. 'Cancelling our breakfast like that, I've never heard of any such thing.'

Mary took a deep breath, feeling suddenly nauseous. 'I need to sit down, Clara, I really do.'

Clara turned to face Mary. 'You have gone a bit pasty-looking. Let's just get up the stairs and you can have a quick lie down.'

Mary nodded her agreement but feared that she couldn't make it all the way up to the room without being ill. With Clara's assistance and several breaks along the way, she made it upstairs. She just managed to close the door before rushing over to her chamber pot to be sick. Clara stood behind her and stroked her hair. 'Do you feel better now?'

Mary shook her head; she felt like she'd been jabbed in the stomach with a blunt stick.

'You probably just need some food inside you. You'll be right as rain after you've eaten.'

Mary wasn't so sure. She slumped down onto her bed with a sigh and shut her eyes.

Lady Rothborne was strutting up and down the length of her bedroom, clutching her black leather Bible. Just like every day of the week, she was dressed immaculately. Today, she was wearing a lavender-coloured skirt with a sweeping train, recently purchased from her favourite London boutique. Despite her advancing years, her boned bodice gave her the desired impression of a firm mono-bosom. She paced the room, struggling to shut out the dreadful rumpus coming from the gramophone downstairs.

She would not be beaten. Not by *him*. She had suffered her late husband, Richard's younger brother for too many years to count. He had made Richard's life hell, forcing and bribing him to pay out more-than-generous annuities and endowments over the years—all of it squandered on gambling and foolhardy, reckless investments. And now, here was history repeating itself in the form of her nephew, Frederick. He was here, turned up in a dreadful automobile that desecrated countryside that had been serene and undisturbed for centuries. He was a mirror-image of his frightful father, plaguing Blackfriars with his vile habits. From indiscreet lips, Lady Rothborne had heard about his licentious ways, dragging the Mansfield name down into the sewers. No, he was *worse* than his father had ever been with his distinct lack of morals and indiscretions.

As Lady Rothborne reached the windows, a flicker of colour in the rose garden caught her eye. She ceased pacing and surveyed the estate. It was Philadelphia, her delightful daughter-in-law, ambling through the ancient beds. The sight of her, the future of Blackfriars, instantly abated the rage that she was feeling. She watched as Philadelphia elegantly stooped to smell an early-flowering rose. *Such a sweet, beautiful girl*, she thought. *I will not allow this despicable man to jeopardise what we have.* She held Philadelphia in high regard, knowing that in her and her precious son, Cecil, the future of the Mansfield family at Blackfriars was assured. *This* branch of the Mansfield family. Frederick Mansfield *would not* fritter overnight what centuries of prudence, labour and wisdom had created. She had previously failed with poor Florence but she would not fail again. She would not. Thinking of Florence again after all these years made her shudder; she needed to change her train of thought back to the present problem of Frederick.

116

Her coffee would be as cold as the inside of the ice-house by now, having been neglected in the library for more than half an hour. But *that* was the source of the music: where Frederick was. Her lady's maid had informed her that he was in there, dancing alone and shamelessly drinking from a wine bottle. Despite his father's selfish and foolish ways, Frederick had enjoyed a respectable upbringing where such degrading behaviour, as was currently being demonstrated in the library, was not tolerated. He flaunted his dishonourable, coarse behaviour and his vile opinions as to the future of Blackfriars, hoping to provoke a reaction. Eventually, he would up and leave, returning to the shadows like a rapacious vulture, waiting for Cecil and Philadelphia to fail to produce an heir. Lady Rothborne had sagely advised Cecil and Philadelphia to do what her dear Richard had always done: do not give him the reaction he craves and he will go away. Sometimes it took days for Frederick to get bored and leave, other times it took much longer.

The music finally stopped. Lady Rothborne closed her eyes and enjoyed the sudden stillness. Standing in the warmth of the sunlight, she held the Bible tightly in her both hands and uttered a short prayer. She thanked God for her family, then repeated her request not to impart to this man what he so badly craved.

Lady Rothborne took deep, long breaths, wilfully absorbing the house's stillness before setting down her Bible and making her way out of her bedroom.

'Miss Herriot, kindly ascertain if the library has been vacated. If so, have a fresh pot of coffee taken in,' Lady Rothborne called to her lady's maid.

'Certainly, my lady.'

Mary was woken by a hand gently stroking the back of her hair.

'Mary!' Clara whispered. 'It's time for breakfast. The music's finished and Mr Mansfield's finally gone to bed.'

Mary opened her eyes. It took a moment to remember where she was. She felt a little groggy, but the nausea had thankfully abated.

'I've made a bit of a hash of it, but I've managed to do all the girls' rooms by myself.'

Mary slowly sat up and swung her feet to the floor. 'Thanks.'

'How are you feeling now?'

'Better,' Mary answered slowly. 'I think.'

'I'm sure you'll feel right as rain with some breakfast inside you. You need to be well, it's your afternoon off.'

Mary smiled and stood up. Maybe Clara was right, a bit of food and she'd be back to normal for her afternoon off. The thought of going home brought on a sudden surge of nausea. *Maybe it's the thought of going home that's making me ill,* Mary thought. She was dreading it but knew she had to go. Caroline would be expecting her wages. Mary hoped that she could manage to find a few precious minutes with Edward today, but it was doubtful. Ever since that magical night in the old folly when he had asked her to be his wife, Mary had seen very little of him other than at the dinner table in the servants' hall. Frederick Mansfield was mainly to blame for their lack of time together. All household routines, including time off, were erratic and unpredictable. She desperately missed Edward. Only a handful of the other servants knew the secret of their engagement. She had told Clara and Eliza last week during an afternoon of needlework, having first sworn them to secrecy.

'Come on, let's get downstairs,' Clara said, linking her arm through Mary's. 'Your fiancé will be worried!'

'Sshh! I don't want people to hear,' Mary murmured. 'I still haven't told my family yet. You'd better not have written anything in that diary of yours!'

'Course not! When are you going to do it?'

Mary shrugged. 'Maybe *after* the wedding!'

The girls giggled as they walked down the corridor to the stairs. Clara failed to spot that one of the bedroom doors, which she had left closed, was now slightly ajar. Through the small gap, listening intently, was the scullery maid, Joan Leigh.

Mary was still feeling unwell, despite having picked at a piece of ham and sipped at a cup of tea. Yet something else was now troubling her. Joan was being unusually quiet, sitting opposite her with some kind of a knowing look on her face. With one eyebrow raised, Joan flicked her head between Mary and Edward.

'Is something the matter with your neck, Joan?' Mary hissed across the table. It was quiet enough for only her to hear.

'Me?' she asked with mock incredulity. 'Me?' Joan held out her left hand and studied her fingers. 'No, I've got nothing to say.' Her eyes glanced up to meet Mary's critical gaze. 'You got anything you want to share with everyone, Mary?' She spoke loudly enough for several servants on the lower half of the table to turn and stare.

Mary's mouth and throat dried up and the nausea returned. *She couldn't know...could she?* Mary glared at Clara, then Eliza, who had turned their attention to the altercation taking place. One of them must have told her. *Why did I ever trust them again?* Mary chastised herself.

'Anything the matter down there?' Mrs Cuff called from the top of the table.

'No, Mrs Cuff,' Eliza replied.

Clara raised her eyebrows at Mary.

'Grow up, Joan,' Mary retorted quietly.

Mr Risler stood from the table. 'Lord Rothborne has been gracious enough to extend your breakfast time this morning and offers his sincere apologies for the delay. As soon as Mr Mansfield has woken, preparations for the hunting trip will resume.' Mr Risler returned to his seat and tolerated the inevitable low level of chatter to rise from his statement.'

'Flippin' right we get a longer breakfast,' Joan remarked to nobody in particular. 'Gracious—I ask you.'

Mary deliberately turned her head, pretending not to have heard her. Mary's eyes met with Edward's and he smiled. Part of her couldn't wait for the household to go to Scotland just for some peace and quiet to descend on Blackfriars. The downside, and it was a *major* downside for Mary, was that Edward had been chosen to accompany the family there. She saw him so seldom now, despite working in the same place, but now she faced almost ten days without even a glimpse of him across the breakfast table.

After the extended breakfast was over, Mrs Cuff led the majority of the female staff to the bedroom suites. She divided the girls into small groups, instructing them on what they were to pack. Mary was paired with Eliza and, under the guidance of Miss Herriot, given the exciting task of packing Lady Philadelphia's outdoor wear.

'The winter coats!' Mary said, excitedly grabbing Eliza's arm as they headed towards Lady Philadelphia's bedroom.

'All those furs!' Eliza responded with a grin. 'Come on, let's get to it.'

As the girls reached the doorway to Philadelphia's bedroom, they stopped still as if held back by an invisible barrier. Lady

Philadelphia was in her room, bending down with her back to them. She turned and smiled. 'Come in, girls.'

The girls stepped into the room and stood awkwardly by the bed. Neither of them had expected her to actually be there.

'Right, the trunk is down here. We're a little short on space, so I must be prudent in what I take. At least, that's what my dear husband tells me,' she said with a pleasant smile. She was midway through neatly folding a pair of elbow-length silk gloves.

Mary reciprocated with a smile of her own and, for the first time since she had started at Blackfriars, fully took her in. Her experiences of Lady Philadelphia were always fleeting or from a distance. The two of them had, mainly by virtue of their opposing standings in the house, never actually spoken to one another. To her surprise, Mary found herself quite in awe of Lady Philadelphia's magnanimous beauty.

'Between the three of us, however, I've had one of the footmen fetch me another case, which my dear husband will be none the wiser about,' Lady Philadelphia said. 'I think it might be best if I hunt through my wardrobes and see what I think I'll need, then give it to you girls to pack for me. How does that sound?'

Mary and Eliza mumbled their agreement and stood waiting with anticipation for the first garment.

Lady Philadelphia returned carrying a bundle of attractive clothing. 'I think most of these will have had their last after Scotland,' she said, passing an ermine fur-lined cloak to Mary.

'What's wrong with them, my lady?' Mary asked quietly, running her fingers through the fine black and white fur. She was quite sure that she had never seen nor touched anything so perfect.

'They're very outdated,' Lady Philadelphia said. 'I'm sure they'll do for those wretched days out watching the men hunting for deer on the Scottish glens, but they'll not do anywhere of note.' She lowered her voice. 'It's more like something Lady Rothborne would wear.'

Mary smiled, delighting in the sense of their shared camaraderie. Maybe she hadn't been silly and immature to believe that she, Mary Mercer could enjoy some of the trappings of high social standing after all.

'These are *much* more the fashion,' Lady Philadelphia said, handing Eliza a full-length coat. 'It's an oriental cocoon. Beautifully made—so elegant, don't you think?'

The girls nodded their agreement and Eliza carefully began to fold it into the trunk.

'Do you think if you stroke it long enough the poor stoat might come back to life?' Lady Philadelphia asked Mary with a laugh.

Mary flushed. She was mid-way through one of her daydreams where she and Lady Philadelphia were attending a grand ball together in London. 'Sorry, my lady. I'm in my own world again. I'm always getting into trouble because of it. It was the same at school.' Mary set the garment down on the bed and gently folded it, just the way she had been shown by Clara.

'What a magnificent thing,' a booming voice called from the doorway. It was Lady Rothborne. She stepped inside the room and picked up the ermine cloak from the bed. 'Simply resplendent.'

Mary and Eliza backed away deferentially, allowing Lady Rothborne to sweep into the room.

'What do you think, Mary?' Lady Rothborne asked.

Mary was taken aback to be included in the conversation *and* to be called by her Christian name. 'I...I...think it's one of the nicest cloaks I've ever seen.'

'Quite.'

Lady Philadelphia smiled. 'I hear you won't be joining us at Boughton House?'

Lady Rothborne shook her head. 'Not this time. I'm a little *over-excited*, shall we say, by the recent comings and goings of our charming visitor; a few days alone is just what I need. I've seen a good forty seasons of deer-hunting—plenty for someone of my age.'

Lady Philadelphia smiled. 'I've got plenty more to do yet, then.'

'Indeed. I shan't keep you,' Lady Rothborne said before gliding from the room.

The girls continued to pack Lady Philadelphia's outdoor clothes until the designated trunks were filled to capacity. Mary wanted to quip that if she went away for ten days to Scotland she would have precisely one winter coat to pack, but wasn't yet sure of her standing, despite the overt friendliness being shown to her. Then the lunchtime bell sounded and Mary and Eliza were thanked for their help and allowed to go on their way.

'Home time for you, then, Mary,' Eliza said.

'Oh yes, in all the fun of packing I'd forgotten.'

Mary closed the kitchen door to Blackfriars and began to walk up the back path towards home. It was a warm day with a gentle breeze and Mary enjoyed having her hair flowing freely across her shoulders, rather than pinned awkwardly under her hat. She crossed the courtyard to the back path and began the short walk home. She took slow, deliberate steps, not wishing to arrive home too soon. As she passed the orchard, her mind was fretting over what or whom she would find when she got there and she failed to see the movement among the blossoming apple trees.

'Mary!' called the voice.

She recognised it instantly and turned to see Edward grinning at her from the abbey ruins. She smiled and rushed towards him. 'I wasn't expecting to see you!' She ran into his open arms and squeezed him tightly.

'I could tell from the grumpy look on your face! You didn't even check I was here,' Edward said, with a hint of dejection.

'Sorry. I was worrying about things—home, not seeing you for ten days—stuff like that,' Mary said, releasing herself from him before kissing him on the lips. 'But you're here!'

'Of course. I couldn't not see my fiancée before I go on my annual hunting holiday!'

Mary rolled her eyes. 'It's alright for the chosen ones. I'm going to be stuck here catching up on all the unwanted, rubbish jobs that get stored up across the year.'

Edward hugged her again. 'At least it'll be quiet and Mr Mansfield will be gone. Come on, let's go and sit down for a minute.' Edward took Mary by the hand and led her to the piece of sandstone which had become their usual seat. On their last visit here, Mary had finished carving into it their initials. *EM and MM*. She sat and stared at the shallow engraving, already missing Edward in her mind. She had already made up her mind to come here next Wednesday on her half-day off and just sit quietly, pretending he was with her.

'Are you okay, Mary?' Edward asked.

Mary shrugged, suddenly and inexplicably unable to speak. A wave of emotion had poured over here and a tear ran down her cheek.

'Hey, what's the matter?' Edward said, tenderly running his forefinger up her cheek to her moistening eye.

'I don't want you to go,' Mary said in a croaking voice.

Edward laughed. 'I don't want to go either, but it's only ten days and then I'll be back. Come on, this isn't like the Mary Mercer I know and love. Where's your fiery, wild side gone?'

Mary managed a short smile. Where *had* her fiery, wild side gone? Had three months of hard labour as a third housemaid *really* been enough to bash it out of her? *No, it can't have been.* She just wasn't coping very well with Edward's imminent departure and the uncertainty of her home life. Her feelings for him had come and grown so quickly that it had turned everything she had known upside down. She was sure that was all it was.

The pair sat in a comfortable silence for some minutes, before each of them needed to go.

'I'd better get back to my duties before I'm missed. They'll be loading the carriages any minute,' Edward said quietly.

'And I'd better get home before Caroline comes storming down here after my money.'

Mary stood and faced Edward. She didn't know how to say goodbye. She could see in Edward's sad face that he was feeling the same.

'Ten days—it's nothing at all,' he finally said, in as cheery voice as he could muster.

Mary could tell that he wasn't feeling it, though she still smiled. 'Yeah, it's not long.'

'Goodbye,' Edward said, leaning in to kiss her.

She allowed herself to be lost in the tenderness of his embrace, to momentarily forget that he was going.

Edward broke away. 'I love you, Mary Mercer.'

'I love you, too, Edward Mercer.'

She pecked him one last time on the lips, then led out of the ruins through the orchard onto the path. With a final smile, she turned in one direction, and he in the other.

Mary continued up the hill towards her house. When she next took a glance round, Edward had gone. She mentally took a hold of herself, took in a deep breath and went home.

It was Caroline who opened the door. But for a veiled headdress, she was still wearing full mourning garments. Mary had hoped that by now she might have returned to Bristol, but knew deep inside that Caroline would remain running the household until their mother returned.

'I was wondering where you'd got to,' Caroline said.

123

Mary was unsure how, but as each week passed, Caroline appeared more haggard and her vitality more faded than the previous time she had seen her. Today was no exception. As Mary stepped through the door she noticed that Caroline's eyes were darker and more sunken and her hair matted and lank.

Caroline slammed the door shut, pushed past Mary and headed into the kitchen. 'Your sister's upstairs,' Caroline said.

The news that Edie was back home took Mary by surprise and made her stomach lurch. She wasn't sure she was in the frame of mind to cope with the compounded concoction of Caroline's evilness and Edie's bitterness. Worse still, she heard an unwelcoming guttural cough coming from the front room: her father was up and out of bed, his melancholia evidently having passed. *Could this day get any worse?* Mary wondered. *I'll drop the money off and run,* she thought. Heading into the kitchen, Mary found Caroline aggressively kneading dough at the kitchen table. Her hair was flailing all around her and she wore a menacing frown.

'Quite how I'm supposed to make bread with so little flour, is anyone's guess. Maybe if you'd got here sooner, I could have gone to the shop to get some more,' Caroline said without looking up.

'I'll go now if you like,' Mary said, quickly latching on to a reason to get out of the house.

Caroline grunted. 'No, thank you. I wouldn't be able to trust you to buy the right thing. Just put the money down there.'

Mary obeyed and emptied her wages onto the table, then turned to leave the room. She made her way down the hallway, destined for the front door. She had done what she came to do, now she could just leave. But, as she neared the front room door, she couldn't quite resist at least saying hello to her father. She hadn't actually seen him for weeks now. Cautiously and slowly, Mary pushed open the front room door. What she saw shocked her and made her gasp. A frail old man, shrivelled in his chair sat before her. Like Caroline, life had suddenly aged him. Mary knew little about melancholia, had no idea that it could do *this* to a person. The man sitting here, staring at the floor, looked old enough to be her grandfather.

'Hello,' she said quietly. When there was no response, she repeated herself, only louder. 'Hello!'

He blinked at the sound and his head twitched slightly, but he made no attempt to look at her or reply.

A laugh came from the kitchen. 'You'll be lucky, Mary!' Caroline called.

This house is falling apart around my ears! I can't stand it! Mary was on the verge of screaming something aloud then dashing dramatically from the house, when she heard her twin sister's voice.

'Mary? Is that you?' Edie called from upstairs. 'Come up.'

Although Mary was glad to leave the front room, she was reluctant to see Edie. She couldn't take much more of this house. She stood by the front door and placed her hand on the latch. Something, possibly the extra special connection she had with Edie, stopped her from running from the madness which had descended here. Instead, she turned and made her way to her former bedroom. As she reached the top of the stairs, Mary wondered what the past weeks had done to Edie. Had she too aged beyond all recognition? Was she still being eaten alive with jealousy of Mary's role at Blackfriars? For the first time in her life, Mary was nervous about seeing her own twin sister. *How has it come to this?* She rebuked herself and stepped in their shared bedroom.

'Mary!' Edie greeted, standing and unexpectedly throwing her arms around her. Mercifully, Edie hadn't aged or turned into a haggard monster—she was exactly the same as when she had last seen her. Except now her face was glowing; she wore a big smile.

Mary held her sister tightly. She was back. *They* were back.

'Guess who's got a job?' Edie said, standing up and swishing her hair back theatrically.

'Have you?' Mary said, delighted. 'Tell me about it.'

'It's *second* housemaid at Durrant House! Can you believe it?' Edie exclaimed.

Mary knew that she was forgiven. Not only had Edie got a higher-status job than her now, it was in Durrant House—a much bigger and more widely known establishment than Blackfriars. That Edie had trumped her was totally fine with Mary, so long as they were no longer fighting. 'Congratulations! Well done. What's it like there?'

'Amazing! I haven't officially started yet, but I *adore* the job and they all adore me. I'm so grateful not to have got the job at Blackfriars. How are you liking it there? Come and sit down and tell me.'

The twins sat side by side, while Mary plucked snippets of truth from the last three months. She selected stories and anecdotes judiciously: she made no mention of her time with Edward and excluded stories which might lead Edie to become jealous or stories which painted a true picture of her unhappiness as a third housemaid, which might have given Edie an opportunity to gloat.

'Sounds okay,' Edie said, not convinced. 'Are you actually enjoying being a housemaid?'

'Yeah,' Mary said feebly. Even *she* didn't believe what had just come out of her mouth.

'What about Edward? Has he mentioned me? Is he getting my letters okay?' Edie asked.

Mary shrugged. She knew the time would come when she would have to tell Edie about her engagement to Edward, but now was definitely not that time. 'I'm not sure. It's funny, but I don't actually see him that much. You know what it's like about female and male servants mixing. It just doesn't happen.'

'True,' Edie said. 'They must be working him jolly hard, he hardly ever writes back to me.'

'Mum will be pleased about your new job,' Mary said, changing the subject. 'Does she know yet?'

Edie shook her head. 'No, but guess what? She can come out—next Wednesday. Do you fancy coming with me on your afternoon off and fetching her home?'

Mary's eyes suddenly lit up. 'Of course, that would be great.' She lowered her voice to a whisper. 'Hopefully then Caroline will push off.'

Edie laughed. 'Oh God, I hope so. You've no idea how unbearable it's been here. I even resorted to staying with Lucy in Eastbourne just so I could get away from here.'

'So that's settled, then, we'll meet back here next week and go and collect Mum.'

Contrary to how she had expected to feel, Mary had enjoyed her afternoon off. She had stayed with Edie for the remainder of the afternoon and evening, the pair of them chatting just like they had used to. Mary felt like at least one of the weights had been lifted from her shoulders. When she had returned to Blackfriars that night, she found the place eerily empty. Evidently the trip to Scotland had gone off as planned, for the only staff she found in the servants' hall for that evening's supper were the first footman, John Wiseman, who was temporarily in charge of the remaining domestic staff, Bastion, Charles Philips, the head gardener and the scullery maid, Joan Leigh. As soon as she set foot into the servants' hall, Mary wished that she hadn't bothered.

'For the sake of keeping things running smoothly,' John Wiseman had said, standing for the occasion, 'I'm going to ask you to sit in your usual seats.'

Mary sagged from the pettiness but knew better than to argue back. She took her seat, opposite Joan at the end of the table, a huge gulf open between them and the other three servants. There was no conversation at all, but Bastion, in his own contemptuous way, made it clear through his grunts, groans and French outbursts that he was livid at having been left behind, the Mansfields preferring to employ a local Scottish chef for their time at Boughton House.

With the silent supper finally over, Mary headed up to her bedroom with Joan irritatingly close behind her.

'Here, do you think Lady Philadelphia's pregnant? That's what Sarah reckons.'

'I don't care for gossip, Joan,' Mary said airily. She did care for gossip but, having been on the receiving end of Joan's tittle-tattle, she decided to take the moral high ground.

'Shall I come in your room while everyone's away?' Joan asked.

'No, thank you,' Mary said. To have that snooping little creature in her room would be simply awful. As much as spending nine nights by herself scared her, she would rather spend a sleepless night alone than have Joan in the room.

'Please?' Joan persisted. They had reached the top of the ninety-six stairs. 'I don't fancy being by myself.'

'Tough. Goodnight,' Mary said, entering her bedroom and shutting the door behind her. With the house so empty, she closed the latch on the door and slid the bolt across. It was the first time in her life that Mary had ever slept totally alone; it was one of the best nights' sleep she had ever had.

Chapter Twelve

Wednesday 12ᵗʰ April 1911

'Miss Herriot, fetch me the oriental cocoon coat, would you, there's a dear,' Mary said to the looking glass in an exaggerated fashion, gesticulating with her hands. She couldn't quite believe her luck. She really *was* in with the Mansfields—they really did see her as more than a domestic servant. Dare she actually say that she was a friend of the family? None of the other servants or even her own family would possibly believe it, but this morning Lady Rothborne herself had invited her, Mary Mercer, for a walk in the rose garden.

'Do you like roses, Mary?' Lady Rothborne had asked her, as they strolled side by side through the formal, rectangular beds.

'Oh yes, I love them,' Mary had answered. 'Especially white ones.'

Lady Rothborne had humoured her. 'Yes, but do you *really* like them? Roses are a species like no other. The sheer number of varieties is truly staggering; each unique…almost with their own personalities.'

They had continued on, taking stock of the passing roses. Mary had watched and mimicked the way that Lady Rothborne seemed to absorb and devour each of the different species.

'I come here when I need to be reminded of the past. Nothing awakens prior associations more than odour in my opinion. There have been rose gardens on this very spot since Tudor times. Imagine, four hundred years of such beautiful specimens. My great grandfather planted many of these,' she said, indicating a bed just beginning to awaken from its winter slumber. 'The old-time perfume of the Centifolia, the dusky sweetness of the Damask that inspired the wallpaper and furnishing of the grand saloon, the refreshing sweetness of the China roses—all planted by him. All absolutely exquisite. And if Mr Phillips and his team do their job properly, those roses shall outlive most of us.'

'But I thought Blackfriars belonged to your husband's family,' Mary had said.

'His and mine. We share a bloodline; we were second cousins,' Lady Rothborne had told her.

'Oh,' Mary had replied. She was taken aback by this piece of news, although she didn't quite know why.

'Rather like you and your cousin, Edward, isn't it?'

Mary's cheeks had turned crimson. 'Yes.'

'And how has your courtship developed? Is it love, I wonder?' Lady Rothborne had questioned.

'I really think so,' Mary had said. Lady Rothborne had, since the first moments of her time at Blackfriars, taken a keen interest in Edward and her. Just days ago, Mary had been summoned to the library where Lady Rothborne had intimated that having *relations* with Edward was a normal and natural part of courtship. Mary had seen little reason to hold back from telling her everything. 'He's even proposed to me.'

Lady Rothborne had stopped and turned to Mary. 'Proposed indeed! How delightful. A Blackfriars wedding. We *must* ensure that you have something delicious to wear for the big day. Perhaps something with a white rose on it. Come.'

Lady Rothborne had led Mary to Lady Philadelphia's wardrobe and thrown open the doors. 'What takes your fancy?'

'All of it!' Mary had said with a laugh.

'Then you are going to have to try some of it on,' Lady Rothborne had said with a smile.

Mary was shocked. 'Are you pulling my leg?'

'Absolutely not. I'm sure Philadelphia wouldn't mind and besides which, she is currently in Scotland watching my son harassing some poor old beast around the Highlands. What about this one?' Lady Rothborne had said, carefully pulling out a beautiful lilac gown and handing it to Mary. 'Go on, try it.'

Mary had seemed reticent, but did as she was being asked. She untied her pinafore and placed it neatly on the floor then unbuttoned her black dress and let it fall to her ankles. Her face flushed as she stood before Lady Rothborne with so little clothing.

'Well,' Lady Rothborne had said, running her eyes up her body.

Mary had turned her back to Lady Rothborne, uncomfortable to be semi-naked in her presence. She quickly reached for the lilac gown and pulled it up over her waist and onto her shoulders. It was a little tight, even though she and Lady Philadelphia were of similar build.

'A good corset will do the trick,' Lady Rothborne had said. 'I don't quite think lilac is your colour, though. Try on some others.'

Mary had looked uncertainly at Lady Rothborne. Despite her hope and growing belief that she was becoming more to the Mansfields than the third housemaid, she still held an uncertainty about trying on

129

someone else's finest clothes without their knowledge. Even she, with her humble wardrobe, would not have appreciated somebody else putting them on without her knowing.

'Go on,' Lady Rothborne had said. 'I have one or two things to attend to, so I shall leave you in peace. I realise you probably do not wish to be seen unclothed by a person elderly enough to be your grandmother. Take your time.'

Mary had nodded hesitantly and watched as Lady Rothborne silently left the room. She had stood uncertainly for a few moments, unsure of what to do. Then she had turned and faced the wardrobe and saw it. A stunning red dress made of silk, with tiny white flowers embroidered on it. She wasn't sure if they were roses or not, but it didn't matter. It was truly beautiful. *Dare I? Really?* Mary's unease had not abated; she couldn't try it on—it didn't feel right. *I could take it out and touch it, though*, Mary had reasoned. Carefully, she had picked the hanger from the rail and held it in front of her. She had to try it on. There was nothing to feel guilty about, she had been *told* to try it on. If she considered it an instruction from her employer, then no harm could be done. Laying the dress gently on the bed, she had unbuttoned the back, slipped it from the hanger and stepped into it. She had stared into the full-length looking glass, staggered at how a simple item of clothing had transformed her into one of the dazzling beauties on the postcards beside Edie's bed. *If only Edie could see me now*, Mary had thought.

Mary took a deep breath and stared at herself in the looking glass, absorbing her reflection. She would certainly need a corset, but apart from that it was perfect. She had found the dress that she would wear when she married Edward. They had not discussed the finer details of the marriage, but she would like it to be soon, and in Winchelsea church. A smile crept over her face as she imagined the day. It would be a warm summer's day—but not too hot. The church would be crowded with family and friends. The Blackfriars servants alone would take up a good few pews. Then there would be the Mansfield family. Maybe not all of them, but certainly Lady Rothborne would be there, possibly even Lady Philadelphia herself. She would dearly love to have the church filled with fresh roses cut from the ancient Blackfriars beds. Mary closed her eyes and allowed her imagination to take over. She was there, on her wedding day to Edward and it was perfect. *Truly* the best day of her life.

She was taken aback when she opened her eyes, but smiled nonetheless. In front of her, quite unexpectedly, stood Mrs Cuff, Miss Herriot and Lady Philadelphia. By the aghast looks on the faces, they had not run into Lady Rothborne yet. Mary suddenly felt silly and foolish, yet she didn't need to—she had been given permission to be here. Still, it would take some explaining.

'Miss Mercer, kindly explain why you are in my bedroom, wearing my clothes?' Lady Philadelphia demanded, stepping boldly towards her. Gone was the charming, kind person Mary had seen when they were last together in this very room.

'I...I...' Mary stammered, unable to formulate an explanation. 'I'm looking for a wedding dress.' As soon as the words were out of her mouth, Mary regretted them. They were silly and unfathomable to the people standing before her, who knew nothing of her engagement.

'Miss Mercer, you're making things worse for yourself,' Mrs Cuff exploded. '*What* are you doing?'

Mary needed to think fast and explain herself fully. She took a deep breath and began her explanation. 'I'm engaged to my cousin, Edward, and Lady Rothborne said that I could find a dress amongst Lady Philadelphia's wardrobe.' It was brief, but it covered it.

A look of profound astonishment and incomprehension passed back and forth between the three women.

Lady Philadelphia let out a horrible, sardonic laugh that chilled Mary and told her in no uncertain circumstances that she had not been believed. '*Lady Rothborne* told you to help yourself to my wardrobe?'

Mary nodded pathetically. 'Ask her.'

'Yes, I certainly would do,' Lady Philadelphia said. 'Except that she isn't here.'

'And hasn't been all day,' Mrs Cuff added.

Mary's eyes began to fill with hot tears. *This can't be happening! This is a huge mistake.* With her lip quivering, Mary tried to speak. 'She *was* here. She left about ten minutes ago, I promise.'

'Miss Mercer, please stop lying, it will serve you no use. You are no longer an employee of Blackfriars, so telling such wild stories will not help your case,' Lady Philadelphia ranted. She turned to Mrs Cuff. 'See that she leaves immediately.'

Mrs Cuff nodded obediently.

The realisation of the situation and its far-reaching implications hit Mary just as surely as if she had been struck down by a speeding automobile. A torrent of emotion was made manifest in a great outpouring of tears.

Mary's time at Blackfriars was over.

Edith Mercer stared into the tiny hallway mirror and smiled. At last, her thick and previously unmanageable hair was obeying her. It fell, in neat ringlets just like Ellaline Terriss's centre-parted locks and she was happy. Using much of her first pay packet, she had visited the best hairdressers in Rye. She had taken the postcard of Ellaline Terriss with her and told the hairdresser to copy the style precisely. Whilst in Rye, Edith also purchased for herself a new summer dress, which she now proudly wore. Just one week from hers and Mary's eighteenth birthday, her skin and body was finally beginning to behave as she wanted. Things were looking up for Edith. After being overlooked for the job of third housemaid at Blackfriars, she had secured a promising and exciting job as second housemaid at Durrant House. With her new job, her new hair and clothes, a surprising wave of confidence filled Edith as she carefully powdered her face. There was just one thing missing: a man in her life. Edward. Although his replies to her letters came seldom and were usually of the briefest in nature, she was sure that he wouldn't be able to resist her when he next saw the woman that she was growing into. Edith remembered how Mary had disapprovingly commented on their potential courtship owing to him being her cousin. But it wasn't unheard of and it certainly wasn't illegal, so the family would just have to get used to the idea. Love was love and that was all there was to it as far as Edith was concerned.

Edith's growing certainty and joviality elevated when she remembered the very reason that she was getting all dressed up: it was the day that she and Mary would be collecting their mother from the sanatorium. She was finally coming home, which hopefully meant that Caroline would be leaving.

She looked at the carriage clock quietly ticking on her bedroom fireplace. Mary would be finishing work in about half an hour. Edith thought about what to do while she waited. She had an idea. Rather than wait around the house, she would walk down to the Blackfriars gates and collect some of the lovely wild flowers growing there and meet Mary on her way up the path. *She will love that*, Edith thought. *I'll pick some flowers for her and some for Mother.* Edith was so taken with the idea that she bound down the stairs and out of the house without saying a word to her father or to Caroline. Her father wouldn't have even uttered a response, but she was sure that Caroline would have some bilious remark to make.

Edith closed the door behind her and stepped out into a beautiful April day. The day was unusually warm and all of the houses that she passed had their windows flung wide open, releasing a burst of the sounds and smells from within. Knowing that her neighbours might see Edith in her new dress with her music-hall-star haircut gave her an extra spring in her step.

The picturesque flowers nestled around the base of the large stone Blackfriars pillars came into view: a stunning concoction of pink fairy foxgloves, white fritillaries, yellow Jew's mallow and pink sorrel, all bathed in a pool of gorgeous sunlight. Edith hurried over to them and, with a warm contented smile, she set about plucking some of the stems from the ground. In just a few minutes, her left hand was filled with the delightful flowers. *Mother and Mary will absolutely love these!* Edith told herself. *But it needs more colour.* She knew places just inside the Blackfriars estate where she could find some superb white field pansies. And then there were the bluebells just the other side of the old abbey ruins. She knew that it was technically trespassing, but everyone in the village helped themselves to the odd flower or pinched a bit of fruit every now and then. Nobody would mind, she told herself as she stole into the grounds.

She walked slowly down the path towards Blackfriars, basking in the warm sunshine and the inner glow that she was feeling. In just a few moments she would meet Mary walking up the path and she would hand her a big bunch of flowers. She was so relieved to have patched things up with her twin. Like all sisters, they had their ups and downs but they shared a bond which could never be broken.

Edith spotted the white field pansies just off the path and headed towards them. She was careful to take just enough to provide balance to her growing posy. As she stood up, she saw a flash of movement in the corner of her eye. She hoped that it was Mary and smiled. But it wasn't, it was a girl who she knew to be the scullery maid.

'What you think you're doing?' the girl called at Edith.

'Just gathering one or two flowers,' Edith said, irked that she had been caught out doing what so many of the villagers did.

'That's thieving, that is,' the scullery maid said.

'Oh go away, you silly girl,' Edith said, beginning to turn her back.

133

'Expect you're looking for your sister, aren't you?'

Edith had no patience and decided to ignore her. It would be much simpler to walk back up the path and wait for Mary outside the gates. She began to walk away when the scullery maid started again.

'You'll probably find her with her fancy man. Her fiancé, I should say.'

Edith stopped in her tracks and turned towards her. 'What are you talking about? Mary doesn't have a *fancy man*. Go back to the scullery.'

'She hasn't told you!' she said with a mocking laugh. 'Your own twin sister hasn't told you that she's engaged to your cousin, Edward! That's funny.'

Edith felt her stomach fall. It couldn't possibly be true. There was no way Mary and Edward were an item. Engaged! The very idea was plainly absurd. Mary would never humiliate her like that; she knew that Edith liked him. 'Don't talk such rot. Will you please just go away and leave me alone?'

'Ask her. She's got a ring and everything. He gave it to her. It was his grandmother's. *Your* grandmother's.'

Every part of Edith wanted to scream at this awful, tittle-tattle-telling vixen, but she maintained her composure and smiled, watching and waiting as she walked up the path and out of the estate.

It was true. She knew it. Her sister—her twin sister—had betrayed her and done the unthinkable. Edith's blood ran cold, as feelings of betrayal were replaced with feelings of anger. With her blood boiling, Edith ran to the old abbey ruins and smashed the bouquet of flowers violently against one of the walls. Watching as a handful of blooms tumbled to the floor, Edith drew the bunch back and again smashed them into the wall. She kept on thrashing them back and forth, angry tears rushing down her cheeks, until she held nothing but a few pathetic stalks.

She would make her twin sister pay. As she stood by the wall giving a view over to the path, Edith spotted the sandstone lintel and the initials etched onto it. That was the last straw.

Lady Rothborne nervously watched from her bedroom window. But for the usual abundance of wildlife attracted to the estate's varied habitats, there was little stirring outside. She could see Mr Phillips and one of the local lads employed as a gardener working in the kitchen garden, but other than that, the gardens were still.

She looked directly below her window and watched as Mary Mercer, audibly in great distress, was ushered out into the courtyard by Mrs Cuff. A slight altercation with raised voices—but not clear enough for Lady Rothborne's ears—took place before Mary marched indignantly up the path towards home and Mrs Cuff headed back inside the house.

Almost not daring to breathe, Lady Rothborne clutched her Bible and watched as a smile appeared on her wizened face.

Chapter Thirteen

Morton was sitting in The Apothecary Coffee House on the corner of Rye's East and High Street, gazing through the small rectangular window panes as an endless torrent of rain fell from the miserable skies. Given the current weather and his position on the Mercer Case, he had assigned today as a computer-based research day and, rather than being cooped up in his attic study all day, Morton had decided that he would rather be working in the cosy and atmospheric coffee shop. Of the plethora of tearooms and cafes in Rye, this was one of Morton's favourites, retaining as it did many characteristics from its rich and colourful history as an apothecary. The modern features of a coffee shop had sympathetically been placed alongside vestiges from the past. Morton enjoyed looking at the banks of original wooden medicine cabinets which lined the room. As he ran his eyes over the neatly labelled drawers, he could only imagine what mysterious illnesses such exotic Latin names as 'B.Capsici,' 'Amylum,' 'Vermicel,' 'G. Benzoin,' and 'Glob Tussi' were once dispensed for.

Outside, the streets were empty. The rain had kept away all but the most ardent tourists and Morton was able to sit in relative solitude by the window with a good excuse to drink copious quantities of coffee all day without being reprimanded by Juliette. He was already in her bad books. His dilemma about whether or not to tell her about the anonymous, threatening package sent to him or the slashing of his car tyres had been decided for him yesterday. It had taken him so long to find a tyre-fitters who had the correct tyres in stock and who were willing to come out to him to change them that Morton knew his lateness home meant either telling her exactly what had occurred or lying to her. Up to now he had omitted to divulge everything, but he hadn't actually lied. As he had finally driven back from The Keep, he played out the impending scenario in his mind. She would tell him about her day at work, then she'd ask about his day. He would *have* to tell her about the tyres. *Oh, and I forgot to say that I also received an anonymous letter through the post which basically threatens your life.* Something along those lines.

'Hi,' Morton had said when he got in.

'Hi. You're late—The Keep must have shut hours ago,' Juliette had remarked, sitting in her uniform on the sofa, reading a dreadful celebrity-gossip magazine.

Seeing her in uniform always unnerved him slightly and made him feel guilty, usually without reason. Today, he had a reason to feel guilty. 'Yeah, it did,' Morton had replied. Literally hours ago. First he had seen all the remnant visitors and researchers leave, shortly followed by the staff: the receptionist had been lovely and asked if he needed any assistance; Quiet Brian had quietly walked by with a barely audible acknowledgment; lastly, Miss Latimer had waltzed gaily past him looking like Mary Poppins. Morton had considered *that* to be the worst part about having his tyres slashed—that she had seen and clearly gloated about it.

'Where did you go then?' Juliette had quizzed.

'I had to have someone change the tyres on my car,' Morton said, knowing full well that using the word *tyres* would immediately kick-start Juliette's investigation. It would just take a few seconds for her to register what he had just said. And it did.

Juliette had put down her magazine and turned to face him. 'What do you mean, *tyres?*' she asked. The investigation had begun.

Taking a deep breath, Morton sat down beside Juliette and told her what had happened. Inexplicably, he decided *not* to start at the beginning, but to start at the end—with the slashing of the tyres.

'But why would someone want to slash all your tyres? Were any other cars vandalised?' she had asked.

'No, just mine,' Morton had said, recalling the sight of the totally deserted car park.

'So, you were *targeted*, then?' Juliette had asked, sweeping her dark hair back over her ears. 'Why would that be?'

'The Mercer Case,' Morton had muttered.

Juliette's eyes had rolled dramatically. 'What now? Come on, Morton, there's *plenty* you're not telling me.'

And so, the majority of their evening last night had been spent going over the ins and outs of the Mercer Case. Morton had mentioned the threatening package he had been sent, half-expecting it to freak Juliette out, but she had taken it all in her stride. Police Constable-in-waiting, Juliette Meade was not at all phased. 'I look a bit rough, don't I?' had been her initial reaction to seeing the picture previously. 'I think I should wear a bit more make-up.'

Surprisingly, Juliette had been more intrigued in the case than anything else—not what he had expected. Even more surprisingly, she hadn't warned him off it. She had just asked that he tell her *everything* that went on with the case, which Morton had readily agreed to do.

'Here's your latte and fruit scone,' the waitress said, bringing Morton back to the present.

'Thank you.' He fired up his laptop, ready to get stuck in: he had a lot of research avenues to pursue today. Flipping his notepad back to the lists of people close to Mary in 1911, Morton re-read each list in the light of recent developments. He had made good progress finding out more about Edward Mercer. His gut reaction was currently that he and Mary were more than just friends, work colleagues and cousins. That placed him *very* highly in the rank of people who might have known what became of Mary. But, as he had died the month following her disappearance without having married or had children, Morton couldn't think of any other areas of research concerning Edward that could currently push the case forward. Looking at the rest of the Blackfriars domestic servants, Morton began a mundane, yet necessary line of enquiry: finding their marriages, deaths and, with luck, living descendants.

He had finished his latte and ordered a second cup in the time that it had taken him to find living relatives to a good portion of the names on the work list. He had drafted letters outlining the bones of the case with a request for any information or photos to descendants of Charlotte Cuff, Walter Risler, Sarah Herriot, Clara Ellingham and Joan Leigh. Owing to his unusual name, Morton had found an email address for Bartholomew Maslow, grandson of Jack Maslow. Morton could find no marriages or children to Susannah Routledge, Agnes Thompson or James Daniels. Charles Phillips had married another Blackfriars servant, Eliza Bootle and they had emigrated with their two children to Australia. Since he did not appear again in the UK, Morton guessed that the chef, Guillaume Bastion, had returned to France. He would print and send the letters first class later today. For the other employees on the list, history had left little to trace easily. If this initial batch of people went nowhere, he would more ardently pursue the remainder of the list.

Next, Morton added the Mercer's immediate neighbours to the 'Friends' list. Of course, he didn't know if they actually *were* friends or not, but they needed to be considered. Running the same types of searches, Morton found living descendants from the adjacent properties and occupants of the two houses opposite to the Mercers in 1911.

Morton's second latte had been finished for some time when the waitress returned to clear his table. A few customers had come and gone since his installation by the window, but the coffee shop was not busy.

'Another latte?' the waitress asked with a pleasant smile.

There was a question. His coffee-addicted brain desperately wanted him to say yes, but, from the dark recesses of his mind, he could hear Juliette reprimanding him for his caffeine intake. She was like some wartime minister, handing out rations of coffee. 'Decaf, please. Thank you,' he said, satisfying himself with the compromise.

Whilst he waited for his drink, Morton focussed his attention on the Mansfield family. Of the main family line, much had already been documented in various sources. Morton cross-referred the various burial dates for the Mansfield family that he had procured from the Winchelsea parish registers with what was available online. Lady Rothborne, her son Cecil and his wife Philadelphia had all been interred in the family vaults of St Thomas's Church, along with their only son, George, who was the last member of the family to appear in the burial register when he was buried in July 2008. The only other family member present at the time of the 1911 census had been Cecil's cousin, Frederick Mansfield. Morton racked his brain to think if he had read anything about him in the guidebook to Blackfriars, but nothing came to mind.

He picked up his laptop case and rummaged among the collection of Mercer Case documents that he had brought with him. He found the guidebook to Blackfriars, flicked to the index and found just one mention of Frederick Mansfield. He turned to the relevant page and found a family portrait taken on Empire Day, 1911. The grainy, sepia image showed Cecil, Philadelphia, Lady Rothborne and Frederick Mansfield standing haughtily outside the front entrance to the main house. Below it was a photograph of the domestic staff taken on the same day, but this one was taken outside the servants' kitchen door. Just underneath the photo was a list of some of those present, although the addition of several question marks indicated that not all of the servants had been identified. Morton kicked himself for having missed that the photographs had been taken in such a key year. A quick Google search revealed that Empire Day in 1911 was on Wednesday 24th May. It was an annual event from 1902, celebrating the British Empire, which tactfully transformed into Commonwealth Day in subsequent years. These pictures had been taken the month following Mary's disappearance and just six days after Edward Mercer had drowned in the Blackfriars lake—just a few yards from where the picture had been taken. Morton held the picture up close. It had not reproduced very well in the guidebook, leaving the faces of the servants small and indistinguishable.

Morton pulled out his mobile and dialled Sidney Mersham's extension at Blackfriars. He was in luck—Sidney was sitting at his desk in the basement archives and picked up straight away. After initial pleasantries had been exchanged, Morton asked Sidney if a larger copy of the Empire Day photographs could be emailed to him. Sidney agreed to do it right away. Morton thanked him and ended the call. He would check his emails as soon as his current research thread had ended.

The phone tap had worked. The man listening to the conversation that had just taken place between Morton Farrier and Sidney Mersham smiled. It was much easier to intercept a phone conversation than he had ever realised. When given the task, he had asked some of his more nefarious friends about how to obtain the necessary equipment. However, he easily found what he needed on a legitimate website for a hundred and forty-nine pounds. Getting the necessary software onto Morton's phone had been the hardest part and required him to enter Morton's house at night to place the software onto his phone. It wasn't the first time in his life that he had made a trip to an ironmongers for the requisite breaking and entering equipment and he doubted that it would be the last, despite a deliberate attempt to try and legitimise himself of late. With the software in place, he had access through an online console to all of Morton's key information: SMS activity, voice calls, emails, GPS location, internet browser history, call recording and the ability to listen and record background noise around the mobile phone. He was going to monitor Morton Farrier's every move.

The young waitress tottered over to Morton's window-seat table and placed a mug down in front of him. 'Decaf latte,' she said. 'Will there be anything else?'

'Not for now, thank you,' he answered. He would likely end up having lunch here, but it was all down to how much he achieved on his list of research areas.

Morton returned his attention back to Frederick Mansfield. His only mention in the guidebook was in the Empire Day photograph and on the genealogical pull-out chart at the centre of the book.

140

Morton double-checked the burial register entries for Winchelsea and confirmed that he had not been buried in the family vault.

Running a marriage and death search for Frederick revealed that he had died young, shortly after marrying in 1922. A further, generalised search brought Frederick up in the *Andrews Newspaper Index Cards 1790-1976*. Morton clicked to view the original image, which was for a newspaper clipping, stating that Frederick Mansfield had been killed in an automobile accident. Little more of the incident was mentioned, so Morton switched to the Findmypast website and searched their British newspaper collection 1710-1953. He quickly found that *The Times* had a more detailed report on the accident. It stated in no uncertain terms that Frederick, excessively intoxicated with liquor, had driven his Rolls Royce Silver Ghost over the cliff-top at Beachy Head in Eastbourne, following a late-night gambling and soliciting foray in Soho. He left his wife, Emmeline and young daughter, Vivien Mansfield. The Mansfield family had declined to make a statement to the newspaper, but Morton guessed that they were mortified by such scandalous revelations.

Morton saved the entry to print out later, then ran a living descendant search to Vivien Mansfield: one daughter, Jennifer Margaret, born 1923, who later married a Jonathan Greenwood. Jennifer Greenwood. The name rang a bell, though he couldn't fathom why. Google didn't help matters either. It was somebody that he had encountered recently. Somebody to do with the Mercer Case. *Was it a servant at Blackfriars?* No, he was fairly sure not. Then it came to him— Mrs Greenwood was the grumpy woman working on the ticket desk at Blackfriars. He was sure that he had heard Sidney Mersham call her Jenny. Could she be the same person as he was now writing to? Did it matter? For some reason, it did matter to Morton. It struck him as odd that a member of the Mansfield family should be working, clearly unhappily, as the modern-day equivalent of a domestic servant. From her interactions with Sidney, she was certainly not treated as anything more than that. And her grandfather was present around the time of Mary's disappearance. He drafted and saved a similar request-for-help letter to her, making no mention of the fact that they may already have been acquainted.

Morton took a couple of mouthfuls of coffee then opened up his emails. One unread message—from Sidney Mersham. The email said simply: *Here you go, Morton. Regards, Sid.*

Morton grinned when he saw the paperclip icon showing that the email contained an attachment. Being quite a large file size, it took a moment to load. Eventually the image appeared onscreen and Morton was able to zoom in close to see the features on each of their faces. He planned to save the image and later on, maybe tonight whilst watching television, to digitally annotate who was who. He looked at each person in turn—they all held the same po-faced, serious expressions common to portraits of the period. However, there was something else in their eyes, which Morton guessed to be sorrow at one of their friends and fellow servant's deaths just six days hitherto. Edward had worked at Blackfriars for three years, so his death must have come as quite a shock to them. He noticed that the man, whom the guidebook had identified as Walter Risler, had a battered nose and a bruised eye. Morton could only speculate as to what had caused his injuries.

Zooming out and taking the staff in as one group of people, Morton could see that they were all standing in hierarchical order. Except for one. Mrs Cuff, whom Morton knew to be the housekeeper and, therefore, the highest-ranking female member of staff, was standing at the end of the line of the servants. When taken with the fact that she no longer signed the Day Book following Mary's disappearance, Morton became curious. *Had she put herself at the end of the line, or had she been put there? Interesting*, Morton thought. Her continuing wages at the level of a housekeeper suggested that she had not been demoted, yet *something* was amiss.

Whilst he had his emails open, Morton composed a lengthy message to Ray Mercer, outlining the details of the case so far. He also asked Ray if he knew anything of his grandmother's visit to Canada in 1925. He held back from mentioning the encounter with Douglas Catt, but did say that he garnered a copy of the letter Mary had apparently written from Scotland. Morton clicked 'send' on the email, then turned his attention to seeing what he could find about Edith Mercer's visit to Canada.

He opened up a new web-browser and ran a search in the 1921 Canadian census for 4 West Street, Halifax. It was four years prior to when he wanted, but he reasoned that whomever Edith was visiting in 1925 may have been residing there in 1921. Within seconds, Morton had the original census onscreen. Unlike many of the older census returns, the 1921 Canadian one was a goldmine for genealogists, asking as it did thirty-five detailed questions about each individual recorded.

Morton felt a buzz of excitement as he zoomed in for an up-close inspection of the entry. Just one person resided at the house, a lady by the name of Martha Stone. He felt a rush of anticipation as he considered that Martha Stone could be a pseudonym for Mary Mercer. Slowly, he moved the cursor along the entry, carefully deciphering the handwriting as he went. It said that Martha Stone rented her house, that it was wooden in structure with four rooms. She was the head of household, aged thirty-one and her birthplace was given as England— the same place as her mother and father. The year of emigration was given as 1911 and she was able to read and write. Her occupation was listed as teacher.

Morton sat up with eagerness. *Could Martha Stone be Mary Mercer?* he pondered, as he stared out of the window. A solitary figure in a long rain coat, black Panama hat and a temperamental umbrella battled with the rain, which seemed to have grown in ferocity, buffeted by a strong wind.

Morton considered the facts. Martha Stone was listed as being three years older than Mary would have been in 1921, but she could easily have lied to the enumerator. The rest of the facts, in particular her year of emigration, tied with Mary Mercer perfectly. At the moment, though, he couldn't be certain that Martha was still resident there in 1925. He added to his list the need to find out whether or not electoral registers existed for Nova Scotia in 1925.

Outside, the man's umbrella flipped inside out. He gave up battling the elements and entered The Apothecary.

Morton returned his focus to his laptop screen. He wanted to find out whether Martha Stone's census entry was backed up with a paper trail in England; if his hunch was correct then there would be none. She had stated that she was born in England in 1890. Therefore, she should show up on the 1891 and 1901 censuses and possibly even the 1911 census. First, he tried the 1891 census: three results for Martha Stone born 1890. The first was born in Birmingham, the second in Derbyshire. To his disappointment, the third was born in Winchelsea. Morton clicked to view the original image. The entry was for the Stone family: James Stone, head, gardener lived with his wife, Flora, no occupation and their one year old daughter, Martha Stone. Morton moved the cursor to the left of the screen and noticed the address: Peace Cottage, Friar's Road.

It took Morton a moment to digest what he had just read and to place it in the jigsaw of the Mercer Case. Edith Mercer, under her married name of Leyden, had simply visited a neighbour, Martha Stone. Morton's initial excitement that perhaps Mary was living under a pseudonym had not borne out. Just to shore up his findings, however, Morton wanted to conclude Martha's story. And, just as predicted, Martha showed up alongside the Mercer girls on the 1901 census, then promptly vanished by 1911. Martha Stone existed in her own right. She could not be Mary Mercer.

Morton was momentarily distracted by the coffee shop door opening again, as the man with the broken umbrella left carrying a take-out drink. A sudden gust of wind pushed through the open door, scattering some of Morton's papers to the floor.

As Morton bent down to pick up the fallen papers, the waitress who had served him earlier placed something on his table. 'Here you go,' she said with a smile. 'A gift.'

'Thanks,' Morton replied. He looked down and saw a brown A4 envelope with his name on it—exactly the same handwriting as the previous threatening packages that had been posted through his door. The waitress was heading back behind the counter. 'Excuse me,' Morton called after her. 'Where did you get this?' He held up the envelope.

'Oh, a customer just gave it to me to give to you,' she said with a smile. She evidently thought she had done him a favour.

'Who was it?' Morton asked, already knowing the answer.

'The guy who just left—with the umbrella.'

'Watch my stuff,' Morton called, dashing out the door into the thick sheets of vertical rain. He tried to recall which way the man had gone. He was sure he went right, so Morton ran, already soaked to the skin, along the high street, his eyes flicking feverishly left and right into shop windows and passing streets, but there was no sign of him. He stopped and spun around, considering if he could have missed him, when he heard the sound of a car engine starting up. A little way further down the street, a red Mazda was beginning to pull out from a parking spot. Without a moment's thought, Morton ran as fast as he could towards the car. He was in luck—another car had just parked illegally in front of the Mazda, meaning that the driver could not make a quick escape.

Morton, utterly drenched, raced to the passenger side window as the car finally became free from its space. He banged on the side of the door and the driver flicked his head towards Morton.

'What do you want?' Morton yelled.

144

He recognised the driver.

Chapter Fourteen

After what had happened yesterday, Morton was happy to spend today close by Juliette's side. When she had got home last night Morton had, as promised, relayed everything of his day to her. They sat in the kitchen with the lights dimmed and a candle burning on the windowsill, as the rain and wind continued to batter the house. They were eating a wild mushroom and spinach lasagne that Morton had cooked when he had returned from his drenching on the high street. He hadn't waited to be asked about his day, but blundered straight in by telling her that something had occurred that she needed to know about.

'You can skip all these bits,' Juliette had said playfully, when Morton began to detail the minutiae of each individual search and his reasons for doing it.

'Skip the boring bits you mean,' he said, feigning offence.

'No, I just know that you've got something in there that I'm probably not going to like.'

Damn, she was good. Skipping over the finer points of his research, Morton had told her about the waitress delivering the envelope and him rushing out into the rain to find the perpetrator. 'And I stared him right in the eyes,' Morton had said.

'And?'

'Douglas Catt. The one and only.'

Juliette had looked puzzled for a moment. 'But I thought you said you phoned him and he was at home.'

'He must have had the phone on a redirect to his mobile.'

'What's he got against you?'

Morton had shrugged. 'You're the police officer, you tell me.' Morton had no idea why he was so hell bent on stopping Morton from researching the Mercer Case. Morton had been wracking his brains for any semblance of a reason Douglas would have, but the only thing that had come to mind was that he knew more about Mary's disappearance than he was letting on.

Juliette had run her fingers through her hair, her eyes searching his face. 'What was inside the envelope?'

Morton had handed it to her, allowing her to sift through it at her own speed and to make her deductions about the contents. And she had taken her time, setting about the contents like a diligent police officer. First, she looked at the handwritten note with the simple

146

words '*Final warning*'. Then she examined another photograph of her getting into the car. 'Jesus, I *really* need to start wearing make-up.'

'You really don't,' Morton had replied.

'The thing is, apart from taking awful photos, he hasn't actually committed a crime by taking photos.'

'What about harassment?'

'The trouble with harassment is you need to show a course of conduct—in other words, it needs to be persistent and you have to have formally told them to stop.'

'Legalities aside, are you really okay with someone photographing you like this?' Morton had asked, more worried about her than the finer points of the law Douglas Catt might or might not be breaking. 'Can't you put a trace on his car or something?'

'Not without good cause and not as a trainee, no, but I will take it to my boss. No arguments this time, Morton.'

He wasn't about to argue, he agreed with her: Douglas Catt needed stopping right away. 'Do it. Until then, you're spending your day off tomorrow, with me.'

Juliette had laughed and pecked Morton on the lips. 'Oh, thank you. We'll have a brilliant time.'

Morton's face had suddenly fallen. 'Why? What were you planning on doing tomorrow then?'

'Not *were* planning, *am* planning. Rye Wedding Fayre.'

'Bloody hell.' He had slumped with some exaggeration into his chair, but actually dreaded the very idea.

'You'll have to come now—you said you would. Besides, I need a bodyguard to save me from being photographed,' Juliette had mocked. She held up the most recent photograph of herself. 'Especially if I look like *that*.'

The wedding fayre was held in an old warehouse on the periphery of the town. The cold uninspiring building was filled with a plethora of stalls selling every conceivable aspect of marriage, all equally abhorrent to Morton. He trudged around the building like a sullen teenager, trailing a few steps behind Juliette who was having the time of her life, delighting at the wares on display at each stall. The rain, which had started yesterday, had continued without stopping and was now drumming noisily on the corrugated tin roof. He wasn't sure if she had dressed for the occasion, or whether Douglas Catt's recent attempts at taking her photo had done it, but today she wore an unusual amount of make-up and had even straightened her hair—very un-Juliette. They had only been there an hour and she had amassed an impressive collection of free gifts, which Morton lugged around like a pack-horse.

'This is brilliant,' Juliette muttered about the whole event, before making her way to the fifth table showcasing the talents of yet another photographer.

Morton sighed. It quite easily ranked amongst the worst possible days of his life. It wasn't *that* bad, really, he just couldn't stand the commercial aspect of marriage. With a slight groan, he realised then that he was turning into his adoptive father, a man who refused to take part in any special occasion, apart from birthdays, because of *commercialisation*. Even when Morton and Jeremy were small boys, he never bought Mother's Day cards or gifts on their behalf; it was only when they went to Sunday school and primary school that their mother began to receive anything. The two boys learnt early on not to bother with Father's Day when their efforts at homemade cards were met with the derisory glimmer of a glance before being tossed to one side. He never bought Valentine gifts for his wife and only really took part in Christmas celebrations begrudgingly and under duress from the rest of the family. Ever since Morton's mother had died of cancer, his father had celebrated Christmas alone, despite numerous offers from friends and family. Every year was the same for him: a quiet walk around the park, a meal of shop-bought fish and chips at home and strictly no television. Since 1990, Christmas had officially been banned from the Farrier household. Morton was determined *not* to turn into him.

'What do you think of this one?' Juliette said quietly, handing Morton an example of the photographer's work. It was a close-up of the bride's shoes and a close-up of a filled champagne glass with a red lipstick mark on the rim.

It was hard for Morton to select among a possible bank of adjectives to describe the photos. He decided to use one that Juliette wanted to hear. 'Stunning.'

Juliette shot an incredulous look at him, turned her head away from the man behind the table and lowered her voice. 'Morton, don't just say what you think I want to hear.'

'I…' he began when his phone began to shriek its ringtone into the air. Saved by the bell. 'Sorry,' Morton said, pulling his phone from his pocket. It was an unidentified mobile number. He answered the call and stepped away from Juliette, who pulled an apologetic face to the man behind the table. 'Hello.'

'Hello, is that Morton Farrier?' a female voice asked.

'Speaking.'

'This is Jenny Greenwood here. I've just got your letter.' Her voice was flat and Morton couldn't detect her reaction to having received the letter.

'Oh yes, thank you for getting in touch,' he said, treading very carefully with his words.

'Well, even though your letter doesn't mention that we've already met at Blackfriars, I'm guessing that you've discovered my little secret?' she asked. There was still no emotion in her voice.

'It did click, when I found out that Vivien Mansfield had had a daughter called Jennifer and she'd gone on to marry a Greenwood, that it was you, yes. Don't worry, I'm not going to ask the whys and wherefores of your situation. I'm really only interested in Mary Mercer—as I set out in the letter.'

The line went quiet and Morton removed the phone from his ear to check if the call had ended, but it hadn't. After a few seconds, Jenny spoke. 'I've got my own reasons for working there, which I will tell you. Can we meet up?'

Morton thought for a moment. He didn't need to see Jenny to discuss why she was working at Blackfriars when she was actually a member of their family. 'Listen, Jenny, you really don't need to explain your story to me. As I said—'

Jenny interrupted him. 'What if part of my story is part of Mary's story?' she asked cryptically.

Interesting, he thought. 'Okay… when do you want to meet, then?'

'My next day off is in two days. That any good?'

'Yes, that's fine. When and where?'

'How about one o'clock at the Winchelsea Farm Kitchen? It's just a stone's throw from Blackfriars and not far from you.'

Morton, ever the tearoom connoisseur, knew of the place. 'Yes, that will be fine.'

'See you then,' Jenny said and hung up.

Morton was intrigued about what Jenny had just said. The implication was surely that Frederick Mansfield was somehow associated with Mary Mercer's disappearance. He was about to put his mobile away when he spotted that he had two new emails. He glanced over at Juliette. She had now moved on to a table filled with every type of wedding cake imaginable. She was in her element; he had plenty of time to open his emails. The most recent one was from Ray Mercer. *Dear Morton, Thank you for your very detailed email. I can see why you are a 'forensic' genealogist! You sound as though you are pursuing avenues I wouldn't even have thought of. I was most intrigued by what you said about my grandmother travelling to Canada. I had no idea about this, but of course it was years before I was even born. She certainly never mentioned it to me. Perhaps just a holiday? You asked after my health—not good I'm afraid. I've been given the details of a nearby hospice, which I'm sure doesn't require much more of an explanation on my part. I know you're working at full speed, so hopefully my lost ancestor will appear from the shadows of the past sometime soon. With warmest regards, Ray.* Morton felt an even greater sense of urgency now that Ray's health was deteriorating. He really needed to go all out on bringing this case to a resolution as quickly as possible. When he considered all that he had discovered so far, he believed he *would* find out what happened to Mary. Before Morton looked at the next email, he peered over at Juliette, who was now busy stuffing her face with cake samples. The email was from Bartholomew Maslow, grandson of Jack Maslow, a Blackfriars servant. *Morton, I received your email. I have something to show you which might be of interest. Meet me in St Thomas's Church, Winchelsea tonight at 8pm.* Morton re-read the email several times. He had found Bartholomew's email address on the University of Brighton's website, although the reply was sent from a Gmail account. *Probably not wanting to use his work email address for personal business,* Morton reasoned. He was excited that his email had hit the right person *and* he had something which might help the Mercer Case. Brilliant. He felt a surge of satisfaction that his relentless efforts were starting to pay off.

'Everything okay?' Juliette asked when he rejoined her.

'Yeah, just had an email from Ray Mercer—he's been told to contact the local hospice.'

Juliette pulled a sympathetic face.

'He really needs closure on this before…' Morton let the words hang in the air before continuing, '…I had another email,' he said, more upbeat. 'From a Bartholomew Maslow, the grandson of one of the servants, and he wants to meet me tonight.'

'That's good,' Juliette said with a smile. 'The jigsaw's coming together.'

Morton nodded. 'Can we go now?'

'We haven't found a present for Jeremy and Guy yet. And I haven't looked at any of those stalls over there,' she said, indicating the far side of the room.

Morton groaned. As much as he wanted to just leave Juliette to it and go and get a coffee somewhere, he knew he couldn't. 'I'm going to go and sit over there by the door and do some bits on my phone.'

Juliette nodded her agreement and he sloped off to a bench beside the door. It was the only entrance or exit to the warehouse, so he could easily keep an eye on Juliette and anyone else intent on taking pictures of her. Morton opened a web-browser on his mobile and began to research Canadian electoral registers. None of the main genealogy websites offered him what he was looking for, so he headed to the Nova Scotia Archives website and sent an email asking if electoral registers existed for Halifax and if so, whether they could check the occupancy of 4 West Street. It would be pushing his luck, but he asked for searches to be carried out 1921-1930 and then emphasised that he was from England and couldn't search the records for himself. In his experience, most archives and record offices were happy to help with research requests, although he recalled one burial search request for a cemetery in Chatham which resulted in a twenty-five pounds fee for a search to be carried out ten years after and ten years *before* the date of death. Madness.

Morton scanned the warehouse and located Juliette. She was happily chatting to two women behind a table on the far side of the room. He slowly cast his eyes over the rest of the place—no sign of Douglas Catt, thankfully.

Morton pondered the Mercer Case. The Scottish connection still bothered him. Mary had, it seemed, been sacked from Blackfriars at a time when most of the household was in Scotland, then written a letter from there saying that she wouldn't be coming back. Yet she failed to turn up ever again in the country. Morton opened up the Scotland's People website and again began a series of searches for Mary, but no credible leads were forthcoming. Unless Mary lived her whole life under a pseudonym, her time in Scotland must have been very brief.

After more than two hours at the wedding fayre, Juliette wandered over to Morton and said the magic words: 'Right, let's go.'

Through bleary eyes, Morton looked incredulously at the accumulation of gift bags that she had acquired during one afternoon in a chilly dilapidated warehouse. He still couldn't quite fathom how this could be enjoyable for anyone.

Morton stepped outside and raised his umbrella to shield against the incessant, driving rain.

151

'Well, I've got loads of ideas for our big day,' Juliette said, as she slipped her arm through his.

'Go on then, enlighten me.'

'I'll need to be asked the question first,' she said with a smile.

Morton leant over and kissed her. 'Okay. Will you, Juliette Meade, please tell me about your ideas for our big day?'

Juliette squeezed his arm and smiled.

The pair hurried through the saturated streets, navigating ever-expanding puddles until they reached home.

Having unlocked the front door, Morton hastened inside and was relieved not to see another envelope waiting for him on the doormat. He looked at his watch. He had another three hours until his meeting at the church with Bartholomew Maslow. Plenty of time to shower and freshen up.

In a tiny box-room that he had self-proclaimed as his office, the man grinned. The room only contained a desk and a laptop, but it was enough. He had just compiled a detailed report of all the activity on Morton Farrier's mobile phone. Everything. He had logged his exact movements, his incoming and outgoing text messages and phone calls, his emails and internet browsing. The file was growing impressively and the man began to feel like a real spy. He laughed at how easily he had intercepted the email to Bartholomew Maslow, then created a false Gmail account from which to reply to Morton. He glanced at his watch. Two hours until his scheduled meeting in St Thomas's Church. Then it would be case closed for Morton Farrier and all activity on his phone would end. The man laughed raucously as he picked up his latest acquisition—a Sig Sauer p232-22 handgun. Aiming the weapon at Morton's communications file, the man pretended to fire.

'Goodbye, Mr Farrier.'

Morton was running late. He had seriously misjudged the time that it would take him to prepare the fish pie that he had cooked for him and Juliette. He zoomed, far too fast, up Strand Hill, almost colliding with an oncoming car when the road narrowed to a single lane in order to pass through the fourteenth-century Strand Gate.

'Shit,' Morton yelled, slamming on his brakes and allowing the other car through. It didn't help that his visibility was severely reduced owing to the incredible quantity of rain thrashing down.

Morton raced around the corner and parked in a similar spot to the one used on his last visit here, just outside the former Mercer house on Friar's Road. He killed the engine and leapt from the car, pulling his waterproof coat collar up to try and get some protection from the dismal weather. The exterior of the church was up-lit by the burnt amber glow from several huge floodlights dotted around the churchyard. Even in the driving rain, Morton thought that the grand church looked majestic and impressive. Apart from the lights beaming onto the church, Winchelsea had very little street lighting and Morton struggled to see where he was going.

'Damn it!' he cursed again, having stepped into a deep puddle that lapped up over his left shoe. He remembered then that his iPhone had a torch function and rummaged around in his pockets for it. He stopped still on the path, fumbling infuriatedly. He'd left his phone in the car.

Douglas Catt, wearing a dark wax jacket and matching hat, was cowering behind a tilted gravestone to the south the church entrance. He had chosen a grave just behind one of the huge floodlights to conceal himself better. He had tailed Morton from his home in Rye, almost rear-ending him at the Strand Gate. He had no idea what Morton was doing here, but Douglas was certain that it somehow involved the church and Morton's ridiculous quest to find out what happened to Mary Mercer—a quest Douglas was determined to end. Douglas quickly pulled out his camera, checked that the flash was not on and took a grainy, blurred photo of Morton. It wasn't a great image by any means, but it would be enough to spook Morton. Douglas watched as Morton stopped on his way towards the church. He had evidently forgotten something. Morton turned around, hurrying back towards his car. Now was his chance to get into the church ahead of Morton and find somewhere to hide. Using the powerful shaft of light to shield him, Douglas moved from grave to grave, always keeping Morton in view, until he reached the chunky outer wooden door. He pulled it open, wincing at the amount of noise emanating from the ancient hinges.

'Bloody thing,' Douglas muttered to himself, hoping that the sound of the wind and rain was enough to mask the sound.

Pushing the door tightly shut, Douglas moved through the vestibule, opened another creaky door and turned into the gloom of the church. The only light was that which filtered in through the stained-glass windows, producing an unnatural, eerie glow around the church ceiling. He quickly cast his eyes around the room for somewhere to conceal himself and decided that a large, gothic pillar might be a good place in which to hide, since it offered him the ability to manoeuvre around it, should the need arise. He crept over to the pillar and ducked down, his eyes set firmly on the door.

From the other side of the church, Douglas heard the unmistakable sound of a stifled cough.

Someone was already here. Whoever it was was started to approach him.

Morton reached his car, climbed in and instinctively locked the doors. Groping around by his feet, he found his mobile. He picked it up and saw that he had a missed call with an answerphone message. He checked the time. It was eight twenty. Even though he was twenty minutes late, Morton decided it would be wise to listen to the message since it might be Bartholomew Maslow. *Hopefully he's running late, too*, Morton thought. Accessing his voicemails, he listened carefully. It wasn't from Bartholomew, it was from a descendant of Sarah Herriot who had been phoning to say that she knew nothing at all of her grandmother's time at Blackfriars; that she worked there at all had been a fascinating revelation to her. Morton saved the message, switched on the torch function and stepped out of the car.

The torch provided sufficient light to guide Morton back into the churchyard towards the door. He was half expecting Bartholomew to be stood in the vestibule ready to greet him and share whatever information he had. Morton very much hoped that whatever it was he wanted to show him was *inside* the church. He pulled open the inner church door and began to feel slightly unnerved. It hadn't really occurred to him just how creepy the church might be when unoccupied after eight at night.

Morton stood in the chancel and allowed his eyes to adjust to the low light levels. He scanned around the vast edifice, expecting to see Bartholomew sitting in the pews, but there was nobody in sight.

His heart began to beat a little faster as he crept along the chancel towards the altar, turning his head nervously as he went. Something didn't quite feel right.

Suddenly Morton's phone beeped loudly with an email alert.

'Bloody hell!' he said, annoyed for having made himself jump. He pulled his phone out to switch it onto silent when he noticed that

154

the email was from Bartholomew Maslow. The first line made no sense and stopped Morton in his tracks in order to read it fully. *Dear Mr Farrier. Many thanks for your email. Yes, you have correctly identified me! Although, I'm not sure what help I can be. I have pictures of my grandfather (Jack) during his time at Blackfriars, which I'm happy to scan and email you. Never heard of Mary Mercer though, unfortunately. Get back to me if the photos are of use. Regards, Bart Maslow.* Morton was baffled. This email was a direct reply to Morton's, with his original message below.

A sudden wash of panic hit Morton when he realised that he had been set up, lured to the church by someone other than Bartholomew Maslow. His heart rate shot through the roof and his breathing became restricted. He needed to get out. Right now.

Morton turned, ready to run from the building. As he did so, something caught his eye. Something on the floor beside the altar. Not something, someone. Someone lying splayed out not moving. Dead.

Morton gasped and froze as he stared at the person on the floor. From the limited light cascading from the stained glass windows, Morton could see a bullet hole in the person's forehead. It was then that he recognised the body: Douglas Catt. As his mind began to try and fathom what on earth Douglas Catt was doing dead in Winchelsea church, he suddenly realised that the killer might still be inside here. Without another second's thought, Morton ran for the door, tugged it open, momentarily praying that the vestibule would be empty. It was. He pulled open the outer door and rushed into the rain. The previously innocuous shadows that bordered the graveyard were suddenly frightening harbours of potential evil.

He took a deep breath and ran for his car. His single focus was on getting in the car and getting away. Then he would phone the police. As he neared his car, the thought entered his head that maybe Douglas had slashed his tyres again, but thankfully that was not the case. Morton climbed into the Mini, started the engine and sped from Friar's Road as fast as he could.

Only once he had descended Strand Hill, did he dare to pull over and make the 999 call.

155

Chapter Fifteen

Saturday 15th April 1911

Edward Mercer could barely contain himself. He and the rest of the Blackfriars household were on the final leg of their journey home from Scotland. He was grateful that Lord Rothborne had decided to return slightly earlier than planned to be with his wife following the illness that had sent her home prematurely. The family and all the domestic staff had stayed overnight in London, ready to take the first train back to Rye. A convoy of six shiny black horse-drawn carriages were cutting their way through the glorious Sussex countryside towards Winchelsea. Edward gazed through the coach window at the patchwork quilt of yellow and green fields that ran endlessly into the horizon. He wasn't really taking in what his eyes were seeing; his thoughts were preoccupied with Mary. His feelings for her had seemed to spring unexpectedly from nowhere, but were now so powerful that they were driving his every thought and action. The time when they could be together, properly and seriously, couldn't come soon enough. The painful absence from her had sown the seed of the idea of getting married as quickly as possible. When he had proposed, they had only discussed the marriage in very general terms, which revolved around their family being informed. But now, Edward didn't care what their family thought about it; he loved Mary and she loved him. Throughout the time in Scotland, the idea burgeoned to the point that Edward had written a letter to the vicar of Winchelsea, requesting a special marriage licence so that they could be married quickly and without the need for banns to be called. They could even marry in secret and *then* tell their family. He couldn't wait to tell Mary—he knew that she would be as thrilled as he was at the prospect. Edward had made up his mind that the two of them would go and speak to the vicar this very afternoon. Lord Rothborne had kindly given *all* domestic staff the rest of the day off, including those who hadn't been included in the trip, meaning that he and Mary could have an entire day off together. It was probably too ambitious, but he wondered if he could take her to Hastings after they had seen the vicar, or somewhere further afield. Although, thinking about it more, he knew that Mary would much prefer to take a picnic and head out into the countryside where they could be alone together. Whatever they did, it didn't really matter. The weather, too was perfect for them—bright blue skies with only the merest smudge of cloud.

'What you grinning at, Mercer?' Jack Maslow asked, as the coach bumbled along an unmade section of the road.

'Nothing,' Edward said, unable to stop smiling. He had told Jack everything about his courtship with Mary, but now wasn't the place to open up about the marriage, since James Daniels and Thomas Redfern were also sharing the coach with them. The gossip had inevitably spread but the last thing Edward wanted was to add fuel to the fire.

'Mary, Mary—my darling, Mary!' James teased. 'How I long to hold you in my arms!'

Edward smiled and ignored the goading. His stomach began to churn as the grand front entrance to Blackfriars came into view. Usually, the servants would have been brought in via the back entrance along Friar's Road, but the grand spectacle of six horse-drawn carriages was an opportunity to remind the village of the prominence of the Mansfield family.

Upon entering the estate, the procession split: the coaches containing the family went to the front of the house and the carriages containing staff and luggage drew up at the kitchen door. As much as Edward wanted to run into the house to find Mary, he still had work to do yet. They could only be dismissed once all the trunks and cases had been safely taken to the correct areas of the house. The mammoth operation of unpacking and life returning to normal was to begin tomorrow.

Edward was disappointed when he first entered the gloomy kitchen to be greeted by Bastion's wretched face and a disgusting smell. He had hoped that wherever Mary was in the house, she would have seen their return and come and welcomed him. *She must be busy somewhere at the back of the house and not know we're home*, Edward thought. *What a surprise she'll have!* He grinned and left the kitchen to help carry the suitcases inside.

'Come on, lads, let's get this done,' Edward said, heading to a coach containing the cases and trunks.

'Yeah, we know why you're in a hurry, Mercer,' Jack Maslow said with a laugh.

Edward responded with a smile, rolled his sleeves up and reached up for the first trunk.

It was almost ten o'clock in the morning by the time all of the luggage had been carefully transported inside. The horses had been led away to the stables and the coaches stowed in the old cart lodge. For Edward, the time had passed agonisingly slowly and there was still no sign of Mary. *It's just like her to keep me waiting,* he thought with an inward laugh.

He headed through the kitchen, which was still filled with the unpleasant aroma of offal being sliced and diced, towards the servants' hall, whistling a made-up tune. As he walked along the corridor, the door to the housekeeper's room opened and Mrs Cuff and Miss Herriot stepped out. 'Good morning,' Edward said cheerfully. 'We're back!' He stepped back to allow the ladies to pass.

'Good morning,' the ladies answered as they wandered smartly past.

'Have either of you seen Mary at all?' Edward called after them. He watched, somewhat alarmed, as both the women stopped and glanced at each other before turning back towards him.

'Has nobody told you?' Mrs Cuff asked.

'Told me what?' Edward said, beginning to panic. 'Is she okay?'

Mrs Cuff nodded. 'She's fine.' She looked again at Miss Herriot. 'You go on, I'll be along in a moment.' Then she faced Edward. 'Come into my room for a moment.'

At Mrs Cuff's request, Edward sat down at her oak writing desk. She took a seat opposite him and sat with a solemn face. He was really worrying about whatever he was about to be told and a thin bead of sweat broke out on his forehead. 'What is it, Mrs Cuff? Please, tell me.'

'I'm afraid that Miss Mercer has left the employ of Blackfriars,' she began.

'What do you mean?' Edward asked.

'I mean that Miss Mercer no longer works here.'

'Why? What did she do?' Edward demanded, straightening defensively in his chair.

Mrs Cuff paused for a moment. 'It's a delicate matter, the details of which should probably be left to the discretion of Miss Mercer. Suffice it to say, something occurred last Wednesday which could not be tolerated at Blackfriars.'

'Where did she go?'

'Home, I would have thought.'

Edward stood, mumbled his thanks and dashed from the room. He bolted along the corridor, through the kitchen and out the door. 'What have you done, Mary?' he said to himself as he ran at full pelt up the back path. He briefly left the path at the orchard and stuck his head in the old abbey ruins, but she was not there.

When he reached his aunt and uncle's house, Edward kept pounding on the door until somebody answered it. 'Come on, come on!' he yelled breathlessly. 'Mary!'

Finally, the door was unbolted and Caroline's face snarled through the narrow gap that she had allowed. 'Edward,' she said, her voice finely laced with disgust.

'Caroline, open the door. I need to see Mary,' Edward said, taking a step closer to the house.

Caroline held the door firm. 'You've got a nerve showing up here after what you and Mary did to Edith. Judas.'

Edward began to lose his temper and raised his voice. 'It's none of your business, just open the door. I need to see Mary.'

Caroline frowned but said nothing for several seconds. 'Why would Mary be here on a *Saturday*?' When she saw Edward's confusion she widened the gap in the door. 'Where is she?' she demanded. 'She owes us her wages from last week.'

'Who is it?' a voice called from behind Caroline.

Edward recognised it as his aunt's voice. 'It's me, Edward. Can you come to the door, please?'

Caroline sneered and stepped back to allow her mother to come forward.

'Oh hello, Edward. Do you want to come in?'

Edward nodded and followed his aunt inside and through to the kitchen.

'Sit down. I've just made a pot of tea. What are you doing up here on a Saturday, then?' his aunt asked. 'Oh, have you just got back from Scotland? How was it?"

'It was okay, thanks. Listen, I've come looking for Mary. Have you seen her since Wednesday?'

His aunt laughed, as she poured two cups of tea. 'What, do you mean she's disappeared? She should be at work. It is Saturday, isn't it?' she said, sounding slightly confused.

Caroline had followed them into the kitchen and stood with her arms folded in the doorway. Edward glanced at her then back to his aunt. 'I don't really know what's happened, but they let her go on Wednesday last week. They've not seen her at Blackfriars since.'

His aunt frowned at him and set down the teapot. 'Well where the devil is she, then?' She turned to Caroline. 'Do you know where she is?'

Caroline shrugged. 'Don't ask me where she's gone. Probably somewhere of ill-repute, knowing Mary.'

'Caroline!' her mother snapped. 'That's enough. I really don't know why you've got it in for her.' She turned back to Edward with an apologetic look on her face.

Edward ignored the nasty comment from Caroline and addressed his aunt. 'We need to find her. All the other servants are off today so I could get some help searching for her.'

'Isn't that all a bit dramatic and over the top?' Caroline asked.

Edward stared at her cold, uncaring face. 'Is it? Your sister has been missing since Wednesday—aren't you a little bit bothered.'

'She's old enough to look after herself. What did she do at work to get sacked anyway?'

'I don't know,' Edward said quietly. 'It doesn't really matter to me. The point is that she's nowhere to be found.'

'Where are you going to look for her?' Caroline asked derisively.

Edward hadn't thought that far ahead yet. He just knew that he needed to look for her. 'I don't know... we could ask around the village. Search around the Blackfriars estate. Maybe she slipped and banged her head or hurt herself somehow.'

With trembling hands, his aunt picked up her cup and saucer and took a sip of tea to steady her nerves. 'Edward's right. This is out of character for Mary. She does do some silly things but she's never run off like this. When's Edie home? Maybe she's heard from her.'

'I think if Edie had heard from her we'd soon know about it,' Caroline said. 'She's livid with her. Understandably, she feels totally betrayed.'

'Caroline, just stop with your harsh words,' her mother instructed in a soft but direct tone. 'Why don't you go and get yourself ready to help look for Mary?'

Caroline exhaled, then silently left the room.

'Just ignore her, she's still very emotional following William's death. She's taken it hard, poor girl,' she said, taking a seat opposite Edward.

Edward looked into his aunt's eyes and a desperate biting feeling overtook him and he began to sob. Something had happened

160

to Mary. He knew that it was something bad. His aunt reached across the table and took his hand.

'We'll find her, don't you worry. You know what she's like—always getting herself into mischief.'

Edward wiped his eyes with the back of his hand. 'But where can she be? This is so not like her. She wouldn't have just left like this, not without telling me.'

His aunt breathed in and out heavily for several seconds. 'I must admit, when she didn't come with Edie to collect me from the sanatorium last week I was a bit worried, but then Edie said Mary hardly ever comes home now on her half day's leave, so I didn't think any more of it.'

'Can you think of anyone she might have gone to?' Edward asked.

She thought for a time, then shook her head. 'Nobody that comes to mind. You probably should get someone to check with your mum and dad—make sure she's not waiting for you there.'

Edward hadn't thought of that and the notion that she was simply with his parents, waiting for him to get back, filled him with a little hope that she was okay. *But how would she think I would find out where she was?* Edward wondered. *Maybe she's left a note for me somewhere.* He chastised himself for not having searched his *own* room for any letter or note that she might have left him—exactly as he had done for her. The sinking feeling that he had been experiencing was suddenly lifted to one of hope. *That will be it—she's left me a note telling me where to find her.* 'I'm going to make one final check of Blackfriars. If I don't find anything, I'll return with help and we'll begin searching for her.'

'Okay.'

Edward stood up and darted from the house back to Blackfriars. 'Why didn't I think of that before?' he mumbled to himself as he ran into the estate.

Breathlessly, Edward climbed the stairs to his bedroom. He headed straight for the bed and lunged for the pillow. Below it, there was no note. Nothing. He then turned the room upside down, emptying drawers and his wardrobe, searching every nook and cranny that he could find. But there was nothing. The room hadn't been touched since he had left for Scotland.

In despair, Edward kicked the bed and then yelped in pain. He stood in the centre of his trashed room, desperately trying to stop himself from crying. He frantically considered his options and any places where she might have gone or clues that she might have left here in Blackfriars. There was only one other place to check: her bedroom.

Descending the stairs two, sometimes three at a time, Edward raced along the corridor and up the stairs to the female servants' quarters.

'Edward!' Eliza yelled angrily when she bumped into him at the top of the stairs. 'What are you doing here?'

'Sorry, Eliza, I know it's forbidden but I must look in Mary's room,' Edward managed to say through gasps for breath. 'She's disappeared.'

'What do you mean?' Eliza asked indignantly.

Upon hearing a man's voice, Clara stepped out of the bedroom that she had shared with Mary. 'What's he doing up here?'

Edward turned to face Clara. 'Mary stopped working here on Wednesday and she hasn't been seen since. None of her family knows where she is and—' he was cut off by another voice further down the corridor.

'She was sacked, the naughty little girl.' It was Joan, who stuck her head out from her bedroom door.

'Do you know why she was sacked, Joan?' Edward asked.

Joan shrugged her shoulders smugly.

'Please, nobody knows where she is,' Edward pleaded.

Joan grinned. 'Apparently, so I was told, Mary was caught by Her Royal Highness wearing all her fancy clothes. Parading up and down in her bedroom, so I was told. Typical Mary—thinking she's better than everyone else.'

Edward was perplexed. *Why would Mary be wearing Lady Philadelphia's clothes? Was that even enough to be sacked?* 'Then what happened?'

Joan shrugged again.

'Joan, just tell him if you know anything, you can see how worried he is,' Clara said.

'She came up here, packed up her things and left. I saw her leaving myself. Gone. She's probably hiding, too ashamed to show her face. She'll not work in a house like this again, I can tell you.'

Clara rolled her eyes, then faced Edward. 'Did she not just go home?'

'No, she never showed up. I was hoping she might have left a note or a clue.'

162

'You're welcome to have a look in our room, but I haven't seen any notes.'

'Thanks—it's my last hope before I really start to panic,' Edward said, as he followed Clara into the room. Eliza also joined them and between them they methodically searched the small bedroom.

'There's nothing here,' Edward said, resigning himself to the situation. Her drawers and wardrobe were empty, her bed was stripped bare: there was nothing of Mary here. *She's gone,* he was forced to admit.

Edith had to get some fresh air. At least that was what she had told her mother earlier today. In reality, she needed to escape her overbearing sister, Caroline. She longed for the day Caroline would return to own house in Bristol. *Why is she even still here?* Edith asked herself, as she traipsed through the Strand Gate, running her fingers slowly over the ancient stone. *She says it's because Mother is still unwell, but it's more likely because she's enjoying being in charge.* A gentle wind wafted through Edith's hair and seemed to calm her thoughts. She stood still and closed her eyes, trying to settle her mind before returning home. She wished things could go back to how they were last year. The seriousness of life seemed to have suddenly come upon her. In just a few days she and Mary would turn eighteen. It was a milestone birthday and they were at odds with each other. Edith inhaled and exhaled deeply, trying—*really* trying to forgive her twin. But she just couldn't yet. She felt utterly deceived by Mary's actions in the past few months. First the job, then Edward. And she didn't even have the courage to turn up on Wednesday to face her—probably snuggled up somewhere with her fancy man.

'It'll work itself out, Edie,' her mother had said, trying to console her. 'Look how it all turned out with the job—you're going to be the second housemaid at Durrant House. Besides which, you're still young. You don't need to saddle yourself with a man yet. Trust me, there's plenty of time for that.'

But her anger and hostility only worsened and deepened. Edith had been alarmed at the rise of her ill feelings towards her sister. Then she had berated herself for such shameful thoughts.

Edith turned the corner into Friar's Road. Something was going on. Something serious. The usually deserted street was bustling with activity. At least fifteen people, comprising neighbours, friends

163

and some servants whom she recognised from Blackfriars, were all milling about and chatting noisily just in front of her house. *Was it her mother? It couldn't be, she had seemed so well since she'd been home. Perhaps it was her father.*

Edith spotted her mother among the crowd and rushed over to her. 'What's going on?' she asked.

'It's Mary, she's disappeared. Apparently she left work on Wednesday lunchtime and never came home. They've not seen her since at Blackfriars. Edward's gathered all these people up to look for her. You've not seen her, have you?'

'No, not at all.' Edith felt a lump rise in her throat, as all of the unkind thoughts and feelings about her twin dissipated. *How cruel you can be, Edith Mercer,* she scolded herself. *You wished ill harm on your sister and now it's happened. She could be lying dead somewhere.* On the verge of tears, she hurried over to Edward, who seemed to be orchestrating a small search party. 'Edward, is it true that Mary's vanished?'

Edward nodded. 'Yes, I'm afraid so. It's so not like her, Edie. She's been missing since Wednesday. We have to find her. Will you help?'

'Of course.'

'Good. Could you make your way out to my parents' house and see if she's there or if they've seen any sign of her?'

'Okay,' Edith answered.

'And knock on doors on the way—there are only a few houses on the main road. If you can, have them check out-buildings, empty sheds—that sort of thing.'

'Do you really think it's that serious?' Edith asked, hoping that he was simply erring on the side of caution.

He nodded. 'I've got a bad feeling about it.'

Edith reached out and squeezed his hand. All ill-feelings towards Edward and Mary had entirely vanished. As she looked into his sad face, she realised that her resentment towards her twin was based on jealousy rather than any real, deep feelings for Edward.

Edward smiled at Edith as she let go of his hand, turned and left the village.

As she made her way along the main road, Edith passed several people knocking on doors in the pursuit of Mary. *Edward must really be in love with her to have organised all of this,* she thought as she walked briskly in the midday sunshine.

164

There were only four properties on the less than two mile walk to Icklesham. Each was a farm, complete with a myriad sprawling outbuildings. When she reached the first property, Edith suddenly felt a little silly at the prospect of asking a stranger to search their property for her missing twin. *Is this really necessary? She's only been missing three days. Knowing Mary, she's taken herself off somewhere to recover from the embarrassment of losing her job then she'll swan back like nothing's happened, wondering what all the fuss is about. It's just like the number of times she was sent home from school for bad behaviour.*

Edith paused in the gabled porch way, not quite able to lift the heavy black door-knocker. 'Come on, Edith,' she said to herself. 'Mary might need you.' She raised her hand and wrapped the semi-circle knocker onto the decorative plate behind it.

The door was pulled open by a short elderly woman with a pleasant face. 'Hello. How can I help?'

Edith smiled. 'Hello. Sorry to disturb you, I'm looking for my twin sister who disappeared last week. Her name is Mary Mercer and she's my height with big red curly hair. You couldn't mistake her. Have you seen her by any chance?'

The old woman shook her head. 'No, definitely not seen anyone matching that description. Sorry, my love.'

'Would you mind terribly just having a quick look in your farm buildings, just in case she's there?'

The woman frowned, evidently not keen on the idea of searching for a trespasser. 'I'll have a quick look now. You wait here. If she is here, she wants to keep well out of my husband's way, let me tell you. He doesn't take kindly to traveller folk and itinerants on his land.'

Before Edith could interject and say that her sister was neither a traveller nor itinerant, the door was closed.

The longer she waited, the more preposterous the search felt to Edith. *What really were the chances of Mary being stowed in the barn of an Icklesham farm? It made no sense.*

'Sorry, my love, nothing,' the old woman said when she eventually returned. 'Good luck—hope you find her. We'll keep an eye out.'

'Thanks,' Edith said, and turned back to continue her walk along the main road.

After the second, then third and fourth farmhouse all returned the same negative outcomes, Edith became more apprehensive. For

165

her part of the search being carried out, everything relied on her aunt and uncle having seen or heard from Mary since Wednesday.

Her aunt and uncle lived in a small white weather-boarded cottage close to Icklesham church. Again, Edith was hesitant about knocking. In the window, she caught sight of her aunt who seemed perplexed to see her.

'Edith! What are you doing here? Just out for a walk?' her aunt called through the open window.

'Not really, I'm looking for Mary. Can I come in?'

Her aunt opened the door and, at the sight of her warm familiarity, Edith burst into tears.

'Oh my poor thing, whatever's the matter? Come inside.'

Despite the clear skies that had mercifully dominated the day, at just after seven-thirty the day began to give way to the night. Edward and the few remaining searchers were standing on Friar's Road outside the Mercer family home, anxious with despair. None of them had spoken for several minutes, each too absorbed with their own theories and conclusions, drawn from the outcome of the day's searches: nobody had discovered anything. Edward had no new leads to go on—there had been absolutely no sightings at all of Mary since Wednesday. To him, it seemed as though she had been plucked from the face of the earth, which worried him immensely. He could cope with her running away, even if it did mean the end of their courtship. What he couldn't cope with was the idea that something untoward had happened to her. He couldn't shake an unpleasant recurring thought: that Mary was lying dead somewhere where she would never be found. That idea had haunted and clouded his every thought. There was now only one possibility left for today and that was Edith. She had yet to return from Icklesham. The fact that she had been so long heartened Edward; he kept expecting the two of them to waltz in, arm-in-arm with a tale to tell.

The streets grew darker, the darkness bringing with it a stark chill in the air. Edward could only just make out the corner of the street and was now starting to worry about Edith. *Should he go and search for her now?*

'What's taking her so long?' Edith's mum asked, evidently thinking the same as he was. 'She should've been home hours ago.'

'You don't think the pair of them are up to something?' Caroline mused.

Edward bit his lip through fear of saying something he might regret. All day Caroline had strutted around, huffing, puffing and complaining that the searches were a waste of time.

'Don't be so silly, Caroline. Why don't you go inside and check on your father.'

Caroline did as suggested and disappeared.

'Is that her?' Edward said, suddenly seeing movement at the corner of the road. He strained his eyes through the dusky gloom to see, as the figure drew closer. It was Edith. Alone. With a despondent look on her face. Edward knew that if she had any news at all, then it wasn't good.

'Anything, Edie?' her mother called as she approached them.

'No,' Edith said. Her voice was edged with despair.

'What took you so long?' Edward asked.

'Your mum had a photo of Mary, so we went door to door in Icklesham but nobody has seen her. I even went back to the farms that I had called into on the way there to show them the photo, but nothing. Has nobody seen her in the village or around the estate?'

'No,' Edward said, almost inaudibly. 'Nothing. She's vanished.'

'I think we need to call it a day for today,' Edith's mother said. 'I can barely see the hands in front of me. Come on, let's go in and have some supper. I'm sure we're worrying too much, you know. I'm sure she'll wander in all sheepish and we'll look back on this day and laugh at how we set the whole village out looking for her.'

Edward and Edith offered their best attempts at a smile but everyone knew that Mary's situation didn't look good.

The setting of the sun that day left a darkness that the Mercer family would feel for years to come.

Chapter Sixteen

Wednesday 19ᵗʰ April 1911

The sun was beginning to burn off a thin mist which had blown up from a squally sea. Slivers of sunlight began to slip in through the panes of the Mercer kitchen window. Edith was sitting with her mother. Both of them were silent. It had been exactly one week now since Mary's disappearance and, as each day gave way into the next without word from her twin, Edith had been growing more and more anxious. Today was their eighteenth birthday, a milestone that they should be sharing together, just as they had shared every previous birthday. In her heart, Edith knew that Mary wasn't going to come home today. She had no clue at all as to her whereabouts but she just felt her absence inside. If Edward's theory that she had fallen and injured herself was correct, then by now… she couldn't bring herself to think the worst. It was just too awful to contemplate.

A clattering of the letterbox and the dull thud of post tumbling to the floor sent Edith dashing into the hallway. Among a pile of birthday cards, she spotted a letter addressed to her parents. It was Mary's handwriting. She dropped the cards and picked it up, turning it over in her hands, then took it to her mother, who was kneading dough in the kitchen. 'Something for you; it's from Mary.'

'Oh, thank God!' her mother cried.

Edith watched anxiously as her mother tore open the letter.

Suddenly, her mother let out an awful cry. 'She's in Scotland and she says she's never coming home!'

Edith snatched the letter and, with quaking hands, carefully read it. *Dear Mother and Father, It is with great sadness and shame that I write you this letter. I have behaved and acted in an unforgivable manner, which, if you were to learn of the whole matter, would bring embarrassment to the Mercer name. Please know that in taking on the role of housemaid at Blackfriars, I only wanted to earn your love and respect. In this, I have failed and ask that you respect my decision to leave Winchelsea. I hope to start a new life in Scotland, where I may be disconnected from the life and pains of Mary Mercer. I pray that I will one day receive your forgiveness. Your loving daughter, Mary.*

'What on earth's she doing in *Scotland*?' he mother wailed.

'Whatever's happened?' Edith's father barked from the doorway. He was half-dressed, standing in his underpants, socks and a ragged shirt. His beard and hair were shabby and matted—the same as he looked every day, irrespective of visitors or occasions. Behind him stood an agitated-looking Caroline.

Edith looked up at her sister and father. 'We've had a letter from Mary. She's in Scotland and she says she's not coming back.'

Her father walked over, grabbed the letter and begun to read with Caroline peering over his shoulder. 'What's the problem?' he asked his wife. 'Reads to me like the most sensible thing she's ever done.' He tossed the letter down onto the kitchen table and hobbled back upstairs.

'But she didn't do anything *this* bad,' Edith muttered quietly. 'She only tried on Lady Philadelphia's dress. From this letter you'd think she'd killed someone.'

'Maybe she's done something else that we don't know about,' Caroline mused.

Edith flung her head around to face Caroline. She had heard enough. 'Maybe you should shut up and go back to Bristol. What are you still doing here? Nobody wants you! Go away!' Edith screamed, flinging back her chair and reaching for Mary's letter. With a great deal of force she barged past Caroline, sending her to the floor as she dashed for the door.

'You horrible little urchin!' Caroline yelled. 'You want horse-whipping!'

'Bloody cow!' Edith yelled, as she slammed the front door shut behind her.

Edith's eyes were wet with tears as she crossed into the Blackfriars estate, clutching the letter from Mary. She still couldn't believe it. Mary was in Scotland. Something about Mary's tone told her that all was not well. It just didn't *sound* like her. She dreadfully wanted the letter to be real because then at least it meant that she was okay.

Edith reached the kitchen door to Blackfriars house and recalled when she had last stood here on a cold day in January, ready for her job interview. Her life had been about to begin. Since then her world had seemed to collapse: Mary had taken her job; her brother-in-law, William had died, leaving her horrid sister, Caroline living with her; her mother had caught tuberculosis; her father had suffered with a severe bout of melancholia; Mary had taken the man with whom Edith had thought that she was destined to be and now this. *What have I done to deserve such an awful time?* Edith wondered.

She knocked on the door.

169

'Oh, hello,' Mrs Cuff said warmly. She was smartly dressed in her full housekeeper's black uniform. 'Any news on your sister yet?'

Edith nodded and Mrs Cuff noticed that she was upset.

'You'd better come in, then. Come to my room for some privacy.'

Mrs Cuff stood to one side and allowed Edith into the busy kitchen. It was strange, the room sounded and smelt exactly the same as three months ago. Servants were coming and going according to the orders being barked at them by the rotund French chef, as a variety of interesting-smelling foods boiled on the hot stove behind him. One of the maids, Joan Leigh, cast a curious eye in her direction, but the rest were too absorbed in their own work to notice her. Mrs Cuff closed the door and led Edith through the kitchen, down the corridor to her room. Taking out her large bunch of keys, Mrs Cuff unlocked the door and indicated for Edith to enter.

'We've had a letter from Mary. It says she's in Scotland,' Edith began. 'But...I don't know. It doesn't feel right to me.'

'What's she doing in Scotland?'

Edith thought it would be much simpler if Mrs Cuff actually read the letter, so she handed it over. 'Have a read.'

'Are you sure? It's private.'

'Go ahead.'

A short silence hung in the room as Mrs Cuff read the letter. She looked up. Edith could see that she felt the letter to be justified, given what Mary had done. 'I know it must be impossible for you to accept that your sister—your twin sister—is so very far away and has expressed her feelings like this, but at least you know that she's safe and well.'

'It doesn't feel right,' Edith said, although she was unable to express exactly *why* it felt that way.

'Do you not think she wrote it, then?'

'Yes, it's definitely her handwriting,' Edith began. Finally, she felt able to articulate something of her uncertainty. 'It's just not her words or her turn of phrase. Not to mention that she wouldn't just run away like that after being caught wearing someone else's clothes. It doesn't add up.'

Mrs Cuff seemed a little taken aback at Edith's nonchalance towards Mary's misdemeanour. 'I think Lady Rothborne felt her transgression to be quite a serious matter. Then there was the dishonesty about it.'

170

'What do you mean?'

Mrs Cuff shifted uncomfortably in her seat. 'Having been caught, your sister refused to admit that her actions were of her own doing.'

Edith's inquisitive face implored Mrs Cuff to continue.

'She insisted that Lady Rothborne had encouraged her to try on outfits that she could wear at her wedding to Edward.'

Edith could tell from her face that Mrs Cuff found even the retelling of the story to be so fanciful as to not justify the breath taken to say it. 'But…'

'I know, it's absurd. From reading this,' she said, holding up the letter, 'I would say it was the guilt over her insincerity that prompted her shame.'

Edith was dumbstruck. Ever since she could remember, Mary had always been prone to impulsive, often fanciful outbursts. Trying on Lady Rothborne's clothes was *entirely* the kind of silly thing Mary would do on a whim. But to lie about it afterwards with such a bizarre tale struck Edith as very out of character. 'Did anyone check with Lady Rothborne?' Edith ventured, knowing full well that she was risking stepping into dangerous territory.

Mrs Cuff took a moment to navigate the potential storm diplomatically. 'A full investigation was undertaken and everybody concerned given a fair hearing. As part of that, yes, Lady Rothborne was consulted.'

There was nothing more for Edith to say on the matter. She now needed to inform Edward about the letter. 'May I speak with my cousin, Edward, please?'

Mrs Cuff nodded. 'If you would like to wait here, I shall fetch him to you,' she said, making her way out of the room. As she reached the door, she turned back towards Edith. 'I am sorry, Miss Mercer. I was quite fond of your sister.'

Edith smiled politely and watched as Mrs Cuff disappeared from the room. As she sat in the stillness of the housekeeper's room, she replayed what she had just been told about Mary's actions. Coupled with the letter, Edith's discomfort grew. Then an idea came into her mind that she was unable to shake. *What if a clue to Mary's disappearance was in this very room?* She was sure that the Day Book, signed off religiously each and every Sunday by the housekeeper and butler, would be stored in this room. *Don't be so silly, Edith!* But the idea persisted and her heart began to race. As if being controlled by somebody else, Edith stood up and walked over to the door. Gently, she pulled it open and stuck her head into the corridor. Silent and empty. The sound of footsteps on the stone floor would give her plenty of notice of anyone approaching. It was now or never. Edith took a breath and rushed over to a large bureau and opened the doors. It was filled with paperwork, ledgers and files. Exactly the right kind of place. Her fingers clumsily began picking through the shelving. She knew the Day Book would be quite a large official-looking document, so she ignored individual loose papers or published books.

'Here it is!' Edith whispered, her hands resting on a soft velvet ledger. She quickly flicked to the last completed week and read the entry for Wednesday. *Lady Philadelphia and some of the female staff returned prematurely from the hunting trip to Scotland. Lady Philadelphia suffering from morning sickness. Discovered one of the housemaids, Mary Mercer, in Lady Philadelphia's bedroom, wearing her finest ball gown and some of the most precious Mansfield jewellery. Servant immediately dismissed. Replacement currently being sought. Lady Philadelphia much improved upon return to Blackfriars. Mrs Cuff.*

So that was the official Blackfriars admission which would consign Mary's misconduct to history. With a heavy heart, Edith set the book back in place, closed the bureau and pushed shut the room door. Returning to her seat, Edith began to worry about how Edward would react to the news. She simply decided to show him the letter and see his response. Would he too feel as she had, that something wasn't quite right about the situation?

Moments later, the door opened and Edward apprehensively walked in. He was dressed in his neat livery, his hair was tidy but his face was worn and wearied. Mary's disappearance had hit him hard.

'Mrs Cuff said you'd heard from her?' he said, even before Mrs Cuff had shut the door behind him.

'A letter came this morning,' Edith said, passing it to him.

Edward took a while to read the letter. Edith watched as his eyes darted around the page, his mind seeming to re-read and question its content.

'What do you think?' Edith asked, trying to keep her tone as neutral as possible.

Edward met her eyes, his own filled with tears. 'It's not from Mary,' he said.

'It's her handwriting,' Edith insisted.

'But it's not *from* her. Do you believe it's her?' he asked, his eyes searching her face to understand her thinking. He didn't wait for a response but continued with his case. 'I'm telling you, Edie, there's no way she—'

'I know,' Edith interposed. 'There's no way she would write a letter like that. There's no way she would have taken off like that. And there's no way she wouldn't have told *one* of us at least.'

Edward seemed to calm a little upon hearing that he and Edith were allied in their thinking. 'Now what do we do?'

Edith shrugged. She had no idea what to do next.

Lady Rothborne watched from the east window as a black coach drew up at the back entrance to the house. From the carriage, Mr Risler, the butler stepped out with his case. Lady Rothborne took a moment to savour the fact that he had returned from Scotland alone: her despicable nephew, Frederick, had thankfully not returned.

A quiet knock came from her bedroom door. She recognised the light tapping as belonging to her lady's maid, Miss Herriot. 'Enter,' she bellowed.

'Your coffee is ready in the library, Lady Rothborne,' Miss Herriot said from the doorway.

'Very good, Miss Herriot. Thank you. Could you have Mr Risler visit me there, please?'

'Yes, Lady Rothborne,' Miss Herriot said, deferentially backing from the room.

Lady Rothborne smiled. *Frederick Mansfield will not be getting his way.*

Chapter Seventeen

Morton was exhausted and no amount of caffeine could counteract it. He was slumped at one end of the sofa cradling a large cup of coffee, resting his legs on Juliette, who was sitting at the opposite end. His mind was still rerunning the events of last night. Over and over. It had been truly awful. Upon discovering Douglas Catt's dead body in the church, Morton had dialled 999 and waited on the phone to an operator until the first police car had arrived. Only then had he dared to turn his car around and venture back to the church. Inside the safe confines of their police car, the first officers on scene had taken his basic details, then referred him to the ambulance crew who had turned up tasked with removing the body. After a few checks, he had been released, apparently not suffering from shock or injury. When he had stepped out of the ambulance it was as though he had entered a wormhole and exited from a place different to that which he had entered. Police tape had criss-crossed each of the entry gates to the church, guarded by policemen and policewomen to keep out a surprisingly large crowd of chattering curious locals. Three white forensics tents had sprung up just in front of the church entrance and between them moved an assortment of personnel in protective white suits and plastic blue shoe-covers. Two further police cars had also emptied their staff into the medley. Morton had been fairly sure that sleepy Winchelsea had not seen anything like this in quite a while.

Morton had looked bewildered standing at the rear of the ambulance, surveying the scene before him. He hadn't really had time to process what had happened. Douglas Catt was dead. *Could it have been suicide?* he wondered. *Was his death something to do with the Mercer Case?* In his heart, Morton thought that it probably was.

'Morton Farrier?' a voice had asked, suddenly cutting through the darkness.

'Yes,' Morton had answered, struggling to make out the face behind the voice.

'Detective Inspector Harding,' he had said. He was a tall serious man in plain clothes with a scowl on his face. 'I need to ask you a few questions.'

Morton had nodded. As the person who had found the body, Morton knew that he would face a barrage of questions. He had also known that, unless it was suicide, for the moment at least he was likely to be the number one suspect.

Detective Inspector Harding had led Morton through a throng of police personnel into the churchyard. Finding a spot away from the prying ears and eyes of the crowd, and with just sufficient light from one of the huge floodlights, he had begun his questioning, all the while maintaining a disbelieving scowl on his face.

Morton had answered the questions as best he could and even volunteered all that had gone on with Douglas during the course of the Mercer Case.

'So this guy has been taking pictures of you and your girlfriend? Threatening you? Then you get a message to meet here and he ends up dead. That all sounds a little strange, wouldn't you say?' His frown had at last disappeared and turned into a smile. But it was a fake smile, one which had spoken volumes of his disbelief.

'Is there any way it could have been suicide?' Morton had asked.

Detective Inspector Harding had laughed. It was a full, belly laugh that was so loud that two nearby policewomen turned to see the cause of the hilarity. 'Only if he was a *very* clever man who could defy the laws of physics.'

'Okay, just a thought,' Morton had replied, feeling somewhat sheepish.

Detective Inspector Harding had ended the questioning by telling him that they might need to speak to him again as the investigation progressed.

'You're lucky they didn't lock you up last night,' Juliette mused, jolting Morton back to the present. 'Your alibi—me—only lasts until a few moments before Douglas was murdered. You *could* be the person who killed him.'

Morton pulled an incredulous face. 'Thanks for that.'

'I'm just saying, you *were* there at the time of the murder *and* you've got motive—the guy threatened you and your occasionally stunning girlfriend—just not stunning in the pictures that he took.'

'I don't rule out being framed for it,' Morton answered. He was acutely aware that what they talked about half-heartedly was actually a possibility. 'That's not my biggest worry, though...'

Juliette looked at him and waited for him to continue.

'I think *I* should have been the one carried off in the body bag last night—not Douglas.'

Juliette nodded slowly as if processing the information, but Morton knew that Juliette would have already reached that conclusion herself long ago. 'Why do you think that?'

'Because whoever sent that false email to me had hacked into my account and arranged the meeting with me—Douglas was just there because he was following me. It was just chance that the killer got to him first. I guess in the darkness of the church the killer thought it was me. Either that or Douglas got in the way—but I doubt it or else the killer would have stuck around until I got there.'

'But I don't get why two *different* sets of people are so adamant that you stop working on finding a housemaid who disappeared more than a hundred years ago. It doesn't add up.'

Morton shrugged. 'I still don't know. All I can think is that Mary Mercer discovered something that finding what happened to her would now reveal...I don't know. It's all guesswork at the moment. Something could obviously still cause real damage.'

'If you're right about all this, you've got a period of grace where the killer thinks you're dead. Use that time to get on with cracking the case.' Juliette pushed his legs off her. 'Now stop moping and get on with it, Mr Farrier.'

'What are you up to today?'

'Not sure yet. I might pop to the shops. Pick up something nice for dinner.'

'Fancy giving me a fresh set of eyes?' Morton asked. Although not a great lover of the finer points of genealogy, Juliette could rarely resist sharing her opinion on the reasoning, motivations and detection aspects of the bigger cases on which he had worked. Today, Morton was glad of some assistance since his own brain was running on flat batteries.

'Why not. Come on, then,' she said, standing up and offering him her hand.

He took her hand and stood heavily, his body weight dragging him down, making a dramatic performance of standing.

Upstairs in the study Morton used his notepad and the wall, covered with Mercer Case information, to talk Juliette through every aspect of his work so far. In her own brooding way and with few words, Juliette broadly agreed with his summations.

'I need to see this in a more linear way,' she said. 'I can't follow your logic when it's all pinned up haphazardly like that. I need a

176

timeline of some sort.' She pulled a piece of A4 paper from the printer and then proceeded to roughly tear it into three strips. 'Right, let's start at the beginning.'

And so, for the next two hours, Morton and Juliette created a crude hand-drawn timeline for the key events surrounding the disappearance of Mary Mercer.

'I've just got something new to add to the timeline. Well, maybe not actually—I'm not sure it helps,' Morton said, wafting his mobile in front of Juliette. 'Nova Scotia Archives have got back to me.'

'And?' Juliette said, poised with a pen and the timeline.

'*Dear Mr Farrier. Thank you for your e-mail. Nova Scotia Archives has printed "Lists of Voters for the City of Halifax" (RG 5 Series E. Vol. 28). It is somewhat large and is too fragile to photocopy. The names are divided by wards and within each ward names are divided by men and women, giving name, occupation and address. I have looked at the years you requested and have the following information, which I trust is of use: 1921-1925 gives the same occupant: Martha Stone, teacher. 1926-1930 Michael Fellows, Fruiterer, Julia Fellows, laundress. Kind regards, Martin Lythgoe, Reference Archivist.*'

'Hmm,' Juliette mused, gazing at the timeline. 'It *is* of interest when you look at what happened in 1925.'

Morton stood beside Juliette, wondering at what extra information she had been able to glean from this latest email that he hadn't.

'Edith Leyton travels out to visit Martha in 1925. That same year, Martha moves out. Possibly a coincidence, or did something between her and Edith happen to make her move on?'

Morton wasn't convinced that the two things were necessarily connected to each other, never mind the disappearance of Mary Mercer. It was looking increasingly like a dead end. 'I'm keeping an open mind on it... But I think Edith visiting her old neighbour in Canada in 1925 is just a holiday. The fact that Martha then moved out afterwards is just a coincidence.'

'I thought you didn't believe in coincidences?'

Morton shrugged. There was *something* about Martha and Edith that pricked at his genealogical intuition.

'Look at this,' Juliette said excitedly. She drummed a finger on the images of Dr Leyden's leases for Wisteria Cottage. 'Guess which year Edith's husband's rent-free lease expired?'

'1925?' Morton suggested.

'Exactly. Something happened to Edith that year, Morton,' Juliette said. She paused and ran her fingers through her hair. 'Okay. What about this. In 1925 Edith sets about trying to find her twin again, having failed for the previous fourteen years. She goes out to see Martha, who knows something about it. Martha gets spooked and runs away. Edith comes home.'

Morton laughed. 'Jesus, I really hope you don't use that kind of logic at work, Juliette. That's ninety percent fiction and ten percent fact. What about the other piece of information about the rental of Wisteria Cottage coming to an end? You didn't incorporate that into your lovely story.'

Juliette thought for a moment. 'Didn't you say she split up with Dr Leyden?'

Morton nodded.

'There you go, then, she splits up and moves out. New adventure to Canada. Done.'

Morton smiled. 'I might just ask Ray when his grandmother divorced Dr Leyden, just out of interest. Other than that, I really don't see much more point in pursuing the Canada and Martha Stone avenue. For the moment, at least.'

'Can't say I didn't try. Drink?'

'Coffee, please,' Morton said with a grin. He knew what was coming next.

'One decaf coffee coming right up,' Juliette said and disappeared from the room.

Whilst he was alone in the room, Morton stared at the wall that Juliette had dubbed haphazard. It might *look* chaotic, but each little pin, Post-it and string connection made sense in Morton's head. At the centre of it all was the photo of Mary. The last known picture ever taken of her. He sent the latest email from the Nova Scotia Archives to the printer and added the information to the wall then emailed Ray Mercer asking if he knew when his grandmother divorced.

'Here you go, sir,' Juliette said as she entered the study and set down Morton's coffee.

'Thank you, madam,' Morton replied.

Juliette clutched a mug in both hands. 'Listen, unless you need me more here, I'm going to go and try and find a present for Jeremy and Guy.'

'We've got two months yet.'

'Yeah, but you know what you're like at leaving things to the last minute.'

Morton avoided her gaze. 'I've been thinking-'

'Oh, God—that's never a good thing,' Juliette said.

'I'm not going to go to the wedding—' Morton began.

'What? You can't—'

'Before you interrupt—I'm just not ready to see her yet. I can't do it, Juliette.' Many anxiety-wrought moments had passed since the day that his adoptive father had told him about the identity of his biological mother. That had been hard enough, but he had also learnt that his Aunty Margaret had been raped. His own, biological father was a rapist. He couldn't even bear to *try* and think that awful truth through. 'I just can't face Aunty Margaret. I don't even know if Dad's told her that I know. You know what he's like.'

Juliette reached out and took his hand. 'Look, I'll support you whatever you decide but I think you'll regret missing Jeremy's wedding. You two have built so many bridges in the last few months. I think he'd be gutted that you weren't there.'

She was right, of course. He and Jeremy were getting on like real brothers for the first time in their lives. And yet, he couldn't get past the fact that he wasn't ready to see his Aunty Margaret with what he now knew about her.

'Listen, why don't you go and speak to your dad face to face? Ask him what your aunt knows and how she feels; it's a conversation that needs to happen regardless of the wedding.'

'Okay,' Morton found himself saying. He knew that he needed to do it, but without Juliette pushing him forward, it would have become another conversation that the Farrier household swept under the carpet, as they always had done with other contentious topics. 'I'll go over in the next couple of days and talk to him.'

Juliette smiled reassuringly. 'Are you coming to the shops to look for a gift?'

'I'll stay, if you don't mind.'

Juliette rolled her eyes playfully and pecked him on the lips. 'Don't do anything silly. In fact, don't leave the house.'

Morton saluted her. 'Yes, ma'am.'

Taking a mouthful of coffee, Morton studied each of the pieces of coloured wool that fed from Mary's picture. He had pursued many research avenues but now it was time to go back to the beginning. Morton picked up his notepad and flicked back to the first pages of

179

notes. He carefully re-read each page, paying attention for any potential oversights. When he was convinced that nothing had been missed so far, he returned to the page with the people surrounding Mary at the time of her disappearance. He was still waiting on responses from living relatives of her family and her work colleagues; the only people to respond so far had been Jenny Greenwood and Bartholomew Maslow. Morton remembered then that he hadn't yet replied to the genuine email from Bartholomew, so set about a quick reply accepting his offer of the photos of his grandfather, Jack.

Morton considered what to do next. He remembered what Juliette had said about staying put for the day. She had said it half-jokingly but the plain reality was that a murder investigation was currently ongoing which involved him. And, if his theory was correct, then somebody out there wanted him dead. No, he was definitely happy to stay home today.

He looked up at the timeline they had created together and focussed in on 1925. *Could Juliette have been right about something going on that year?* Although he had just asked Ray Mercer about Edith's divorce date, he set about finding the answer for himself. He knew that some divorce records were open to the public but were not yet available online. Morton accessed the National Archives website and quickly found that divorce case files were available for 1858-1937. He completed the relevant search request documents and clicked 'send'.

The man was sure that he had found a new career in espionage or covert operations. He could now be hired out for good money. As he caressed the Sig Sauer handgun on the desk in front of him, he replayed last night's events and the ease with which he had put a bullet through Morton Farrier's skull. It had been exactly like playing *Grand Theft Auto* on the computer. Hold the gun, pull the trigger. Dead. Simple as that. He felt no remorse. Why should he care about some dumbass genealogist who was snooping in places he had no business snooping? It was the end of this particular job and his employers had told him to return to his normal duties. He looked at his name badge. Mark Drury, security guard. Well, that was all about to change. Now he was Mark Drury, hit-man. Mark Drury, spy. He grinned as he held the gun up and pretended to shoot random objects around the room. Now that Morton Farrier was dead, Mark had been told to destroy *everything*. Every last bit of evidence, the phone tap—everything.

'Here we go,' Mark said, opening up the cardboard wallet containing all his reconnaissance that he had presented to his boss before being given the green light to take out Farrier. He had borrowed a shredder and proceeded to feed it the contents of the file. Piece by piece was chewed and devoured by the machine so that all that was left was the cardboard wallet itself.

Mark turned to his laptop and brought up the online console. Navigating to the administration panel, Mark moved his cursor to the 'Format All Data' icon. Then he spotted that something wasn't quite right.

Morton Farrier's mobile was currently active.

Chapter Eighteen

Morton was sitting in a quiet corner of the Winchelsea Farm Kitchen—a traditional shop specialising in local meats, cheeses, jams and produce, with one half of the premises functioning as a charming tearoom. He was slightly early for his appointment with Jenny Greenwood and was growing more and more intrigued by whatever it was that she had to tell him. He checked his emails whilst he waited but there were no new messages. He re-read the email he had received earlier this morning from Bartholomew Maslow containing three attachments related to his grandfather, Jack's, time at Blackfriars. One was a close-up image of Jack with a nondescript background. The second was of much greater interest to Morton. It was another close-up of Jack with another man. Bartholomew had been good enough to also scan and email the back which revealed old-fashioned script: *Me and my best chum, Edward.* Morton was looking at a sepia photograph of Jack Maslow with Edward Mercer. Curiously, at some point since the photograph had been developed, somebody had crudely hand-tinted three basic colours: red, green and blue. Interestingly, whoever had undertaken the paint job had given Edward red hair. The post this morning had also brought a written response from a descendant of Walter Risler. The letter was rude and to the point. *Dear Mr Farrier, Indeed I do object to your writing. My grandfather's business is none of yours. I have never heard of Mary Mercer. Roy Risler.* He could smile about it now, but its arrival this morning had incensed him. In his fourteen years as a genealogist, Morton had never received such a discourteous response.

'Morton? Hello?'

The voice made Morton sit up with a jerk, spilling some of his latte. Jenny Greenwood was standing in front of him. 'Jenny—hi. So sorry. I was drifting away.'

'So I see! I was waving and talking to you but you were on another planet.' She looked at her watch. 'Sorry I'm a bit late. I expect you've seen all what's going on out there. It's like a flippin' circus.'

'Yeah, I had noticed,' Morton said. The scene of the crime had certainly calmed down from yesterday but the church was still cordoned off with a small police presence and requisite group of interested locals. Later he might tell her about his involvement in the

182

murder but right now he just wanted to hear what Jenny had to say. 'Would you like a drink at all?'

'I'll get it, don't worry. Would you like anything?'

'No, I'm fine with this for now, thank you.'

As Jenny caught the attention of a passing waiter, Morton tried to shake his lethargy.

'Right,' Jenny said, seeming also to want to get straight down to business. 'So you found out that the wayward Frederick Mansfield is actually my grandfather.'

Morton smiled and nodded. He *really* hoped this meeting wasn't just about her connection to the Mansfields. He didn't interrupt.

'As I'm sure your detailed research has discovered, he died penniless in 1922, leaving my poor grandmother with a baby to raise alone. He had frittered *everything*. Family heirlooms, paintings, a valuable Egyptian ceramics collection, jewellery—he either sold it, swapped it or hocked it. But when he died, my grandmother took some consolation from the fact they at least lived in a comfortable house which she could sell to buy something smaller and more practical. Then she discovered that he'd squandered that too. Had he not died, they would have been forced to up and leave within a few weeks anyway to pay his mountain of debts.'

Jenny's story, much of which Morton already knew and didn't feel the need to transcribe as yet, was interrupted when the waiter brought over her Earl Grey.

She thanked him, then continued. 'That Frederick was not a great husband or father can't be contested, and I think my grandmother and mother were probably better off without him, as awful as that sounds.' Jenny paused to pour her tea into the bone-china cup. 'The problem lies in the fact that my mother probably was—no *certainly* was owed a sizeable fortune in inheritance.'

'Right,' Morton said, unsure of where this conversation was going. 'But you said Frederick died with debts and no money. Did your mother acquire some money after he died?'

Jenny shook her head. 'No, the inheritance should have come my mother's way in 1959.' Jenny stared at Morton, waiting for him to make the connection that she evidently thought he should be able to make.

Morton racked his brains. The date did ring a bell, but his brain was swimming with names and dates. It was obviously a

Mansfield-related date, so Morton pushed himself to think through the relevant people alive around that time. Then he got it. 'Was that when Cecil Mansfield died?' he asked uncertainly.

'You got it!' Jenny said, seemingly impressed.

'Okay,' Morton said, trying to connect the dots. 'So he died in 1959 and the estate passed to his son, George Mansfield.'

'Exactly.' She sounded as though her answer were sufficient.

'And it shouldn't have?' Morton ventured. 'It should have passed to your mum?'

Jenny looked suspiciously around the tearoom, then nodded. 'Why?'

Jenny took a moment to answer, suddenly appearing nervous. 'You're going to probably find it a bit of a fanciful tale—wishful thinking on my part—but...' Another pause. 'Take a look at this.' Jenny placed a Next carrier bag on the table and carefully withdrew a stapled A4 document, which she handed to him.

Morton took the pages from her and began to read. It was an official document of the British Military—labelled E.504, Militia Attestation for Cecil Mansfield. The first page was a standard admission file for the 3rd Royal Sussex Regiment, noting Cecil's residence at Blackfriars, his age of seventeen years and the answers to various closed questions concerning eligibility to join the military. The foot of the first page was signed by him and a witness and dated 2nd February 1897. Morton flipped to the second page, already having an inkling as to why Cecil had joined the military at this moment in history. The next page was a description of Cecil upon enlistment:

Apparent age: 17 years and 3 months
Height: 5 feet 3 inches
Weight: 108lbs
Chest measurement: 32 inches
Complexion: Dark
Eyes: Hazel
Hair: Ginger red
Religious denomination: Church of England
Distinctive marks and marks indicating congenital peculiarities or previous disease: None

At the foot of the second page, Cecil was signed as medically fit by a medical officer. Morton remained silent, trying not to make a

184

judgement as to what this form had to do with Mary Mercer, but rather to digest and understand the historical information that it contained. He flipped over to the third page, which was entitled 'A Statement of Services of No.7355 Name: C. Mansfield.' The sheet noted Cecil's attestation, embodiment, and finally his discharge on the 21st October 1902 for being medically unfit. The final page in the document concerned his military history. As Morton had suspected, Cecil had seen service in South Africa in 1901 and St Helena from the 15th June 1901 until 11th September 1902, for which had had been awarded the 'South Africa Medal & Clasp.' Under the heading 'Wounded', Cecil's reason for discharge became clear: 'Severe G.S. wound to groin.'

'Initial thoughts?' Jenny asked when he finally looked up from the papers.

She really was making him work hard. Morton took a mouthful of drink before answering. 'Cecil volunteered for the 3rd Royal Sussex regiment to serve against the South Africans in the Boer Wars. He was discharged as medically unfit after a gunshot wound to the groin,' he surmised.

Jenny seemed disappointed. 'Come on, you can do better than that,' she said with a smile. 'You're a forensic genealogist.'

Morton smiled. 'Okay. I think you're implying that a gunshot wound to the groin would preclude him from having children and since his son, George, was born in 1911, I think you're suggesting that he cannot biologically be his. If that were the case, then the Mansfield fortunes should have, according to inheritance laws, passed to your grandmother or mother in 1959.' Morton suddenly felt on a roll. 'I think you're working at Blackfriars in the hope of finding proof of this amongst their archives.'

Jenny smiled. 'Pretty well spot on, yes.'

Morton was still confused. 'Right, so…?' He let his question hang in the air, allowing Jenny to continue her story.

'I've done some fairly extensive research at the National Archives, ferreting around various private papers, unit diaries and what have you and, although Cecil is never mentioned by name, one particular battalion commander comes pretty close to a graphic description of injuries which fit with Cecil. The injuries he describes would have left the man in question unable to father a child.'

'So who do you think is George Mansfield's father, then?'

'That's one question, but not the one you need to be asking. The question you need to ask is, who is George's mother?'

185

Morton was taken aback. *Surely she isn't suggesting...* 'Really?' he said, a little too incredulously.

Jenny shuffled uncomfortably in her seat and took another glance over her shoulder. 'Really. You might find it an outlandish theory, but I don't believe that either Cecil or Philadelphia were George's parents.'

'But he looks so much like them—the hair...' Morton stopped himself when he realised what he had just said. Mary Mercer's physical description, with her red hair, dark complexion and hazel eyes matched Cecil's appearance almost exactly; she would have been perfect to have been chosen to bear a child with Mansfield features. *But what about the father? His genes could surely have overridden hers?* He recalled the photo of Edward Mercer that he had just looked at. A flash of feeling, like swallowing a cup of freezing ice-water, fired through Morton's insides. *It couldn't be...*

'You're getting it, aren't you?' Jenny said, sipping her tea, but still maintaining eye contact.

'Jenny, this is one hell of a huge leap from Cecil *possibly* being unable to have children to Mary Mercer being George's biological mother. *Huge.* Why was Philadelphia at least not the mother?'

Jenny shrugged, as if this were an unimportant point to raise. 'I think you know the answer to that because you suspect who the father might have been.'

'I think, but have absolutely no evidence of this, that Mary Mercer was romantically linked with her cousin, Edward Mercer,' Morton revealed.

'Did he look like her?'

Morton withdrew his mobile phone, opened up the email from Bartholomew Maslow and showed Jenny the hand-tinted photo of Jack and Edward. 'Guess which one's Edward,' he said sarcastically.

Jenny grinned. 'There you have it, then. You've answered it for yourself. Philadelphia wouldn't have degraded herself with another man when two people under her own roof and with a passing resemblance could give them the child they needed to continue the Mansfield line—keeping it firmly away from my philandering grandfather.'

Something bothered Morton. 'How did you suspect, though, that Mary Mercer was the mother of George?' Morton asked.

'I didn't, until your letter arrived last week,' Jenny said, taking another sip of tea. She rummaged again in her Next bag, like it was a bag of magic tricks that she could only access if Morton asked the right questions. She removed some more sheets of paper but held on to them while she spoke. 'Whilst conducting my own research, I happened upon this article from 1908—three years after Cecil and Philadelphia married.'

Morton took the piece of paper. It was a photocopy of an extract from the *Sussex Express* and, rather alarmingly, read strikingly similarly to a mixture of the reports of Edward's drowning and Mary's disappearance.

Suicide by Drowning

Miss Florence McDougall, seventeen years of age, was found drowned in the lake of the Blackfriars estate on Tuesday of last week. Miss McDougall had been an employee there for two years but had, according to her employers, been suffering from depression. In the days prior, Miss McDougall had privately threatened to take her own life. Her lifeless body was spotted by the head gardener, Mr Charles Phillips, who noticed her distinct red hair on the water surface. The Coroner's jury found that the deceased had committed suicide whilst of unsound mind.

'That image—of the poor girl's red hair splayed out on the lake at Blackfriars haunted me,' Jenny said. 'Whenever I see the lake now, I see her hair.' She paused for a moment. 'I don't know why, but something about Florence captivated me. The more I thought about how Cecil and Philadelphia couldn't have had a child, the more obvious it seemed that they would have found someone close by with some physical characteristics that would throw off suspicion that the child might not have been theirs. Anyway, I couldn't persuade Sidney Mersham to let me look in the archives, so it was on the back-burner when I received your letter.'

Morton nodded. 'Do you think that Florence and Mary were *willing* participants?' he asked, already fearing the answer.

Jenny screwed up her face. 'It doesn't seem like it to me.'

'But if Mary had unwillingly had her child taken from her and survived—why didn't she return for him or just not give him up?'

'The answer to that might forever be consigned to the vaults of history, Morton.'

Time passed with neither of them speaking, both absorbed in their own thoughts.

Morton thought about the Scotland connection. *Maybe she went there in order to give birth. But then where did she go? Evidently not the same way of Florence McDougall and Edward Mercer, since she turned up in Winchelsea in 1962.* He considered the letter that Mary had written from Scotland about having done something which caused sadness, shame and embarrassment. *Could this be it?* It was certainly more substantial than trying on an employer's clothes. Then he considered that he had waltzed into the Mansfield archives with very few questions. 'But why, then, did the current Mansfields allow me unprecedented access to their archives, when they wouldn't even allow their own employee?' he said.

Jenny smiled. 'Have you never heard of the saying 'keep your friends close but keep your enemies closer'?'

She had a point. Then Morton remembered that Sidney had *not* willingly let him see the Day Book for the time of Mary's disappearance—he had only learnt of what had happened that day through deception.

'But...' Morton had too many questions to know even where to begin. The theory had more holes in it than a colander. 'Okay. So, let's say you're correct. How on earth would we set about proving it? What we have on paper—concrete evidence—amounts to nothing at all. We'd look like a laughing stock. I'm taking it you've got your eye on a pretty sizeable court case?'

'Perhaps. But that's a long way down the line. You tell me how we proceed from here.'

There was a question. Morton held Jenny's gaze, as he thought about all that he had just been told. He hated the fact that there was so little evidence—it went directly against his whole genealogical ethos. Yet, despite this, his instincts told him that Jenny *could* be onto something. If she were correct, then they would have one hell of a job proving it. DNA would be the simplest answer if he were following a direct male lineage, but the switching between sexes from Ray Mercer's generation to Edith and Mary's parents left only one type of DNA test available: the autosomal test, which looks at the twenty-two pairs of non-sex chromosomes. From what he knew about the test, it was shaky at best. As the generations increase, the odds of sharing autosomal DNA decrease. Not to mention the fact that no member of the Mansfield family would willingly agree to a test. For the moment, Morton ruled out the use of DNA to prove or disprove the theory, which left him with very few options for the time being.

'I think,' Morton began. 'If your theory is right, then the answer will come when I find out what happened to Mary. Speaking of which...' He glanced at his watch. He had arranged to meet with the vicar of Winchelsea in fifteen minutes' time. Whilst most documents pertaining to the church had long ago been transferred to East Sussex Archives, the vicar had told Morton that a small bundle—mainly comprised of letters—was still held at the vicarage. 'I've got an appointment with the vicar of St Thomas's church in a moment, so I need to dash.'

Jenny's eyes lit up. 'Bit presumptuous, but can I come?' she asked.

Morton was slightly taken aback at the question. He usually liked to work alone, although an extra pair of hands might just be useful on this occasion. 'Yeah, sure. Okay.'

Jenny smiled. 'Drink up then.' She finished the last dregs of her tea and stood to pay.

'Let me get these,' Morton said, fumbling for his wallet.

'Nope. My treat. You're the only person beside my husband who thinks I'm not totally bonkers.'

'Okay,' Morton said, packing up his belongings. He held onto the Next carrier bag until Jenny had finished paying. 'Thanks for that. Here's your bag.'

'Keep it—it's a photocopy of all my research which is relevant to Mary.'

'Thank you,' he said, pulling open the door and stepping out into the quiet streets. The bright day had turned slightly overcast, with thick clouds shielding the sun.

'I wonder what on earth went on there?' Jenny said, as she and Morton looked into the churchyard. The entrances at each corner were still sealed off with police tape. It looked as though the forensic tents were being taken down and the operations scaled back. Just one police car and three policemen remained.

Morton grinned. 'I might tell you later. Come on, let's go.' Morton turned to leave when something caught his eyes. It was a name on a headstone. His eyes darted back to the name carved into the simple grey memorial.

'What's the matter?' Jenny asked, realising that Morton was transfixed by the grave.

'This grave. It can't be.'

Jenny leant over and looked. 'Martha Stone, 1890 to 1902.' Jenny switched her attention to Morton. 'Do you know her?'

189

Morton nodded. He knew her alright. She was alive and well, living in Canada in the 1920s. He needed to think. Fast. He quickly took a picture of the grave, then addressed Jenny. 'Let's go—I might need your help this afternoon. I'll explain later. For now, we need to go and see this vicar.'

'Okay,' Jenny said, sounding slightly confused.

Morton led Jenny across the street to a rather grand peg-tile-covered house. It was detached and had an immaculate garden filled with bright red roses. A pink climbing rose with a thick trunk splayed out across the front of the house. 'This is it,' Morton said, checking the address with what he had scribbled on his notepad. He rang the bell and waited.

A moment later, a squat man with white hair, wearing a cassock and dog collar, opened the door. 'Morning,' he said cheerfully. 'Mr Farrier?'

Morton nodded and shook the vicar's hand. 'Yes, thank you for seeing me. This is my friend, Jenny.'

'Nice to meet you, Jenny,' he said, shaking her hand. 'Come in.' The vicar stepped to one side to allow them in. 'I might have to cut this short if I get a visit from our friends over there.' He nodded his head over to the church and sighed. 'First time I've ever been barred from my own church. Terrible business.' He showed them into a small room at the front of the house. It was a simply furnished one, which Morton guessed was used for parish business rather than personal use. It had three fabric chairs, which had seen better days, and a small table. On the walls was an assortment of watercolours of scenic views around Sussex.

'What happened?' Jenny asked.

'Murder,' the vicar said, taking a long breath. 'I don't know the full extent yet. A man was shot dead. You can't imagine anyone in this town with a *gun*.'

'Have they caught the murderer?' Morton asked.

The vicar shook his head, making his jowls shake like a boxer dog. 'Not that I know of, no. It's terrified my poor parishioners, I can tell you.'

'I bet it has,' Jenny commented.

'Well,' the vicar replied, facing Morton, 'as I said on the phone, we've only got a few parish chest bits and pieces but pretty well everything of importance, official church records, etcetera were handed over years ago. It's mainly letters to and from the diocese. Don't get your hopes up.'

'Don't worry,' Morton said. 'Just checking every avenue.'

'I won't be a moment. Take a seat.' The vicar strode from the room, leaving Morton and Jenny to sit at the table.

'So, is Martha Stone something to do with this case you're working on, then?' Jenny asked.

'Possibly. I need to get to The Keep pretty quickly after this. Fancy coming along?'

'Oh, yes please!' Jenny said enthusiastically.

Morton smiled. 'I'll bring you up to date on our way over.'

The vicar pushed open the door with an apologetic look on his face. In his hand was a bundle of papers bound by a red ribbon. 'It really isn't much,' he said, setting the bundle down on the table and proceeding to unpeel the binding. 'I'm afraid, for security reasons, I'm going to have to stay in the room while you look at them.'

'That's fine,' Morton said, leaning over to inspect the bundle. He felt like a child in a sweet shop when presented with historical artefacts, desperate to delve in. He took the first document and Jenny took the second. He could see instantly that the piece of paper was of no use. It was simply a letter written from the diocese to the church about a village event commemoration in 1978. Morton set the paper down and took the next, a bundle of papers which he skim-read. They were a series of letters about the erection of a tablet commemorating the life and distinguished service of one of their organists, who had died in 1948. Jenny set down her document and took another.

'I did warn you,' the vicar said with a look of slight embarrassment.

'It's fine,' Morton said. 'We're just very meticulous.'

After ten minutes of fruitless searching, the end of the pile drew closer when Jenny suddenly sat up straight. 'Morton,' she said, a hint of excitement in her voice. 'Look at this.' She handed over a letter.

'Dear Rev. Knowles, I am writing to you to request that you prepare a marriage licence so that I can be married at your earliest convenience. I enclose the sum of 7s 6d, which I believe to be the cost. I am currently in Scotland with the Mansfield family, but I would like to marry my fiancée, Mary Mercer as soon after my return to Winchelsea as possible. I hope this is all as it should be. Yours sincerely, Edward Mercer.'

191

'He somebody of interest?' the vicar asked, sitting up with curiosity.

'Very much so,' Morton replied. The letter proved that he and Mary were an item. They were engaged. Marrying by licence often, but not always, implied a rushed marriage. *Was Mary pregnant and they were marrying quickly to avoid the scandal of having a child out of wedlock?* Morton studied the letter again. It was dated Monday 10th April 1911. It disproved one of Morton's initial theories: that Mary had taken herself off to Scotland to be with Edward. He can only have learned of her disappearance upon his return with the rest of the household. And then he was dead just over a month later, drowned in the Blackfriars lake, just like Florence McDougall. 'Mind if I take a photo of it on my phone?'

'By all means,' the vicar answered.

'Would a copy of the licence exist somewhere?' Jenny asked hopefully.

'I'm guessing that the reason this letter is still here is because the licence wasn't granted. Vicars couldn't, and indeed still can't, issue marriage licences. This Edward chap of yours was in such a hurry that he wrote to the wrong place. The Bishop of Canterbury would have been the person to issue the licence. If it had been granted, then the marriage would likely have taken place soon after. Your best bet is to see if they actually married. The marriage certificate will tell you if it was after banns had been called or by licence.'

'They didn't marry,' Morton said.

'Oh, I see. He seemed keen enough. Maybe young Mary wasn't quite so keen.'

'Maybe,' Morton said, not wishing to waste time conveying the details of the case.

Jenny carefully held the letter whilst Morton took the picture.

'Right, let's finish the bundle and then we'll let you get on,' Jenny said to the vicar.

Morton and Jenny continued looking through the remaining papers, both working in silence as they considered the implications of chancing upon Edward's letter. They reached the end of the pile, with no further trace of the Mercers or Mansfields.

Morton thanked the vicar and handed him a ten-pound note. 'For your trouble.'

'It was no trouble, but thank you,' the vicar said, holding the front door open for them.

'Well—that sure was a discovery!' Jenny beamed once they were out of earshot. 'That proves that they were a couple. And we know they looked alike.'

'It doesn't prove that she was pregnant with his child, which was then given over—willingly or otherwise—to Cecil and Philadelphia.'

'We'll see,' Jenny said with a wry smile.

As they walked towards Morton's car, he couldn't help but feel a hint of admiration for Jenny and her determination to prove her theory through her own personal endeavours. If it all came to nothing, it would still be a pleasant afternoon spent in the company of someone who shared his passion for uncovering historical truth.

Mark Drury was agitated and angry. Last night had not gone to plan and he was pissed off. He was sitting in his van clenching his jaw, impatiently waiting. Suddenly, the GPS signal from Morton Farrier's phone was moving. A small green dot representing Morton's signal moved apace across a map on Mark Drury's laptop screen. The laptop was open on the passenger seat of his car. Mark was little over half a mile from Morton's present location in Winchelsea. Turning onto the main road, Mark began to follow the signal. With the technology sitting beside him, he had no need to ever get into Morton's view and could comfortably hang back and allow the GPS signal to guide him to wherever he was going. In the glove compartment was Mark's Sig Sauer handgun, loaded and with a silencer. After a severe reprimand from his boss, Mark knew that it had to end today.

Chapter Nineteen

Thursday 18th May 1911

Two weeks of solid sunshine had given way to violent storms. Dense black clouds raged outside and the windows of Blackfriars were pounded by the heavy rain.

'Goodness, I think we might have to light some fires tonight, if this continues,' Mrs Cuff said, as she walked beside Edward along the corridor towards the housekeeper's room. It was half past eight in the evening and the servants had just finished their tea.

Edward agreed with an inaudible mumble; he knew that she was just trying to make small talk, despite obviously having something more significant to say to him. It had to be a personal issue—if it were work-related then Mr Risler would have spoken to him. Maybe it was about Mary, Edward hoped. He had known all day that something hadn't been quite right with Mrs Cuff; her lingering, uncertain looks implied that something was on her mind. Now he was about to find out what.

When Mrs Cuff entered her dimly lit room, she rubbed her hands together and tried to put on a smile; Edward could see that it was all in an attempt to make him feel at ease, although he felt anything but at ease. 'Don't tell Mr Risler, but I shall certainly be lighting a small fire tonight,' she said with a quiet laugh.

Edward smiled. 'What is it you wanted to see me about, Mrs Cuff?' he asked, willing her to get on with whatever she had to say.

'Take a seat. I just wanted to see how you were getting on…since Mary left.'

'Not very well,' Edward answered flatly as he sat opposite her in the gloomy room.

'It must be very hard for you. And for her sister.'

Edward nodded. 'It's unbearable. We've looked everywhere for her. At great expense, poor Edie's even had Mary's picture copied and sent it to all the major shipping ports to ask them to search their passenger records. She's contacted carriage companies, charabanc companies. The local police have all but closed their case because of that wretched letter from Scotland.'

'You never did believe that she was in Scotland, did you?'

Edward shook his head vehemently. 'Never. I know you did, but—'

Mrs Cuff interjected. 'Well, that was why I wanted to speak to you.'

Edward looked puzzled but remained silent.

'I *did* believe the letter, yes. I *hoped* the letter was genuine—desperately, in fact.' She took a pause and stared at Edward, as if unsure of whether to proceed. 'It reminded me all too much of Florence McDougall.'

'Who's she?'

'A young lady who worked here just before you started. Lovely girl, she was.'

'What happened to her?' Edward asked, just as a ferocious gust of wind rattled the window, making them both jump.

'She disappeared.'

'Oh,' Edward said flatly. 'Was she ever found?'

Mrs Cuff nodded. 'Unfortunately, yes. She turned up a few days later. They found her dead in the lake here.'

'That's awful,' Edward said looking shocked. From what Mrs Cuff had said earlier, he didn't like the sound of where this conversation was going.

'It was awful. The poor girl…' her voice trailed off, as if she were unable to vocalise the past. She shuddered. 'The coroner ruled it as suicide and the unfortunate episode passed. Time moved on as it always does, taking with it any uncertainties about the situation.'

'What kind of uncertainties?'

'Nothing specific. It was only when Mary disappeared that it set me wondering. You see, Mary looked a lot like Florence, which I thought was just a coincidence, but then it got me thinking back to Mary's interview: she didn't have one. Edith was interviewed and found suitable for the job, then Lady Rothborne stepped in and offered it to Mary instead. I mean no offence to Mary, but she didn't really have the right experience to be a housemaid, unlike Edith. Then, when she disappeared I remembered Florence…so, I was relieved when Mary had written a letter to say she was well and in Scotland.'

'You sound as though you've had a change of heart,' Edward said.

'I have. I didn't know if I should tell you or not…but, after Florence…'

'Please, Mrs Cuff—you have to tell me.'

Mrs Cuff sighed, accepting that she was about to start a chain of events over which she would have little control. She lowered her voice to the point that Edward had to lean forward to hear what she was saying. 'I overheard something yesterday that made me sick to my stomach. I couldn't quite believe it and spent all of last night tossing and turning, unable to shake it from my mind. It's too unbelievable.'

'What did you hear?' Edward implored.

Mrs Cuff took a moment and he could see that her hands were trembling slightly. 'I heard Mr Risler saying that the plan had worked. He said that he had posted Mary's letter from Scotland to her parents to make it look as though she was there.'

Edward gasped. 'So she was never in Scotland?'

Mrs Cuff shook her head solemnly.

Countless questions and thoughts sped through Edward's mind. His firm belief that Mary would never have run away to Scotland without him was right. Risler had posted the letter. *But why? Who was he working with?* 'Who was Mr Risler talking to?'

'Lady Rothborne.'

'What? I don't understand,' Edward said loudly. 'Why would Lady Rothborne and Mr Risler want to lock Mary away?'

'Edward, be quiet,' Mrs Cuff urged.

'Sorry. I don't understand.'

Mrs Cuff leaned closer. 'Did you know that Mary was pregnant?'

'Pregnant? Are you sure?'

'Absolutely. I've seen her with my own two eyes.'

'But... that's not a reason to lock someone up! I'm going to marry her. She's not the first unwed girl for that to happen to...'

'I don't think that what's happened is through moral condemnation.'

'Pardon?' Edward was truly lost.

'I think that she's being used as a surrogate. Her baby will then be given to Lord and Lady Rothborne.'

'But that's not right,' Edward protested. 'Mary would never agree to that!'

'That's why I've told you. I fear that poor Florence was being used in the same way and that didn't end well for the poor girl.'

Edward failed to comprehend all that he had just heard. He wanted to scream and cry and shout, but most of all, he wanted to find Mary. 'Do you know where they're keeping her?'

Mrs Cuff shook her head. 'Somewhere on the estate. There can't be too many places.'

Edward leapt up, jettisoning his chair backwards.

'Wait, Edward,' Mrs Cuff called, just as he reached the door. 'Listen to me, when you find her you both need to go—you need to leave Blackfriars forever. Maybe even leave Winchelsea for a while; I don't think either of you are safe here.'

Edward nodded. It suited him to get away anyway. He would find Mary, go back to her house to pack, then onwards to his house. The vicar of Winchelsea might still have the marriage licence that he had asked for upon his return from Scotland. They could marry quickly, then head off somewhere together as man and wife. As he went to leave the room, Edward turned back to Mrs Cuff. 'Thank you.'

She smiled and watched as he darted along the corridor. Her smile faded as a deep dread and foreboding washed over her. She listened to his heavy footsteps travelling down the corridor to the Butler's Room, where she knew Edward would find Mr Risler. Mrs Cuff stood up, closed the door and slumped backwards with her hands over her ears.

Edward Mercer had always approached the Butler's Room with the deferential decorum that had been drummed into him from the moment he had arrived at Blackfriars in 1908. He would knock lightly, stand back a step with his head slightly bowed and his hands behind his back. But not now—primal instinct instead of a sense of duty made him kick the door back as hard as he could, sending it flying inwards.

'What in God's name!' Mr Risler exclaimed, leaping up from his chair. He had been quietly reading a newspaper, which he dropped to the floor. '*Mercer!*'

Edward saw no need for a polite conversation or explanation. Mary was out there somewhere, waiting for him. He attacked Risler with the proficiency of a top-class boxer, almost dancing on his heels as he rushed towards him. The speed of the first punch lifted Risler clear off his feet, sending him crashing backwards into his wooden table. Risler yelped and tried to speak, but his mouth met with another powerful right hook. He tumbled to the ground, curled into a foetal position and covered his face with the squeal of a helpless animal as he braced himself for the next impact.

Every muscle in Edward's body was focussed on this moment, channelled by his one-track thought of finding Mary. He bent down, dragged Risler up by the collar and held his bloodied face just inches from his own. Edward could see fear and panic in Risler's dark eyes. He could feel his beer-laced breath on his face. 'Where is she?' Edward demanded.

'Who?' Risler whimpered. '*Who?*'

Edward let his right hand go, allowing his left hand to hold Risler's dead weight, drew his right arm back and smashed it into Risler's face. Edward's bloody knuckles met his nose with a horrible crunch. 'Where is she?' He could see that Risler's panic was growing and his resolve was shrinking. Edward drew back his hand again, ready for the next punch.

'Stop, please,' he begged. 'It wasn't my idea.'

Edward let Risler go and watched as he fell to his feet, like some pathetic beggar. 'Please.'

'Where is she?'

'The folly,' Risler spat.

With a jerking movement, Edward pushed Risler backwards, sending him crashing to the floor. His heart racing wildly, Edward ran at full pelt through the corridor and into the kitchen. From behind him he heard Risler calling, swearing and shouting.

'Hey!' Bastion screeched as Edward ploughed straight into Joan Leigh, sending an armful of crockery smashing to the stone floor. '*Eh! Mais, toi, qu'est-ce que tu as? Sorte de ma cuisine—espèce d'imbécile!*'

'Edward!' Joan yelled, stooping down to pick up the fallen crockery, but she was talking to an open door.

Edward was oblivious to the torrent of rain which saturated him to the skin seconds after leaving the house. In the diffused light from the illuminated windows on the east side of the house, Edward was just about able to make out the contours of the path. The most direct route to Mary would be to head to the edge of the lake then swim across it to the island. But Edward couldn't swim so he needed to take the boat. When he reached the lake, he was surrounded by a blanket of darkness. If there had been any kind of moonlight, then it was being shielded by the rolling black clouds above him. He was dismayed to have to slow his pace in order to negotiate the narrow path. One wrong foot and he would be in the lake. He was sure that by now Risler had raised the alarm. *Maybe I should have knocked him out cold*, Edward thought as he ran beside the water. The only sound came from the rain thrashing down on the surface of the lake.

A low noise came from the direction of the house. Edward turned to see a shadowed figure standing in the light of the kitchen.

Time was running out. He pushed his legs harder—he was almost at the boathouse. As he turned back, he noticed too late that the path had taken a minor turn and his left foot fell off the path and onto a slope of wet mud.

'Damn!' Edward yelled, as he tried to counteract an inevitable slide into the lake. He twisted his body and lurched to the right, reaching out to a thick clump of irises protruding from the bank. Clawing out with both hands, Edward managed to stabilise himself. He pulled himself back upright and winced at the pain shooting up his leg from his foot. *The boathouse is so close!* Edward slammed himself, as he hurried as best he could, trying to put minimum weight on his injured left foot.

Finally, he reached the door to the boathouse. Mercifully, it was open. When he hurried from the house and briefly considered his rash plan, he thought he would have to kick the door in, but with the pain searing in his foot, that would have been impossible. Edward shoved the door open and carefully lowered himself into the rowing boat. Taking the pair of oars in his hands, he used one to push off from the side. The boat slowly glided out from the confines of the boathouse into the thick sheets of rain; finally, it emerged fully onto the lake and Edward was able to extend the oars into the water.

'I'm coming, Mary,' Edward muttered. Just a few more minutes and they would be reunited. That idea spurred him on, made him pull harder and harder on the oars.

A sudden, deafening clap of thunder made him jump and he dropped one of the oars into the water. 'Damn it!' he yelled, reaching over into the freezing water.

A ferocious snap of lightening shot from the angry skies down into the woodland behind Blackfriars. That one glimmer of powerful light was enough for Edward to catch something awful in his peripheral vision. A figure in the water approaching his boat. The frame suggested that it was Risler. He was gaining on him fast.

Edward thrust the oars into the water and began to heave and thrust with all his might. It terrified him that his aggressor was protected by the joint wall of total darkness and the resonance of the hard rain.

Edward was just a few more strokes from reaching the island jetty when the assailant's wet hand grasped onto the side of the boat. Edward noticed too late and by the time he had raised his right foot to slam down onto the grappling hand, a second hand had gripped the side, hauling Risler's saturated body up behind it. Risler whipped his hand away and lunged at Edward, who tumbled into the boat from the force of his actions. Risler pulled himself into the boat and leapt onto Edward.

It took Edward a moment to regain his composure. As he had just demonstrated, Risler was no way a match for him and Edward used this knowledge to bolster himself mentally. He drew in a quick, deep breath and shoved Risler's heavy body from on top of him. Risler managed a weak punch, which glanced off Edward's chin.

Another crack and rumble of overhead thunder masked Risler's yelp, as Edward's tensed biceps thrust Risler backwards, banging his head on the boat's internal ribbing. Edward wasted no time and sent his right fist into Risler's face. After another punch, Edward stopped to take stock of the situation. Risler was whimpering in the bottom of the boat. *Should I just finish him off?* Edward wondered, desperate to reach Mary. He had visions of getting to the island only for Risler to follow him into the folly. He needed to finish the job. Edward drew his right hand back, ready for the punch when he suddenly lurched back, tumbling off the side of the boat.

Someone was pulling on the back of his collar.

A lightning strike briefly lit up the lake, but it only added to the confusion, as Edward fell backwards, plunging into the cold depths beside the boat. He was momentarily disorientated, reaching and fumbling about under water. His fingers touched something. The boat. He kicked and pushed towards it, feeling for the slated contours. Finally, he surfaced and took in a huge lungful of air. He desperately flung his head around, searching the murky lake for his second attacker. He turned his head towards the folly as a pair of heavy meaty hands lunged at his neck from behind and began to force him under.

Edward kicked furiously, trying to counteract the pushing action of his attacker, as the water began to nibble at his chin. The grip on his neck was such that Edward couldn't turn or use his arms to neutralise the force being exerted. His only choice was to keep kicking to stay afloat and try to prise the hands from his neck.

'Mary! Mary!' Edward shouted in desperation, before the first mouthful of water entered his lungs. He knew then that those would be his dying words and that they would be heard by nobody other than his assailants. He knew they were his dying words. He had no fight left to match the strength of the person shoving him under.

The water covered his mouth.

Every muscle in his legs screamed for more oxygen than his lungs could provide.

There were just moments left.

Using the final reserves of his energy, Edward clawed at the powerful hands that held him, but it was no use. The hands were locked firm. Whoever it was behind him didn't want him to die by strangulation, they wanted him to drown. At that moment Edward saw himself as an hourglass, the sand quickly passing from top to bottom; the time remaining in his life had reached the final grains. He thought of Mary and their baby. He saw himself at their impromptu wedding at Winchelsea church. He saw the baby's christening at the same place a few months later.

Edward smiled as his lungs filled with water.

Moments later, Bastion released his grip around Edward's throat. It was done.

Chapter Twenty

Taking no chances this time, Morton parked his Mini directly in front of The Keep entrance. It was a disabled parking bay, but he just didn't care. Having brought Jenny up to speed with the entirety of the Mercer Case on the journey over, she too didn't query his parking choices. The pair marched confidently into the archives, placed their coats and other items into the lockers and then made their way into the Reading Room.

Morton visibly slumped when he spotted his old adversary, Miss Latimer, once again on sentry duty. 'Oh God,' he mumbled as their eyes met.

Jenny turned to him. 'What's the matter?'

Just he went to answer, Jenny turned towards the desk and her eyes lit up. 'Deidre!'

Miss Latimer grinned. 'Jennifer Greenwood!'

Morton looked on incredulously as the pair bound towards each other, then embraced as if they were best friends who'd been separated for years.

'We haven't seen you here in a while,' Miss Latimer said. 'Still digging?'

'Oh yes! Actually, I'm here with my friend, Morton Farrier to follow some exciting new leads.' She turned to Morton. 'Morton, have you met Deidre Latimer—surely you must have done?'

Morton nodded. 'Yes, we're acquainted.'

'Thought you must know each other well—I expect this is a second home for you, Morton!'

Morton tried to smile but a vague pained look appeared on his face instead.

'It was actually Deidre here who got me into this genealogy lark,' Jenny continued. 'We're old friends from way back and when I told her of my *interests,* she pointed me in all the right places. I expect she's been as helpful in your work, Morton?'

Morton, seemingly paralysed by this most uncomfortable situation, couldn't find the words which struck the delicate balance between truth and lies. Luckily for him, Deidre stepped in.

Flashing an incredibly false smile in Morton's direction, she turned to Jenny. 'So what's this exciting new lead, then?'

Jenny, always on her guard, turned and checked around her then lowered her voice. 'I'll see how we get on today and let you know. Let's just say that my theory about Cecil and Philadelphia isn't looking so implausible all of a sudden.' Her volume returned to normal. You know, we really must meet up for dinner sometime.'

'Well, I'm free after work today if you'd like?'

'I can't today, I'm afraid—I came in Morton's car.' She turned to Morton. 'Unless you'd care to join us?'

Morton waited for his life to flash before his eyes. This had to be a near-death experience. Dinner with Deidre Latimer would be one of the worst types of tortures imaginable. At the moment, he could not think of a single thing that was a worse idea. He tried to disguise the look of sheer horror on his face. 'Er... I really can't,' Morton stammered. 'I need to get back...'

Deidre, replete with her own look of horror, stepped in again. 'Listen. You don't want to inconvenience your friend, Jenny. Let's go out for dinner together and I'll run you home afterwards. How does that sound?'

Jenny looked at Morton for approval.

'Absolutely,' he said, 'go ahead. That suits everyone.' Anything, anything, anything but him having to spend time with Deidre Latimer.

Jenny nodded her agreement and laughed. 'Okay, that would be lovely.'

'Marvellous,' Deidre said. She glanced at her watch. 'I'd best let you get on with it, we close in two hours' time.'

'Could we have a log-in please, Deidre,' Morton said, unable to help himself.

'Not a problem,' she said with a strange smile. As she walked away, Morton thought that he heard her crack her old joke of calling him *Moron* under her breath.

She turned back to her desk, picked up a small sliver of paper and handed it to Jenny.

'Thank you,' Jenny said with a smile, and they made their way to the banks of computer terminals in order to call up the necessary documents. 'She's such a lovely lady, isn't she?'

'Very thorough and knowledgeable,' Morton answered diplomatically.

A handful of researchers sat at the computers, eagerly transcribing and taking notes from the screens in front of them.

Morton headed to the first available computer, offered the chair to Jenny and slid one along for himself from the adjacent computer. He quickly typed in the log-in details provided by Miss Latimer.

'What's first, then?' Jenny whispered.

'If I concentrate on Martha, can you see what you can find on George Mansfield? Locate references for his birth, marriage and death certificates and I'll order them later. See if you can find his baptism and marriage at Winchelsea—shouldn't be too hard to locate. I've already got his burial record,' Morton said, as he signed into The Keep's website and ordered the admission records for St Thomas's School, Winchelsea 1873-1950, as well as the log book covering a similar period. At the back of his mind the whole journey had been Martha Stone's grave and the extraordinary idea proposed by Jenny. He had already ruled out a DNA test, which left him with the basic, traditional routes.

'Two steps ahead of you on that one,' Jenny said with a grin. 'One of the first things Deidre suggested I do, when I first became suspicious about George's parentage, was to determine what had been presented as facts on his certificates. I've got his birth, marriage and death certificates at home.'

Morton nodded. 'Could you email a copy of them to me when you get a moment?'

'Of course, I'll do it tonight.'

'Right, what about a baptism record?'

'Haven't looked for that, so I'll make a start now.'

'And is the marriage certificate you have the copy of made from General Register Office, or taken from the original register?'

'GRO copy. Do you want me to look up the original?'

'It wouldn't hurt,' Morton said. 'They should be identical except that the GRO copy has been transcribed. I prefer originals where I can because they have the actual signatures of the bride, groom and witnesses.'

'Very thorough,' she commented with a chuckle.

'Can I leave you to it?' he asked.

'Absolutely. I'll see what else I can dig up, too.'

'Jolly good. See you shortly,' Morton said, carrying his laptop and notepad over towards the Reference Room. He swiped his card on the silver pillar and the glass door slid open for him.

He found the room busier than on his previous visit, with researchers diligently and silently beavering away at their own genealogical quests. He often surreptitiously glanced at the documents being pored over, wondering at the nature of the research taking place.

Having found a seat on the back row, Morton fired up his laptop, set up his notepad and pencil and checked online to see if his documents had been delivered. They were both listed as 'Available', so Morton headed over to the help desk.

'Morton, how the devil are you?' Max Fairbrother asked jovially. Having been the senior archivist for more than thirty years at the old East Sussex Record Office and now The Keep, Max was on familiar terms with Morton.

'Morning, Max. Good, thanks. You?' Morton said, studying Max's bizarre choice of attire. He had a shocking Hawaiian shirt on with a pair of bleached ripped jeans. For a man in his late fifties, he looked plainly ridiculous.

'Very good, thank you. What can we do for you, today?'

'I've got some documents ready.'

'Brilliant,' Max said, as if it were the best news that he had ever heard. Ever since a previous case that Morton had worked on, where he had overlooked an indiscretion on the senior archivist's part, Max had gone out of his way to assist Morton. Max and Deidre were polar opposites as far as Morton was concerned. *Maybe things will change now that I've got Jenny for an ally*, Morton thought as he handed over his Reader's Ticket. Max took his ticket and scanned it. 'Any preference for which one first?' he asked.

'Admissions register, please.'

Max dramatically thrust back his wheeled office chair into the back room.

Morton rolled his eyes but said nothing. Max's mid-life crisis was evidently continuing, he thought.

'Here we go,' Max said, handing over the document. 'Any probs, give me a shout.'

'Thanks, will do,' Morton said.

Back at his seat, Morton eagerly opened the file. It ran in chronological order and listed name of child, number, admission date, date of birth, name of parent/guardian, address, previous school and date of withdrawal. Morton carefully ran his index finger down the names of the children, then back up the names of the parents, to ensure that he covered any discrepancies. When he reached the 1890s, some familiar names appeared. Charles Phillips had started at the school in 1891, Clara Ellingham and Jack Maslow started at the school in 1893 and Eliza Bootle in 1894. Also in 1893 Morton found the entry for Martha Stone, who had started at the school on the 8th November that year. Her leaving date was noted as the 18th February 1902—the day that she had died. He took out his digital camera and took photographs of all relevant pages before continuing his search. In 1896 he found the entry for the Mercer twins. Both entries were identical but for the forename. The girls were admitted to St Thomas's school on the 1st May 1896 and their address was listed as 3 Friar's Cottages, Winchelsea. Their parents were listed as Thomas and Katherine Mercer and their date of withdrawal was listed as the 26th April 1906. Morton photographed the page, then continued searching and photographing the subsequent pages in order to build up a clear picture of other children present in the school at the same time as the twins. He would then do as he had done with the staff at Blackfriars, and try and make contact with living descendants. *One of them must have known what happened to Mary.* From a quick initial assessment of the entries and withdrawals from the school, Morton estimated that there were probably between twelve and twenty children at the school with Mary and Edith. He added previously unknown children to the friends list, then continued to search the register until its conclusion in July 1950.

Morton carried the register back to the help desk, returned it to Max and was then issued with the log book for the school. It was an A5-sized, leather-bound book that retained the typical musty smell of such an old document. He could spend hours poring over such wonderful embodiments of history, but knew that he needed to prioritise his searching to the relevant time period. Sitting back at his work station, Morton opened the ledger and flipped to 1896. The book was a day-by-day account of the comings and goings of school life, recorded by the headmaster, Mr P. Vaughn. Morton read the entries with keen historical interest. Despite their lack of direct connection to the Mercer Case, it painted an interesting and colourful picture of Mary and Edith's early life.

25th January 1896
No fewer than 9 children have left the school lately, their parents being obliged to leave the village in search of employment. The children, who have left, were among the best in their various standards.

206

2nd February 1896

Police Constable Groves came this morning about some boys using catapults &
damaging the church clock. They were cautioned and their instruments taken away.

4th May 1896

Average lower than last week, owing to the "measles" having broken out afresh,
and amongst the elder children. It has hitherto been confined to the outskirts of the
village—now it is in the midst of us.

15th October 1896

School routine resumed as usual though the holidays have been lengthened owing to
the delay in picking, caused by rains, the school was not fully attended.

19th January 1897

No more than 6 children presented themselves…

30th May 1897

The attendance is very thin indeed. The children are employed with their parents in
the hop gardens—knitting discontinued.

25th November 1898

Four boys away "beating" for Lord Rothborne. Anything seems to be allowed in this
village…

23rd January 1901

Gave a short lesson on the death of our beloved Queen, who peacefully passed away
on Tuesday evening at 6.30 in the year 1901 at Osbourne House, Isle of Wight.

3rd March 1901

Singing lessons on Friday morning instead of the usual arithmetic lesson. Mary
Mercer and Martha Stone kept in the whole dinner-time on Friday for playing
truant on the previous afternoon.

Morton read the previous entry several times. It was simple and yet
spoke volumes about the two girls and their friendship. He hoped that
whatever had happened to Martha would be noted in the coming
pages. He returned to the ledger and carried on his searches into 1902.

8th February 1902

The school is very cold this morning. The correspondent says we cannot have any
more coal. The week opens with a very thin attendance owing to the prevailing
epidemic of influenza.

10th February 1902

Still no coal, and the school very cold. Obliged to let 2 boys saw up Hop Poles to
warm the rooms a little, infants nearly crying with cold.

18th February 1902

I regret to say that influenza has again broken out amongst the children and one child, Martha Stone died this morning.

Morton stopped reading and stared at the entry, transfixed.

Chapter Twenty-One

How was this possible? As if the headstone had not been proof enough, here it was in black and white: Martha Stone had died. And yet, in 1911 Martha Stone had apparently emigrated to Nova Scotia, where she had remained until at least 1925.

Morton's mind went into overdrive as he began to make tentative links between the facts that he already knew, the theories proposed by Jenny and the newly acquired knowledge of Martha Stone's death. At the moment, it was still tentative to say the least. He needed more—much more—to even *consider* suggesting anything to Ray Mercer.

Morton photographed the entry and moved on. On the following page, Martha's burial was noted.

1st March 1902
The little girl (Martha Stone) who was taken ill a few days before the annual inspection was buried to-day. The children sent a wreath & a cross which were placed on her grave. The teachers also sent a wreath & cross.

After photographing the page and continuing his search, Morton quite soon found another entry that made him sit up with interest.

18th March 1902
One girl, Mary Mercer punished, by wearing two placards on her coat, before the whole school, for appalling conduct during her dinner-hour. Her recent conduct has been the subject of a managers' meeting last week.

Morton could only speculate at Mary's behaviour. One possibility was that Martha's death had had a severe impact on her.

'Anything?' Jenny suddenly asked, peering over his shoulder at where his index finger pointed. 'Oh. Naughty girl!'

Morton turned. 'Yeah. I just found Martha's death—she died of the flu.'

She lowered her glasses and looked at Morton. 'Are you now thinking that Mary travelled to Canada under a pseudonym, using her dead school friend's name?'

'It's certainly a theory,' Morton said nonchalantly.

'Oh, come on, Morton,' Jenny persisted. 'It's looking *much* more probable than a theory.'

Morton was indignant in his belief that he should never accept something as fact without substantial proof. His usual ideal was three pieces of separate evidence. 'We'll see. How are you getting on?'

Jenny turned her nose up. 'Not great. I found George's baptism fairly quickly. It was in November 1911, just a few weeks after his birth. I've taken a photo of it, but there's nothing unusual about it—same for his marriage. I've spent the rest of the time on the Findmypast website digging around, but nothing so far.'

From the desk in front of him, Morton noticed his phone light up. Juliette was calling. 'Just need to take this—can you watch my stuff for a moment?'

'Of course,' Jenny replied.

Morton answered the call with a hushed whisper. 'Hang on,' he said, as Max pressed the door release, allowing him to leave the Reference Room. Once safely in the lobby, Morton returned the phone to his ear. 'Hi, Juliette. You okay?'

'Yeah, fine. You?' Juliette said.

'Interesting day—will tell all later,' he said, taking a seat at one of the small round tables. 'I'm doing some research at The Keep at the moment. Oh, that reminds me—I'm going to call in on Dad on the way home—do what you suggested and talk to him about Aunty Margaret and the wedding.'

'That's good. I'll be finishing work in about an hour. Listen, I just wanted to ring to tell you that I've been making discreet enquiries at work today about the investigation into Douglas Catt's murder. At the moment they're none the wiser about why he was shot. One theory is that he was in the wrong place at the wrong time, like you wondered. But, Douglas seems to have a *lot* of enemies and the killer wasn't a professional hit-man, like you thought he might have been.'

'How do they know that?' Morton asked.

'He just made a lot of mistakes. The kill wasn't clean, he left footprints and DNA material, and grainy CCTV from the pub over the road shows him tripping over a gravestone in the churchyard. A bit hapless and bungling really. Even so, be careful, because he's not been caught yet and, if you're right, then he could still be after you.'

'Will do,' he muttered. All the while he was ensconced in the archives he felt safe enough. He was more worried about her, but he

210

knew that she couldn't be safer anywhere else than surrounded by dozens of police officers.

'The other reason I was ringing was because, whilst I was in the station today, I had a chance to speak to Susan Catt. I caught her quickly as she was leaving following another interview.'

'Did you ask her why her husband was so desperate for me to stop my work?' Morton asked.

'Well, in a bit more of a diplomatic, pillar of the community kind of way, yes. She wouldn't reveal anything to me but she wants to meet you. I'll text you her mobile number in a minute.'

Could be interesting, Morton thought.

'Just be careful,' Juliette warned. 'Meet her somewhere public. I don't trust her at all.'

'You don't think she killed Douglas, do you?' Morton asked incredulously.

Juliette laughed in a mocking way. 'No chance. I said the killer was hapless, not a dappy wet fish. Plus, she's got a very good alibi for the evening of the murder.'

'Fair enough.'

'Got to go—about to go off on patrol now. See you later. Love you.'

'Love you too—see you tonight.'

'Be careful!' she warned.

'I will. Bye.' Morton ended the call and sat for a moment thinking about the next steps that he needed to take. He should go online and find Martha's parents in 1911. If the census enumerator had done his job properly, and they had told the truth, then their entry on the 1911 census should show that they had lost a child. It would be worth checking if passport applications existed and disembarkation records for the period, too. *Could Mary have escaped Blackfriars, leaving her child behind and run off to Canada under a false name?* As much as he had initially doubted the theory, more and more evidence was rising to the surface to prove, rather than to disprove it, at least the latter part of that theory.

Morton made his way back to the Reference Room, swanning past Miss Latimer just like the good old days where their mutual hatred needed no disguise.

'Right,' Morton said when he reached Jenny at his workstation. 'I'm going to see if historic passport applications are available online— I'm fairly sure that the National Archives has some on their website. If

211

so, would you mind trawling them to see if you can find anything for Martha Stone or Mary Mercer in 1911?'

'I'd be delighted,' Jenny said, rubbing her hands with glee.

Morton opened up a web browser and navigated to the National Archives website. He used their search facility to look up passport applications and quickly found what he was looking for. 'Here,' he said to Jenny. 'FO—for Foreign Office—611. Then go to file 21, which covers the period 1909-1912. It's a free document but pretty large by the looks of it,' he said as he clicked to download the file. 'Three hundred and sixty-three hand-written pages.' Morton turned to Jenny with a grin then began scrolling down through the file.

'Shouldn't take long—it's in alphabetical order,' Jenny noted.

'Hmm, but only by first letter. You then need to search through pages and pages of haphazard surnames beginning with M and S. Is that okay?'

'Oh yes, absolutely!' Jenny said. 'I'll get right to it.'

'Great,' Morton said, watching Jenny head back into the Reading Room. Normally, he liked to research *everything* for himself, but with this slightly outlandish theory and the approaching closure of the archives for the day, he was happy to delegate some of the less important work to someone else.

Morton used the Ancestry website to gain the necessary reference to order Martha Stone's death certificate; he then placed the order on a priority service. The certificate would be unlikely to give him any new information, but he wanted to really make sure that there was only one Martha Stone and that she had died and was buried in Winchelsea, thus making the Martha Stone living in Nova Scotia someone living under a false name.

Next, Morton turned his attention to the 1911 census. Within seconds he had the record of Martha Stone's parents. They were still living in Peace Cottage, Friar's Road. The census return showed that they had been married for twenty-three years. One child had been born alive. One child had died. There were no surviving children to James and Flora Stone.

Morton saved the image of the census return, now having sufficient evidence to show that Martha Stone had died and that *somebody* was living under a false name in Canada. Somebody that Edith Leyden visited in 1925.

Opening up a fresh web browser, Morton ran some generic Google searches into gaining false passports for the period around

Mary's disappearance. He discovered that photographs of the passport holder were only added in 1914, so Mary could easily have passed as someone else born within just a few years of her. Morton knew, as many genealogists knew, that it was only until very recently that *anyone* could gain an original birth certificate if they could provide enough of the background family details included on them. One hundred years ago, it would have been even easier. Mary would have known the Stone family well enough to have been able to answer the basic questions asked in order to gain a birth certificate and then a passport.

A while later, Jenny returned. 'Nothing under Mercer, but I found this,' she said with a telling grin. She held up her digital camera with the rear-viewer facing Morton. He strained his eyes to see. November 26th 1911, Stone, Miss Martha. It was brief, but firm proof that *someone* had been issued with a passport under that name.

'Take a seat,' Morton instructed. 'Let's see if this Martha Stone appears on passenger lists.'

Jenny pulled up a swivel chair and tucked herself up close to Morton's chair. 'It's getting very exciting!'

Morton smiled and opened up a search for outward passenger lists 1890-1960. He typed in Martha Stone, date of travel 1911. One result. Morton clicked to see a scan of the original page.

Returns of passengers leaving the United Kingdom in ships bound for places out of Europe, and not within the Mediterranean Sea.
Port of Departure: *Bristol. Date of departure: December 12th 1911*
Ship's name: *Royal Edward*
Steamship line: *Royal Line, Canadian Northern Steamships Limited*
Where bound: *Halifax, Canada*

Morton scrolled down the list of passengers until he found her.

Martha Stone, 3rd class, housemaid, single, English, aged 21.

Both Morton and Jenny stared at the screen for some time before either of them spoke.

'What date was George Mansfield baptised?' Morton finally asked.

Jenny switched her camera back on and scrolled through the images that she had taken. 'Twenty-first of November.'

213

'And you thought that was about three weeks after his birth?' Morton quizzed.

'About that. I remember that he was definitely born in November 1911.'

Morton nodded. 'Okay. Nine months prior to that takes us to...' he stopped and thought for a moment. 'February 1911—when Mary and Edward were working and living under the same roof. Two months later, Edward tries to get a marriage licence but Mary disappears. One month after that, he turns up dead in the Blackfriars lake. Then nothing happens.'

'Until we reach November,' Jenny continued, 'when George Mansfield is born. Soon after, a female, who knew Martha Stone very well, travels to Canada, where she remains until at least 1925 when Edith Leyden travels out to see her.' Jenny paused. 'And then Martha Stone's trail goes cold.'

'Let's try and find her,' Morton said, returning his focus to his laptop. He opened up the Canadian Ancestry website to search the millions of records available pertaining to Canada. First, he tried Nova Scotia death records 1890-1960, but his search returned zero hits. 'So she didn't die in Nova Scotia before 1960,' Morton mumbled, before widening his search to the rest of the country. Of the few possibilities that appeared on screen, it took just a few minutes of cross-referencing in other records to eliminate them.

Jenny sighed. 'Doesn't look like Martha remained in Canada, does it?'

'Well, not necessarily,' Morton said. 'We don't have any more censuses available to us and, if she died in Nova Scotia after 1960, then she wouldn't show up. She could very easily have lived in the next house and we'd not know about it. I could pay the Nova Scotia Archives to search for her, but judging by their email, it would be quite a lengthy process.' He was already processing his next step and began quickly tapping at the keyboard. 'Here we are. Canada Voter's Lists 1935 to 1980.'

Jenny watched with nervous anticipation as Morton typed Martha's name into the search box. Several results in five-yearly blocks appeared onscreen. 'Looks like she's in Ontario in 1935,' Jenny said excitedly. 'Click it!'

Morton smiled and did as he was told. 'Stone, Miss Martha, teacher.'

'Living at...' Jenny pushed her glasses back onto the bridge of her nose. '102 Wellington Street.'

Morton returned to the previous screen, scrolled down to the next block of entries and selected 1940. 'Still at the same address,' Morton confirmed. He then repeated the process, checking and finding her living at the same address every five years.

'She's gone,' Jenny said, when the 1965 Voter List failed to show Martha. He continued his search until 1980 but there was no sign of her.

Morton frowned and double-checked the results list but to no avail. 'So... Martha lived in Ontario from 1935 until sometime between 1960 and 1965. Death records online only run to 1938, so there's every possibility that she died there. When I get home tonight, I'll run some searches and contact cemeteries in the area.'

'What about passenger lists?' Jenny asked. 'She could have come back to England.'

'Yeah, that thought had crossed my mind,' Morton said. 'The problem is most available passenger lists end in 1960, when we know she was still alive and well in Ontario. I'll look into it more later. The fact that she was a teacher up until 1960 in one city is interesting. There might be records for her. There's also a good possibility that children she once taught might still remember her.'

'And how do you plan on finding them?' Jenny laughed.

'I'm not—I'm going to get them to come to me. That's what forums and message boards are for, Mrs Greenwood!' Morton teased.

Jenny smiled and watched as he returned to the Canadian Ancestry main page, then navigated through to the Message Boards whose tag line read *The world's largest online genealogy community with over 25 Million posts on more than 198,000 boards.* Faster than she could even read the words, Morton tapped out a quick request for anyone who knew of, or was taught by Martha Stone to get in touch.

'There—done!' Morton said as he hit the enter button.

Jenny and Morton smiled conspiratorially at one another.

'Ladies and gentlemen,' Max Fairbrother shouted from behind the help desk, 'the archive will be closing in five minutes. That's five minutes.'

'Guess that's us done, then,' Jenny remarked, the disappointment evident in her voice.

Morton could see how saddened she was by the day's being over. 'You've got your nice meal with Deidre to look forward to.'

215

Jenny visibly cheered. 'Oh, yes. Are you sure we can't tempt you? She might even be able to suggest something on the case that we hadn't thought of.'

'Quite sure,' Morton insisted. 'I'm planning on calling in on my dad anyway. You two go ahead and have a good catch up. I'll keep you up to date—don't worry.'

Jenny smiled. 'Come on then, let's go. We're almost the last left!'

'I'm *always* the last left,' Morton groaned, as he shut down his laptop and scooped up all his belongings.

'Bye, Max,' Morton called as they left the Reference Room.

'Cheerio, buddy,' Max replied.

Miss Latimer was still on duty, guarding the Reading Room like a vicious Rottweiler, snapping at people to hurry up and leave. She smiled when she spotted Jenny. 'Be with you in a moment.'

'Lovely,' Jenny answered, before following Morton into the busy cloakroom. 'Well, it's been a lovely day, Morton. I'll get George's certificates over to you tonight and then we'll take it from there.'

'Great,' Morton answered. 'I've had a good day, too. It's been nice having someone to work with. Have a lovely evening.'

'Thanks. Bye.'

'Bye.'

Mark Drury was feeling anxious. He was getting impatient waiting for Morton to appear. All afternoon he had sat in his car, fiddling with his phone and watching as the GPS device tracked Morton's every move, even within the confines of the archive. *What the hell can anyone want to do in a crappy old library all day?* Mark asked himself. *How bloody boring is this bloke?*

Finally, the steady stream of people leaving the building suggested that it was closing time. The GPS signal confirmed his theory. He thrust the gun into the waistband of his jeans, got out of his car and made his way inside the building.

'I'm sorry, sir, but the archive is closed now,' the lady behind the reception desk called to him as he strode past.

'Just left something in the locker,' Mark said, flashing the receptionist an oafish smile. He could see that the look on her face suggested that she questioned if she had ever seen him before now, but she declined to comment further.

216

Mark made his way to a locker out of her view and began to pretend to fiddle inside it. From this vantage point, at the tip of the bank of central lockers, he could see if Morton approached from either side.

There he was.

Mark pulled his head back slightly and watched as Morton passed the end of the lockers and headed into the toilet. Now was his chance. He patted the gun, which was sitting comfortably on his right thigh and waltzed down between the lockers towards the toilet. He briefly considered taking him out in the toilet, but quickly dismissed it when he spotted CCTV cameras pointing at the main entrance. *No, I'll flash the gun, march him out to his car, then take him off somewhere quiet.* He grinned and made his way to the toilet.

'Mark!' a voice suddenly proclaimed.

He couldn't contain his surprise and jumped at being recognised. *Damn it.* 'Hi, Jenny,' Mark said coolly. 'What are you doing here?'

Jenny grinned. 'I was about to ask you the same thing. This doesn't strike me as your cup of tea somehow.'

'Yeah, just doing some stuff,' Mark said vaguely, looking around the room for a clue as to what actually went on inside the building. His eyes settled on a digital display. 'Boats and stuff.'

Jenny nodded with a vague look of understanding on her face. It was evidently enough not to arouse her suspicions. 'Oh, lovely.'

'See you later,' he said, hurrying past her and out the door, cursing to himself for having been caught. There was no way he could do anything now that he had been recognised. *Damn that stupid bitch!*

Mark reached his car, climbed in and wound down the window. A bead of sweat ruptured on his forehead and under his arms, as the adrenalin raged around his body, poised for what he had just been about to do. *This has got to happen. Today.* He thumped the steering wheel with his fist, then had an idea. He would go ahead of Morton and wait for him at home. He grinned, pulled a quantity of phlegm down the back of his throat, spat it out of the window and sped out of The Keep car park with his tyres squealing on the tarmac.

Morton parked outside his dad's semi-detached house in Hastings with apprehension. He switched off the ignition and just sat, staring at the house for a moment. Although his relationship with his father had

217

improved a great deal since he had been told about his biological mother's true identity, Morton still felt pangs of anxiety when left alone in his father's presence. It was at times like this that he relied heavily on Juliette to assuage the awkwardness of the situation. When he looked back on the years between his adoptive mother's death and having his true past revealed to him, Morton realised that he had often treated his father with an immature flippant attitude, bordering on contempt. It was no justification by any means, but Morton had spent much of his life feeling like the fifth wheel of the Farrier household and that his adoptive brother, Jeremy, was consistently treated as the miracle child who could do no wrong.

Morton rubbed his tired temples and breathed slowly and deeply. It was time to grow up and move on from the past. In just a few weeks' time, he would turn forty. Forty years old and he had no wife or children to show for it. *Did that matter?* Before he had met Juliette, he had always put his career first and the thought of being saddled with a wife and child had once filled him with genuine horror. And yet now, he wondered if his only objection to marriage and, maybe one day having children, was because he had always believed that that was the way his life was destined to be. Was it really all based on an outdated notion that he no longer believed in? He wasn't sure.

'See what you do to me, Dad,' Morton mumbled to himself. It was true that the only time he became so introspective and maudlin was when he returned to his father's memory-filled house. This house embodied his childhood, his teenage years, his mother's death and the news of his being adopted. With a flash of clarity, he realised that this was the place that enveloped his past and could govern his future—if he allowed it to.

A loud beeping from his phone jolted him from his mawkishness. It was a short text message from Juliette, giving him Susan Catt's mobile number. Morton looked at the number, deliberating about whether to call or text. After such a long heavy day and with what he was about to potentially face, he didn't feel as though he had the energy for a phone call. He typed out a quick text to her, suggesting that they meet somewhere in the next few days. He clicked 'send', pocketed the phone, then looked up at the house again. His father was waving at him with a huge frown dominating his face, as he looked left and right to see if Morton had been spotted sitting in his car staring at the house. Morton smiled, took a deep breath and climbed from his car.

'Hi, Dad,' Morton said cheerfully, as the front door opened.

'What the devil are you doing out there?' his dad barked. 'You looked daft as a brush, looking up at the house without getting out. I hope Dave and Sandra aren't in.'

'Sorry, just thinking,' Morton said as he stepped inside the house.

'Dave's running the Neighbourhood Watch now that Geoff's passed on, so I expect you've been clocked.'

'Oh dear,' Morton said sarcastically, then quickly reprimanded himself for his tone.

'Do you want a cup of tea?' his father asked when they reached the lounge.

'Coffee, please,' Morton answered.

'You don't have sugar, do you?'

'No,' he said, biting his tongue. *Surely his own father should know after thirty-nine years that he didn't take sugar?*

'Go into the lounge and I'll bring it through.'

Morton sat in the quiet room, deliberately choosing the armchair by the window rather than the sofa which faced the awful family portrait hanging above the fireplace of him, Jeremy and their mum and dad. Not only did he hate the way that he looked in the portrait, but it always reminded him of his mum's death, as it was the last picture that existed of all of them together before she died. Having chosen the seat so as not to have to look at the portrait, he found himself craning his neck to see it properly. He looked his mother in the eyes and allowed happy memories to return. He smiled at her as his eyes filled with tears. 'I miss you, Mum,' he whispered.

'Here we are,' his father's voice boomed as he entered the room carrying a tray. 'Only got chocolate bourbons, I'm afraid.'

Morton quickly ran his sleeve over his moist eyes. 'That's fine.' He watched as his father's doddery hand placed the cups and china plate of biscuits on the coffee table between them. After suffering from severe heart trouble last year, his father had, albeit very reluctantly, had a change of lifestyle. He had joined the local gym and cut back on his cooked breakfasts and he now looked much better for it. 'You're looking well.'

His father waved his hand dismissively. 'It's all that rabbit food I'm eating. Do you know what the dietician suggested I eat once a fortnight? Millet! Ha!' he said with a laugh. 'Does she think I'm a budgie or something?' He laughed again. 'I ask you.'

'It's obviously working, though,' Morton said, taking a bourbon. He observed his father and waited for the inevitable comeback along the lines of *If this is going to make me live longer, then I'd rather not live*, but it didn't come. It seemed his father's attitude as well as his appearance had shifted. *Maybe broaching the subject of Aunty Margaret won't be so painful after all*, Morton hoped.

'How's work?' his father asked.

'Great, thank you. I'm working on a really interesting case at the moment,' Morton began. Ever since his last high-profile case, his father had suddenly sat up with interest. He had even told the neighbours with a hint of pride that his son was the forensic genealogist who had brought down the Windsor-Sackville family. Up until then he had regarded Morton's career with derision and open scorn.

'Go on,' his father encouraged.

Morton recounted the highlights of the case, carefully choosing the parts which sounded the most exciting.

His father looked impressed. 'Very enthralling.'

With his story over, a slight pause hung in the air, as both men sipped their drinks. Morton used the gap in conversation to broach the subject of Aunty Margaret. *Here's where it all goes horribly wrong*, Morton thought. But he had to do it. The past would forever have a grip on him until he began to resolve the issue. Forever delaying meeting Aunty Margaret was not an option. Neither was discussing at his brother's wedding, her rape at the age of sixteen. Even worse would be to pretend that nothing had changed. 'I wanted to ask you something about the wedding,' Morton ventured carefully. 'I...I'm not sure about what I can say to Aunty Margaret...' Suddenly, his mouth had dried and he struggled to swallow.

'She very much doubts she'll be coming to the wedding,' his father said flatly.

'Oh?' Morton said.

'She's got lady troubles,' he said, with an indistinct gesture towards his waist. 'She's due to have a big operation in a few weeks to... sort it all out. She's been told she can't do much for about six weeks, so unless the operation gets moved, the wedding's sadly out of the question.'

Morton wasn't sure how to process the news that his Aunty Margaret wouldn't be at the wedding. On the one hand, he was greatly relieved that there would be no awkwardness between them and he could just relax and enjoy the occasion. On the other hand, it was delaying the inevitable. He would have to see her again one day...

A short silence began to draw out, gradually emphasising the elephant in the room to which Morton had just referred. He felt as though someone was slowly strangling him from behind, pressing and squashing his vocal chords. *Say it!* But no words would come. He looked over at his father and waited for him to swallow his mouthful of tea. Finally, their eyes locked. *Say it!*

'I expect you're dithering around asking me what she knows,' his father said, unexpectedly.

Morton nodded, still unable to speak.

His father set down his tea and cleared his throat. 'I told her about the situation when I got out of hospital last year; she knows everything,' he said.

Morton waited for more to follow, but, true to form, his father felt that no further explanation was required. It struck him as interesting that he had heard nothing from her since being told—just the usual Christmas card with the annual syrupy round-robin letter to tell everyone how their family had fared during the past year. It definitely didn't include the lines 'Discovered that my nephew, who is actually my biological son, now knows the truth!' *Did that mean she had taken the news badly?* He had to ask, as painful and uncomfortable as it might be for his father. 'How did she take it?' he asked quietly.

'She was a bit upset at first,' he said. 'She needed time—I think she still does. Her main worry is that you understand her reasons. I assured her that you understood.' He looked seriously at Morton. 'You do understand, don't you, Morton?'

Morton nodded that he understood, although deep down he didn't know *how* he felt about it. The bottom line, despite all the reasons offered, was that his own biological mother had abandoned him at birth and, as far as she was concerned, wanted nothing maternally to do with him. She had then gone on to have her own two daughters. As a forensic genealogist, he couldn't ignore the facts.

His father smiled. 'Then that's it—everything's fine. Back to normal.'

But it wasn't fine. And it wasn't back to normal. Before he could ask any more questions, his father swiftly changed the subject.

'How's Juliette?'

And that was it, subject changed. Morton knew better than to steer his father back to the previous conversation, so he accepted it. 'She's fine, getting on well with her police training.'

'Oh right. Tell me about it.'

An hour later, just as dusk began to stretch and pull at the shadows, Morton stepped into his front door. 'Hi,' he called out, kicking off his shoes. There was no answer and the house was quiet. *She's probably asleep on the sofa. Or gone out for a jog or to get something for dinner.* With his laptop under his arm, Morton stuck his head into the lounge. The room was empty, so he pulled out his mobile and tapped out a quick text. *Home. Where are you? xx* He clicked 'send' and began to make his way up to the study. He probably had a few minutes to get a bit more done on the Mercer Case before she returned. He was quite looking forward to adding all the new details to his study wall. Just then, he heard Juliette's phone beep upstairs. She was in the study.

Morton padded up to the top of the stairs. The study door was slightly ajar. He pushed it open. 'Hi...' he said, then stopped quickly. Juliette was sitting in his office chair, bound with blue rope, her mouth gagged with tape. Standing over her, with a vulgar grin on his face, was a man he recognised but couldn't immediately place. He held a gun to Juliette's temple. She was trying to appear threatening and defiant but Morton could see the terror in her eyes.

Chapter Twenty-Two

Wednesday 1st November 1911

It was working. Her astute plan was working. The future of the Mansfield family was being secured, their tenure on Blackfriars and their centuries-long high standing in society would continue for generations to come. A Mansfield baby—God-willing, a boy—was due imminently. Lady Rothborne was alone in her room, perched nervously at the edge of her bed, waiting. She had eaten nothing all day and her stomach was starting to cramp. *When will there be news? Dr Leyden was called to Philadelphia's room more than an hour ago. There must surely be something to report,* she thought. She had personally requested that Dr Leyden himself keep her updated with news of the arrival. As time passed, she began to fear the worst. *What if there were complications?* She strengthened herself and sat up straight. She needed to exercise patience.

And, sure enough, her patience paid off when, forty minutes later, there was a light tapping at the door. Lady Rothborne smiled a small, faint smile. 'Come in.'

An incensed snarl beset her face when she was not greeted by Dr Leyden, but by Mr Risler. 'I specifically asked not to be disturbed,' she growled.

Mr Risler lowered his head deferentially. 'I do apologise, Lady Rothborne. I thought it prudent to keep you informed of some developments.'

Lady Rothborne stood, her body rigid and commanding, despite her aging years. 'Developments?'

'Your nephew, Frederick Mansfield, has arrived unexpectedly. He seems under the influence of alcohol and is most insistent at being present at the birth.'

Lady Rothborne felt her pulse quicken and her throat tighten. 'That's the most absurd, disgusting idea that I have ever heard. Disgraceful man. Alert Lord Rothborne and request that he get rid of him at once.'

'Yes, Your Ladyship,' Mr Risler said.

Turning her back to the door, Lady Rothborne began to make her way to the window. When her bedroom door did not shut, she

223

turned to see Mr Risler still standing there with an apologetic look on his face. 'What is it?' she demanded.

'There's something else,' Mr Risler began. 'Mrs Caroline Ransom is in the kitchen demanding to see a member of the family.'

Lady Rothborne scowled. 'Tell her to go away. Who is she? Demanding to see one of the family. Why did you even entertain such a person, Risler? And on such a day as today.'

'She's the sister of Miss Mercer,' Mr Risler said, shifting uncomfortably. 'She's under the impression that Miss Mercer is here and is expecting a child at any moment.'

Lady Rothborne's perfect poise faltered and she stumbled.

'Your ladyship,' Mr Risler called, hurrying to her aid.

'Get off,' she scolded, sitting herself down on the bed. 'Who knows that she's here?'

'Just myself and Monsieur Bastion at the moment.'

'Take her to the library and see to it that nobody is made aware of her visit. I will speak with her presently. I trust that is all the *developments*?'

'Yes, Lady Rothborne.' Mr Risler bowed his head and backed from the room.

Clenching her fists to control a slight tremble that had wracked her whole body, Lady Rothborne stood stoically. She knew that in the next few minutes, the fate of her family's future would be sealed: history was about to be written.

Elegantly and gracefully, Lady Rothborne left her room. From the disturbance emanating from the floor below, she surmised that Cecil had been unable to prevent her dreadful nephew from reaching Philadelphia's chamber. She prayed that she was not too late.

Standing outside Philadelphia's bedroom, her disapproving eyes fell upon Frederick with his open shirt, dishevelled hair and a general stench of fetid alcohol. He was grinning from ear to ear, as if he had just been told the greatest joke on earth. Behind him, forcing one arm bent back between his shoulder blades, stood his angry cousin, Cecil.

'Hello dearest Aunt,' Frederick slurred. 'I've come to pay my respects.' With a wriggle and a fierce wrench, Frederick released himself from Cecil's grip.

With the force of an angry bull, Lady Rothborne strode to Philadelphia's door. 'You will *not* be permitted entry into a lady's boudoir in this house at any time,' she hissed. 'You most certainly will *never* be permitted entry when such an intimate event is taking place.

224

Your father would be disgusted.' Lady Rothborne stood tall and firm in front of Philadelphia's bedroom door.

'Ouch!' Frederick moaned, turning back towards Cecil. 'No need to be so brutal, Cousin dearest. I just wanted to wish my dear Philly well.'

'It is uncouth, it is vulgar and it is *not* going to happen,' Lady Rothborne ranted. 'Kindly take to your room with a glass of water for a few hours.'

The distinct burst of a new-born baby's cry resounded from the bedroom, cutting through the commotion. Everyone stopped and stared as a happy sweat-covered Dr Leyden pulled open the door. 'A boy,' he said breathlessly. 'Come and meet him.'

A subtle nod of the head by Dr Leyden at Lady Rothborne told her that she could permit Frederick's entry into the room.

Lady Rothborne, Frederick and Cecil walked behind Dr Leyden into the bedroom. Looking hot and tired, Philadelphia sat up in bed carefully cradling her new baby in her arms. She was smiling and seemed oblivious to the new arrivals.

Lady Rothborne heaved a sigh of relief when she saw the tiny baby with its small tuft of bright red hair. A boy. A Mansfield boy in fine health. Under normal circumstances, she might have allowed herself to shed a tear but there was still work to be done. Only part of the story was written.

Cecil rushed to his wife's side and gently kissed her on the lips, before kissing his new-born son.

Lady Rothborne turned her attention to Frederick. He was transfixed by the baby and all the colour had drained from his face. 'I think it's time you left Blackfriars,' she said quietly. 'For good. No more impromptu visits. No more annuities. You need to stand on your own two feet. Goodbye, Frederick.' She determined right there and then, that the family would no longer suffer this man.

Frederick opened his mouth as if to speak, but nothing came out. He staggered from the room, slamming the door behind him.

The baby screamed his startled response and Lady Rothborne smiled. Her next problem was Caroline Ransom.

Mrs Cuff sat in the servants' hall beside Risler's vacant seat. All the other servants were seated and silent, just as she had demanded them to be. Mrs Cuff stared at her empty plate. She had requested no food when the under-butler had offered it. She felt sick and had no appetite.

225

The mood amongst the servants was, after many months of despondency and sorrow following Edward Mercer's death, positively euphoric. Even the generally more glum staff were delighted at the prospect of a new baby arriving at Blackfriars. The older members recalled that the last birth had been with Lord Cecil himself, way back in 1880. Before she had ordered silence, there had been excited talk of parties, champagne and extra holiday days. She couldn't stand it. The euphoria was based on a horrible, sordid lie. After what had happened to Edward when she had told him the truth, Mrs Cuff had vowed to keep silent on the matter and allow events to evolve and unfold without her interference. But this morning, with all the hype and excitement rippling and bubbling through the hierarchies of the house, she could take the disgusting ruse no longer and had slipped unnoticed out of the house to the Mercer household.

Mary's older sister, Caroline had answered the door with a grimace. 'What?'

Mrs Cuff had looked uncertainly at the surly, unwelcoming face and turned to leave.

'What do you want?' Caroline had called after her.

Mrs Cuff had stopped and knew she just needed to say it. Come what may, she needed to unburden herself. She had moved closer to Caroline and lowered her voice. 'I know something about Mary. May I come in?'

Caroline had shown Mrs Cuff into the tiny lounge and directed her to a chair.

'Mary's in Scotland. What about it?' Caroline had barked.

Mrs Cuff, for many reasons, had needed this to be over quickly. She had had no time or desire to discuss the subject in detail. 'Mary's being held—I believe against her will—at Blackfriars. Any moment now she's going to give birth and the baby will be kept by Lord and Lady Rothborne, who are unable to have children of their own.'

Caroline, as expected, had been stunned into shocked silence.

Mrs Cuff was brought back to her present surroundings in the servants' hall by the gentle thud of the door closing and heavy footsteps heading towards her. She looked up and saw the beaming face of Mr Risler.

The sound of wood scraping stone resounded around the room as the servants pushed their chairs back to stand for the entrance of the butler.

Mr Risler indicated that they could sit. 'I have some wonderful, delightful news!' he chirped. 'It is my great pleasure to announce the safe arrival of Master George Richard Mansfield.'

Mrs Cuff smiled, unable to look anybody in the eyes and joined in with the chorus of clapping and cheering that erupted around the room.

'On this occasion...' Mr Risler began to say over the din, but nobody was listening. Talk had returned to parties and time off. Mr Risler bent down and spoke to Mrs Cuff. 'I was going to say, on this occasion they would be permitted to talk!'

Mrs Cuff offered a weak, pathetic smile.

'Not excited about the news, Mrs Cuff?' Mr Risler asked, raising a knowing eyebrow.

'Of course,' she answered flatly. Any moment now, the Mercer family—maybe even the police—would arrive and stop this awful charade.

Chapter Twenty-Three

Morton was paralysed to the spot with fear. Every muscle was frozen. He didn't do well in fight or flight situations such as this. He focussed on Juliette's puffy red eyes. She had been crying but didn't look hurt. He tried to think what she would do if the situation were reversed. Negotiate. Be nice to him. Buy time.

'You finally turned up, Mr Farrier,' Mark Drury laughed. 'Your poor old bird here has been waiting ages for ya.' He lowered his head towards Juliette's face. 'He must have gone the wrong way back from that big library place in Falmer. Or, do you reckon he's got another woman on the go somewhere?" Mark grinned. 'Expect you'll be glad when I've shot him.' He laughed in a hollow, exaggerated way.

Juliette squirmed in her seat and tried to speak, but all that came out was a muffled, nonsensical sound.

'What is it you want?' Morton asked, trying his hardest to stay calm. 'Money?'

'Naa,' Mark answered. 'Cup of tea maybe. But don't worry, I'll make it myself when I've finished here.' He laughed again and drew a quantity of phlegm from his nose.

That was when Morton was able to place from where he knew him.

'I ain't come for nothing except to kill you. Don't get much simpler than that, really, does it? It was a bit of a surprise finding *her* here, so I'll have to take her out as well, but never mind.'

'Please—I can get you money—lots of money for you to just walk away,' Morton pleaded, his eyes darting around the room for something—anything—with which to hit the assailant if it came to it. He was almost certain that negotiation would fail and he would need to take action to keep him and Juliette alive.

'I told ya, I ain't here for money. You or her first?' Mark asked.

Morton's brain was racing at lightning speed, as he tried to work out what to do next for the best. From past experience, fighting wasn't a great option and so far he could see nothing in the room that could be used as a weapon.

'I asked you a question—you or her first?' Mark shouted.

'Er… me,' Morton stammered. 'But before you do it, could you answer me one question?'

'No,' Mark said with another laugh.

Morton was running out of time. 'I know you work as a security guard at Blackfriars, so I assume the order came from there…' Morton let his words hang in the air, hoping that it would catch the intruder off-guard. He remembered that Juliette had said he was hapless and not a very good shot. Morton had quickly assimilated a hasty plan and it relied very heavily on that information's being correct.

'How do you know I work there?' Mark asked, lowering the gun slightly.

'I've seen you there. Was it Lord Rothborne that sent you to do his dirty work?'

Mark scowled. 'No, he ain't got a clue about none of this.'

'Who then?' Morton persisted.

Mark sniffed and smiled. 'Suppose there's something quite poetic about the last words you hear being the name of the person who wants you dead.' Mark laughed again.

Morton saw his chance.

With all the power he could muster, he launched his laptop from under his arm, aiming straight for the assailant's hand which held the weapon. The laptop flew through the air. Mark saw what was happening a moment too late, raised the gun to take a shot, just as the laptop cracked down on his wrist. He squeezed the trigger and the barrel flipped upwards in a jerking motion, as the bullet glanced his forehead and penetrated the ceiling. The gun tumbled from Mark's hand and fell to the floor. Both Mark and Morton dived for it, but Mark, being closer, had the advantage and his hand reached out towards the hand grip.

Morton watched as, in a flash, Juliette rocked her chair from one side then to the next, sending herself crashing down onto the intruder. It was enough to buy Morton a few precious seconds. He reached down, grabbed the gun and backed himself away to the door.

With a hulking shove, Mark pushed Juliette off him; her head hit the floor with a painful thud. 'You ain't going to use that,' Mark sneered. 'Go on, shoot me.'

'Stay where you are,' Morton shouted.

Mark slowly began to pull himself up until he was standing.

'I said don't move,' Morton yelled.

Still Mark ignored him, a loutish grin wide on his face and made a step towards him.

Morton knew that he had to act but he also knew that he couldn't bring himself to actually kill someone. He lowered the gun slightly and pulled the trigger.

Mark let out an agonising scream as the bullet passed into his right foot.

'Sit down or I'll shoot your other foot,' Morton warned, surprising himself with the commanding authority in his voice.

Mark fell to the floor clutching his foot, moaning and writhing in pain.

Morton, with the gun pointing at Mark, carefully stepped over to Juliette and removed the gag from her mouth. She gasped and drew in a great lungful of air. 'Are you okay? Did he hurt you?'

'I'm fine, a little bit dazed from hitting the floor just then,' she said.

Morton moved behind the chair and began to untie the rope. Moments later, Juliette was freed and Morton offered her the gun.

'You keep it, you did a really good job, Morton. I'll phone the police.'

'Hang on a moment,' Morton directed. He had suddenly became aware of the vast quantities of adrenalin rushing around his body and he felt his limbs begin to quiver. He definitely was not suited to a career in law enforcement. However, he wanted to make one final use of his power.

Juliette looked at him in surprise. 'What are you going to do?'

'Shoot him and plead self-defence,' Morton said firmly.

'But…' Juliette began, 'you can't. Don't!'

Morton aimed the gun at the assailant.

'Stop!' Juliette shouted.

Mark looked up pitifully, having removed his shoe and sock he was now cradling his foot in his arm, as though it were a new-born baby. Wet streaks coursed down his cheeks. 'Please, don't shoot me.'

'Who sent you?' Morton demanded.

Mark needed no extra threats. 'Daphne Mansfield.'

'Why?' Morton asked. He already knew the answer.

'She didn't tell me the ins-and-outs of it, just that she wanted to protect the next generations of Mansfields at Blackfriars. That's all I know. Honest.'

Morton nodded to Juliette and she called the police.

It was game over for Mark Drury.

230

Four hours had passed since the drama had ended and the police had carted Mark Drury away. Lying in his dark bedroom with only a glimmer of moonlight creating bizarre shadows and shapes on the ceiling, Morton was wide awake. Juliette was sleeping peacefully beside him, as if being taken hostage and threatened with a gun was just another ordinary day. He supposed that it was the kind of situation for which she was being trained. She had fallen asleep within seconds of her head hitting the pillow and now Morton was left wide awake, mulling over the latest developments in the Mercer Case. He remembered, then, that Jenny was going to send over the certificates for George Mansfield's birth, marriage and death. He could easily and quickly have checked his emails on his phone, but he convinced himself to head back up to his study to look at them on his laptop in the context of the whole case.

Having made himself a decaf coffee, Morton made his way to his study. With a slight trepidation, he pushed open the door and switched on the light. The violent scenes from earlier in the day, made manifest in the blood-stained carpet, replayed in his mind and he considered just how close he and Juliette had come to being seriously injured or worse. Although Juliette and the armed police who stormed the house all praised his actions and bravery, in reality he knew that his survival was more down to Mark Drury's incompetence than his own gallantry.

With his laptop fired up and thankfully unharmed from being launched at Mark, Morton opened his emails and sipped his coffee. Above an email with attachments from Jenny were two other emails. He started at the top and worked his way down. The first email was from a Thomas Day. *Dear Morton, I received your letter about my grandmother, Joan Leigh, with great interest. I have been researching the family tree for a number of years now, so take an active interest in such things! My grandmother died before I was born, so I only have a limited amount of information on her and scant amount for the precise period you are researching. I attach a photo of Joan in her servant's outfit, which would have been taken around 1914. From what I can gather from my mother, Joan wasn't overly keen on her time at Blackfriars and was ready to leave when she met my grandfather, Andrew Day in 1915. I'm not sure this is of any use to you, but I wish you luck in your search! Yours faithfully, Thomas Day.*

Morton opened the attachment of Joan Leigh in her uniform. She was standing beside a man dressed in a First World War soldier's uniform, which confirmed that the picture had little value for the

231

Mercer Case, although Morton always appreciated putting a face to a name. He printed the picture and added it to the wall under Joan's name.

The next email was from a Henry Goacher. *Hello Morton! Received your letter about my granny, Clara Ellingham. Dear old lady, she was. You're in luck! Granny kept a diary her whole life and, much to my wife's consternation, I have a whole bookcase full of them! I've always intended to publish them one day as a kind of social history—perhaps when I retire. Anyway, I've had a good look through the diary for 1911 and Granny makes several mentions of your Mary Mercer—is she a relation of yours? I have scanned and (hopefully) attached the relevant pages. All for now, Hen Goacher.*

Morton found himself holding his breath as he clicked to download the seven attachments, each entry saved as a photo. Onscreen appeared the first entry, written in a typical Edwardian scrawl. It took a moment for Morton to break into the style and letter formation before he could read each entry. He scanned for any salient elements.

3rd Jan. *The short time having my own bedroom is now over. A new girl, Mary Mercer has started as third housemaid. Seems nice enough but no previous experience. Her sewing is awful! Still, good to have a bit of company in the evenings I suppose.*

18th Jan. *Mary Mercer really is a mischievous one! Today she was caught in Lord Rothborne's bed! Fortunately he was not in it at the time...*

30th Jan. *Mary really has been down of late. She hasn't taken well to being a domestic servant—think she has dreams and ideas above her station. I'm having a great difficulty getting off to sleep owing to her constant crying at bedtime.*

8th Feb. *Found a note under Mary's pillow from her cousin, Edward declaring his love! Hopefully now she might cheer up a little. Whispered my discovery to Eliza but that wretched scullery-maid, Joan, overheard and has been teasing Mary.*

10th Feb. *Mary confided in me today that Edward took her to the folly the other night and proposed! How delightful.*

5th April. *I've got a growing suspicion that Mary might be in the family way. I haven't spoken to her about it, but she is much more guarded when changing and the last few mornings she has been ill. Do hope not, for her sake.*

15th April. *Returned from a great time in Scotland. Bit of a to-do at B'friars— Mary's packed up and gone. Vanished. She didn't go home and now Edward's sick with worry—even organised search parties to look for her. Eliza and I joined in, a little half-heartedly I must confess, but to no avail. Guess she's run off somewhere—maybe to have the baby in peace?*

Morton printed each entry then re-read them. They added further proof that Mary and Edward were an item and gave further credence to the idea that Mary was pregnant by April 1911. Morton stuck the sheets to the wall, then clicked to open the last email—the one from Jenny Greenwood. *Here they are! Had such a lovely day—please keep me posted!! Jenny x.* He opened the three certificates, paying the closest attention to George's birth certificate. He had been born 1st November 1911 to Cecil and Philadelphia Mansfield. As he went to stick it to the wall, Morton noticed the timeline that he and Juliette had created. Just then, another key piece of the jigsaw fell into place. He couldn't quite believe what he was seeing; the Mercer Case had just taken another twist.

The photograph taken on Empire Day in 1911 caught his eye and he remembered how Mrs Cuff had distanced herself from the other servants. Morton was sure that she had learned the truth about what had taken place all those years ago and was surreptitiously sharing her feelings with history.

Morton looked at his watch: 1:46 a.m. He still didn't feel tired but knew he needed to give up soon and at least *try* and get some rest. Just before he stopped for the night, Morton decided to bring the Mercer Case right up to date and so he set about printing and sticking to the wall all his recent discoveries. Up went the photo of Jack Maslow and Edward Mercer, as did the information from the vicar of Winchelsea and the Voter's Lists showing Martha Stone. He considered again that Martha had vanished between 1960 and 1965. One key event occurred in that period: Edith's death. He knew from Ray Mercer that she had returned for her twin's funeral in 1962. Maybe she stayed. Morton ran a death search for Martha Stone in the British death indexes and found her. She died in the same quarter of the same year, and in the same registration district as Edith. Morton ordered her death certificate on a priority service.

As he switched off his laptop and turned out the study light to make his way back down to bed, Morton considered that it was almost time to arrange a meeting with Ray Mercer.

Chapter Twenty-Four

18th December 1925

Edith Leyden quickly finished dressing in the dim light of her bedside lamp. With a fleeting glance in the mirror, she placed her red cloche hat on her head and buttoned up her matching red coat. A burning nervousness and excitement inside her overcame the chill of the early morning. She had taken the room for one night in the tiny terraced boarding house on the outskirts of Liverpool city centre. The cab that she had ordered was due in a matter of minutes.

Having made a quick final check of the stark room, Edith picked up her small suitcase and made her way down the dark stairs. She had settled her bill last night and had no need to disturb anyone this morning therefore. She quietly closed the front door behind her and stepped down onto the cobbled pavement.

The streets were black, peppered with the muted amber hue coming from the gas-lamps dotted at regular intervals. In the distance, tall chimneys pumped grey tendrils of smoke into the night sky. Edith drew in a long, steady breath and considered what she was about to undertake. After years of searching as to the whereabouts of her twin sister, the answer had been close by all along. And now, in just seven days' time, the twins would be reunited.

Two round white lights suddenly appeared at the end of the street, growing in size as the vehicle appeared from the gloom. A blue and black Austin Seven drew alongside Edith and, leaving the engine running, a man popped out from the driver's door. 'Morning, madam!' he chirped in a thick Liverpudlian accent. 'Off to the waterfront?'

Edith nodded. 'Yes, yes please.'

The driver scuttled round and opened the passenger door for her, allowing her to step inside before shutting it tight behind her.

Edith's excitement grew as the cab pulled away into the quiet street; it was her very first ride in a motor cab and somehow it made her adventure seem all the more important.

'Where you off to, then, love?' the driver asked.

'Canada. I'm going to see my sister,' Edith answered.

'Ah, that'll be lovely, that will,' he said. 'Has she been out there long?'

'Fourteen years,' Edith said. Fourteen long horrible years. Not a single day had passed when she hadn't thought about her. She pulled out a small piece of white paper handed to her a few days ago by the private investigator, whom she had hired to search for Mary. She unfolded it and read. It simply said, '4 West Street, Halifax.' She had read the address a dozen times and had no need to bring the piece of paper, but it made it all the more real for her. That was where her sister was now residing, having taken the name of her long-dead school friend, Martha Stone.

As Edith looked out of the cab window at the rows and rows of terraced housing, she thought about how she had searched high and low for Mary. She had tried every conceivable avenue, never accepting, but always expecting failure. She would have saved a fortune in money and precious time with her sister if she had known that the answer was under her nose all along. The answer was spat at her by her drunken husband when they were in the midst of an angry row. Joshua had known what had happened to Mary ever since the day that she had disappeared in 1911. A secret that he had harboured for fourteen years.

Almost four weeks ago, Joshua had arrived home at gone-midnight, having spent the evening drinking with Lord Rothborne. The abhorrent sight of her husband drunk had been one that she was growing increasingly accustomed to seeing. She despised the total shift in his personality when he was drunk: he would leave their home at Peace Cottage as the man she had fallen in love with all those years ago but he would return a foul, spiteful man with an unpredictable temperament.

When he had arrived home that night, Edith had been knitting in front of the glimmering fire in the lounge. She had learned from painful experience that pretending to be asleep when he arrived home often resulted in him forcing himself upon her. Much better was to diffuse the situation and pack him off to bed first.

'You waited up again,' Joshua had said jovially as he closed the front door.

Edith had seen instantly that he was drunk to the point of being unable to stand properly. 'Yes, I waited,' she had said, mustering a false smile. 'I think you need to get to bed, Joshua.'

Joshua's smile had turned into a tiger's snarl. 'Why? You think I'm bloody silly, don't you, Edie?'

Edith had set her knitting down into her lap. 'No, Joshua, I don't think you're silly; I think you're tired and need to get to bed.'

'Come on, then, let's go to bed,' Joshua had challenged.

235

'You go, I'll be up in a minute,' Edith had answered, trying to hide her nervousness about where this conversation was headed.

'No, you come now!' Joshua had shouted.

'Shhh, you'll wake Charles,' Edith had said.

'Oh, your poor son,' Joshua had replied. 'Let him live a little. You protect him like he's a porcelain doll. You parcel him off to bed like he's a baby. Cecil lets Georgie stay up with us.'

Edith had looked mortified. 'Not drinking and gambling, surely? He's only fourteen.'

Joshua had rolled his eyes scornfully. 'He's a grown-up lad—more of a man than your wet Charlie upstairs,' he mocked, before mumbling, 'which is odd.'

'Why's it odd?' Edith had retorted. 'I look after my boy.'

'They've got the same blood, though,' he said.

Edith had stared at him, wondering at his last remark. *Had he just said that her son, Charlie, had the same blood as George Mansfield?* 'What do you mean by that?'

'Are you really that bloody stupid and naïve?' Joshua had whispered, moving closer to her face. 'They're cousins! Mary had a little lamb.'

'You're lying!' Edith had snapped.

Joshua had laughed and made his way upstairs.

Edith had wanted to call after her husband, but knew there would be no point. The next morning would be like every other following his drinking; he would remember nothing of it. Edith had intended to keep it that way. She knew that if she wanted to ever see Mary again, she needed to be clever about it. It had become her secret. Her mystery to solve.

'Here we are then, love,' the cab driver said, bringing the car to a sudden stop. 'The Aquitania Pier.'

Edith lurched back to reality. The driver opened the door and she stepped out into another world. Despite the subdued dawn light, Edith could see a hive of industry taking place with everything revolving around the magnificent ship which loomed large in the background. She suddenly became aware of her immediate surroundings. More cars and horse-drawn carriages than she had ever seen in one place were lined up at the edge of the road, spilling people and luggage onto the slipway beside them. People, seemingly of all nationalities, bustled around chatting and carrying cases towards the big ship. Edith was mesmerised. She quickly settled up with the cab driver and stood clutching her case, staring at the liner. RMS Celtic II. Her home for the next seven days.

'Come on, Miss, move along!' an American-sounding voice called from behind her. 'She'll sail without you!'

Edith turned to see a slender lady, elegantly dressed, with a cigarette holder pressed tightly between her lips. She puffed out a long thread of smoke. 'Sorry,' Edith apologised.

'I was just kidding,' the lady said with a wink. 'She's quite something, wouldn't you say?'

'Truly amazing,' Edith replied, quite taken with the enigmatic woman.

'Seven hundred feet long,' the American said. 'Twenty-thousand tons. You can see why it's one of the White Star Line's 'Big Four'.'

'Yes,' Edith answered. 'Where are you going?'

'Back home to New York,' the woman replied. 'And you?'

'Halifax,' Edith replied, her gaze shifting from the boat to the American. She was savouring the few moments that she had with this enchanting woman, for she knew that as soon as they boarded, their differently classed tickets would ensure that they never got to meet again on the voyage. 'I'm going to see my twin sister who lives there.'

The American drew in a long drag of air through the cigarette, then raised her head and expelled it slowly. 'How delightful to have a twin. Well, it was lovely to meet you. *Bon voyage!*' she said, and marched passed Edith. Seconds later, she was absorbed into the growing crowds beginning to cross the narrow gangplank onto the ship.

It was time to go.

Edith picked up her suitcase, found the correct boarding gate for her class and joined the noisy procession of passengers about to enter the magnificent boat. Without her husband's knowledge, Edith had withdrawn a substantial amount from their joint savings account to purchase a single-berth room in second class for herself.

'Tickets!' a friendly steward cried from the mouth of the gate. 'Have your tickets ready, please, ladies and gentlemen!'

Edith removed her ticket from her handbag and held it aloft for the steward's inspection.

'Lovely, thank you, madam. Enjoy your trip.'

Edith smiled and followed a family of four up the gangplank, listening to their excited chatter, then, with some apprehension, stepped onto the boat. It was really going to happen.

Edith knew her room number off by heart—202—but she double-checked her ticket just to be sure. She could easily have asked for directions to her room, but she preferred the idea of exploring the boat independently.

She crossed through a warren of corridors and interconnecting doors, feeling certain that in seven days she would never get to explore all the hidden nooks and crannies that a ship of this size must hold. Despite the extravagant amount that she had spent on the voyage, Edith's ticket did not afford her the luxury of a window; her cabin was buried far below deck, somewhere near the centre of the ship. But Edith was happy with it. The room was very comfortable, comprising a single bed, a settee and, between the two, a washstand and make-up mirror.

Fifty-five minutes later, the deep thundering moan of the ship's horn resounded in Edith's cabin, announcing imminent departure. Edith decided to wait until the ship was sailing before she braved the decks, which right now would be heaving with a sea of faces watching as their loved ones slowly disappeared from view. Inexplicably, Edith couldn't bring herself to join them. It made her think of Mary taking a similar voyage, with nobody there to wave her off. Nobody to care about her.

Edith waited until the ship had been sailing for an hour until she left her cabin for the first time. The thronging decks had thinned out and she found a quiet spot on the port side where she could be alone. Looking out to sea, there was nothing but a gently rolling ocean. No land behind her. No land in front of her. Her thoughts turned to Joshua. She had left him with no uncertainty that their marriage was over. She had been betrayed and, despite his begging and pleading, nothing that he could ever do would repair the damage. Edith stared at the ring on her left hand. After raising a son as a single mother and having been rejected by her family for it, she had hoped that her marriage to Joshua Leyden would be forever. With a heavy heart, Edith removed her ring and held it between her thumb and forefinger. Everything it symbolised was gone. Drawing back her hand, Edith launched the ring into the sea; its insignificance not even creating a visible splash on the ocean surface.

Edith fumbled at the collar of her coat and withdrew the silver locket that was hanging around her neck. She held it tightly and stared into the horizon.

Chapter Twenty-Five

Morton had just left a brief, yet informative meeting with Susan Catt: the final piece of the jigsaw was complete. He was now sitting in his Mini in the car park of Hastings Cemetery. There were four other cars but no sign of their occupants. His window was down and he was savouring the peace and quiet. Beside him, on the passenger chair was a bulging file containing everything pertaining to the Mercer Case, all filed in chronological order and prefaced with a typed, four-page summary explanation of his findings. He had duplicated everything and posted it this morning to Jenny Greenwood. In his rear-view mirror, he spotted a green Vauxhall Corsa pulling in. It was bang on the scheduled meeting time. Morton stepped from his car and waved at the woman behind the wheel. She acknowledged him and parked her car beside his.

'Hi,' Morton said, greeting the woman. 'Morton Farrier.'

'Melissa—Ray's daughter,' she said with a broad smile. 'He's very excited about all this.' She moved around the car and opened the passenger door. She was tall with shoulder-length brown hair and wore smart clothes and heels.

'Hello, Morton,' Ray Mercer said.

'Hi, Ray,' Morton replied, approaching the old man. His face had become more drawn and thin since their last meeting, evidently the cancer was strengthening its grip on him. Morton was thankful to have been able to bring the case to a close so that Ray could know what became of his great aunt. Morton offered his hand and received Ray's thin bony hand in his.

'Would you like to sit in my car for a moment and I'll talk you through what I've found?' Morton said, pulling open the passenger door for Ray. He turned to Melissa. 'Sorry, will you be okay in the back?'

'No worries at all—I'm just looking forward to *finally* finding out what happened to this elusive Mary; I'll sit on the roof if I have to!' Melissa climbed in, carrying a small bunch of roses.

Morton handed the file to Ray and angled himself so he could face both Ray and Melissa. 'Well, it's all in there—all evidenced for you to look at in your own time. But basically, the nitty-gritty of it all is this,' Morton said to his eager audience. 'At the time of her disappearance, your Aunt Mary was, in modern terminology, in a relationship with her cousin, Edward Mercer.'

'Really?' Melissa said.

'Yes, and they intended to marry, but never did because, in May 1911, Edward drowned in the lake at Blackfriars—the place where they both worked.'

'Oh my goodness,' Melissa commented. 'How awful.'

'But, Mary was pregnant at the time—very likely by Edward,' Morton said, taking a moment to ensure Ray was following.

Ray nodded. 'What happened to the baby?'

'Well, there are no babies registered to Mary Mercer in the timeframe when she would have given birth,' Morton said.

'Then what happened?' Ray asked with a curious frown.

Morton leant across and opened the file to the birth certificate of George Mansfield and allowed Ray and Melissa to read it for themselves.

'Nine forty-eight a.m, 1st November 1911, George Richard Mansfield, son of Cecil Mansfield, Earl of Rothborne and Philadelphia his wife,' Ray highlighted.

Melissa gasped. 'She gave it away to another family! So this lord is our cousin!' she said excitedly. 'Can you believe it, Dad?'

'Are you sure this baby is Mary's? It says here that the parents are Lord Cecil and Lady Philadelphia Mansfield. There's no mention of Mary.'

'I'm very sure. Cecil was certainly unable to have children…'

'So Mary gave up her baby?' Melissa interjected.

Morton paused for a moment. 'Well, from what later transpired, I'm inclined to believe that she had no choice, that she was held against her will somewhere on the Blackfriars estate in Winchelsea.'

Another gasp from Melissa.

'I think she was selected to work as a third housemaid at Blackfriars purely on the basis of her appearance—she bore a resemblance to Cecil Mansfield—certainly from the records I've uncovered, she was no good at her job.'

'Then what happened?' Melissa asked impatiently.

'Whether she was allowed to leave freely, or whether she escaped, I'm not sure, but in December 1911 Mary set sail from Bristol to Canada, where she remained for most of her adult life. She worked as a teacher and—'

'Hang on,' Ray interjected. 'I searched every inch of passenger records for that period—there was no Mary Mercer.'

'She travelled under a false name—the name of a school friend, who had died of influenza in 1902. The school records are all in that file and they show that the two girls were close friends. Mary lived under the name of Martha Stone until her death.'

'How sad,' Melissa said.

Morton nodded in agreement. 'But, she does appear to have had a good life. She became a teacher and I've been in touch with a couple of people who were taught by her. They said she was one of the kindest, most gentle people they'd ever met. She also had a mischievous sense of humour—there are a couple of anecdotes in the file. They also sent me this,' Morton said, revealing a sheet of paper with a class photo printed on it. The picture was of a group of children formally facing the camera with a sign saying 'Velmont Juniors 1958'. Standing alongside them, with a mop of wild red hair, was their teacher, Martha Stone. 'That's Mary.'

'I feel like I know her from somewhere,' Ray said.

'It's the family resemblance,' Melissa said. 'You can see it's definitely her.'

'I've analysed the photo against the one you have of her as a child—you'll see the report in there,' he said, pointing at the folder, which was still open on George Mansfield's birth certificate. 'It's definitely her. It's Mary.'

Melissa interrupted a few seconds of silence. 'So, do I take it that she's buried here, Morton?'

'Yes, but don't get your hopes up. It's a common grave. She was buried here under her assumed name but there's no headstone for her.'

'We'll soon change that,' Ray mumbled.

'Before I show you the grave,' Morton said, 'there's one more thing. Turn the page in that folder.'

Ray did as instructed. 'Another birth certificate?'

Melissa got it faster than her father. 'Oh. My. God.'

'Twins,' Ray breathed quietly.

'Five past ten a.m., 1st November 1911, Rebecca Victoria Ransom, born to Caroline Ransom and William Ransom—deceased.'

'But this makes no sense!' Ray blurted. 'The birth's registered in Bristol! The other was registered in Rye!'

'They're both fabricated—Caroline took one baby and the Mansfield's took the other,' Morton said.

'So that side of the family knew all along,' Ray muttered incredulously. 'I knew it.'

'According to Douglas's wife, Susan, he only discovered it by accident a few years ago and vowed that nobody else in the family would ever find out. I think he was ashamed of his grandmother's actions, actually and that was what motivated him to keep it quiet. Just after his mother, Rebecca, died in 1993 he found a letter written to her from Caroline confessing everything. Well, almost everything. She didn't mention the huge detail of Rebecca having a twin brother.'

'Did Mary allow all of this to happen?' Melissa asked, incensed.

Morton shrugged. 'That I can't be sure of. My gut instinct is no. I think it's no coincidence that Mary leaves Bristol—the home town of her elder sister—under a false name: she didn't want to be found. And that's the way it remained until 1925 when your grandmother went out and found her. We can only guess at what happened out there in 1925, but that was the year your grandmother divorced Joshua Leyden and the following year Mary moves away.'

'This is far beyond what I was expecting, Morton,' Ray exclaimed. 'My goodness. The poor girl.'

The car fell into silence, as Morton allowed his two passengers to absorb the information he had just shared. He hoped it wasn't too much for Ray to take in, considering his frail health.

Ray exhaled loudly. 'Come on, let's go and see her grave.' He turned to Melissa. 'If I can't get a headstone sorted out, promise me you will.'

'Of course, Dad.'

'It's over the other side of the cemetery, so I'll drive us closer,' Morton said, starting the engine. 'I asked the office to put a marker on it, so hopefully we can find it.'

Morton slowly wove his way through the cemetery until he reached the right place. He pulled the car over into a parking bay. 'Grave division E, section R, Row B, number eighty-seven. I think that's it, over there,' Morton said, indicating a section of grass close to the boundary wall of the cemetery. He killed the engine and hurried around to open the door for Ray.

'I've got my cane—I'll be fine,' Ray muttered, as he climbed out of the car. He stood still and gazed at the great expanse of grass around them, only sporadically dotted with headstones. 'Is this all unmarked graves around here, then?' he asked.

Morton nodded. 'People too poor to be remembered.'

Ray shook his head. 'Was she that poor, then?'

'The local authority paid for her funeral as they had no idea who she was apart from her name. All her worldly goods were left behind in Canada.'

Ray looked at Morton with a mixture of understanding and incomprehension.

Melissa, holding the flowers in one hand, linked her free arm with her father's and followed Morton to a spot close to the low wall.

'Here it is,' Morton said, solemnly pointing to a wooden stick, on which had been written 'M. Stone. B87.'

Ray stood with his head bowed for a moment as he stared at the grave.

Melissa handed him the bunch of roses. 'Do you want to put these down, Dad?' she whispered.

Ray took the flowers and set them down in front of the grave marker. In a tearful, quivering voice, he said, 'I've found you at last, Aunt Mary.'

Morton smiled and mouthed to Melissa that he would wait in the car. He walked back and sat in the driver's seat, watching the pitiful old man hunched over the grave, his daughter's hand gently stroking his back. Ray said something to Melissa, then she too walked over to the car.

'He wants a few moments by himself,' she said, as she sat in the Mini beside Morton. 'You really don't know how much this means to him, you know,' Melissa said. 'All my life I've heard of this mysterious woman and now it's solved, thanks to you. You've made a dying man very happy.'

'It was a pleasure,' he answered.

'So when did Mary die, then?'

Morton paused before opening up the folder to the last page: her death certificate. 'Day of Edith's funeral,' he said quietly, knowing the reaction it would cause.

'What?' Melissa said. She looked down at the certificate. 'Oh my God.'

Chapter Twenty-Six

25th December 1925

Mary Mercer—living under her pseudonym of Martha Stone—sat by the warm, open fire in the small front room of her cottage in Halifax, Nova Scotia. She was repairing the hem on her skirt, which she had snagged earlier on in the day whilst cutting some flowers from her white rose beds. As she ran the fine cotton through her dress, in an uneven running stitch, she thought of her previous life as Mary. When she had first escaped to Canada in 1911, she had put so much effort into detaching herself from her past that Mary now felt like an entirely separate being—like a long-forgotten acquaintance. She had become so disconnected from her that she seldom thought of her old life in England. Strangely, thoughts of her previous existence seemed only to surface when she performed perfunctory tasks, like sewing, that had dominated her time at Blackfriars. At first, she had disallowed her mind to wander back and would force herself to change the direction of her thoughts. Gradually, as her life in Canada developed to include friends that knew nothing of her former life, she would occasionally allow herself the indulgence of a brief recollection of happier moments. Over time, the choking blackness that had once dominated began to fade and she found herself able to cherry-pick from a handful of happy past memories.

Mary finished her sewing and placed it on the floor by her feet. A blast of cold air tumbled down the chimney and she pulled her cardigan tight. She stood up to draw the curtains. She tugged the first curtain across and was just about to reach across to the second when she thought she saw something unusual in the street outside. She stopped and pressed her face up to the window.

Mary shuddered and felt her body go limp as the blood drained from her face.

A shadowed figure stood pitifully in the blustery snow outside her door.

It couldn't be...

The silhouette looked familiar. Like it belonged to Edie.

But that couldn't be...

She stared hard, trying to discern the facial features.

It was her...without any doubt, it was her...

She had been found. The day that she had feared and yet knew was inevitable, had arrived.

She stared at the motionless figure, snow settling on her body as if she were a statue.

Mary began to shake as the past came thundering back into her head, like an unstoppable locomotive.

Trembling all over, Mary went to the front door and pulled it open. She saw with certainty that it was indeed her twin sister standing before her.

The past—with all the darkness that encompassed it—had come to the present.

'Edith,' Mary said simply.

Edith suddenly lunged from the shadows and threw her arms around her sister, as tears flowed from her eyes. 'Oh, Mary! It is you! It's been so long. I've missed you so much.'

Mary. It was the first time that anybody had called her that in a long time. She tried to smile, she tried to reciprocate the embrace, but the deliberate fence that she had spent fourteen years building, refused to yield to the past.

Edith released her grip and Mary looked her up and down. The time that had elapsed since their last meeting had changed her appearance little. The subtle make-up that she wore gave her a beauty that Mary hadn't previously noticed.

Similar thoughts must have passed through Edith's mind. 'Look at you, you've not changed much. Still got that wild red hair!'

'How did you find me here?' Mary asked quietly.

Edith smiled. 'It's a very long story. I've got so much to tell you and talk about!'

Mary nodded. 'Come and sit down,' she said, leading Edith into the front room.

'This is nice,' Edith said, casting her eye around the room, which comprised two patterned armchairs, a coffee table, grandfather clock and a writing bureau. The only picture on the wall was a painting of the Rye workhouse—a reminder of the life waiting for her if ever she returned home. A simply decorated Christmas tree close to the window completed the room.

'Thank you,' Mary said, shifting uncomfortably in the doorway. 'Would you like a drink?'

'Tea would be lovely. They served some dreadful version of tea on the ship.'

Mary tried to smile. 'I'll be back in a moment.'

Edith smiled and sat in one of the armchairs, fretting over her sister's reaction to her arrival. Mary was hardly excited to see her. *It's understandable,* she told herself. *I arrived here with no warning—of course she's going to be surprised and a little taken aback.* Edith knew that she needed to back off a little and give Mary time.

Mary returned carrying a tray with a pot of tea, two cups and saucers and a plate of sandwiches. 'They're turkey with cranberries from Maine—not sure if you're hungry.'

Edith smiled and picked up a sandwich. 'Only a bit peckish. They put on a full Christmas dinner on the ship. Magnificent thing—the RMS Celtic II, it was called. You wouldn't believe the size of it, Mary.'

Mary sat down in the armchair beside Edith, perching on the edge of her seat as she poured the tea. Edith watched her sister's shaky hands and wondered at her nervousness. 'Are you okay?' she asked.

Mary tried to smile again. 'Yes,' she answered feebly.

An awkward silence sat like a heavy cloud between the sisters. Mary knew that she was standing at a deep chasm with her past thundering towards her like a pack of unstoppable wild beasts. If she was going to have a future, she needed to turn and face the past. Only then could she make the leap to her future. 'So, how did you find me?'

Edith took a sip of tea, then exhaled slowly before beginning. 'After a lot of searching. Years of private detectives found nothing. Then the answer came suddenly from Joshua. He—'

'Joshua?' Mary interjected.

'Sorry—my husband—Joshua Leyden, the doctor—'

'You married *him*?' Mary blurted. 'But he...' She couldn't finish her sentence as hot tears welled in her eyes and her throat closed to the words she needed to say. *That man...*

'I know what he did now, Mary,' Edith said, placing a hand on her sister's leg. 'But I didn't know it when we married. I thought he was a decent man when we got together; I loved him and I thought he loved me. We had several years of happiness but his drinking just got worse and worse and then one night he just announced that Cecil and Philadelphia Mansfield were raising a child that you had given birth to. I couldn't believe it, Mary—I really couldn't. He wouldn't tell me any more that night and I knew he'd only reveal things if he was drunk.' Edith stopped and took a sip of tea. 'So, the next night I plied him with a bottle of whisky and then he opened up with the vile truth about what had happened—that you'd given birth to twins. Is it really true, Mary? That Caroline took the other one? Is Rebecca really not hers?'

Mary couldn't take it any longer and she burst into tears. Years of holding in the horrible truth came flooding out, as if an emotional dam had just ruptured inside her.

'I'm sorry, Mary—this must be so painful,' she said, leaning over and placing her arm around her sister. 'I'm so sorry.'

Mary started to speak, but the words wouldn't come. She needed to ask all the questions that had tried to bubble to the surface over the years, but that she had quickly stifled. She took a deep breath. Now that Edie was here, she had to do this. 'Yes it's true. My children were taken from me...'

'Oh, Mary. Why ever didn't you tell me?'

'I just couldn't. Does she know you're here? Caroline, I mean.'

Edith shook her head. 'Nobody does. I left Charles with Mum and Dad and told them I was going on holiday.'

Mary wiped her eyes. 'Who's Charles?'

Edith smiled. 'He's my son—your nephew. That's how I know you can come back to your old life, Mary. You don't need to hide away as Martha any longer – eventually nobody minded about me having Charles.'

Mary was confused. 'But why would they—you're married—to a doctor at that.'

'I wasn't at the time,' Edith said. 'And he's not Joshua's boy, either.'

Mary met her sister's gaze, her eyes imploring her to continue.

Edith's head slumped down. 'He was the result of one mistaken evening. It was a desperate time. You'd been missing for several months. I'd been out looking for you and came back to Winchelsea upset at yet another failed search. That was when I bumped into Walter and he took me for a drink. One thing led to another...'

Mary withdrew her hand from Edith's in shock, praying that she had misheard. 'Walter?'

Edith nodded. 'Walter Risler.'

Another rush of emotion surged out of Mary in a painful wail. 'No, Edie, no!'

'Whatever's the matter?' Edie said, trying to calm her sister.

'He...he...he was the one who kept me in the folly,' she cried.

Edith pulled Mary in tightly. 'I'm sorry,' she whispered. 'I didn't know. He was so nice to me...'

The pain of discovering her twin's inadvertent complicity in the dark days of her pregnancy clouded and fogged her thoughts. *Another sister tangled in the complications of 1911.*

'Why did you up and leave, Mary? If you'd just told me we could have kept the twins,' Edith said quietly. 'I would have helped you.'

'No, Edie—I couldn't have kept them—I would have ended up in the workhouse, just like Gran. That's no place to raise two babies. Caroline said that the boy would have the best life imaginable with them and that I could help her raise Rebecca in Bristol, so that was what I opted for. She said she had discussed it with Mum and Dad.'

Edie shook her head in anger. 'That woman! I can assure you they have absolutely no idea that Rebecca isn't hers. Honestly, I can count on one hand the number of times we've seen her and Rebecca since you left...I understand why you would want to run away from her.'

'But that's just it, Edie, I had no choice. When we got to Bristol Caroline said it would be less scandalous if she said that the baby was hers. It was just about feasible with William's death in January. I agreed just so I would at least get to see my daughter every day, but then she made life so unbearable for me and pretty well stopped me from seeing Rebecca.'

'Why didn't you just take Rebecca and run? Back home...or somewhere to make a fresh start?' Edie asked, softly stroking Mary's back.

'I thought about—I really did...and I wish now that I had but I was scared stiff, Edie—terrified of ending up in the workhouse. Caroline was an awful person, but she was a good mother to Rebecca. In the end, I thought that Caroline could offer her a better life than me, so I decided to run away.'

Edie's eyes met Mary's. 'Rebecca looks the spitting image of you. So does George—your son.'

Mary shuddered inside. Her children were suddenly coming to life and becoming real people. The boy had a name. *George.* She hadn't allowed herself to dwell on them as children turning into young adults. And now she knew that they looked like her. 'Are they well and happy?'

Edie nodded. 'Yes, but they'd be happier with you. You can come back and live with me for as long as you need.'

249

The very idea went against everything that Mary had worked towards since leaving England. She knew that she didn't have the inner strength to re-open that closed chapter of her life. With a trembling voice, she said, 'Edie, listen to me carefully. I can never go back to England until…the past is gone. Every day my heart has ached for those children and what might have been. The life I might have had with Edward. But I shut it out, close down those feelings because it can never be. I've got a life here now, far away from all those people. I'm a teacher. I've got friends. In my own way, I'm happy.'

Edith sniffed and sobbed at the news she feared she might have come all this way to hear. 'Please, Mary. We can move away from Winchelsea and leave the past behind.'

'Edie, don't you get it? *You're* part of it. You had a child with that horrible man and then married the doctor who pinned me down and snatched away my children the very moment they first drew breath. No matter where I could be in England, I'll always be reminded of Mary Mercer and her past.'

'But you *are* Mary Mercer,' Edie said.

'No, not anymore. I'm Martha Stone.'

Edith looked exasperated. 'Martha was a good friend of ours who died, Mary—don't you see? You're just hiding from the past by pretending to be a dead girl.'

'Stop! Please!' Mary begged. 'Listen to me.' She paused and took Edie's hand in hers. 'You're my sister and the only thing outside of Canada that I care about—'

'But your children?' Edie interrupted.

'They're not my children anymore—they were stolen from me and they've lived for fourteen years believing that they are who they are. Do you honestly think they'd thank me for trying to take them away? That we could suddenly play happy families after all these years? That Caroline and the Mansfields would just sit back and let me take them with no evidence whatsoever that they're mine? Edie, not a single day has passed when I haven't imagined taking them back and us building a life together, but it *cannot* happen. Think. Who would benefit? Not me, not them, not their parents.'

A long protracted silence clung to Mary's words as the two sisters looked at each other and sobbed.

Mary broke the silence. 'You're welcome to stay here for a few days but then you must go back to England, back to your life and forget all about me. If I ever return to England it will be when all traces of the past have disappeared.

Chapter Twenty-Seven

Monday 8ᵗʰ October 1962

The funeral was over. Mary had watched the mourners leave the church and file in a long black procession to Edith's house, where refreshments were being provided. Returning to Winchelsea for the first time in more than fifty years was unbearably difficult and had really taken its toll on her health. She was sixty-nine years old now and, for the first time in her life, was beginning to feel her age. But today it would all be over: the past would finally be put to rest.

She was sitting on a wooden bench just beyond the low stone wall of the church on Friar's Road, as conflicting memories—sad and happy, past and present—flashed into her mind. An elevated discussion from within the churchyard made her turn. With surprisingly dry eyes, she watched as the church sexton and another helper prepared to shovel the mound of clay-brown soil into the void above Edith's coffin. Mary watched as they began to attack the pile, their shovels scooping up clods alternately. There was almost a musical rhythm to their work.

In just forty minutes, Edith's coffin was interred and the gravediggers had gone, leaving a plethora of bouquets and wreaths on the grave.

Mary stood and quietly entered the deserted churchyard. She wove her way slowly across the grass, around headstones and footstones until she reached the grave.

'In loving memory of Katherine Mercer, born 2ⁿᵈ March 1870, died 8ᵗʰ December 1932. A wonderful mother and wife. Also, Thomas Mercer, husband of the above, born 21ˢᵗ April 1870, died 1ˢᵗ November 1938.'

Her parents' grave, and now her sister's grave.

Mary stifled her tears with a handkerchief as she leant a single white rose against the grey stone. Wrapped around the rose was her silver locket containing Edith's photo. Images of the pair of them receiving them for their birthday filled her head. *How happy we once were,* Mary thought.

'Hello,' a male voice said softly, startling Mary.

She turned to see a young man—she guessed in his twenties—with a handsome face and a neat dark quiff. He was dressed in black and his red swollen eyes told Mary that he was here to mourn her twin.

'Hello,' she replied stiltedly. She had no wish to speak to anyone, lest they discover her identity.

'You knew her, then?' he said, indicating the grave.

Mary nodded. 'From a very long time ago, yes.'

'She was my granny,' the man said, with a slight whimper at the end of his sentence.

Now that he had said it, Mary could see some of Edie's angular features in his face. 'Charles's son?' she asked.

'That's right—did you know him?' he said.

'I didn't ever meet him, no.'

The man looked disappointed. 'I barely knew him. He was killed in the war when I was only nine years old.'

'That must have been awful for you,' Mary said.

'It wasn't the best time of my life,' he muttered. He looked at Mary with a quizzical look. 'You seem familiar. Have we met?'

Mary's stomach suddenly lurched. She *could* tell Edie's grandson everything but that wasn't what she had come to do. That was never the plan. She laughed. 'No, definitely not. I must have one of those faces.'

The man seemed satisfied. He smiled and offered his hand. 'My name's Ray—Ray Mercer.'

Mary shook his hand. 'Martha.' She took a breath and, with one last look at the grave, began to turn. 'It was nice to meet you, Ray.'

'Likewise.'

Mary ambled through the churchyard and had almost reached the gate when she spotted something from the corner of her eye. It was a large stone tomb with a life-size angel perched on the top. It hadn't been there when she was a child, so she was intrigued to take a look.

Mary gasped and clutched at her chest. It was the grave of Lady Rothborne, Cecil and Philadelphia Mansfield. The very people who had blighted her whole life. The initial revulsion that she had experienced quickly turned into relief. They were gone and had no hold over her.

Mary left the churchyard without looking back. It would be her one and only visit. She walked down Friar's Road, absorbing every detail of the passing houses. Very little had changed in the fifty-one years that had elapsed. She stopped outside her former home and stared up at her bedroom window. Memories of that fateful day in 1911 when she had accompanied Edith to her job interview returned.

It was the one day in history that, if she could, she would go back and change. She would have stayed at home, curled up in front of the fire with a good book and never set foot in Blackfriars.

Mary continued her journey down the road until she reached the back entrance of Blackfriars. The large black gates were now rusted and set permanently open. Apprehensively, she walked in and began her journey down that familiar path, as if only a few months had passed since the last time. The orchard came into view and Mary stopped in her tracks. She had to visit the abbey ruins one last time.

Crossing through the orchard, Mary reached the ruins. She entered them, half expecting to see Edward's beaming smile appear from behind the archway. But it was deserted. She noticed the slab of sandstone where she and Edward had often sat was still in roughly the same position. She crouched down and carefully ran her fingers over its surface. Fifty years had weathered away the carved initials, leaving only an indistinct indentation where they had once been. She smiled as more memories poured into her mind. The mental wall that she had raised against her past was beginning to crack. Time was running out. She bent down and gathered up a handful of large pieces of sandstone and began filling her pockets until they bulged, like ripe fruit about to burst open.

Heading back to the main path, Mary saw Blackfriars for the first time. She shuddered and stared. Somehow it seemed larger and more terrifying than it had once appeared.

With the building in front of her, she turned and could see the lake. In the centre was the folly that had held her captive for so many months. As if being operated like a puppet, Mary walked towards the water in a trance.

The past was returning.

She reached the water's edge and, oblivious to the members of the public milling around her, placed a foot in the water. Spikes of freezing pain bit at her ankle, but she did not feel them. Putting her other foot in, she began to wade into the lake. The water rose, quickly climbing over her stone-filled pockets up to her chest.

'Hey! What are you doing?' a shocked voice called from the bank. 'Someone get help!'

'What's she doing? She's going to drown!' another voice cried.

Mary didn't hear the voices; the cold water had risen over her ears. Yet she kept moving on, stumbling over debris on the lake bed, onwards. She opened her mouth and allowed the water to rush inside her, expelling the last remnants of air from her lungs.

The wall in her mind cracked and she was back in the harrowing dark days of 1911.

She had packed up her suitcase and left her room empty, her employment at Blackfriars over. She had no idea why Lady Rothborne had encouraged her to try on Philadelphia's dresses only to deny all knowledge. Of course, she knew now. As she had left the building and made her way back home, Bastion and Risler had gagged her then dragged her into a boat where they had incarcerated her in the folly, locked away like some helpless princess. The folly. It had been her prison for so many months. Nobody had visited her, only Risler had brought her food and drink and Dr Leyden had come to check on her pregnancy. One night she thought she had heard Edward calling her name. She was sure it had been him. Then Risler had said that Edward was dead. When the day came, she had been carried into the main house to give birth. It was only then that she had heard the word 'babies' used for the first time. She had been carrying twins. Edward's twins. Just when she had given up any hope of being able to keep her children, Caroline had arrived and held her hand throughout the birth. She had just caught a glimpse of a shock of red hair on her boy's head as he was handed over to Philadelphia Mansfield. The second baby, a girl, had been handed to her elder sister. She had lost her Edward and now she had lost her children. She had no fight in her and the thought of the workhouse was always at the forefront of her mind. She would rather die than end up there. She got herself a passport in Martha Stone's name, packed her suitcase and left Bristol on a ship bound for Halifax, Nova Scotia. A new life beckoned.

Mary Mercer heard the words this time.

'Somebody get an ambulance!' the man's voice shouted.

She opened her eyes and saw a blurred image of Edward. She smiled. Then her vision cleared and she could see that it wasn't him. She was in the arms of a man on the river bank.

'Hello, are you okay?' the voice asked. 'Thank God, I got you out in time. You were about to drown.'

Mary knew. 'My son,' she said softly and then closed her eyes.

The man—George Mansfield—watched as the woman in his arms quietly faded away. 'Will somebody get an ambulance!' he shouted.

But he knew it was all too late.

He cradled the woman's head in his lap and gently stroked her red hair.

255

Biography:

Nathan Dylan Goodwin was born and raised in Hastings, East Sussex. Schooled in the town, he then completed a Bachelor of Arts degree in Radio, Film and Television, followed by a Master of Arts Degree in Creative Writing at Canterbury Christ Church University. He has completed a number of successful local history books about Hastings; other interests include reading, writing, photography, genealogy and travelling.

Books by Nathan Dylan Goodwin:
Non-fiction:
Hastings at War 1939-1945 (2005)
Hastings Wartime Memories and Photographs (2008)
Hastings & St Leonards Through Time (2010)
Around Battle Through Time (2012)

Fiction (The Forensic Genealogist series):
Hiding the Past (2013)
The Lost Ancestor (2014)

Further information:
www.nathangoodwin.co.uk

Follow me on Twitter: @nathangoodwin76
Like me on Facebook: www.facebook.com/nathandylangoodwin